THE WOUNDED SHADOW

Books by Patrick Carr

THE STAFF AND THE SWORD

A Cast of Stones
The Hero's Lot
A Draw of Kings

THE DARKWATER SAGA

By Divine Right (e-novella only)
The Shock of Night
The Shattered Vigil
The Wounded Shadow

THE
WOUNDED
SHADOW

PATRICK W. CARR

BETHANYHOUSE
a division of Baker Publishing Group
Minneapolis, Minnesota

© 2018 by Patrick W. Carr

Published by Bethany House Publishers
11400 Hampshire Avenue South
Bloomington, Minnesota 55438
www.bethanyhouse.com

Bethany House Publishers is a division of
Baker Publishing Group, Grand Rapids, Michigan

Printed in the United States of America

ISBN 978-0-7642-1348-9 (trade paper)
ISBN 978-0-7642-3138-4 (cloth)

Library of Congress Control Number: 2017961599

This is a work of fiction. Names, characters, incidents, and dialogues are products
of the author's imagination and are not to be construed as real. Any resemblance to
actual events or persons, living or dead, is entirely coincidental.

Cover design by LOOK Design Studio

Author represented by The Steve Laube Agency

18 19 20 21 22 23 24   7 6 5 4 3 2 1

To Jesse Tidyman, James (Whit) Campbell,
MacKenzie Sample, and Stephen Graham

That you would be so generous with your time
and so extravagant in your friendship is amazing,
and I can't help but be humbled by it.
I've loved working with you more than
I can possibly communicate . . .
but that won't keep me from trying.

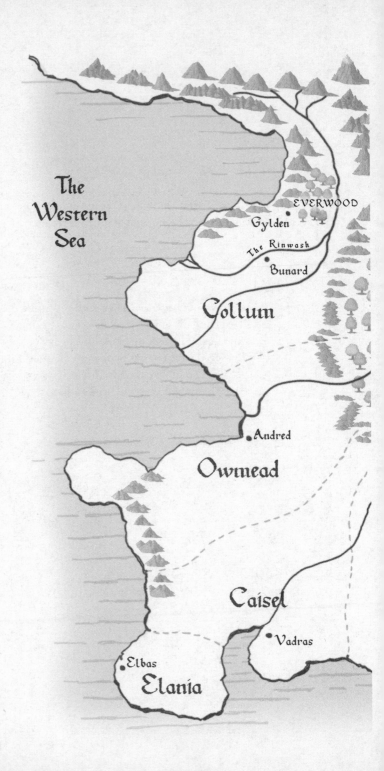

The
Western
Sea

Gylden

EVERWOOD

The Rinwash

Bunard

Collum

Andred

Owmead

Caisel

Vadras

Elbas

Elania

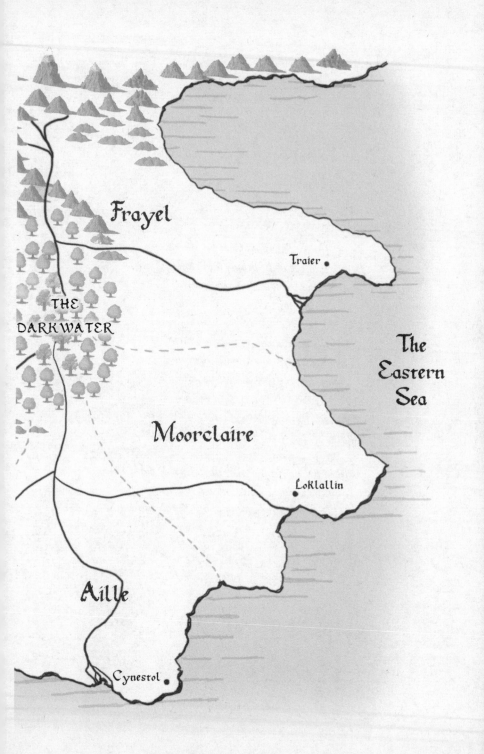

Frayel

THE
DARKWATER

Traier •

Moorclaire

The
Eastern
Sea

Loklallin •

Aille

Cynestol •

The Exordium of the Liturgy

The six charisms of Aer are these:
For the body, beauty and craft
For the soul, sum and parts
For the spirit, helps and devotion

The nine talents of man are these:
Language, logic, space, rhythm,
motion, nature, self, others, and all

The four temperaments of creation are these:
Impulse, passion, observation, and thought

Within the charisms of Aer, the talents of man,
and the temperaments imbued in creation
are found understanding and wisdom. Know and learn.

Chapter 1

Ealdor emerged from the shadows to palpable silence—the lines of his face and the iron-gray stubble of his beard familiar, and his gaze intense enough to see through walls. The Vigil members and our guards held their breath, as if the simple act of breathing might unbind the image of the Fayit and destroy him. I took a step toward my friend—nothing more than an image in my mind but real nonetheless—and extended my arm. He stepped forward to greet me, his right arm extended as well, a prelude to the gripping of forearms.

I followed the motion . . . and froze. I knew Ealdor wasn't really there, that what I always saw in his presence was nothing more than the power of the Fayit touching my mind and creating the familiar illusions of contact, but in the past Ealdor's illusions had been perfect, indistinguishable from the corporeal interactions with other, more common beings.

But not now.

His gaze followed mine, tracking down the length of his sleeve until he came to the bare skin of his forearm and hand.

His skin wavered like mist. I could see the stone of the floor and walls through him. Horror and anger chased each other across his expression, neither of them finding purchase until he withdrew his arm from the gesture of greeting and curled his fingers into an evanescent fist that he held in front of his face. "No, not now!" He growled the words in a voice that hummed with power, and I stepped back.

I'd never seen Ealdor angry. More, I'd rarely seen him don an emotion other than the contented peace that took turns calming and infuriating me. But for all the resonant power that thrummed in his voice, his hand and arm refused to solidify. In defiance of his command, ethereal insubstantiality took him, turned the entirety of his appearance to mist.

He straightened, raising his clenched hands. "Here is what you must do," he said. But his face twisted as if torturers I couldn't see worked to ensure his silence. "To defeat the Darkwater . . ."

A spasm twisted his face, and he shook his head. Screams of pain tore their way from his throat as he yelled in a language I couldn't understand. He dropped his arms, his face etched with tears and enough sorrow to fill uncounted centuries. He shook his head in surrender.

"Ealdor!" I screamed. "Wait. I don't understand."

Then he disappeared.

I turned, seeking knowledge or solace from Gael or Bolt or one of the Vigil, but no one spoke past the shock of having seen the Fayit. Pellin and Toria sat openmouthed and gaping. I would have been tempted to gloat, but something with Ealdor had gone terribly wrong. Too many thoughts filled my head, and the walls within my mind threatened to collapse. I needed space to think.

Rising, I pushed through the chairs and, without waiting to see if anyone would follow, made my way into the sultry afternoon air. Moist breezes off the southern sea warmed my skin, but cold filled my heart. Peripherally, I noted that Gael, Bolt, and Rory shadowed me.

"I need to think." A memory of an inn in Bunard where I'd always been welcomed thawed a bit of the ice in my heart. I looked to Bolt. "Is there a place like Braben's here?"

He nodded and set our path toward the center of Edring.

CHAPTER 2

Pellin sat at the table, waiting for the sounds of Dura's departure to fade, holding himself still against the reeve's possible return. Across from him, Toria and Fess maintained the same posture. After a few moments, Custos and Volsk rose with mumbled farewells to make their return to the library in Cynestol. But Toria and Fess remained—their gazes avoiding his but watching him all the same.

Pellin sighed and pushed his chair back in preparation for his departure.

"You didn't tell him," Toria Deel said.

Still seated, he stopped to answer the accusation, wishing she'd been more specific. "No, I thought it best not to."

Toria nodded without indicating agreement. "Eldest, I fail to understand the logic of this needless deception."

No. Definitely not agreement. "Needless? I think not." He chose his next words with care. Toria had yet to confirm his suspicions about Ealdor's visitation, and he would not allow his shock and wonder to betray him. "Lord Dura, despite his strengths, is still a question to us," he said, turning the conversation from Ealdor's unexpected reality and instruction, to Dura's vault.

Surprising him, Toria turned to her apprentice. "And what do you think, Fess?"

"Me?"

In another time Pellin might have smiled.

"You are one of the Vigil," Toria said. "It is possession of the gift, not the longevity of it, that entitles you to speak your mind."

He shook his head, and the unruly thatch of blond hair atop it shifted in response. "I have no opinion to offer . . . yet."

Toria's face mirrored Pellin's own surprise.

"I don't have centuries or even decades of experience to draw upon." Fess shrugged. "If you are asking me about Willet, he was known to us in the urchins for years before he became a lord and then one of the Vigil. That's my polite way of saying I've known him longer than you have. He has a way of seeing to the heart of people, imagining himself as that person, and then reacting the way they would."

"Undoubtedly, he has a very strong talent for others," Pellin said. Grateful for the opportunity to steer the conversation away from Ealdor and his improbable message, he waved his hand in a circular motion. "Please. Continue."

"Lady Bronwyn said as much while we were traveling together. I think, somewhere deep down inside, Willet knew what it was like for us in the urchins. That's why he helped us so much. The church fathers called it a gift of empathy."

Pellin gave Fess an indulgent smile. "I've read them. Many of the church's early clerics were expansive in their theological speculations. There's no mention of any such gift in the Exordium of the liturgy."

Fess met his gaze, steady, without looking away. "And is Aer bound by the Exordium?"

"That stroke was well laid," Pellin said. Toria's expression might have held a tinge of frustration, as if the conversation had failed to answer her deeper questions. He put his hands on the table and rose. "Now, if you will excuse me, the events of the day have left me fatigued."

Allta followed him out of the huge dining hall and to his quarters, stepping in and bolting the door, despite the fact they had seen no sign of dwimor in Edring. Instead of preparing for bed, Pellin took a seat at the small table in the anteroom, pausing to pour a glass of a full-bodied wine currently in favor in the south.

"Eldest?"

Pellin nodded toward the door. "I think I'm expecting a guest, Allta—at least one, but possibly two." He lifted the wine and let a sip flow over his tongue, picking up hints of dark berry through the oak. Allta took a seat opposite him without questioning further. A half hour later someone knocked, firm but spaced, indicating neither frustration nor haste.

"Two, it would seem," Pellin said. "Allta, please admit Toria Deel and Fess and then rebolt the door."

Toria entered with Fess behind her, his eyes scanning the room for threats in the way of the guards. The past few days training with Allta had only hardened the boy's detachment from his former good humor. Strange that Fess seemed to prefer his role as guard over that as one of the Vigil.

Pellin rose and poured each of them a glass of wine. When Fess made no move to join the two of them at the table, he nodded to Allta. "We are guarded and the door is sturdy, Fess."

The youngest member of the Vigil sat before taking a single sip from the glass in front of him, no more.

"I can understand why you didn't speak of certain matters in the hall, when all were present," Toria said without preamble, "but why the continued reticence? I waited for you to speak to this matter, Eldest. Why did you not? Ealdor spoke to you, didn't he? He told us to—"

"Stop!" Pellin held up a hand. "I didn't speak of it because Ealdor didn't," he said. "Dura's reaction made it plain that he heard nothing in the Fayit's cry except a wail of pain and frustration. In the moment Ealdor screamed his instructions, we heard something Dura did not. Do you think this was by accident?"

Toria favored him with one slow inclination of her head. "But how does that imply that Ealdor did not mean for us to share that knowledge with one another?"

There—she'd asked the question he'd hoped she wouldn't. "I can only say that some intuition guides me." He held up his hand to forestall her rebuttal. "There is wisdom in such a course, Toria Deel. If any of us are taken, we would be unable to betray the others."

Her hair—dark as pitch, like most of those from Elania—waved with the force of her disagreement. "Eldest, should we be so quick to trust this Fayit? We know nothing of him except what we've gleaned from Dura's memories. Memories, I hasten to add, that we believed were the product of Dura's tortured mind before today."

Instead of answering her objection, he addressed the fact behind her presence in his quarters. "You each received instruction, did you not? And unless I miss my guess, the two of you received the same direction."

They exchanged a glance that might have meant anything, but Pellin's intuition told him this wouldn't be the first conversation they'd had about Ealdor's appearance.

"Yes," they said in unison.

"Then we have our separate tasks," Pellin said. "Allta, Mark, and I will leave tomorrow." He pulled the green scrying stone from his pocket. After Bronwyn died, they'd given her stone—a duplicate of Pellin's and one of four—to Fess. The Chief of Servants in far Collum held the fourth and final stone, leaving Dura without access to immediate communication. Not for the first time, Pellin questioned the wisdom of that decision. "Contact me if you must, but without undermining the Fayit's intention."

The next morning, Pellin, Eldest of the Vigil, and perhaps the last who would ever hold the title, rode between Mark and Allta. They avoided the chaos of Cynestol by taking the port road around the city. Soon they would board ship and for the seventh time in his life, Pellin would step upon the southern continent, the birthplace of man. Only this time he wouldn't be there to keep the fragile tie intact between the northern church and its southern counterpart but to try to answer the unanswerable.

Mark shook his head as he gazed west toward the incomprehensible sprawl that constituted the largest city on the northern continent, Cynestol. "There's a lost opportunity, if ever there was one," the urchin said.

Pellin was almost sure the mournful tone of the boy's voice was an affectation. Almost. "What opportunity is that?"

Mark looked at him in surprise. "Why the war, of course. With your position and my skills we could steal half the treasury with no one the wiser. I could live like a king for the rest of my life without ever having to orchestrate another con."

Weeks earlier, Pellin would have turned on his apprentice in disgust and offered some sort of remonstrance. That was before. He paused a moment to consider that thought. Before what, exactly? Before Bronwyn had thrown his objections to apprenticing the urchins back in his face? Or was it before Mark had stymied his theology with his experience and indifference? No. It had been just after that. Outside the doomed village of Broga, Mark had sprinted off to save Pellin and Allta from a throng of broken villagers, each with a vault, all screaming for their blood.

Such sacrifice demanded forbearance. Instead of worrying over the boy's larcenous instincts, Pellin allowed himself a measure of amusement. "Should we turn the horses and make for Cynestol?"

Mark looked at him, his young face already too skilled at hiding his thoughts for Pellin to pick up any indication of what he truly felt. Then a grin snuck up the sides. "No, Eldest. It's more fun to steal the money than it is to spend it, and that kind of wealth draws all sorts of unwelcome attention," he said without irony. "I think my conning days are probably behind me."

Pellin smiled. "Don't be too sure. The world changes, and the mission of the Vigil will have to change with it. In the past, we've considered ourselves almost military in function. It may be that your skills will be what are required in the future."

"Truly?" Mark asked.

He nodded. "I'd be a fool to deny the possibility."

At that, Mark settled himself on horseback and proceeded to doze. Allta pulled his mount closer. "That was well done, Eldest."

He blinked. "What?"

Allta pointed to his sleeping apprentice. "Offering the boy encouragement instead of berating him for wanting to steal. I don't think Cesla or Elwin could have done it any better and probably not as well."

Two things about that startled Pellin. How could he be startled after seven hundred years? First, that Allta would expend the necessary verbiage to tell him, and second, that he seemed to think such an inconsequential bit of conversation would be important. Perhaps Cesla and Elwin's skill with people wasn't connected to their gift. Maybe it was simply a way of encouraging people that could be learned.

"Custos is right," he said to his guard. "There are things that can't be learned from books."

Allta nodded, but his glance strayed to the shining domes of the city. "When we left I assumed that we were headed to Cynestol to speak with the Archbishop."

Pellin shook his head. "No. I meant what I said. I have no intention of coming close enough to Vyne to allow him to 'protect' me. We'll be going a bit farther south."

Allta pursed his lips. "The only place farther south is Port City."

He didn't answer his guard's implied question at first. In truth, he would have preferred delaying the discussion until they were at sea. As a Vigil guard, Allta had sworn his life to protect him, but as Pellin had already learned, that oath could turn the guard's obedience on its head.

"You mean to go to the southern continent?"

He sighed. "There's no help for it, my friend. The command of the Fayit leaves little room for doubt." At the look of consternation on Allta's face, he sighed and reined in. Allta stopped and faced him, and Mark's horse, chosen on the basis of its herd instinct, walked a few steps farther before, curious, it turned and came back. Pellin shook his apprentice. "Wake up, Mark. I have news to give you."

His apprentice pulled himself upright and took a moment to express his disappointment that the landscape had changed so little since he'd fallen asleep. "What news, Eldest?"

"Our purpose," Pellin said. "You'll need to know it in case I fall and my gift passes to you."

He wasn't sure whose objection came to him first, but he cut his hand through the air and Allta and Mark gave him silence. "I do not mean for you to shoulder my task, Mark, but the purpose behind it must be passed on to what remains of the Vigil."

Mark and Allta nodded, mollified.

"But the truth," Pellin continued, "is that there is now no one in the north who can accomplish what the Fayit has asked me to do."

Allta looked to Mark before speaking. "And you believe his quest for you was different than rest?"

Pellin nodded. "When Ealdor spoke to me, I had a sense that he meant to keep our conversation a secret, just as he communicated to Dura, Fess, and Toria Deel."

A sliver of doubt, like a shard of glass stuck in his finger he could feel but not see, cut him as he said this. "I can explain our different experiences in no other way." He hadn't meant to digress to this topic, but they had nothing but hours and days of travel before them and perhaps it was just as well. "We did not speak of it directly, but I have no doubt the command I heard was markedly different than the one Toria Deel and Fess heard."

Mark nodded. "Sense. After he appeared, Fess followed Lady Deel from the hall to speak with her. I tried to hear what they said to each other, but they were in the center of the courtyard and I couldn't get close enough to eavesdrop without being seen."

"Your curiosity is understandable," Pellin said. He stopped before he could add his customary remonstrance about spying. Doubtless the boy already knew his feeling on the subject. "In truth, I was tempted to speak to them about it, but the wisdom behind Ealdor's actions was apparent."

"It's what a military commander would do," Allta said. "What is not known cannot be revealed."

Mark grunted. "We operated similarly in the urchins to keep the city watch from finding us after we'd stolen something too valuable." He paused to scratch beneath his arm. "That's scant comfort. It means the Fayit thinks there's a good chance one of us will be taken."

"Which brings us to the point," Pellin said looking south to where the smell of the sea drifted to him. "We're going to the southern continent."

"What did the Fayit tell you to do?" Allta asked.

He took a deep breath. "Something no one in the Vigil has been able to do in its long history. I have to discover a way to break Dura's vault without destroying his mind."

Mark shook his head. "Why not ask Dura? From what he's said, he broke Queen Cailin's vault right after Bas-solas and she survived."

Pellin nodded in approval. The boy's thoughts ran along the same path as his own. "Unfortunately, Dura doesn't know why Cailin survived, but even if he did, there would be an additional reason to go south. We have to break the vault without losing the information within it."

"The Fayit said this?" Allta asked.

Pellin nodded. "Of the Vigil that remain, I am by far the most experienced. Toria Deel is six hundred years younger in the gift than I am, Willet and Fess seven hundred. And while I do not possess the prodigious memory of our friend Custos, there is no knowledge within our library that can aid me in this. If the knowledge is to be found, it will be on the southern continent with our brothers there."

Pellin made some pretense to confidence, but even so Allta and Mark quieted. When they stopped for the lack of light still some distance from Port City and took rooms, his guard and apprentice still showed no desire to talk.

Mark was the first to break the silence. "How far is it to the southern continent?" he asked as they ate that evening. Their inn had the benefit of being indistinguishable from countless others in Aille. If someone had tracked them here, they would have had to follow them the entire distance from Edring to do it. Even so, Mark kept up a steady scan of the interior, searching for dwimor.

"Almost two hundred leagues," Pellin said." A bit over a week by ship with a good captain and fair wind—longer with a full load."

"What if it's not fair?" Mark asked.

A memory of Pellin's last crossing rose before him, of rough gray-green seas and swells that sent their vessel up and down the troughs like a child's toy while he fought and failed to keep his stomach under control in the crew's quarters. "It should be fair now, but the journey south is best avoided during the winter."

"What's it—" Mark stopped. His eyes fixed on the front entrance of the inn. Allta had already noted his manner and turned toward the door, his hands moving beneath the table to his weapons. Pellin had just begun the motion when Mark turned back to them, his face and voice calm.

"There's a dwimor by the door. Don't," he said as Allta started to rise. "It's already seen everyone in here. I don't think it's here for us." Pellin watched his apprentice take another glance around the room, his gaze roving across the patrons without landing anywhere. Clever, the dwimor wouldn't know it had been seen.

Pellin lifted his glass to his lips, let the wine wet them without drinking. His hand shook, but he ignored the splashes that stained his clothes. "What's it doing?"

Mark cocked his head as he took a bite, the motion smooth. Pellin prayed a quick thanks to Aer. The boy had ice water in his veins.

"It's moving toward the kitchens. I guess even dwimor have to eat."

"Take him," Pellin said.

"Her," Mark corrected.

"Regardless," Allta said, "the risk cannot be taken. Mark, you will follow the dwimor and kill her."

"No," Pellin said. "If Mark can take her, I can delve her. Who knows what we might discover?"

His guard shook his head. "Eldest, consider. If Mark should fall to the dwimor, I will have no way to protect you here or for the remainder of the journey south."

Pellin sighed. Once again, his guard had managed to plot the safest course of action, offering prudence while he proposed risk. When had he become so reckless? Pellin turned to confirm Allta's order. "Curse that little thief," he breathed. "He's done it again."

Mark was already gone.

"Impressive," Allta said. "I should have heard him slip away."

A clatter of dishes and a scream came from the kitchen. Allta rose, conflict written plain on his face—between his desire to aid Mark and his duty to protect Pellin at all costs. Men and women in the inn ran toward the sound of struggle, two of them wearing a reeve's insignia.

"Here now," a deep voice called. "What's this?"

"I'm telling you the truth, you stupid growler," Mark's voice came from the kitchen. "She was robbing you. Look at all that food."

Allta led Pellin toward the kitchen at a run. Mark's voice paused for a moment, followed by a thump.

"What was that for?" another man yelled. "Are you trying to kill her?"

"She's dangerous," Mark said. "You really don't want her to wake up."

Allta shouldered the crowd away, and they came into a circle of men, some almost as big as the guard, surrounding the figure of Mark standing over the now visible form of a young woman.

Pellin itched to remove his gloves, but the crowd of men around Mark had grown ugly, their protective instincts roused by sight of a defenseless girl being attacked. He dug into the pocket of his cloak, his fingers searching among the emblems stored there for the symbol of the Merum faith. His fingers brushed across the silver medallion of the intersecting arcs and brought it forth. "Gentlemen," he said in a voice that cut through the mutters, "may Aer be with you."

The men turned, catching sight of the worked metal that signified the rank of bishop, and as one, most of them bowed. "And also with you," they chorused. This far south the Merum church held almost absolute sway. Only one or two of the patrons crammed into the space refused to bow, their faces stiff with refusal and nervousness.

Pellin pointed at the innkeeper hovering over Mark, a large-bellied bull of a man who had no idea how much danger he was in. "The boy is my servant."

The man took two quick steps back, bumping into those behind him, and Pellin stepped toward Mark, tapping the emblem on his chest, hoping his apprentice understood. "Tell me what happened, lad."

Mark bowed in a way that spoke of familiarity and long habit. "I saw this one"—he nudged the unconscious girl—"sneaking into the kitchen, moving like she didn't want anyone to see her, and I think to myself, 'She's not up to anything good.' When I follow her in, I see she's stuffing food into her cloak like she's trying to empty the place. That's when I rapped her behind the ear, but not before she takes a swing at me with her dagger. Quick she was. I was on my way to tell you, Your Magnificence, but he stopped me." He nodded toward the pot-bellied man.

"I don't allow brawling in my inn," the man said as he bobbed his head. "Not even among boys or women."

Pellin pursed his lips as if thinking, fingering his medallion the whole time. "I need to question the girl. It may be that there is a story behind her thievery. If so, it may be that the church can provide some mercy."

"Begging your pardon, Bishop, but why not just call the watch?"

Pellin forced himself to laugh, praying Mark had hit the girl hard enough to keep her unconscious for a few moments longer. "I hardly think we need to disturb them for a hungry little girl. Here." He held out a silver half-crown. "This should cover your losses from this disturbance. Come, Mark. Allta. Disarm her. I'm old, and I'd rather do this sitting down, and I'm sure we'll get more of the truth from her if she's not surrounded by a crowd of onlookers. Bring her."

Mark did a quick search, relieving the girl of a pair of very functional daggers. Allta lifted her so that she rested in the crook of his left arm, his right hand free and close to his sword. Pellin led them from the kitchen.

CHAPTER 3

The sound of tearing cloth filled the room as Allta ripped the bed covering into strips that Mark used to tie the dwimor to the chair. Her head lolled from side to side, and Pellin squinted against the uncomfortable sensation of having someone fade in and out of perception right in front of him. His head started to hurt.

When her head came up and her eyes opened, his gaze slid from her. If he'd been asked to count the people in the room, he never would have seen the girl. Mark, on the other hand, appeared to have no such trouble. The sounds of struggle and the chair rocking on the floor echoed in the room until Allta put his weight on the girl's seat.

His guard put the blade of his dagger to what Pellin judged to be her throat, forcing her to stillness for a moment before he jerked the dagger away with the sound of air being displaced. A drop of bright red blood appeared in midair and fell to spatter against the floor.

Pellin drew in a breath. Only Allta's physical gift had kept the assassin from killing herself. "Can you speak?" he asked. The effort of trying to bring her into focus made his eyes hurt.

Nothing. No sound came from her—not a word or sigh. He might have been talking to the chair for all the response he received.

Mark moved around until he stood in front of her chair, looking, Pellin supposed, into eyes that had been drained of all color. He turned to Pellin and shook his head. "I don't think she's going to talk, Eldest. It's as if she doesn't have the ability."

Pellin nodded in resignation. "I had hoped it would be otherwise, but Cesla—we—did the same hundreds of years ago to keep the identity

21

and the origins of the dwimor secret." A weight descended upon him as he stripped off his gloves. "Very well, let's see what's in her mind. Bare her arm."

He reached out, the motion stirring the air across his fingertips, until he made contact. Her skin felt human enough. No hint of the emptiness within her mind tainted the warmth her pulsing heart gave to her flesh, but the vision of her fading in and out of his visual perception stymied his gift. He tried to find her gaze, but he couldn't hold those colorless orbs in his sight. Sighing, he closed his eyes.

Pellin rushed into the delve, his thoughts diminishing as he felt himself absorbed into the remnants of the woman's personality. He stood in near absolute emptiness—still himself, still Pellin, Eldest of the Vigil, a man who'd lived for centuries. He turned in the emptiness, searching for the accustomed river of memory that should have taken a part of him at the first touch, the collection of a lifetime of experiences and emotions that defined each and every soul he'd ever delved, no matter how forsaken.

He found it finally—what was left of it, at any rate—a trickle down by his feet. He crouched to inspect it, hoping for some sign, though he knew better than to expect such hope. A thread drifted past him on the stream, dark as obsidian, but short, the recollection comprising it brief in duration. Beneath it, a vault of purest black lay, covered in the symbols of the forest. Another memory followed, also black and short-lived. He reached out his hand and lived the memory as if his own.

"You are dismissed, Myra," Queen Chora said in a voice that could have frozen water.

She fell to her knees, would have clutched the queen's feet had she not kicked her hands away with disdain, her dancer's grace evident even in that gesture. No amount of pleading could convince the queen of her innocence. "But I never touched him," she begged.

"You expect me to believe the word of a common servant over that of a prince?" Queen Chora yelled. "You dare? Take your dismissal and go, and be thankful I do not send you to the headsman."

Pellin stood in emptiness again, the memories too few to create the familiar sensation of consciousness he'd come to expect when delving. He waited until the trickle of Myra's memories brought him the next strand. He reached out and felt blackness take him again.

"No," Countess Relgin said. "I will by no means hire a servant dismissed by the queen." The countess leaned forward until Myra could almost taste the wine on her breath. "No house in Cynestol will hire you, girl. Can you blame them? The queen has told us how you put your hands on the prince."

"But I didn't!" Myra cried.

The countess stiffened. "Are calling the queen a liar?" She looked Myra up and down. "You're young enough. Perhaps you can find work as a night woman."

The memory ceased, and he waited for the next strand, impatient, though he knew that outside the delve, no more than a single heartbeat or two had passed. When it came, he grasped it and despair took him.

She skulked in the streets of Cynestol, begging for food, unable to find work and unwilling to become a night woman. Everywhere she went people accused her of trying to seduce the prince until she fled from them all to hide and hunt the alleys at night. The desire to take Queen Chora and imprison her, force her to live this same humiliation burned through her.

When the memory stopped, he sighed, looking, waiting for another strand, but when it came he found himself reliving the first memory again. Turning, he searched the emptiness of the girl's mind until he found her vault once more.

Surveying the black scroll, he saw it to be like the others, covered with the same writing he'd seen in all who'd been tainted by the evil, written in glyphs that bore no resemblance to any language he'd seen. Redemption was impossible.

He willed his fingers to break contact and he straightened, once more standing in the middle of the room he'd taken with Allta and Mark. Allta's look probably matched his own, resigned and stoic, but Mark wore an expression filled with the wonder the gift of domere often inspired in the uninitiated.

He stood, pondering the girl he couldn't see.

"Eldest?" Allta asked. "What's wrong?"

"A mystery, my friend. There is so much we don't know. A millennium is hardly enough time to make a scratch." He sighed. "We heard no bells signaling Chora's death. I think she was on the way to kill the queen." Even as he said it, his conclusion felt wrong. But why?

"Eldest," Mark said, "she was stealing a *lot* of food."

Pellin took a deep breath. "Meaning she wasn't alone or she intended to wait before making her attempt on the queen. There's not much to work with. The process of making her a dwimor has emptied her mind, making it impossible to retain any memories except what Cesla intended."

He looked at Allta, who responded with one curt nod. All that remained was for him to take his apprentice out of the room on some pretext so his guard could dispatch the girl as quickly and cleanly as mercy allowed. "Mark," Pellin called, "why don't we go downstairs. Perhaps we can persuade the innkeeper to find us something sweet."

Mark didn't move or answer, his eyes fixed on the girl, though Pellin couldn't tell if she met his gaze.

"You're going to kill her, aren't you?" Mark asked.

A stab of regret pained him before he shunted it aside and nodded. "I'm sorry. There's nothing left of her except a desire for vengeance." He rolled his shoulders in an attempt to shed the responsibility Mark's regard placed upon him. "There's nothing left of her except hatred and a name that's not real."

"What is it?"

He thought at first of refusing to answer, but perhaps this would be Mark's way of grieving. Pellin reminded himself his young apprentice was acquainted with bloodshed. Along with several other members of the urchins, he had helped to defeat Laewan during the slaughter of Bas-solas. "Myra," he said. "He gave her the name Myra."

Mark nodded. "I don't read as much as Fess, but I know that means *sorrow*. Why do you have to kill her?"

Pellin shook his head, tried not to let his frustration show. "Mark, there's nothing left of her life. Everything has been emptied out of her mind except the barest need to survive and a hatred of Queen Chora."

Mark shrugged as if Pellin's argument was irrelevant. "Then give her a different life. Give her a different name to live to."

Defeated, Pellin sat on the bed. He didn't want to have this conversation. Wounds on his soul he'd tried to forget tore open anew. "Let me try to explain." He met Mark's gaze, his apprentice's sky-blue eyes so earnest they were almost desperate. "How long does it take a carpenter to make a chair?"

Mark shook his head. "It depends on the chair."

Pellin nodded his approval. "Good, that was well-reasoned." He pointed to Myra. "Let's suppose it's a fairly simple chair."

"A few days," Mark said.

"How long would it take you to destroy it?" Pellin asked. "How much time would you need to reduce all that work to nothing more than kindling for the fire?"

Mark turned away from him to contemplate the woman only he could see. "But you have all those memories in your head. Couldn't you just give her some of those?"

Pellin's heart ached to give his apprentice what he wanted. "Mark, the gift of domere doesn't work that way. When I delve a person, when any of the Vigil touch another, we see the memories and emotions of that person's life as a river. We reach into the river, grasp a memory, and become that person at that point in time. To accomplish our task we track that memory forward or backward until we can determine their guilt or innocence." He shook his head. "But there's no way for us to absorb all the memories that make up a person, just as there's no way you could drink all the water in a river. We don't have room enough in our minds to hold so much. Even as it is, taking only what we need, some of the Vigil lose control over their own minds at the end, too tired to maintain their own identity."

"What do we have to lose?" Mark asked. "What does she have to lose?"

"Oh, Aer," Pellin almost pleaded. "Mark, look at yourself. All of your memories are tied to your physical being. What would it be like to give Myra memories from a different body? You're asking me to give her memories that will drive her insane."

Mark shrugged away his answer. "We have a saying in the urchins, Eldest. When is the best time to die?"

Pellin shook his head. "When?"

His apprentice gave him a rueful smile. "Later."

Behind the dwimor, Allta chuckled, his voice a rumble of amusement. "Well spoken."

Pellin pulled a deep breath that held hints of woodsmoke and ale and sighed his resignation. "I'll try." How could he deny the request of his earnest, kindhearted apprentice. "Allta, as gently as you can, please render her unconscious. I have some somnal powder in my pack."

He sat on the bed, waiting while Allta and Mark tried to coax water mixed with sleeping powder into a girl only one of them could see, a slip of a girl who would kill them all without a hint of remorse because she'd lost the ability to feel it.

After seven hundred years of living, everyone he met reminded him of someone he'd met before. Several times he'd met descendants of nobles or *gnath*, people without a gift, who resembled a distant relative from antiquity so closely that he suspected the dead of walking his memories.

Who would she resemble? Might he have seen or met some of her ancestors in his long sojourn? Deep within, so deep he might have denied it existed, lay the hope that he wouldn't recognize anyone associated with her. What Mark had asked of him lay beyond his ability. Centuries with his gift hadn't given him Aer-like wisdom—only experience, and all of it told him this was doomed to fail.

"I think she's ready, Eldest," Allta said.

Pellin stood and circled the young woman he could now see, committing her features to memory. Her heart-shaped face and dark hair would have been considered attractive in any time period, though the current fashion trended toward smaller facial features. He thumbed open one of her eyelids. Her irises, clear as glass, gave no hint of their original color. He would just have to trust to Aer that the memories he placed within the girl would feel right. "How tall is she, Mark?"

The boy shrugged. "About my height, Eldest. Perhaps a finger's width shorter."

Pellin pulled the other chair close and removed his gloves, though he made no move to delve the girl just yet. "You may as well be seated, gentlemen. This will take more than a moment."

He turned his thoughts inward and entered the construct that existed in his mind, a vast library of five levels and four wings emanating from a central open space. He lifted his arms, palms down, and floated. The strictures of Aer's physical universe didn't apply here, and he'd long ago found it quicker to fly than walk. When he'd first come to the Vigil, Formona and the others had instructed him on the construction of his sanctuary, how it might have to hold the accumulated delvings of a thousand years.

He'd planned accordingly. Each wing held two hundred and fifty years of accumulated memories, divided into groups of five decades for each level. He flew along the hallways, his fingers brushing each door just long enough to get a sense of the physical appearance of the person within.

It was over more quickly than he would have thought, but he had two possibilities, neither of them good. "Mark." He tried not to sigh. "I'm willing to make the attempt, and I will strive to make it work, but there is a choice to be made."

The boy's eyebrows dipped as if in suspicion. "What choice, Eldest?"

"Most of the memories held by the Vigil are from those who've committed some crime, not surprising, since that is the task Aer has laid upon us with our gift."

He didn't have to finish. "You're going to give her the memories of a criminal," Mark said. A moment later he shrugged. "That would have described me a few short months ago."

"We don't delve mere thieves," Pellin snapped. "You know that."

Mark's face went stony, and for a moment he resembled a Vigil guard. "I do know that. What's the choice?"

"Criminal or victim," Pellin said. "They both resemble her, but the memories are old and partial, as we discussed before."

Mark stared. "You're asking me to choose?"

Pellin nodded. "It's customary within the Vigil for the one who proposes a course of action to bear the cost of its decisions." Behind him, Allta might have made a sound of disapproval.

To his credit the boy didn't try to argue or rationalize his way out of the responsibility. "Victim," he said. "It will give her a better chance at healing. Besides, she's seems to be one."

"Well enough," Pellin nodded. He leaned forward, placed his hand on the dwimor's arm, and opened the door to memories from a long dead girl. "May Aer have mercy on our souls," he whispered.

CHAPTER 4

In the cavernous desolation of the girl's mind, Pellin searched for her wellspring, the source from which the river of memory flowed for any soul walking the earth. At his feet, a pitiful trickle with a few solitary black strands flowed past him and disappeared only to reappear a few seconds later, the implanted memories that had turned the girl into Cesla's tool. Each time it completed its cycle, he followed it a bit farther upstream until he found its source. He hadn't told Mark this had been tried before. And before.

And before.

He did not require Custos or any other historian to tell him that failure waited.

He had tried it himself.

During the Wars for the Gift of Kings, as Agin and his kin ravaged the north, it had been Pellin's duty to heal those volunteers who had fallen just short in their quest to become dwimor. He had taken the task upon himself. Even now, centuries later, he could still remember the bone-aching weariness that had come with the labor, how he'd forced himself to stay in the delve longer than he'd ever dreamed in his misguided attempt at healing.

The stream with its black threads bubbled forth from the girl's wellspring, and he sighed. He would have to destroy the memories Cesla had implanted in her mind while simultaneously releasing the chosen set of memories from his construct. He knelt, his hands poised on either side of the source of the girl's identity and waited.

When those black memories bubbled forth, he grabbed them, held them in one hand as he thrust his other as deep into her wellspring as he could. With a thought he slashed those memories of hatred and injustice and opened the door in his mind, letting the replacement memories stream forth, living her life again. Against reason, he hoped the swap would be enough to destroy her vault, but it remained.

Her name had been Cerena Niwe, a girl from the northern part of Aille, near Treflow, when Pellin had been new enough to the Vigil to carry his years as any other man. In truth, Cerena's memories carried slightly more chance of success than any other. When Pellin had delved her, the victim of a cleric's unwanted attention, he had yet to master his gift. In his zeal he'd absorbed far more of her memories than he should have. That single delve had been the only one he'd been able to attempt that day. In the long years since, he'd learned to refine his search, to focus his gift to an edge sharper than any healer's scalpel so that he only need absorb the memories required to determine innocence or guilt. In the first days of his service, he'd been a broadsword.

He loosed the memories of a girl who'd been dead for nearly seven hundred years, pushing them as deep into the assassin's wellspring as they could go. When the last memory flowed from his mind to hers, he closed the door within his construct and released his hold.

He blinked against the light of the room, his eyes still remembering the phantom darkness of the girl's empty mind. Allta and Mark looked at him, waiting, he supposed, for some sign of success or failure. The girl lolled in her chair, her body limp against her restraints.

"The memories are deep within her wellspring," he said. "It will take a while for them to come forth." He sighed. "Her name is Cerena. Cerena Niwe."

Mark looked at the girl, his expression so still it might have been mistaken for indifference had Pellin not spent nearly every waking hour with him for the past few months. "Shouldn't we know more about her? So we can be her friends?"

Pellin had been about to say "It won't matter," but Mark's earnestness stopped him, filling him with an obscure sense of shame, as though he'd surrendered in the face of evil. This girl, whoever she had been, was a victim of evil's deception. Who was he to say that finding her, an incredible unlikelihood, had not been arranged by Aer?

Even if the threefold God hadn't set their paths to cross, this girl sat as a living metaphor for the entire continent, a land being force-fed evil until it succumbed.

"She's from a village near Treflow," Pellin said. "Aenwold. Her father was a grain merchant. When he died, the local priest offered to take her on as his secretary to help her family. It was rare in those days for anyone outside the priesthood to know how to read or write."

Mark nodded. "You said she was a victim. Let me guess, the priest had other interests besides her clerical skills." He shook his head. "The church."

Pellin felt the stab of the boy's disgust, recognized that emotion by his own long familiarity with it. Unlike his apprentice, Pellin did not believe Aer was indifferent to suffering, and he had an answer for this. "To some people the church, then and now, offered easy access to power, Mark. They joined her ranks out of the desire to exercise that power or to obtain some measure of wealth." He shook his head. "It is the same with any organization, though it is most often associated with the nobility."

"Then the church should cleanse itself," Mark said without taking his eyes from the girl.

Pellin nodded. This too was an argument he knew well. "And many agree with you—I, for one. But remember what the church is, lad—a collection of lost souls who have recognized their plight, many of whom can no more heal themselves of their moral disease than a man or woman can cure themselves of the wasting sickness. They come to Aer, Iosa, and Gaoithe for that healing. Some receive it quickly while others struggle with their weaknesses their entire lives, carrying that fight all the way to their grave."

Mark opened his mouth to object once more, but Pellin held up a hand. "But in this case, your desire for justice was fulfilled." He pointed at the unconscious girl. "I have her memories up through her victimization by the priest because I was called upon by the Archbishop of the Merum to determine the truth."

"She was a victim, you said. What happened?" Mark asked.

"After I determined the priest's guilt, Cerena was freed from his dominion and paid recompense. Because it was early during my time with the Vigil, and I still had the energy for such, I checked on her a few times over the years. Amazingly, though I am not aware the priest

PATRICK W. CARR

asked for such, it seemed she forgave him and moved on. She married and had children and lived to the end of her days."

"And the priest?"

Pellin nodded. "He also lived to the end of his days."

"Doesn't everyone?" Mark said.

Despite himself, Pellin laughed. "It's an old phrase that means someone has lived a long life. I don't know that the priest enjoyed it so much, though he might have been grateful for it. I never saw him again. The Archbishop kept him under penance until the day he died, working alone in the fields near Cynestol."

Mark nodded in satisfaction. "It's strange to think she'll have the chance to relive her life centuries after it happened."

If only, Pellin thought.

CHAPTER 5

Pellin watched the girl, breathing shallowly and still bound to the chair, his heart grieving what he had done. "She will wake at any moment," he said to Mark. "It is difficult to say just what her reaction will be. To her own eyes, she will certainly look different than she remembers. Blindfold her, and have a gag ready. We don't want to draw any more attention than we have to."

Mark nodded as he took from his bag the cloth that all of the urchins carried to shield their eyes from lamp and daylight before going out to steal at night. He tied it firmly over the girl's eyes and waited. "How many times has this been tried?" he asked.

Pellin stepped into the river that comprised his own long life, panning for those memories. "In the lore of the Vigil, it's been recorded at least a dozen times, though it's certain that it has been attempted more often. Those who hold the gift of domere are no less human than anyone else. We have no desire to commit our failures to pen and parchment."

"Has it ever worked?" Mark asked. He kept his gaze on the girl.

"No," Pellin whispered.

His apprentice nodded slightly, his face somber. "Is there a prayer you could offer for her?"

He shook his head, though Mark still hadn't looked away from the girl. "There is nothing in the liturgy that covers circumstances such as these."

"Is it possible to surprise Aer?" Mark asked.

"No."

"Then He knew this would happen?"

"Yes."

"Then there must be some prayer you can offer for her that He will hear," he said, his face tight.

"And do you believe He cares?" Pellin asked.

"Who can speak for Aer?" Mark said. "But I care."

A knot formed in Pellin's throat that refused to loosen. "Perhaps this will suffice." He raised his hands and recited the Exordium, the preface to each liturgical prayer in the church. Afterward, he lifted his voice, both in benison to the girl and in pleading to the threefold one. "Into your hands, O Aer, we commend this one, and we plead that where she found disease, she will find healing. Where she found hatred, she will find love. Where she found sorrow, she will find joy." He paused, knowing Mark would remember every word. The boy would test events against the words of his prayer, but Pellin had committed himself to this. "And where this poor soul found death, Aer, we pray she shall find life."

Mark turned at last from his contemplation of the girl. "That sounded like the prayer for the dead."

He nodded, knowing Mark would recognize it, expecting no less. "I changed it to something more appropriate."

"Thank you. I used to hear that prayer in Bunard whenever one of the urchins died, mostly in the winter. The priests always rushed through it." He shrugged, but something savage worked its way free from his indifference. "It was cold, and there was no reason for them not to. No one stood in attendance, and the priest couldn't know I was there, hidden in the shadows."

A sound came from the chair, like the softest mewing of a kitten. The girl lifted her head first, then tried to move her arms. A grunt, the prelude to struggle, sounded low in her throat. Mark darted forward to untie the ropes around her arms and legs. Allta drew his sword, the whisper of steel against leather soft in the room

Her head swiveled toward the sound.

"Do you know your name?" Mark asked.

She shook her head at first, then cocked it to one side. "Ce . . . Ce . . . Ce . . ."

"Your name is Cerena," Mark said.

The girl nodded, and for an instant, improbable impossible hope flared in Pellin's chest.

But then her legs twitched and she raised her arms, one trailing the other in uncoordinated jerks to rip the blindfold from her eyes. She held her shaking hands in front of her face, settling for an instant before the momentary expression of calm fled and her visage crumpled. She gasped, drawing breath to scream, but Allta was quicker. He placed a cloth infused with somnal syrup over her nose and held it there until her limbs went slack.

"Is this what happened before?" Mark asked in a small voice.

Pellin sighed, nodding. "Her memories of Cerena's physical body, no matter how close to her own, aren't hers, and her mind cannot reconcile the difference."

"You ended up killing them all, didn't you?"

He didn't bother to dodge the accusation or offer the claim that others had made the decision to create the dwimor and that he had only tried to heal them. Mark probably wouldn't care. He was certain he didn't care himself. As Eldest of the Vigil he carried the responsibility of past decisions as well as his own. "Yes, usually with the apothecaries' aid, but in the end all of them died by our hand. There is no need for us to be present for this, Mark." He turned. "Allta."

"No," Mark said. "There will be time to kill her later."

"Why?" Pellin asked.

Mark turned to him, his eyes bright with tears in the lamplight of the room. "Because she's a victim. Cesla emptied her mind as if he were pouring water from a pitcher."

"Apt," Pellin said. "She's just an empty vessel now, or nearly so. What would you have me do?"

To his surprise, Mark shook his head. "Nothing. If you will allow it, Eldest, I will tend to her on the journey south."

"No," Allta said stepping forward. "This *I* will not allow. We cannot afford the attention she will bring. Her screams and flailing will draw eyes and questions. The Eldest of the Vigil is in my care. The girl dies tonight."

Instead of answering Allta directly, Mark turned to Pellin. "What if I can keep her quiet?"

Pellin sighed. "If you can, then you will have bested the Vigil's efforts. Even that was beyond us." He nodded. "A day. I will give you a day to bring her mind under some sort of control." He would have stopped, wanted to stop, but his heart grieved what Mark intended, and he would save his apprentice this defeat if he could. "Please, don't do this."

Mark faced him, his face as resolute as any Vigil guard. "If it is alright, Eldest, I would like to keep her sleeping until dawn. I will take her outside the village once she wakes so that her screams will attract less attention."

"Until tomorrow, then," Pellin nodded. "Allta and I will take our meal downstairs. We will bring food back to you. You will call us if you need us?"

Mark nodded and pulled a chair to sit in front of the girl.

Outside the room, Pellin turned to Allta. "Let the innkeeper know the girl has a sickness that's causing her some pain. There's no need for specifics. Perhaps that will cover whatever noise she makes until we leave."

Oddly, despite the circumstances and struggles with Mark, Pellin's heart felt light, lighter than it had in some time, and he smiled as he realized the reason.

Allta caught the change in his mood. "Eldest?"

Pellin gripped his arm. "I believe that Mark will be my apprentice in truth, Allta, not just in name."

His guard's eyebrows registered his surprise. "He doesn't care much for the church, Eldest, and his belief in the reality of Aer is impersonal at best."

"Hardly," Pellin said. "I've finally divined Mark's greatest struggle. His belief in Aer is so viscerally real to him that he can't understand how a church professing those same beliefs could be so consistently indifferent." He nodded. "Come, we will bring dinner up to our room. The three of us will share our meal tonight and hold vigil over the girl."

"And tomorrow?" Allta asked.

Pellin sighed, shouldering his burden of past failures once more. "Tomorrow, despite what I just told Mark, I will offer my utmost effort to saving a girl who cannot be saved. Only such extremity of effort will convince Mark of the church's good intentions. After that, he will grieve the girl's death, but not our failure."

Pellin woke twice that night to see Mark watching the girl sleep, the somnal-infused cloth held ready in one hand, a single candle flame keeping watch with him. In the morning, Pellin stirred to see

Mark bent close to the girl who still slept, his mouth next to her ear, speaking in low, steady tones. Allta stood by the door.

They left the inn, Allta carrying the blindfolded girl until they mounted their horses to continue to the port, but Mark steered them west, directly away from the village and Cynestol, until they'd left the densest portion of civilization behind.

The girl stirred where she sat ahead of Mark on his horse. Instead of bringing the sleeping cloth to her face as he'd done before, his apprentice dismounted and helped the girl down.

She reached toward her face, her motions jerky, uncontrolled.

"Don't," Mark said.

The hands stopped, fluttering in the air as though the girl couldn't decide whether to obey. They started toward the blindfold again.

"If you can understand me," Mark said, "then I want you to lower your hands."

For a moment, they continued upward, as if their momentum was too great to be halted by mere words, but they stopped just short of the cloth before dropping heavily to her lap.

"Good," Mark said. "I have you blindfolded because you've been injured. Nod if you understand what I just said."

The girl nodded.

"Can you speak?" Mark asked.

Her mouth opened, but she exercised even less control over her tongue than she did her arms. "Ahhh!" Thrashing, she struggled to rise, but her arms and legs refused to cooperate. Mark moved behind her and folded her in his arms. His touch only made the struggles worse, and several times her flailing hands caught him in the face, leaving marks that would purple within a day.

"Shhh," he whispered. "You'll be alright."

Something in his tone or touch must have gotten through, the girl ceased her struggles to begin weeping softly instead.

"Let me tell you a story," Mark said. "Once there was a young woman who sat with a storyteller who repeatedly told her a tale of hatred and revenge. At first, she was pleased that the storyteller would make a story about her, but as time went on she noticed that more and more of her real life slipped away, until all that was left was the tale. Filled with a false desire for vengeance, the storyteller sent her out to do his bidding, to kill."

"But a brave man, a man of great years and wisdom, saw her and took away the lust for revenge, giving the young woman a different story. The man of great years and his friends hoped this would heal the woman, but it wasn't to be. The memories weren't really hers. When she tried to move, everything felt as if it belonged to someone else, and her arms and legs jerked like a marionette's."

Pellin stood transfixed as the young woman, cradled in Mark's arms, cocked her head, intent on each word.

"Yet the woman survived," Mark continued. "And after a time she learned how to speak and move and discovered that there was a life waiting for her that was all her own."

For a moment Pellin dared to hope that Mark's story and physical presence might be enough to calm her, but when he loosened his grip, she flailed, throwing him loose. Convulsions gripped her, and the sound of her head and limbs beating against the ground wrung his heart. Allta stepped forward, but Mark recovered and waved him back.

Like a fighter beaten but undeterred, Mark came within the circle of the girl's convulsions, accepting blows until he could gather her in his arms once more. Blood ran down his chin from a split in his lip, but he ignored it until the young woman quieted, her chest heaving. Only then did he duck his head to wipe the blood away.

"I think she might be thirsty," Mark said to Allta. "Would you give me my waterskin?"

Only years of familiarity allowed Pellin to understand the emotion locked behind Allta's expression. He handed Mark the skin, then turned quickly away to scan the surroundings for any signs of danger. They were still alone.

When Mark held the spout to her lips she started, jerking away, but soon she drank, her neck cording with the effort.

Pellin went to his pack and retrieved a loaf of honeyed bread. "Here," he said. "She must be hungry, and this will sit easy on her tongue, even if she doesn't remember the taste."

Mark nodded. One eye was beginning to swell shut. "Thank you, Eldest." He took the bread and broke off a piece without any crust and held it carefully to her lips. When she took that, he repeated the process, intermixing sips of water until she showed no more inclination to eat or drink.

When she started to struggle again, Mark repeated the story he told her earlier, rocking back and forth, though the young woman he held matched him in weight and size. She drowsed in his arms and fell asleep.

"How did you know holding her like that would calm her?" Pellin asked. He still didn't believe the girl could be saved, but her extremity served to reveal aspects of Mark's character he had only glimpsed before now.

"I didn't," Mark said, "but there have been children who have come into the urchins over the past few years who were in similar straits." He stretched his face, working to open his swollen eye. "Though none of them were as big as Cerena, or as strong."

Allta rejoined them, the reins of all three horses clenched in one fist. "Can she ride?"

Mark nodded after a pause. "I think so, but if I release her, she'll wake and probably start struggling again."

With a nod, Allta handed the reins to Pellin, then scooped both Mark and the girl in his arms to set them atop Mark's horse.

CHAPTER 6

They turned south and rode at a brisk walk toward the southern coast. Whenever Pellin checked on his apprentice, he saw the boy's lips moving, but the words were too soft to hear. Sometime between dawn and noon, the girl stirred from her sleep, her limbs jerking at first with the startlement of consciousness before settling under Mark's reassurance.

"Eldest," Mark's voice called to him. "How far are we from Cynestol's port?"

"At this pace we will arrive just before dusk. Too late to take ship, I'm afraid," Pellin said.

Mark nodded as though that information somehow suited him. "With your permission, Eldest, can we stay at an inn with baths?" He wrinkled his nose. "We both need it."

Pellin nodded in appreciation of Mark's discretion. His nose had told him as much as his apprentice had admitted to. "Frequent bathing in Cynestol is a more accepted practice than it is in the northern climes. Every inn has public baths—and private, for those willing to pay a bit extra."

For the first time since Mark had entered Pellin's service as apprentice and guard, temporary or otherwise, embarrassment discolored the boy's fair skin. "Will they have attendants, Eldest? Women, I mean."

Pellin nodded. "No doubt."

They hit the coast road a few miles east of Port City and came in sight of the harbor just before dusk. The docks were still a couple miles distant, but the sprawl of the continent's largest city and its shipping center had spread here as well. Everywhere he looked, carts rumbled past in both directions filled with goods coming from or going to the ships that awaited them, and people from every kingdom of the northern continent and even a few merchants from the southern continent roamed the streets.

They stopped at the first inn they found, a two-story structure of weathered wood and heavy beams that might have been salvaged from a ship. The girl started at the noise, but each time Mark spoke into her ear and she stilled.

"Why does it look like that?" Mark asked, pointing at the inn.

Pellin took in the ponderous sight of the Fair Wind and laughed, remembering. "Storms from the southern sea are rare," he said. "It's known for being placid, but on occasion, especially as winter approaches, they can be quite severe."

They rode around back to the stable yard, where Allta lifted Mark and the girl down to set them standing on the ground between the inn and the long, low shed of the stable. A woman came out of the back of the inn, her nose wrinkling as she passed by Mark.

"I'm Misara Anan. You'll be needing rooms, then?" she asked. "And baths?"

Pellin nodded. "One room, please, large enough for the four of us, and private baths."

She looked at their plain clothing. "That'll be one silver half."

He put two silver half crowns into her extended hand. "And we'll need a change of clothes for the girl."

She nodded. "She's about my daughter's size." She pointed to the blindfold. "What's wrong with her eyes? I don't allow guests with the pox to stay here. I don't care how much money you have."

A cloud passed over the sun, throwing the portion of the yard where Mark supported the girl into shadow. Mistress Anan looked up and made the ancient sign against evil. Pellin stifled his instinct to speak against her superstition and forced himself to don a comforting smile. "She has a condition that affects her vision. I assure you, the girl is not carrying any malady into your inn."

The woman's face darkened to match the shadow in the courtyard. "An innkeeper hears everything, Master Pellin. I've heard tell of people who come back from the forest. They can't abide the light, and when the sun goes down they kill."

Pellin nodded. "An interesting tale indeed, but I assure you, the girl is no danger."

"Do you have an attendant who can assist her with her bath?" Mark asked.

She looked at him, her expression curious. "Why don't you do it?"

Pellin interrupted before Mark could respond. "The girl is somewhat modest."

The innkeeper shook her head. "Northerners. Aye. Take the room at the far end of the inn on the first floor. I'll send my eldest, Nosura, along."

Mark guided Cerena to the inn, the girl stumbling with every step as Pellin and Allta followed. For a wonder, she didn't cry out or fall as they passed through the taproom with its noisy patrons. They entered a room with five large beds and a large copper-lined bath that could accommodate three or four people. Pellin breathed a sigh of relief, nodding toward a privacy screen that could be used to shield the bathers. "Mistress Anan seems acquainted with the customs of the north."

Allta moved to answer a knock at the door a moment later, and a girl of fifteen or sixteen entered. "I'm Nosura. Mother said you needed assistance."

Pellin nodded. "Yes. This is Mark"—he pointed—"and his sister, Cerena."

Nosura wrinkled her nose. "She's soiled her clothes."

"Yes," Mark said, his voice even.

"Not to worry," Nosura said. "I have a cousin. She had an accident and we helped care for her. Let's get her undressed and bathed."

Mark guided Cerena toward the bath with Nosura following. All went well until Mark attempted to disengage himself from Cerena's grasp. Cerena clung to him as she made desperate noises like the whine of an animal.

"Shh, it will be alright," Mark said, crooning to her over and over again.

But no amount of reassurance could calm her. After half an hour of trying to persuade Cerena to release Mark, Nosura shook her head. "I'm sorry, Master Pellin, but I have other duties in the inn."

He waved her away. "Thank you for your efforts, Nosura. We will handle Cerena's bathing."

After the door closed behind her, Pellin turned back to Mark to see his apprentice, stiff-postured and dour, in Cerena's grip. "I suppose you'll say we need to kill her."

Pellin shook his head. "By no means. You've made more progress with Cerena than anyone ever made restoring a dwimor." He sighed. "However, we must find a solution for her current state. If she cannot adopt the rudiments of her morning regimen, crossing the strait to the southern continent will be difficult."

Allta nodded his agreement. "Sailors are not known for their patience."

Mark nodded, guiding Cerena toward the step leading up to the bath. "Alright. I will get her cleaned."

"Well and good," Pellin said. "But how will you keep her from soiling herself?" As soon as he asked, he regretted the question, seeing Mark bow beneath its weight. "Never mind, lad. One thing at a time."

Mark managed to get his boots off along with his cloak, but any attempts he made to disrobe for the bath sent Cerena into a panic, her mouth open in a rictus of horror. "Why is she doing that?" Mark asked.

Pellin opened the door to Cerena's memories, sifted through them before shutting them away again. "The priest who took her against her will possessed a particular appetite. He always had her bathe first."

Mark loosed a stream of heartfelt curses that Pellin thought impressive, given that their intended target had been dead for almost seven hundred years.

"I hope neither of you are in a hurry," Mark said after he'd run out of imprecations. "Her baths are going to include me in my clothes."

"You've done this before," Pellin said.

Mark nodded. "Yes, Eldest. The urchins didn't have access to baths, but we made generous use of the Rinwash in the poor quarter. There were quite a few of the younger ones who were in similar shape to Cerena. She's not the first girl I've had to bathe." He took a few steps into the bath. The progressive touch of the water agitated the girl, but each time Mark would speak in her ear until she calmed. Hints of past lives intruded on Pellin, images of similar, poignant moments, moments of sacrifice. "Perhaps I can help," Pellin said, leaning over the water as he removed his gloves.

The proximity of his voice sent Cerena deeper into Mark's embrace until his apprentice could hardly move. "How, Eldest?" Mark asked.

"I'm going to look into her mind and see how much is there. Perhaps she has enough accumulated memories of you to allow me to excise those responsible for her fear of bathing."

Heedless of the water, he reached out to touch Cerena's arm. She jerked at the unfamiliar contact, but not so much as to break the delve. Pellin rushed into her mind and stood as before in a cavern without sides or roof. Only the sensation of insubstantial ground below his imaginary feet provided any spatial orientation.

Strands comprising her river of memories flowed past him in colors that spanned everything from gold to black, testaments to the nature of those remembrances. That there should be any memories comprised of gold astounded him, and he bent to touch one.

His awareness dropped away and he became Cerena. A woman held by the voice that spoke to her in long dark nights of terror comprised of blindness, unfamiliar limbs, and a past that carried disjointed memories. Over and over again the voice—more than a child's but less than a man's—spoke to her, keeping the darkness at bay.

"Once there was a woman who went to a storyteller," the voice said, and the familiar tale covered her with warmth like a blanket in the midst of winter. At the end the voice changed, becoming quieter, but no less insistent for that. "Remember," the voice said, "you are loved." And the arms around her gave her a comforting squeeze. "No matter what has happened in your past, no matter who you might have been, this day is yours to start anew. More important than any man or woman or storyteller is this: You are loved and cherished. Not for how you look or what you can do, but simply because you are."

Pellin let go of the memory, dizzy with its remembered intensity, and looked down. There still wasn't very much of a river to comprise the girl's consciousness, hardly more than a newborn's and most of the memories he did see, didn't belong to the girl, but to long-dead Cerena.

Perhaps Cerena's memories were more of an impediment than an aid at this point. He bent, searching through the river for those memories of Cerena that were tied to her physical presence. If he could have sighed in the cavern that comprised her mind, he would have. It was the nature of memory that each recollection was tied to physical being. If he destroyed all of them, the girl would be reduced to nothing. Response would be impossible.

But perhaps there was another way. Thrusting his hands into the river, he removed those memories of Cerena that were connected to speaking. The task required a finer touch than he had ever used before. For the girl to make the quickest recovery, memories of language must not be destroyed. Only those memories that tied Cerena's expression of language to speech, those very memories of her moving her mouth to make sound, only those could be destroyed. Over and over, he let the river of memories cascade through him until he'd removed every memory that might keep the girl mute.

He broke the delve. Despite the chill of the water, sweat cascaded down his face, and he turned to find Allta next to him, concern on the guard's face mirrored on Mark's. He put his hand on the edge of the tub to steady himself. "I'm well."

"You were in the delve for over an hour, Eldest," Allta said.

"Ah." He took a breath, the sensation unfamiliar after so much time in another's mind. "So long?" They nodded. "Well, it was more than a little difficult at that." He went on to explain what he'd done and his reasoning behind it.

Cerena still stood in the water, shivering though Mark held her, letting the water wash away her indignity. Sometime during Pellin's sojourn in her mind, Mark had managed to wash her hair despite the presence of her blindfold, and deep red highlights revealed themselves in the brown color.

Pellin accepted Allta's hand and stepped away from the tub. "If this works, you'll have to give her a new name, of course. Cerena will be a thing of the past. It may be that Cerena's memories are keeping her from reconnecting with her body." He sighed. "It wouldn't be the first time my preconceived notions have been wrong."

Mark guided Cerena from the tub and wrapped her in one of the blankets. He would have let go entirely, but she clutched at his arm, wrapping her own unsteady limbs around it. "Will this work, Eldest?" Mark asked.

Pellin laughed, amused at his own ignorance amid the boy's assumption of wisdom. "Mark, you've done more with that poor broken girl than any of the Vigil were ever able to do with the dwimor we created. Not once were we able to come close to restoring them." An idea began to form in his mind, a terrible risk. "Let me ask you, is she getting any better?"

Mark shrugged. "I don't know. I think so, but I might just be trying to convince myself." He turned to face Cerena, his expression somber. "There was a girl in the urchins a few years younger than me who got a cough one winter. We all took turns caring for her, and I thought she was getting better right up until the morning I went to wake her and she didn't move."

Pellin nodded. "What will you call her?" he asked. "She deserves her own name."

Mark nodded. "I've never named anyone before." Pain filled his light blue eyes. "It seems very important to me somehow. Will you help me?"

"Of course," Pellin bowed. "I would be honored. You know, our language covers a long, long history." Cerena's gilded memory returned to him. "I know a name I think you would like. It hasn't been used in very long time. Elieve."

Mark tilted his head and his lips moved, testing the sound. "What does it mean?"

Tears stung Pellin's eyes and he had to swallow twice before he could muster the strength to answer. "It means *loved*."

Mark put his ear by the girl's head and spoke, but not so quietly that Pellin couldn't hear him. "Your name is Elieve. You are loved." He repeated this perhaps a dozen times as his charge stood unmoving at his side.

Quiet hung over the room as they dried themselves. Tomorrow they would board ship and cross the sea to the southern continent, the origin of man.

Mark had knelt to dry Cerena's feet, and so didn't see, but Pellin did. The girl's lips moved, working, and even through the cloth of the blindfold, the acuteness of her effort was plain.

Pellin didn't breathe or move for fear of disturbing her, but a moment later, Mark must have sensed her struggle. He rose.

"E-el-el-li," the girl stuttered, then stopped, her mouth tight with frustration.

"Elieve," Mark said, his voice thick. "You are loved."

CHAPTER 7

Pellin, flanked by Allta on one side and Mark with Elieve on the other, surveyed a three-masted ship the following day. The captain—a broad bluff of a man with stump-like legs and the light olive coloring of those from Caisel—looked as though he could have weathered the worst of storms without a thought. As they approached the boarding plank, the captain called imprecations on a poor unfortunate sailor who been a shade too slow to obey an order.

"Curse your worthless, maggot-ridden hide, Jory! The next time you hear me repeat myself it will be because I thought throwing you overboard was so funny I had to laugh twice. You understand me, yah?"

"Aye, uncle." The boy was faced the other way, and his reply barely made it to Pellin's hearing.

"Call me Captain Onen, boy, or I'll have you on kitchen duty for the next year." He turned to Pellin, still wearing the sneer that had sent Jory scrambling into the rigging to help unfurl the sails. "My sister's son," he growled. "I love him dearly, but the lad's never going to make a good sailor. The call of the sea is just not in him." He took in Pellin's clothes and stance with a quick glance. "Who are you?"

Pellin nodded. "I understand the boy's plight, Captain. It took me a long time and many trips before I acquired my sea legs. My name is Pellin. I'm looking for passage to Erimos."

The captain scowled as he pursed his lips. "Are you telling me I need to be more patient with the boy?"

"Ah, no, Captain," Pellin smiled. "When I say a long time, I'm

46

not measuring it in years. Do as you think best. I understand you're bound for the southern continent."

"Aye, but I don't usually take on passengers." He shot a pointed look at Mark, who still held Elieve close. "They're fussy. I don't like the smell of vomit on my ship." He waved a hand at his nephew. "It's bad enough I have to put up with Jory's puking hide, yah?"

Pellin felt for his purse. "I heard you were the best captain with a fast ship."

"Aye, but travelers to the southern continent usually go farther east. Erimos is a trading port, and you don't have the look of a merchant."

He ignored the implied question. "I'm prepared to make it worth your while, Captain Onen."

"Humph." Onen looked at the weight of Pellin's purse. "And how would you know how much my while is worth?"

Pellin smiled. "I'm counting on you to tell me—though I expect you'll try to deprive my descendants of their inheritance if you can, yah?" He smiled with his brows raised.

"You've been to Caisel, then?" the captain asked. "You have the look of a Cynestol man."

Pellin nodded. "I've done more than a bit of traveling, Captain. I've probably spent more time in Caisel than you've lived. Do you wish to negotiate the terms of our passage with or without bargaining?"

"Without. It's faster." Onen's eyes narrowed, and he shook his head. "One silver crown each to the south and back."

Pellin stared at the captain. "My compliments, Captain, on your house. I haven't seen that ruse used in some years, agreeing not to bargain and then using an inflated price anyway—high, but not so high to arouse suspicion from most. That bit of trickery is old enough that most men wouldn't recognize it."

Onen smiled. "My granda taught it to me when I was a lad. You must be older than you look."

"We won't need passage back, Captain," Pellin said. "I don't know how long we'll be there."

The captain shook his head. "Have you not heard? The leaders of the one church down there have shut off the interior. No one from the northern continent is allowed to travel past the ports."

A fist closed around Pellin's heart. "Have they said why, Captain?"

Onen scowled as he shook his head. "The southern churchmen

keep their own counsel. They have no need to explain it to a grizzled seaman like me."

Pellin took in a deep breath laden with the smell of salt and sea-weed. "Three crowns to the south, Captain, for the four of us. If needed, we'll pay the same rate for passage back." He looked at the ship. "How heavy are you running?"

Onen's gaze turned speculative. "Three-quarters of the holds are filled with wheat."

Pellin checked the waterline on the ship. With a decent wind, it would make the trip at an adequate pace. "Two weeks, wouldn't you say?"

"Aye," the captain said. "You've served on board, then, yah?"

"No, Captain, but I have an appreciation for the gifts and talents, however they're shown. You have a talent for nature, and you love the sea. May we board?"

At the captain's nod, Pellin waved at Allta and Mark, and together they descended to the cabin set aside for passengers. Allta looked at the compartment—functional, if a bit worn. "It seems the captain offers his ship to passengers more than he lets on."

"Yes," Pellin said. "Mistress Anan told me as much." He spied a pitcher and water along with a chamber pot. Sleeping would prove to be a tight affair on board a ship where space came at a premium. "Mark, do you have everything you need to tend to Elieve?"

After a moment, he nodded. "Yes, Eldest, though I may need more water to keep her clean."

Pellin frowned. "Try to get her to use the chamber pot. The captain is likely to be stingy with his fresh water supply. If you can't, use as much seawater as you can before using fresh."

Mark nodded, looking uncomfortable. "How long do you need to wait before removing the rest of Cerena's memories?"

"I don't know, lad. We're in uncharted territory. For all our centuries of experience, there is much of the mind that remains a mystery to us. I'm afraid if I take too many of her memories from her, Elieve will slip into *breostfage*."

Mark frowned. "Slip into what?"

Pellin shook his head. "I'm sorry, Mark. That word probably hasn't been heard since I first joined the Vigil. It means *mind death*. The mind must have a certain amount of memories to be able to function. Even in the act of creating a dwimor, the creator must be careful to provide enough memories so that the assassin can accomplish their mission."

"How do you know how much is enough?"

"By the river within the mind. Gaps within the flow cause the river to slow, become sluggish. If the gaps become too large, it shuts down completely. Dwimor live on the edge of mind death." He waved one hand to dispel memories that accused him. "That's one of the reasons we went through so many when we first created them."

Mark nodded, his face creased in concentration. "What's the fastest way to create memories?"

Pellin nodded his approval. "You have a keen mind. That question has been studied much by the Vigil over the years. I don't think the answer will surprise you. Of the five senses, the eyes provide more input than any of the others, but because of that, the memories they create are the weakest."

He watched his apprentice, saw him sorting through the unasked question, considering. "Smell?"

"Yes." Pellin nodded. "Or touch. They create the strongest memories because they connect to so many others."

For the first time, Mark appeared uncomfortable with Elieve's ever-present clutch, but with a shake of his head, he straightened. "So if she's to heal, I need to have her experience as many strong memories as I can so that when Cerena's are removed, Elieve will remain."

"Makes sense, lad," Pellin said. "I doubt any of the Vigil could reason it out better. The journey to the southern continent should take about two weeks. Halfway there, I'll delve her again. Then we'll just have to see."

He turned to Allta. "I need to speak to the captain. Let us leave Mark here with Elieve."

"Le-Elieve," the girl stuttered, her voice raspy with effort.

Pellin stopped, turning to the girl. "Yes," he said. "Loved."

Allta climbed the stairs to the deck, preceding him, but when they reached the open air, Pellin caught him with a hand on his arm. "We may have a problem I hadn't considered before."

"Eldest?"

"The girl, Elieve, was chosen to be an assassin."

Allta nodded. "Yes."

"That means she is possessed of at least a partial gift of devotion.

It's the presence of that gift that allows one of the Vigil to create a core of blind, excoriating hatred within their mind." He shuddered at his own memories, wished they belonged to another. "Without the violent target for her devotion, Elieve's soul will find another focus for her gift." He sighed. "Indeed, I think she's already found it."

"The boy." Allta nodded in understanding. "Is it dangerous?"

Deep within Pellin's chest, but not so deep that he could deny it or rationalize it away, lay the fear the twist of Elieve's gift would yet bring grief. "I don't know. When the time is right, we must attempt to place some emotional distance between the two of them. After that, I'm afraid Elieve's ultimate healing is still in the hands of Aer."

Allta nodded before changing the subject. "If the ports are blocked to the inland passage, Eldest, how will we get to the southern Vigil?"

He sighed. "I have means of sending word, but it will mean a delay."

His guard stood next to him at the rail of the ship, unspeaking, but Pellin could sense a tension in him that heightened with each passing moment until Allta turned away from the rhythmic swell of the waves. "Eldest, why did we bring the girl?"

Standing this close to his guard forcibly reminded Pellin of just how big Allta was. Thick shoulders from countless hours of training stretched his shirt and cloak, and he stood on legs as sturdy and strong as tree limbs. Yet for all of that, he moved with the grace and quickness of a dancer. The deadliest man alive.

"Why should we not?" Pellin responded. "The girl is in need, and Mark seems able to fill it." He considered his guard. "I could ask you a similar question. Why did you allow Mark to bring her? So long as his attention is divided, the boy will be less likely to spot dwimor coming for us."

Allta nodded. "I already defied you once, Eldest, on the edge of the Darkwater."

"I remember," Pellin said.

"Defiance is a habit unsuited to a Vigil guard," Allta said. "Plus, I do not see how any dwimor could track us. The threat seemed to be minimal."

Pellin turned to survey the passing sea once more, but Allta refused to be deterred. "Why is she here with us, Eldest?"

After a pause he said, "Something amazing has happened, Allta. Mark has managed to bring a dead girl back to life."

"Hardly dead, Eldest."

"You think not?" he asked. "Perhaps my gift and time in the Vigil have given me a different perspective. When does a person die?" Without waiting for an answer, he went on. "The healers would say it's when their heart stops beating or they stop breathing, but I've seen death from the Vigil's perspective."

"What does it look like, Eldest?"

"It's a cavern, dark and empty, where a river of memories should run, a flow filled with the colored strands that make up a person's life. It's a wellspring run dry, never refreshed, never renewed because all their memories have been destroyed."

"From what you've said, that doesn't quite describe Elieve."

He mused. "Doesn't it? You weren't there when we created the first dwimor in desperation and death during the Wars for the Gift of Kings. We were going to starve, and Agin had us bottled up in the north. We were desperate." He struggled to take a breath as if the sea air had suddenly become too thick to breathe. "We tried to save our early failures, Bronwyn and I, but to do so we had to completely erase the memories that drove the dwimor to kill and replace them with memories delved from others.

"But the link between body, mind, and soul was and is more complex and delicate than we understood." He shrugged.

Allta nodded, but whether in agreement or simple acknowledgment, Pellin couldn't tell. "Then how could Mark succeed?"

Pellin eyed his guard. "How could a boy succeed in saving a dwimor when all the skills and effort of the Vigil failed? If you know enough to ask the question that way, then I suppose you know that answer already."

"He loves her," Allta said.

"Yes," Pellin nodded. "I've suspected for some time that Mark held within him a capacity for such extravagance. It was his *heart* that guided him to Elieve's rescue. Think of it, a young woman with no past, given a second chance at life."

He turned to face his guard, surprised at the clarity of conviction that came upon him like a thief. "What is your primary purpose, Allta?"

"To safeguard the Vigil, no matter the cost."

"Good." Pellin nodded. "Then perhaps you will understand my

next command in that context. You must keep Mark alive above all else. My heart tells me the future of the Vigil rests with him."

"He does not hold the gift, Eldest."

"A temporary deficiency that I intend to correct when the time is right. Do you understand and agree?"

Pellin waited until the growing silence coerced Allta into giving him one slow, grudging nod before he returned to his contemplation of the sea.

CHAPTER 8

In the days after Ealdor's miraculous appearance and even more startling disappearance, Toria peppered me with questions and speculations as if I could divine meaning from Ealdor's strange behavior. After the second day of her interrogations I took to greeting her with my bare arm extended, my offer to be delved plain.

Two times she accepted. After that it became pointless. Even Fess, new and cruelly young to the Vigil, delved me at Toria's insistence. If I hadn't been scared witless by Ealdor's appearance and behavior, I would have wept at his solemnity. After the fifth day I changed my mode of greeting. When Toria and Fess passed me in the hallway, I said, "I don't know," as their lips parted to ask yet another question that I couldn't answer.

Bolt kept his accustomed place at my side, but I hardly noticed. Somewhere in our expansive villa north of Cynestol, he'd lost his habit of dispensing soldierly wisdom. Perhaps Pellin's sudden and unexplained disappearance, as though he'd become one of the Fayit himself, had something to do with it.

Wag seemed to care for nothing except when we might hunt next. His thoughts carried visions from his dam of running the border of the forest, his strides eating the ground until his paws hardly touched it. With Custos having returned to his research within the Vigil library in Cynestol, only Gael, ever and always Gael, sought my company. I could no more answer her questions than Toria Deel's, and she trusted me enough to know that I'd said everything I would or could, but that didn't keep her from asking them.

"What happened to him, Willet?"

Despite the events of almost a week past, she still had the power to shape my name in a way I felt with my skin as much as I heard with my ears.

I rolled my shoulders as if I could shed the weight of responsibility that rested there. "I don't know. When I saw him in the Everwood, Ealdor looked perfectly normal." Ironic laughter burst from me for an instant. "Normal for him, anyway. He didn't leave footprints, and he managed to move through the church without disturbing any of the debris." I shook my head. "But when I saw him in Bunard afterward, he did something he's never done before. He walked through me to prove he existed only in my mind."

"Why would he need to do that?" she asked.

I'd already had this conversation with Toria and Fess, but they hadn't worded the question exactly that way. We'd taken the question of how to bring him back and had pounded away at it until nothing remained, but we'd never asked what Ealdor needed. I came to a stop, afraid that if I kept walking I might lose the opportunity to see . . . something.

"Need," I said. "Suppose Ealdor needed me to believe he wasn't real." I shook my head. "But why? I believed he was real for years before Bronwyn took me to his church and showed me it was impossible." Even now, I could feel the absence of my friend like a hollow place in my chest. "In all the years of celebrating haeling and confession I was as certain of his reality as I was my own."

Gael nodded. "What changed?"

I thought back. "The Everwood." The answer might have come from someone else's lips it was so quiet. "He told me something I didn't know." I looked at Gael, at the glorious shining blue of her eyes and gave voice to the insubstantial thread of intuition that ghosted through my mind. "I think Ealdor broke the rules when he told me about the bation leaves."

She nodded. Gael knew the sequence of events from that point nearly as well as I. Without the bation leaves to keep Wag alive, we would have never been able to track Cesla to Vaerwold, where the only remaining witness to Elwin's murder was being held. Only Branna had survived the string of killings in Bunard that had wiped out those who could identify Elwin's killer.

"We're almost back where we started," I said. "Cesla is alive, and knowing that was so important that one of the Fayit was willing to risk . . ." I stopped. "What? What's he risking?"

"His life?" Gael asked.

"Or worse," I said. "Maybe he's risking his existence. You saw him. He wasn't dying, he was fading, as if he couldn't hold on to himself anymore."

"It couldn't have been the first time he broke the rules," Bolt said.

I turned, surprised to find him leaning against the wall, but of course he'd never left. "What do you mean by that?"

"How did you learn his name?"

The soft hiss of my breath in the air announced my answer. "I don't know. Neither do Pellin or Toria Deel. They both delved me, sifted through every memory of Ealdor without finding the beginning. It's as if someone whispered his name in my sleep."

Bolt's expression didn't change, but his body stilled in a way that usually prefaced killing, and the hair on my neck urged me to leave. "Maybe someone did."

I nodded, but it took Gael a moment to catch up. "You think Ealdor's name came from Willet's vault?"

My guard shrugged. "The Vigil is nothing if not thorough. If Willet had a memory of meeting Ealdor for the first time and learning his name, they would have found it."

I didn't much care for having my guard and my betrothed talk about me like ten pounds of mutton at the butcher's, but we were running out of options. "I could call him."

Bolt shook his head. "Pellin forbade it."

I shrugged. "What good is a sword if you don't draw it?"

His brows lifted a fraction. "I like that. It's pithy and it's appropriate, but Pellin's right. Ealdor couldn't maintain his contact with us. How many more times can he appear before he fades completely?"

"How can we possibly know that?" Gael asked. "It could be once or a hundred."

Deep inside, not in my mind, but in my chest, I felt a whisper, like the softest caress of a breeze against my skin. "I could try to find an abandoned church," I said half joking. "Maybe I'm not supposed to summon him at all. Maybe he's supposed to come to me."

Gael shook her head. "This is the southern coast. We're fifteen miles from Cynestol, and you can hardly tell where the city stops and the next town begins. There are no abandoned churches here."

Bolt looked at me for a moment without blinking. "There's one, in Aeldu, a village half a day east of here. The swamp overtook it."

"Do you think that's a good idea?" I asked. "We're practically within spitting distance of Cynestol and the Archbishop. I'm surprised Vyne hasn't scooped us up already."

Bolt rolled a shoulder, dismissing my objection. "We'll take Rory in case there are dwimor about. If we leave at first light we should make it back by sunset."

I could feel an unfamiliar smile working its way through me. "You know Pellin and Toria Deel would forbid this if they could. What prompted this rebellion? I thought Vigil guards were the soul of unquestioning obedience."

He shook his head with a hint of a smirk that on anyone else would have been a full-fledged grin. "It's a recent development. I'm probably keeping bad company."

The next morning we saddled four horses Bolt had hired for the day, clean-limbed cobs that pranced as though they'd just been broken. A suggestion of orange lit the wispy clouds overhead as we worked to muffle the tack.

Rory, still less than confident as a rider, scowled as his bay tossed his head. "Stupid growler. You're trying to kill me, yah?"

Bolt watched the horse lift in a half rear and stamp the ground with both feet. "Consider it part of your education. Sometimes speed comes at a price."

Gael swung into the saddle with a grace and confidence that quieted her mount. I felt more like Rory. "Couldn't you find horses that were a little less enthusiastic?"

"I wanted fast, not tame."

I nodded, but I missed Dest. We'd been together for years, and I used to talk to him when companions were scarce. I couldn't seem to hang on to friends, no matter how many legs they had.

Bolt didn't bother to hide our path out of the village. Almost as ancient as Cynestol itself, Edring was one of innumerable villages attached to the great city and occupied a series of hills to the northeast. If the Archbishop discovered the village we were hiding in, it would be a short search, even if he took the time to go building to building. We rode east into the sun, but the orange-yellow light failed to encourage me, despite the fact that I'd had seven nights of uninterrupted sleep.

"What's Cynestol like?" I asked Gael.

"That's a short question with a long answer, Willet," she said. "The customs are different, especially in court." She gave me a smile that was just short of laughter. "The good news is they tend to view our northern propensity for challenges and dueling as somewhat barbaric."

I frowned. "That's not what I meant, but since you brought it up, how do they settle disputes between nobles?"

She smiled without showing her teeth in a way that curved her lips into a bow that her gift made unfairly graceful. How was I supposed to concentrate?

"They get married," she said.

"What?"

"She's right," Bolt said. "It's their national passion. The nobles in Moorclaire raise hounds, those in Bunard fight, but the nobility in Aille get married. Alliances are formed and split based on each family's extensions into other families. The fact that the Crown allows marriages to be dissolved for almost any reason means keeping track of those alliances is an ordeal. Queen Chora has a whole ministry devoted to the job. Then again, she has a ministry devoted to almost everything."

"Sounds like a nightmare," I said. "And I should know."

Gael laughed, and I let the clean high sound wash over me like a benison. "I don't think it's the type of place you would enjoy, Willet, but Kera and I savored every visit. It's where we mastered the nuances of our game."

We rode for four hours, and as the smell of salt intensified, the landscape gradually changed from sandy scrub to marshland. An hour before the sun reached its zenith, Bolt pointed to a spot in the distance that wavered in the heat. "There."

I couldn't see anything except shimmering air and said so.

"You don't know what to look for," my guard said. "From this point on, make sure you stay on the road. The ground on either side isn't as solid as it looks." To demonstrate, he dismounted and tossed a rock the size of his fist onto ground that looked to be perfectly solid. The rock bounced once and stopped for a pair of breaths before sinking out of sight, leaving the sandy soil perfectly undisturbed. We fell in line immediately.

Bolt picked his way through the marsh along a path that might have been a road in the past. I couldn't see much difference. The smell of the sea came to us on the breeze, but it wasn't the cold, clean scent I'd experienced in Vaerwold. This was heavy with the humidity of the south and held so much decay within it, I wondered how it managed to stay off the ground.

After another mile, we put enough of the shimmering waves of heat behind us that I could just discern the outlines of a village. Houses made of yellowish clay formed a broad arc defining the boundary of the village, but I couldn't make out the rest of the details.

"I don't think I've ever seen a village laid out in a circle before," I said.

Bolt shook his head. "You wouldn't have. None of the villages, towns, or cities in Collum is old enough." He pointed at the sweep of buildings ahead of us. "This is Aeldu. We don't know if it's the oldest village on the continent, but if it's not, it is close. It's been deserted for the last hundred years."

We were close enough to now make out hints of color that had been used to decorate the houses, suggestions of blue and green that still showed beneath the brown stains of weather. "Why?" Gael asked.

"Something changed," Bolt said. "Either the sea rose or the land sank, but the villagers couldn't keep the salt water from poisoning their fields. Eventually it crept into the village itself. Everything was taken." He sent an unblinking glance my way.

"Are we still talking about the village?"

He abandoned his regard of Aeldu long enough to consider the question. "Are we? I don't know. Maybe if the villagers had fought a little harder they could have held on to their lives."

"How do you stop something as big as the sea?" I asked.

"I don't know, but if you don't try, you certainly won't."

"Pellin doesn't know what to do," Rory said.

During his silence as we rode, I'd forgotten he was with us. I'd also forgotten just how perceptive the little thief could be.

We coaxed our horses forward, and the ground under their hooves squelched with each step as we passed through the outer ring of houses and came to a smaller inner ring of buildings somewhat larger than those on the outside.

"These were homes as well," Bolt said.

"For those who were wealthier." I nodded. "That never changes. Money gets you access to power." We passed through two more rings that I recognized as belonging to craftsmen and merchants before we came to the center of the village, a broad church that could have housed every occupant of Aeldu and then some.

I knew why Bolt had brought me here, but until that moment I'd been less than hopeful that Ealdor would appear. Now I feared that if I didn't see him, I never would.

"The entire village is a children's game," Gael said. "It's laid out in four circles."

"I thought it was supposed to be a circle of four," Rory said.

"No," I said, feeling inside my mind for the door of memories that belonged to Custos. "The game is so old, we don't know what it's supposed to be, or even if it matters. More than one account of the children's game says whoever calls the Fayit must die."

"It hasn't happened yet," Bolt said.

I nodded. "It's the *yet* that bothers me."

The church squatted in the middle of a plaza, but the stones of the encircling street were mostly covered with mud. I dismounted, and a swarm of gnats floated up to surround me like some warped idea of a halo. No one else moved. "You're not coming?" I asked Bolt.

He shook his head. "I don't think we're supposed to. You don't need protection. Nothing's here except us."

Rory slapped his neck. "And the bugs."

Bolt nodded. "Watch for snakes, Willet. If you see a blue one with a wedge-shaped head, give it a wide berth."

I was about to say that the snakes in Bunard didn't crawl on their bellies, but that wasn't entirely true, so I let the comment pass. Two sets of steps led up to the church in groups of six and nine, of course, and I passed beneath a wide gray stone lintel that still showed a pair of intersecting arcs, the universal symbol of the faith. Broad double doors of thick reddish wood greeted me, closed. I grabbed the tarnished lever and pushed, but weather and disuse had swelled the panels. I backed up a step and, in a gesture that felt like sacrilege, rammed my shoulder into the right-hand door.

Toria stood in the small stable yard behind the estate in Edring, preparing for the journey Ealdor had assigned. A century of changing location every decade had taught her the importance of preparation. A quote from Elwin when she'd first come to the Vigil hung in her mind. *"If I had seven days to make a journey, I would spend the first making sure I was prepared."* And this journey would be longer still. Aer willing, she and the rest of the Vigil would return from their travels.

"Strange," she murmured.

Across from her, Fess raised his head from his inspection of their supplies. "Lady Deel?"

She started at the sound and turned, struck again by how impossibly young Fess looked for the burden that Aer had placed upon him, for the burdens he had taken upon himself. For a moment she considered demurring, but there might be few opportunities for unguarded conversation on their trip north, and despite her position within the Vigil, she needed companionship as much as anyone.

No. She was Elanian, born and bred. She required companionship more.

"Lady Deel?" Fess prompted again.

"I was just thinking how, after watching him lead the Vigil these past months, I've never seen Pellin so sure of himself," she said. "It seems ironic."

Fess almost smiled. Almost, but not quite. "Ironic that he seems more decisive in following the Fayit's guidance than he ever did enforcing his own?"

She nodded, noting the formal turn his speech had taken since Bronwyn's death. And Balean's. "Yes. I hope he's not making a mistake."

"It is difficult to argue with someone who's been alive so long they make Pellin seem young by comparison," Fess said.

"Does age equate to wisdom?"

He gave her a direct look. "I've no experience with which to answer. Few in the urchins live long, Lady Deel. They die from the wracking cough in winter, or they're caught stealing from the wrong man. Even if they live, age forces them to leave the urchins and join their lot to the thieves' guild or the night women, where the chances of a long life are just as thin."

His bleak assessment roused more in her than he'd intended, and she blinked to clear her eyes. "That seems a very wise answer to me, Fess. Perhaps if we survive this war, we can venture north and west to Bunard once more and see how Lord Dura's bargain fares." To secure the aid of the urchins during the slaughter of Bas-solas, Dura had wrung a concession from the church—they would adopt every urchin who was willing into homes where the children might find love and a future.

He nodded. "I'd like that, but I have the feeling that the city and the people in it will be as strange to me as I would be to them."

"We should—" she began, but Fess held up a hand.

He cocked his head. "Someone is out front." He paused. "Make that several someones."

She knew better than to question him. The footfalls of their company were known to him, and they weren't expecting any other visitors. "Bring Wag," she ordered. "If they are not friends, we must be on our way."

She followed him, thankful for the dirt and hay that silenced their footsteps. Her heart set a cadence that urged her to run. She groped at her waist for the only objects she couldn't afford to leave behind, her scrying stone and her purse.

With Wag at their side, they ran out the back of the stable toward the wall and the gate that opened onto the back street. Throwing the bolt, they slipped through, casting glances to either side. She took enough time to close the gate, wincing at the sound the hinges made.

She reached out and grabbed a handful of Fess's shirt. "Don't run. You'll attract attention."

"I was raised in the streets, Lady Deel. I know better than to call attention to myself that way, but walking won't disguise a sentinel."

She nodded, turning toward the nearest alley. "Let's get off this street and circle around. I want to have a look at our visitors."

Moments later they crouched behind a large planter, watching men who moved with the fluid grace of the gifted, each wearing similar clothing.

"Do you know them, Lady Deel?"

"I have a suspicion that they're church guards," she said, turning away. "That would mean the Archbishop wants something badly enough to send them. But it doesn't matter. We're leaving."

Fess didn't stir from his crouch. "Lady Deel? What about Lord Dura and the rest?"

She couldn't help but hear the tone of accusation in his voice. "How many men did you see, Fess?"

His features closed into a scowl. "Perhaps a dozen, with more already inside."

"Too many for us to fight," she said. "We will have to let Lord Dura and the rest settle this with their wits."

"We can't just—"

"We can and will," she said, "or have you forgotten Ealdor's instruction?"

"What about Modrie?" he asked.

She paused, weighing options and possibilities. "She has plenty of food and water. Willet can tend to her better than we."

"What about the horses and supplies?" he asked.

"No time. I have money enough in my purse to replace them."

"Is this what happens with the gift of domere?" he asked. "With all that time, do we all become stone inside?"

She chose to answer his question instead of his accusation. "The gift is given in the hope that those who receive it will manage to retain their humanity."

CHAPTER 9

Time and rain in the south had been just as merciless as the forest in
the Everwood, both conspiring to reduce their churches to nothing
more than a shell. Though the church here had been built to last for
centuries, even the best construction had to be maintained. The red
tile roof had withstood the elements better than thatch would have,
but it hadn't lasted through a century of disuse.

As I picked my way through the narthex and entered into the sanctuary proper, I tried not to think of the parallels between the village church
and myself. Spots of light came through holes in the roof, where tile and
plaster had failed at last to keep the outside world at bay. "The pews
are gone." I don't know why that surprised me. The sea had been implacable, but slow. The priests had probably taken everything of value.

I scuffed my foot in the sludge that covered most of the floor and
noted the similarity to Ealdor's church in Bunard. A broad central
aisle provided the main access to the confessional rail and the altar,
while smaller aisles on the outside ran past empty holes where I assumed stained-glass windows had been.

The altar was gone too, though for some reason they'd left the
confessional rail. Evidently the exodus from this church in Aeldu had
been more orderly than Ealdor's little parish. I kept an eye out for
snakes but didn't see any as I made my way to the dais at the front,
stepping to each puddle of light like a child playing hops.

Of Ealdor, there was no sign.

I sat on the top step of the dais with my back to the empty spot
where the altar had been and waved away the dust that rose from my

movement to tickle my nose. The church, abandoned and derelict like the ones in Bunard and the Everwood, depressed me. "This is getting to be a bad habit." I half expected an echo, but the dirt and cobwebs muffled the sound.

"Greetings, Willet."

Ealdor didn't walk out of the shadows this time. Maybe he'd decided to surrender that pretense, or maybe he just didn't like the shadows here. At any rate, he appeared on the top step, sitting next to me as if he'd been there all along.

A beam of sunlight from a jagged hole in the roof illuminated my old friend, but I could see a stone buttress through his right shoulder, as though the little church, ruined as it was, possessed a substantiality that he did not. "You're fading."

He shrugged, and the buttress behind him waved like grass in a pond. "No one lives forever." My friend paused for a moment, considering. "At least so far."

Something in his manner, the diffidence combined with the slightest hitch in his voice, told me this was more than jesting. "Are you telling me someone is immortal? Who is it?"

He met my gaze, and his eyes held a depth of sorrow that all my misfortune couldn't hope to match. "You know the rules, Willet."

I nodded. "You can only tell me what I already know. Alright, is there any wiggle room in this rule?"

He put out his hand to catch a stray beam of sunlight, and I saw light on the floor beneath his arm. "Evidently not," I sighed. "Then I won't ask you any questions."

I groped for what to say, hesitant to push my friend into forbidden territory. "You broke the rules when you came to us in Edring," I said, my eyes stinging. "I'm sorry, Ealdor. I'm so sorry. Custos told us that we needed a circle, and I didn't even try to put one together. I just called you."

Ealdor nodded, and bit of sunlight flared behind his eyes, making them appear lit from within. "That was a mistake, but it was mine, not yours."

"But I saw you," I said. "You would have stayed if you could." I paused. What I was about to say, I didn't *know*, but strongly suspected. Would the rules allow him to confirm my intuition? "But if you'd stayed, you would have faded completely."

Ealdor eyed me for a moment, and I reminded myself that he wasn't really there in the church with me, but in my thoughts. I could almost feel him rummaging around in my head before he answered. "Yes. The rules are severe."

"Who made them?" I asked before I could catch myself and thrust my hand out to keep him from answering.

"You don't have enough information yet to puzzle that one out, Willet. Take a step back."

I shook my head. "It's impossible. There are too many questions screaming at me. I don't know which ones are important, much less which ones I can figure out."

"You're a reeve."

"Was a reeve," I corrected.

Ealdor smiled. "I'm not talking about your profession or circumstances, Willet. I'm talking about your nature." He sobered, and something unimaginably desperate hollowed out his gaze. "Please. There's more at stake here than you can know."

I squeezed my eyes shut and held up a hand in forbidding. "That's not helping." I took a pair of deep breaths that made me shudder as they came and went. I was rolling the bones with my friend's life and countless others. "Alright, let's go back to the beginning. Something has gotten loose from the Darkwater," I said. "Cesla said he came to a lake and stood on metal. And he delved it."

Ealdor nodded once, slowly.

I pulled a memory from my first conversation with Custos about my gift, how the ancients had described it as tunneling, like someone mining. The first commandment said not to delve the deep places of the earth. "It's the same word for both, tunneling and delving." Then I had it. "It's a prison. The Darkwater is a prison, and when Cesla delved it, something inside the prison sensed it and took him." I pushed myself off the dais, the room in the air too thick to breathe. Ealdor didn't flinch. "Oh, Aer help us. That was why we weren't supposed to delve the deep places of the earth. It was never about silver or gold, it was to keep whatever was locked in the Darkwater Forest from getting out."

I stopped my frantic pacing. Something about that last bit didn't ring quite true. "No." I shook my head as if I could deny the disaster that was about to fall on the world. "If that was true, then there would be no need to continue luring people to the forest." A memory of Myle holding a sliver of metal near a harp came to me. "Aurium. The prison is made of aurium, and whatever is inside isn't truly free until the prison is breached."

I sat down, horror draining the strength from my legs. I spat a curse. "Cesla. What kind of arrogance makes a man break the most basic commandment of the liturgy?"

Ealdor shrugged. "You already know the answer, Willet. Cesla placed his own ideas and inspiration above the liturgy. Perhaps he thought Aer had given him a new commandment."

With an effort, I pulled my thoughts back from Cesla and his stupidity and concentrated on the clues that were in front of me. "It's not hopeless," I said looking at Ealdor. "If it was, there would be no point to you showing up." An unexpected flare of hope blossomed somewhere in my chest—small, but there. "There's a way for us to win." Just as quickly, it guttered and died. "But if you can't tell us, how will we find it?"

Ealdor stilled. "Let me point out two things you already know. Cesla is no longer himself. He is a combination of whatever is imprisoned in the Darkwater and the human known as Cesla."

"Well enough." I nodded. "We've known that ever since Vaerwold. What's the second?"

A tremor worked its way across his right hand, marring the perfect peace Ealdor had worn ever since I'd known him. "How will you know what's important to him, how to stop him?" He put his hand into a beam of sunlight and flexed it. Only after he turned it palm up and examined each finger did he sigh in relief.

I opened my mouth to reply and stopped. Ealdor's obvious question had carried some threat to his corporeality, some danger to his presence. Cesla. Two intelligences within one body. If there existed a way to stop him, and Ealdor's appearance testified that there was, then Cesla would know of it as well. "And he'll take steps to prevent us." I finished the train of thought out loud.

I looked at my friend, grieving over those parts of him that had become translucent. "He'll strike at whatever threatens him." I sighed. "You know that means we'll have to react. We'll be chasing him from behind, just as we did before."

"I know, Willet, but if I continue to break the rules of summoning,

I'll fade completely. I won't even be able to tell you what you already know. I'll just be gone." His head dipped, and he wet his lips. On anyone else that gesture would have signaled nervousness, but one of the Fayit . . . ? I'd never seen Ealdor show that emotion.

"Now I need to ask you a question, Willet." He leaned toward me. "How do you know my name?"

"I don't—" I stopped at the look of panic that washed over him. Had he become less real than he'd been just a moment before or had I imagined it? Of all the things he might have asked or spoken of, he'd chosen this. If I said I didn't know, then Ealdor had guided me toward some hint of knowledge I hadn't possessed before. "How does anyone learn someone else's name?" I said. "You told me."

He nodded and my heart fluttered with relief in my chest. Ealdor possessed the gift of domere as surely as if he were one of the Vigil. He'd looked into my thoughts far too often for there to be any other explanation. He knew Pellin and Toria and even Fess had all delved me, had searched me for the origin of his name. And none of them had found it.

He winced, exhaling as if he'd been struck and the buttress behind him became easier to see.

"Oh, Aer, help us. Even that cost you?" I asked. He held up a hand.

"It's not as bad as it could have been," he said, "but the rules divine some measure of intent."

In that moment, his gaze held me as if he'd already died and had left his body of mist behind. The familiar abstraction, the glamour that came over me in the presence of the dead, exerted its hold and I slipped into the stare of his blue eyes. "What's out there, Ealdor?" I whispered. "What will you see on the other side of eternity?"

His laughter broke the spell, and I shook my head to scatter its traces. "Don't worry, Willet, you'll see it when it's time." He looked up toward the empty spot where the altar had been. "Time. It's amazing how you can think you have so much of it and then realize it's been slipping away faster than you could imagine. Would you like to celebrate haeling with me?"

"This is why you came to me here," I said, gasping with the intuition. "There's something about celebrating haeling that sustains you."

He smiled and for a moment I could have pretended we were back in Bunard before Elwin's death. "That was very well done, Willet.

Doesn't the church say that the celebration brings healing? It's more real than you know. Even among the Fayit the mysteries of Aer held us. Shall we?"

I nodded, trying to ignore the stinging in my eyes. Without a gesture or a word, an altar of uncut stones, similar to the one in the Everwood, appeared on the dais, and Ealdor's worn purple stole graced his shoulders once more. I joined him behind the illusion and raised my hands to bless the empty church.

"'The six charisms of Aer are these,'" I pronounced, wondering as peace, unexpected as a ray of sun during a storm, found a home, however temporary, in my heart. "'For the body, beauty and craft. For the mind, sum and parts. And for the soul, helps and devotion.'" After I finished haeling, Ealdor vanished, taking his altar with him, but the peace remained and I finished the coda, my arms raised to receive whatever blessing Aer might give.

I left the church and descended the two sets of steps back to the plaza, their grouping of six and nine reminding me of the burden I had to satisfy before I could summon Ealdor for knowledge I didn't already have. I needed a circle of six gifts or nine talents, and they all had to be pure. I tried not to let the fact that there no longer existed pure gifts or talents in the world deter me.

I tried, but I failed.

Gael, Bolt, and Rory looked at me with varying degrees of expectation in their gazes.

"He came to you," Bolt said. Not a question.

I nodded. "It's like most things. There are glad tidings and ill."

"Better to hear the ill first," Bolt said. "It gives you something to look forward to."

Rory shook his head. "In the urchins, we always give the glad tidings first. That way if you die, you've missed out on the bad news."

I saw Gael start to say something, her eyes stricken, but Bolt cut her off, nodding in simple agreement. "Sense. I think I'll start eating dessert first."

"We always do," Rory said.

"I like peaches," Bolt said. "Especially in pies."

"I'm fond of currants," Rory said. "There's nothing like currant brandy to take the chill off."

I shook my head. "Are you two done?" I looked back the church.

"The glad tidings are that we can win. Ealdor wouldn't have come to us otherwise."

Bolt nodded, but his eyes were hooded, suspicious. "And the ill?"

"He can't tell us how. The rules binding his existence forbid him from answering our questions unless we can satisfy the strictures of summoning. That means assembling a circle of perfect gifts or talents. If he tries to break the rules again, he may disappear completely." I pulled a shaky breath. "He's lost so much of himself already."

Gael's hair lifted in the breeze, mirroring her frustration. "That's not overly helpful. That leaves us to guessing. We could spend lifetimes trying to find a way to fight the Darkwater."

"If it were impossible, he wouldn't have come to me," I said. "And we won't have to guess Cesla's intentions. Whatever has gotten loose from the forest will strike at whatever threatens him most."

"*Kreppa*," Bolt said. "And we're supposed to magically interpret that into some course of action?" He shook his head in disgust. "'When your enemy dictates the course of war, you've lost.'"

I recognized his military adage from somewhere, but I couldn't place it. "Whose is that?"

"Magius, one of the generals who fought Agin and lost in the Gift of Kings War."

"That's not exactly heartening to know," I said. The Vigil's answer to Agin had been to create something new, the dwimor, assassins who couldn't be seen except by children. Whatever had taken Cesla had gained access to that knowledge. Three times I'd almost been killed by people I couldn't see when they were right in front of me.

CHAPTER 10

We didn't speak much on the road back to Edring, consigned as we were to waiting for Cesla's next strike before plotting our course of action. For reasons I couldn't quite define, I didn't make mention of Ealdor's question about how I knew his name. That it carried unimaginable importance, I couldn't deny; Ealdor had risked and lost some of his nebulous existence to ask it. Yet it wasn't the loss of a bit more of his presence that scared me so much as the implications of the obvious, terrifying answer.

If Pellin, with over seven hundred years of existence and experience with the gift couldn't find the memory of learning Ealdor's name in my mind, that meant there was only one place it could be.

Inside my vault.

Somewhere within the black scroll lay the knowledge of Ealdor's name and more—or else he wouldn't have risked the last of his life to tell me. To get to that knowledge I would have to allow Pellin or Toria to break my vault and hope that against all odds and experience, I survived. As soon as that thought crossed my mind, two others accompanied it. A memory came to me of Bronach, a simple tanner woman from Bunard sitting on her stool, her mind shattered beyond repair after I'd broken her vault. Tearing the unreadable black scroll into pieces too small to reckon had robbed her of the last vestige of her humanity.

Just as it had every other vault I or the rest of the Vigil had broken, save one—Queen Cailin.

Toria or Pellin would have to make the attempt. I would never allow

70

Fess to break my vault, though I trusted him more. At ten and six, he was the second-youngest person ever to come to the gift, despite the hopelessness of his upbringing in the urchins. I carried the burden of every soul I'd consigned to mindlessness and death. Fess had already endured his share and more of misery in life. He didn't need any more.

The wind picked up out of the south, lifting the wealth of Gael's black hair to wave like a cape of darkest velvet. A stab of grief pulled the air from my lungs. The gift of domere that I owned would extend my life for centuries while she would live out her allotted decades. I had another impossible task to go with finding a way for us to live out our lives together. Not only did I have to let the Vigil break my vault, but they had to do it in a way that left the knowledge it contained intact.

I couldn't help it. I laughed, gales of grief and rage flooding out of me at the ridiculous unfairness of my situation.

"Willet?" Gael moved her horse closer to mine, put her hand on my arm.

I gasped for breath. "It's absurd. The whole thing. It wouldn't even make for a good tale because it's unbelievable. Only the mind of Aer could create it."

Gael caught my mood first. She knew me that well, knew what I needed so desperately in that moment. Catching my gaze, she lifted her chin and laughed as tears coursed down her cheeks, sharing her grief for her sister, Kera, for me, but refusing to let it define her. She laughed.

Rory joined in a moment later, his voice warbling between the clear high tones of boyhood and the deeper thrum of the man he would become. His losses and failures were known to me. Abandoned, he had headed the urchins, an informal guild of child beggars, thieves, and pickpockets who'd wrested life, however temporary, from the poor quarter.

Only Bolt didn't laugh—though I thought I saw longing in his gaze. I'd never delved my guard, had no idea the depth of sorrow that he must have carried. I'd seen him laugh, genuinely laugh, exactly once in all the time he'd guarded me. It had looked painful.

We made our way back to the Edring, where Toria would no doubt pester me with questions about my conversation with Ealdor. The one thing a traveler could rely on in this hillside region was that the roads never ran in a straight line—instead they'd been laid out as if they followed the flow of water from the frequent rains. Newcomers spent weeks learning their way around the cobblestone paths that ended at destinations that defied prediction. Bolt knew the village as well as the sword he carried, an effortless familiarity.

We rounded a corner, entering the shade of jaccara trees growing from a planter in the center of the street. As we approached our estate from the north, Bolt reined in and dismounted as if we'd arrived. "Get down," he said in a conversational tone, "but slowly." He lifted his head, gesturing over my shoulder. "We have trouble."

Two men, dressed in nondescript clothing that blended with the sand-colored wall surrounding the estate, stood outside watching a couple of boys play catch. It took me a second to notice that while the heads of the men were pointed toward the boys, their eyes scanned the streets.

"That's a roll of ones," I said. Soldiers—the good ones, anyway—have a way holding themselves even when they're not standing at attention that draws the eye. It's a readiness for violence they maintain even when they're not on patrol. "Do you know them?" I asked Bolt.

He shook his head. "No. They have the olive skin tones of Aille, but for all of that, they could be attached to the crown, the church, or anyone."

"It's not just the men," Rory said. "Look at the boys. They're nearly the same age as me, and they're, what, ten feet apart? There's no fun in throwing a ball that far. What do we do?" To emphasize his question, he pulled a dagger, spinning it around one hand before making it disappear again.

Gael touched my arm. "Give me a moment." Then she walked away. I watched as she left the little square and then reappeared to approach the soldiers from the west, carrying a basket of cut flowers as if she'd just been to the market. We watched the soldiers as my betrothed walked toward them.

"It won't work, yah?" Rory said. "How many people with her coloring live here?"

She would have known that. "I think that's what she intends. If they've been sent to take us, they'll have our descriptions and act accordingly, but if they're only watching, they'll let her pass."

Gael went past the guards and through the gate. Half a heartbeat later, the guards followed her. I moved to follow, my hand on my sword while my heart struggled within in my throat. Bolt stopped me, not threatening, but I could hear him growling a stream of invectives under his breath.

"Will you please say something that makes sense?" I asked. Across the distance of the square, another pair of men sauntered up from a side street to take the place of the two that had followed Gael inside.

"They're cosp," he spat. "Physically gifted soldiers who serve as guards for the Merum order in Aille." His lip curled in disgust. "After the crown and church disbanded the Errants, the Archbishop decided it would be a good idea to buy the service of those who were similarly gifted."

"Are they as good as Vigil guards?" Rory asked.

Bolt shook his head. "No, but they don't have to be. Archbishop Vyne commands enough of them to fight us to a standstill or worse."

Rory turned, leaning toward the guards with his right ear. "I don't hear any sounds of fighting."

"How did they find us?"

"Custos," Bolt said, "or more likely Peret Volsk." He ground the name like a curse. "The librarian blends in, but that popinjay doesn't."

Rory shook his head. "Churchmen. None of you have enough sense to learn how to check for a tail. That one thinks too highly of himself."

Bolt nodded. "He always has."

I'd inadvertently delved Volsk months before, uncovering his treachery, but behind the door in my mind where his memories lay were other memories that gave the lie to Rory's assessment. "Not anymore," I said. Bolt didn't push me for an explanation and I didn't bother to provide one. His enmity for the Vigil's former apprentice and golden boy went too deep for forgiveness.

Without warning, Rory sneezed, bending double while his cloak fluttered with the motion. Only Bolt and I could see his hands when he straightened, a dagger clutched in each. "We've got more behind us," he murmured. "And they're headed this way."

Bolt didn't move but sighed, his hand finding his sword in the midst of an idle scratch. "How many?"

Rory's hands fluttered beneath his cloak again and came back as empty as his expression.

"Too many for us to fight, I take it?" I asked.

Bolt turned without making an effort to hide his motion or intention and nodded. "Eight. And they're all gifted. We might as well join Gael. We might win a fight, but we'd have to put any number of them down, most of them for good."

What he didn't bother to say was that I would be the most likely to die, since I had no physical gift. For good measure I took a quick glance at the eight behind us, scanning each face to see if my suspicions proved true. Then I caught a glimpse of the setting sun. Where did Ealdor go when he wasn't pretending to appear to me? "You'd think talking with one of the Fayit would be enough excitement for one day." I grabbed the reins of Gael's horse, adding them to those of my own. "We might as well go see what the Archbishop wants with us."

From the south, bells began to toll. I only heard a few at first, soft with the intervening distance, but more joined in until the sound came toward us like a wave. "Aer help us," Bolt said. "I think I know."

My questions slid from him, ignored, as we walked out from beneath jaccara trees, the three of us striding across the square with our horses trailing us as if we weren't sweating with the need to pull steel. At the gate I turned to one of the two men lounging there and put the reins in his hand. His eyes went wide and then wider still when Bolt and Rory followed suit. "I'm going to want my horse back. Oh, and he likes a bit of apple with his oats."

We stepped past them into the entryway and the men following behind us closed in, blocking the sun. "One of these days that mouth of yours is going to get you into trouble," Bolt said.

"You mean it hasn't already?"

"I mean trouble I can't get you out of."

"Well, luck might be smiling on you today," I said. "We have no idea what's waiting for us."

"I do," he said, but again, he offered no explanation for the sudden grief in his eyes.

We walked across the courtyard with eight of the Archbishop's gifted trailing us.

"They've got the house and the rest of our group buttoned up," Bolt said. "Otherwise, they'd have drawn steel before now."

The broad doors to the entry swung open at our approach, showing another half-dozen church guards trying to pretend they were ordinary people. I shook my head. As if ordinary people all wore the exact same ordinary clothes.

"Not a lot of imagination there," Rory said. "I bet none of these men has ever pulled a bluff in their life, much less a con."

We stepped into the dining hall. Domed in the style popular in Cynestol, it held a pair of tables made from single slabs of wood each two hands thick, a pace and a half across and fifteen paces long. Big as the room was, it barely contained the crowd. Men and women—some of them young but all with very functional-looking swords and daggers at their belts—clustered around us. Gael sat in the middle of the closest table, but her posture radiated restrained motion. She glanced at me before her gaze returned to a whippet-faced man with a long nose at the head of the table.

Toria and Fess were nowhere in sight.

"Come, Lord Dura," the whippet-faced man said. "Sit."

Nothing in his voice hinted at a reason for the presence of so many armed men in the house or how they had found us. Rory and Bolt took seats across from Gael as I took the one next to her. I reached out to give her hand a comforting squeeze, and she gave me an indulgent smile. "Until we know what's going on, I probably should keep my hands free," she whispered to me.

"Excellent," the man at the head of the table said. "We worried for your return, Lord Dura." He lifted his right hand and crooked a finger. One of the guards, with more time and scars than the rest leaned forward. "You can clear the room now, Batten, and seal the doors."

The man stroked an untouched glass of wine in front of him with that same finger. "An introduction is in order, of course. I am Lieutenant Hradian. Your names, I already know from the descriptions given me with the exception of this flower." He nodded to Gael.

Gael inclined her head in a gesture I recognized from court. "I am Gael Alainn, of Collum."

"A lady, no doubt," Hradian said. "Your manners speak of court, and your grace speaks of other gifts as well. Your group numbers significantly fewer than I was led to expect." He nodded toward the empty seats around the table. "This charming estate shows signs of recently hosting nearly a dozen." He made a vague gesture toward the general vicinity of the stable. "As well as a pair of large dogs, of which only one remains. Where are your companions?"

At our stoic stares, he continued. "I assure you all, you have nothing to fear from me or from His Holiness."

The tide of bells, muted by distance and the walls of the estate, intruded upon our conversation as the church the next street over began tolling in unison, the heavy iron bell the only one to peal. Across from me, Bolt's face blanched, though his expression never changed.

"You've brought enough gifted to decimate an army," I said. "What exactly does Vyne want that requires our service—voluntary or otherwise?"

Hradian nodded. "His Excellence does not confide in me." For a moment he broke his gaze to cast a measuring glance toward Bolt, and something akin to speculation bordering on wonder passed over his eyes before he continued. "Archbishop Vyne wanted me to assure you that he has told me nothing about you except your descriptions and other trivial details that would allow me to find you." He nodded toward Gael. "He failed to mention the lady."

I nodded. "You've surrounded us with armed men, Lieutenant. I'm sure you can see how that would make me suspicious. Exactly how do you intend to prove that you're from the Archbishop and don't mean us harm?"

Hradian nodded. "He told me to expect this question and that in the presence of so many gifted, no answer would suffice."

I smiled. "Clever man. It seems strange that the Archbishop did not send a letter with you."

The look of speculation I'd seen in Hradian's eyes returned, sharper, before he answered. "When I asked the Archbishop for such a letter, he said something strange." He glanced at each of us. "He said that if we were taken or attacked in any way, he didn't want to betray you." Hradian leaned forward, like a racing hound straining at the lead. "Cynestol boasts hundreds of thousands and the rest of Aille holds that and more, but I was given fully half the cosp to make this journey."

He looked at each of us in turn, as if he could will us to answer his unspoken questions, his dark eyes intent above the sharp nose that dominated his face. "The Archbishop's counsel is his own," he said, "but it is my job to protect him, even from his own counsel. I have enough men to force all of you to Cynestol."

"Without proof that you've come from the Archbishop, you die first," Bolt said. For an instant I saw something eager in Hradian's gaze.

"But those weren't your orders, were they?" I asked. As entertaining as a pitched battle that would get us all killed might be, Ealdor's costly information still hung in my ears.

The bells pealed outside the window. I might have heard voices between each strike of the heavy clapper against the sound bow. "Why don't you tell us why the bells are ringing, Hradian? Is the Archbishop even alive?"

He nodded, and I heard a long sigh whisper from Bolt as he squeezed his eyes shut against some private pain. Hradian looked at me as if I'd somehow managed to read his private letters, but he gave me one slow nod.

"There were supposed to be others here," he said. "I was told to seek an older man or, failing that, an Elanian woman. In their absence, I have little choice but to bring you, Lord Dura."

I favored Hradian with a humorless smile. "It's so nice to be wanted. I'll try not to disappoint His Stupendousness."

Hradian stiffened at the jibe. "The Archbishop is to be referred to as Holiness or Excellence, and nothing else. I and the rest of the cosp serve him with our lives. He is the leader and spiritual head of the largest order on the continent and wise beyond your reckoning."

I shook my head. Despite the distance from Bunard, Hradian's arrogance, even on behalf of another, could have been Duke Orlan's or any other of the countless nobles who despised me. "And yet, for all his wisdom, the Archbishop surprised you," I said, "when he forced you to put children in the vanguard."

Hradian gave me an unblinking stare. "Lord Dura, you are commanded to accompany me to Cynestol this very hour."

CHAPTER 11

Hradian had hardly blinked when I insisted he leave a man behind to take care of Modrie, but he'd been more than serious about the need for haste. Any and all attempts on our part to pack, or even eat, were forestalled, and we were on horseback riding from Edring as dusk approached. On our left, the sun slipped below the horizon, and the light died with a flare of red against the clouds, like an omen of blood.

I shuddered. When had I become a superstitious man?

Hradian barked an order, and the leading wedge of the cosp lit torches to guide us. Hooves thundered on the cobblestones as we closed the distance to Cynestol. I tried once to pry additional information from the lieutenant, but the pace and the noise precluded any conversation. Bolt looked as serious as I'd ever seen him.

"How far are we from the city?" I asked him.

"Another two hours from the cathedral—there is no way we can keep this pace."

"I didn't think we were that far away."

He grimaced, the expression lurid in the light of the torches. "We're not, but Cynestol spreads widely and it never sleeps. Even at night much of the city is crowded and progress slows to almost a halt."

An hour and a half later, or something close to it, we crested a hill and stopped, brought to a halt by a wall of sound. Cynestol filled a broad bowl in the landscape, surrounded by a rim of low hills. Within that depression thousands of iron bells peeled their grief, and the entire city of Cynestol vibrated with the multitoned cry of anguish and loss.

Hradian reined in, all expression sliding from him until he might have been cast from stone. With the sharp bark of an order, the entire group of cosp dismounted and, as one, knelt to face the east, each man or woman's hand rising to inscribe the intersecting arcs on their forehead. It wasn't until I stepped closer that I heard him reciting the antidon for the dead in a low voice.

Bolt stepped in beside me, his customary stoicism in place, barely. "Tell me," I said. "What kind of woman was Chora?"

There was no movement that might have betrayed his thoughts. "The last time I saw her, she was hardly more than a girl, but she had a talent for self and space that made her a beautiful dancer even before Sylvest died and she inherited the gift of kings." He paused as the sound of bells gathered and broke, washing over us. "Better if it had been the prince, or even the Archbishop," he said softly.

But not softly enough. Hradian wheeled, his expression stricken and his hand on his sword, but my guard only shrugged. "No insult intended, Lieutenant. Archbishop Vyne is an old man and no fool. He would long since have arranged for his successor, but if Queen Chora has died without passing her gift to Prince Maenelic, then the largest kingdom on the continent is about to descend into chaos." He stopped to look at me. "The timing here feels more than a little coincidental."

"That's quite a piece of understatement, even for you," I said. "If Sevin were taking wagers for the watch, I'd give him whatever odds he wanted that Chora died right as Ealdor came to me in Aeldu."

"Or even when we decided to set out for the church," Gael said.

When we descended the hill, the first thing we saw was a full garrison of soldiers camped on the road illuminated by watch fires that circled away from us into the night. Hradian cursed under his breath as he rode forward to speak to the men guarding the makeshift gate.

During the next quarter of an hour we watched him argue with the grizzled commander, his posture changing depending on whether he attempted to order, bargain, or plead his way past the barricade. When he rode back to us his face wore a mixture of relief and frustration, or maybe the dancing shadows on his expression from the flickering torchlight just made it seem that way.

"What news, Lieutenant?" I asked.

He took a deep breath and exhaled through his nose. "The city is under curfew. No one in or out except by daylight and after a thorough search."

"They're trying to catch the killer," I said. I caught Hradian's eye. "That order didn't come from the Archbishop, did it."

Hradian gave me another one of those looks as if he suspected me of prying open his head and reading his thoughts. "No. It comes from the captain of the queen's guard." He stepped toward me in a way that put Bolt, Gael, and Rory on alert, but I held up one hand and they relaxed, a little anyway. "How did you know this, Lord Dura?"

His reaction made me wonder just what Vyne had told him about the Vigil. Had the Archbishop suspended the rules and revealed our ability? "Relax, Lieutenant Hradian. It's doubtful the Archbishop would send you to retrieve me and then keep you from entering the city. It's obvious that he's not the one who ordered the curfew."

Hradian shook his head at me. "The Archbishop might have ordered such a curfew, in light of the queen's death. How are you so sure?"

I didn't know how much the lieutenant knew, and I wasn't about to create trouble for myself. "The reason Archbishop Vyne ordered children to accompany you is the reason he wouldn't bother with ordering a curfew to try and catch the killer."

"And why is that?" Hradian pressed.

"Because he knows it wouldn't work." I walked away before he could ask me anything else.

We bedded down close enough to the watch fires of the soldiers to provide light and waited for dawn. Except for Rory. Our thief pulled a length of chiccor root from his pocket and stuck it in his mouth, staring into the night as he spun a dagger back and forth across his hand.

As I lay on my back staring up at the dots of light in the sky, Gael scooted in close and put one hand on my chest. Her voice came to me like a blessing, her face close to my ear. "Is this what we've come to, Willet? Being guarded by children?" She glanced at Rory.

I nodded. "So it seems. Odd as it is, I still feel safer here than in Laidir's court in Bunard."

We drifted to sleep soon after.

At dawn, Hradian and his men led us between the cold braziers and the soldiers to crest a low rise, and we drew closer to Cynestol, the crown of the northern continent. I'd expected it to be big, had known that the chief city of Aille could hold half a dozen copies of

Bunard within its walls, but distance and haze had obscured it the previous day.

"Aer in heaven," I breathed. "It's . . . it's . . ."

"Huge," Bolt said. "I've never liked it much."

"Why not?" Rory asked. "It's got to be the biggest and richest city on the continent."

Bolt shook his head. "That's just it. Cynestol has everything that can be had on the northern continent and everyone who lives here knows it. There's a saying that if there's an indulgence you can't find in Cynestol, it's because it doesn't exist. Its citizens are all very impressed with the wealth and size of their city, as though it imparts some sort of virtue."

I pointed. "That's not impressive?"

Gael patted my arm. "You'll get used to it after a while, though I have to admit it took me the better part of a month. Think of it as several cities in one."

I shook my head. "I'm having a problem thinking of it at all. It makes my eyes hurt."

We struggled to make headway against a flood of foot traffic that clogged the entire width of the road and spilled over the sides. It couldn't have effectively accommodated half the people that were trying to use it. "Is it always like this?" Rory asked. "I could spend a year here as a pickpocket and live in leisure for the rest of my life."

Bolt shook his head. "The king, Sylvest, passed less than a year ago, and now the queen is dead as well. The people of Cynestol pride themselves on their detachment, but they're nervous, and understandably so." He jerked his head toward Hradian. "Though the good lieutenant hasn't said so, the news is worse than that."

I looked at the crowd and felt my heart make the long descent from my chest to the pit of my stomach. "She died before she could pass the gift of kings on to her heir."

Rory scowled. "How do you know that?"

I pointed at the people streaming past us, hurrying to get away from the city. "Because if Chora's gift had passed to her son, these people wouldn't be running away. New ministers will probably use the opportunity to settle old scores."

Rory's grin turned feral. "Forget picking pockets. I should ask Pellin to let the Mark come back to us."

Bolt's glare could have withered a stump. "Boy, if there are dwimor in this crowd, you're the only one who can spot them."

To Rory's credit, he sobered, but that probably wouldn't mollify Bolt. He would most likely subject Rory to an extended "training session" once we were safely tucked away in the city.

The wall surrounding Cynestol wasn't particularly high. I doubted if it could withstand a siege for more than a week, but Aille could easily muster enough men to put any other nation's standing army to shame. Tiled rooftops shone in the sun in a thousand different colors, and most of the buildings, large or small, were constructed out of huge blocks of sandstone.

"I'd like to move faster," Bolt grunted, nudging his horse forward. "We'll be lucky to make the cathedral before noon."

"What about the east gate?" Gael asked. "If I remember correctly that route usually has much less use."

Bolt nodded. "That might help. I'll suggest it to Hradian."

We soon came to a road that circled the city on three sides and detoured toward the sun. Closer, I amended my opinion of the city walls. They were higher than I had first estimated. The sheer size of Cynestol made them appear lower from a distance. How did they feed so many people?

The sun was an orange ball that had risen to two hands above the horizon when we entered the east gate. I was used to the noise of marketplaces, and this one was no different. What I hadn't expected was the heat. Bolt was the first to strip down to nothing more than shirt and breeches, but the rest of us followed in short order. Despite the adaptation, I could feel the heat reflecting from the buildings like a hammer. Already, my clothes were stuck to my skin with sweat. Hradian and his men hardly seemed to notice the air laying on us like a wet blanket.

"How do these people stand it?" I asked.

Gael managed to look beautiful despite the sweat cascading down her face, or maybe because of it. "It's quite interesting, actually. The weavers here have mastered the art of creating a material so light you'd scarcely know you were wearing it. It's a guild secret. I've tried more than once to pry it out of them, but it's closely guarded." She shrugged. "Of course, we guard the secret to our waterproof wool just as closely."

The mention of wool sent another wave of sweat cascading down my face.

"It's not so bad once you get off the street," Bolt said. "Most of the buildings are constructed with breezeways that capture and magnify even the slightest wind."

I suffered in silence, taking regular pulls from my waterskin until we came within sight of a huge flat-topped hill holding a building that could have rivaled the entire tor.

Bolt's expression turned even more sour than usual. "Behold the magnificence of the six-sided cathedral of the Merum."

"You're in an unusually foul humor," I said, "even for you."

"I don't like coming here," he replied, but he didn't bother to elaborate.

"Why not?" I prodded.

He continued to stare over the top of his horse. "They know me here—at least they used to. Maybe the last of those have had the decency to die by now."

I looked at Gael and Rory, but neither of them appeared to know anything more than I did.

CHAPTER 12

Toria Deel rode next to Fess as they journeyed north across the rich landscape of Aille. Wag followed just behind their horses, his nose in the wind, his gaze sharp enough to infer intelligence that no ordinary dog could own. The last of his kind on the northern continent. His littermate Modrie lived, but Willet had been forced to destroy her mind in Vaerwold.

She shook her head. So much had been lost, and there was still so much more that could be. That thought brought her back to Fess. Though she hadn't spent as much time with the young urchin as Lady Bronwyn, she couldn't help but notice the marked change in his personality since he'd been the unwilling recipient of both Balean's physical gift and Bronwyn's gift of domere.

The laughing carefree boy rarely seen without his smile had disappeared as if he'd never been. He rode at her side and might have been a ridiculous parody of the stoic vigilance of one their guards had he not been in earnest.

What had happened to him?

She considered the question. The most obvious answer might be true—that Fess's part in the death of Balean had altered his view of the world, fracturing his image of himself in ways that couldn't be reversed or restored. As tempting as that supposition was, she didn't wholly believe it. During the festival of Bas-solas, Fess had helped defeat Laewan. Along with the other urchins, he'd temporarily accepted the physical gift of the Vigil guards and had used that deception to kill him.

84

Laewan, corrupted by Cesla and showing physical gifts he should never have possessed, had been cut down by countless dagger strikes from Fess and the other urchins they'd employed. Yet afterward, Fess had been the same as always. The urchins were accustomed to hardship and even death. In spite of that, Fess had shown a remarkable capacity for humor and even joy. What had changed?

Unbidden, a memory worked its way free of her control, the words of Pellin, praise Aer. Memories of Cesla held too much condemnation. *"Never underestimate the power of a question, Toria Deel. Next to our gift, it will reveal more about a person than any other tool or stratagem, and it's more honest."*

She mused, rocking back and forth with the steady gait of the horse beneath her. Questions were indeed powerful, if she knew the right ones to ask. She already knew what had happened to Fess, Bronwyn, and Balean on their journey to the Darkwater. Any query she posed would merely confirm the facts she'd gleaned from Fess when she'd delved him, and facts wouldn't serve her. The knowledge lay deeper, but he wore his newfound reticence as readily as his former garrulousness.

"Fess?"

"Yes, Lady Deel?" He answered with her title, as he always did, but without breaking his survey of the landscape. She would have to find a query of sufficient importance to overcome his reluctance to speak.

"Tell me, what do you think of Ealdor's instruction?"

His brows lowered, and his expression assumed a gravity that she prayed would never look natural. "From what vantage point do you wish me to consider the question?"

This aspect of him, the acuity of his intellect, had surprised her as well, but it explained why Lady Bronwyn had been drawn to him. When the former member of the Vigil had taken on Fess as apprentice, Toria had assumed it to be due to pity, like an old woman caring for a cat found on her doorstep. Bronwyn had seen more. Fess had a turn of mind that would make him a fine scholar, if he lived.

"All of them," she answered.

He made one last check of the horizon before turning to her. "Assuming that what we think is true actually is true, Ealdor's appearance is frightening. The Fayit is willing to surrender an immortal existence to warn us of the threat."

A familiar misgiving, one that she'd felt at Ealdor's appearance, returned. She chose, reluctantly, to voice it. Perhaps honesty on her part would be returned. "I find it difficult to trust him."

"Ealdor?" Fess appeared surprised. "How so?"

She broke away from his gaze. "He reminds me too much of Cesla, all secrets and the appearance of honesty, telling us just enough to do as he wishes but not enough to know everything we need."

"I was under the impression the Vigil worshipped Cesla as the second coming of Iosa," Fess said.

She tried to ignore the flippancy behind the reply, but it struck too close to the mark. "Perhaps we did for a while." She shrugged. "Everyone except Pellin and Bronwyn. According to them and Elwin, Cesla's power was like nothing the Vigil had ever seen before."

Fess blinked. "I didn't know the gift came in different strengths."

She sighed. This was a familiar conversation, though not with Fess. "It doesn't, at least we don't think so, but Cesla's talents and temperaments seemed to be perfectly suited for the gift we carry. His talent of others, for example, was almost frighteningly strong."

"It sounds like the Mark would have liked him."

She shook her head. "I doubt it. Cesla was skilled at manipulating those around him, but neither he nor they would have called it that. With a gesture and smile, perhaps a casual touch on the arm or a friendly pat, he would turn the rest of the Vigil's disagreement into support. For centuries he ran the Vigil like a kingdom, where his word was law."

"That doesn't sound like Ealdor at all," Fess said.

She smiled, but there was little humor in it. "You wouldn't think so, and they look nothing alike, yet if the legends of the Fayit are to be believed, they possessed all the gifts and talents and temperaments at once. I find myself mistrustful of being moved about on the ficheall board like a pawn."

Fess's expression sobered. "Isn't that what Aer does, Lady Deel?"

"As is His right," she answered without thinking. "Cesla and Ealdor are not Aer."

"It seems to me, the end result is pretty much the same."

"Then why did *you* consent to follow Ealdor's instruction?" she asked.

A stand of cedar trees off to the left of the road drew his attention for a few moments before he answered. "Surely you must admit that safeguarding the Darkwater is important."

The enormity of their task bored a hole through her middle, left her feeling drained and inadequate. She envied Fess his ignorance, however temporary. "It is difficult to see our contribution to the defense of the forest as anything other than inconsequential at this point." She held up a hand as his eyes widened in shock. "Don't mistake me. I believe the gift is powerful and has subtle uses the Vigil has only begun to explore, but the power of domere is an intimate exercise. We touch a single person at a time and determine their guilt or innocence. Our gift is a scalpel. The defense of the forest requires a broadsword, and probably more than one."

"The sentinels?" he asked.

She nodded. "And they are denied to us unless we can successfully petition our counterparts on the southern continent to help."

Fess glanced back at Wag. "Why would they not?"

She sighed. "That's a short question with a long, mournful history. If you talk about the split of the church, most people on the northern continent assume you're speaking of the Order Wars between the four, but centuries before that the church split into the Merum in the north and the One Church in the south. That split still colors interactions between the two continents. Trade, religion, travel—nothing is free from its influence.

"We have only two of our four-footed guardians left to us. Wag's sister has been stripped of her gift. Modrie is hardly more than an oversized dog. A single sentinel, while formidable, can hardly safeguard the entire forest."

She turned in her saddle to face him. "That brings us to the point, Fess. Ealdor obviously failed somehow in his own task to keep the forest from being delved. Why should we follow his instructions?"

He shrugged. "I don't know what else to do. Willet trusts him."

She closed her mouth around her rebuttal. Willet Dura had a vault. "Yes, he does, but Lord Dura gives depths to the word *reckless* that I've never encountered before."

She waited for Fess to reply, but it appeared the topic of the Ealdor and his instructions had come to its end. She spoke before the boy could clothe himself in his stoicism. "Fess, why don't you smile anymore?"

"Lady Deel?" Suggestions of pain showed in his eyes before he turned away to resume his scan of the horizon.

She sighed, had hoped the simple earnestness of her question would shock Fess into giving her an unguarded answer. "The lives of those within the Vigil are long, Fess."

"So Lady Bronwyn told me."

"Too long for you to deny yourself," she said softly.

Instead of acknowledging her observation, he turned her question back on her. "Who were you before you became one of the Vigil?"

"A postulant of the Merum order in Elania." She took a deep breath. If this was what Aer required of her to restore Fess to himself, she would comply. "I was young, not much older than you, when I came into the gift. Before that, I spent my days in study and service, but I had no plans to serve the Merum with the rest of my life. It's customary in Elania for young women to receive their education from the church, but most depart after a few years to pursue marriage or trade. I had no gift that would have elevated me to the nobility, but I did possess talents for self and others. That drew the attention of the bishop in Elania and eventually, the Eldest of the Vigil."

"And what would you have done with your talents had you not joined the Vigil?"

"Fess, I was practically a child," she said. "What does a girl of sixteen know?" She almost laughed. "I thought I wanted to be a sculptor's assistant. The marble of Elania is prized for its pure white color veined with specks of copper that give sculptures a lifelike cast. I thought nothing could be more beautiful."

He nodded but showed no inclination to answer the question she had posed.

So she asked again, "Why don't you smile anymore?" and settled herself to wait in silence, hoping the question's weight would be enough to prompt him. Minutes went by as they rode and he performed the ceaseless scan of the landscape, searching for threats.

Perhaps a mile later, he spoke, a single sentence that negated any further attempts at conversation. "Because I'm not happy." His voice carried just enough breath to make it to her ears.

A few hours later the road entered a copse of trees, and Fess's gaze sharpened as he searched the woods for threats. Nothing stirred beneath the canopy except for squirrels or other small game, but Fess jerked, facing a bend in the road.

"Someone's coming."

A moment later she caught the percussive sound of plodding hoof-beats and the creak of a wagon. Fess pulled to a halt and signaled her to do the same and they waited. She measured time by the call of birds until the wagon came into sight, a rickety affair pulled by a horse that should have seen its last pasture long ago. The man on top held the reins with one hand. His other arm hung useless at his side.

"He's wearing Aille's colors," she said.

The man's gaze came up off the road just once before guiding his horse to the right. He gave no other sign that he'd noticed her and Fess or that he cared.

Toria put her horse in his path, forcing him to stop. "Soldier." He lifted his head, but his eyes hardly saw her. "Are you come from the Darkwater?"

His head dipped in a single nod. "Aye."

"What happened?"

Enough of his abstraction fell away for him to laugh caustically. "Our idiot of a commander received his first and last lesson. Darkness belongs to them." He didn't bother to elaborate.

The rasp of his laughter could have peeled bark from a tree. "That sort of sentiment doesn't usually go over well with officers," she said.

He smiled at her, but behind his eyes she saw horror working to get free. He turned to poke one of the bodies stacked behind him. "You don't mind d'ya, sir, if I offer an opinion on yer glorious leadership?" The driver jerked as if at an unexpected response and bent to put his ear close to the dead man's mouth.

He straightened to leer at her. "He says he doesn't mind." He laughed. "We've had quite the conversations, we have, the commander and I. An idiot in the field he might be, but there's no denyin' he's a great listener. Always gives me his undivided attention, he does."

Fess moved forward and extended his hand. "Fair travels to you, soldier."

A bit of the soldier's frantic leer faded as he accepted the gesture. "You're riding into a killing field, lad, and no doubt." Without warning, he spun in his seat and struck the dead officer with his fist. "Against King Rymark's instruction, the captain there thought it would be clever to dress us in black and cover our faces in charcoal to scout the forest at night. Idiot. Even if those in the forest couldn't see us, we wouldn't have been able to see them either, as if we could aim our bows by sound alone. We were slaughtered, two hundred men and women, except for me. My ma always told me I was lucky. I guess I had enough blood coming out of my arm that they figured I'd bleed to death." He shrugged. "Or maybe they'd had their fill."

She nodded. An unhealthy flush marred the man's complexion. "How many of them came out of the forest against you?"

The soldier's expression hardened. "Two."

Fess pointed at the pile of bodies. "What's so special about these eight that you have to cart them back to Cynestol?"

The soldier shook his head. "They're nobles. They may be stupid and arrogant enough to get everyone in their command killed, but an accident of birth means they get carted back to the city instead of buried in some unmarked grave up north. Can't have them touching common men, not even in death."

Memories of war and dying fought to escape from behind the doors where she'd locked them away. "What's your name, soldier?"

"Maledetto." He laughed.

Toria nodded to him. "As you say. Find a healer at the next village for your arm. It's infected."

His eyes narrowed. "And how would you know that?"

"It stinks," she said.

With his one good arm, he shook the reins and the horse continued its slow plod south. Toria watched him go. "If he doesn't get healing for that arm, he won't make it back to Cynestol, whatever his name is."

"He told you his name," Fess said.

She pulled a deep breath through her nose, hoping to erase the stench of death from the cart, but it still hung in the air. "Maledetto means *cursed*."

CHAPTER 13

After we gained the safety of the walls of Cynestol, most of our escort peeled off in ones and twos until we rode in the company of only Hradian and eight of the cosp, half of whom were of an age with Rory. Hradian's presence managed to get us past most of the small-jobbed, small-minded functionaries who considered it their mission to keep the common man away from the cathedral and the Archbishop. Our journey was marked by a succession of clergy who rose in rank the farther we penetrated into the cathedral. When we arrived at the Archbishop's "office"—a word that was far too small to convey the proportions of the actuality—Hradian and his soldiers withdrew as if they'd been about to step on sacred ground and be struck dead for it.

Bolt stopped short at the sight of the Archbishop's secretary. "He's new."

"Is that bad?" I asked.

He sighed. "It probably means Amicus has died. I don't know why I'm surprised. He was older than I. Don't grow old, Willet. You won't like what comes of it."

My circumstances as one of the Vigil, any of whom might ultimately reach ten centuries, probably meant Bolt had made a joke at my expense, but when I looked his way, his expression remained as closed and stoic as ever.

Our current escort, an aged bishop by the name of Serius, bowed his greeting to the man behind the desk, who nodded absently because

91

he was too busy looking at us as if we might have brought a disease into the cathedral.

"Cardinal Jactans," Serius said, "these men were brought here by Lieutenant Hradian and wish to see the Archbishop on a matter of urgency."

Cardinal Jactans appeared to have a talent not spoken of in the Exordium. He could ignore anything he chose. Serius's tone and posture had no effect on the secretary. "Everyone wishes to see the Archbishop, and it's always urgent—at least that's what they claim. Hmmm. You're sweating and your skin holds the pallor of those from the north. What is your business with Archbishop Vyne?"

I nodded. "Our business is of an urgent and sensitive nature, and I'm not authorized to share it. However, I'm sure Archbishop Vyne will apprise you of it in due time, and I'm certain he wishes to see us immediately."

Jactans stared down a considerable length of nose, his lips pursed in disapproval. "No. I think not. The Archbishop is currently engaged." He nodded toward a thickly upholstered bench that ran the length of the wall opposite his desk. "You are welcome to wait, of course, but I feel compelled to inform you that it often takes days for the Archbishop's calendar to clear." He cleared his throat. "Even for matters of urgency."

Serius looked at us as though he wished to apologize, and for the first time his gaze slid past Gael and me and the rest of us to peer at Bolt. The two men were of an age, though my guard did a far better job of carrying his years than the bishop.

"I know you," Bishop Serius said.

Bolt tried to shake his head, but the bishop stepped closer, peering into Bolt's face from a handsbreadth away, his finger stabbing the air with his disagreement. "Yes, you're him."

I came alongside my guard. "Him who?"

Serius looked at me as if I'd suddenly transformed into the village idiot. "You have Tueri Consto as your guard and you have no idea who he is?"

"He more or less assigned himself to me." I looked at Bolt. "You never told me you were from Aille."

"I'm not, but you never asked where I was from, and I haven't been back to Cynestol in a long time." He sighed, looked to Serius, and nodded toward Cardinal Jactans. "Do you think you could impose upon the gatekeeper to let us pass?"

Serius nodded deep enough so that it was almost a bow. "Certainly."

We followed Serius, ducklings in his wake.

"Cardinal Jactans," Serius said, "you must admit these men at once. This man is Tueri Consto."

Jactans didn't appear impressed.

"I go by Bolt now."

Serius wrinkled his nose as if he'd caught a whiff of something foul. "Nonsense."

Jactans looked my guard up and down. "You're telling me this is Tueri Consto, the last Errant?" He snorted. "Surely you jest. This man is hardly taller than I am."

Bolt sighed. "I get that a lot."

Gael looked at Bolt, her blue eyes wide and vivid against her fair skin. "You're dead."

"Not yet, though it's been a close thing a time or two. This is why I don't come back here," he muttered.

With a sigh, he reached into his tunic and pulled forth the silver medallion I'd seen once before, when he'd accepted Duke Orlan's challenge in my stead. With a toss he sent the heavy tarnished silver crashing onto the ordered desktop of Cardinal Jactans. "If the Archbishop finds you've kept us waiting, he'll be displeased."

Jactans stiffened, though he didn't go so far as to stand. "I take orders from the Archbishop and only the Archbishop. Not northerners with tarnished trinkets."

Bolt nodded. "As you say. I'm going to have a seat, and when the Archbishop does see me, I'm going to tell him exactly how long you've kept me waiting." He flicked his glance to Bishop Serius. "At that point I'll probably add a recommendation about your replacement."

With a smile that never advanced past the corners of his mouth, he stepped away from Jactans's desk and moved to the pew along the wall, signaling the rest of us to follow.

"Will this work?" I muttered.

Bolt shrugged. "It doesn't matter. We're not in that much of a hurry. Plus, I've noticed that one of the ways to get something from people you don't like is to threaten them with the consequences of their own decisions." He nodded to where Jactans sat at his desk, his lips pursed as he examined Bolt's worn medallion. "And I meant what I said about suggesting Serius for the job."

Gael took the seat on the opposite side of my guard. "But you're dead."

Bolt's self-satisfied look soured. "Will you stop saying that? I disappeared. There's a difference. You're a smart girl—I'm sure you can work out what happened when I changed jobs, so to speak."

She shook her head, unwilling to be put off. "But all the Errants died. I've read the accounts of the attack on Queen Chora. All four of you—Tento, Valens, Beald, and Consto—died saving her."

"Almost all." Bolt's gaze grew distant, a look I'd seen on veterans as they sat over their ale remembering comrades who'd fallen. "Can we talk about something else?"

"I'm sitting next to a legend," Gael said.

This last comment was too much for Jactans. His chair scraped across the floor as he rose, Bolt's medallion in hand, to scurry over to the towering double doors of the Archbishop's office and step through.

"Finally," Gael muttered. "A moment longer and I would have had to kneel at your feet and kiss your boots."

My guard smirked. "I thought you were laying it on a little heavy."

She patted his check. "Only a little. I never really thought you were dead. Even the manuscripts in Bunard are clear on the fact that Tueri Consto disappeared after the attempt on Queen Chora's life, but Jactans didn't know that."

The door to the Archbishop's office opened, and Jactans came bustling out to bow to Bolt and the rest of us. "My humble apologies for the delay. The Archbishop will see you immediately, of course."

Bolt held out his hand to the secretary. "Might I have my medallion back? It's a bit worn, like me, but I've had it for a long time."

Jactans bobbed his acquiescence. "Yes. Yes, of course."

We stepped through the polished mahogany doors and into two thousand years of accumulated opulence. A long rosewood table that I could have used as a shaving mirror held a dozen gilded chairs across from a desk big enough for a squad of soldiers to stand on. The northern wall was filled from floor to ceiling with books, and I wondered idly if there were any there Custos hadn't read. As I reminded myself to stop in to visit my old friend, I craned my neck to look at the mural on the ceiling, some twenty or thirty feet above eye level.

Stained-glass scenes from the liturgy filled the southern wall and cast a rainbow of colors on the white marble floor.

Rory stood goggling at the altar against the east wall. All the implements were solid gold, and every edge of the dark wood had been gilded in the metal as well. "The sale of one serving plate could feed all the urchins for four years or more," he whispered.

"Don't get any ideas," Bolt whispered back. "This is probably the most powerful man on the continent. He might not appreciate it if any of his toys went missing."

The Archbishop himself sat at the desk, to all appearances waiting patiently for our shock and awe to run its course. A fringe of pure white hair ringed the tanned and age-spotted dome of his head and a short beard and mustache matched the fringe, but his eyebrows still held hints of jet that had been its color in his youth.

After a brief glance at Bolt, his gaze latched on to me, and he stood. "Greetings, Lord Dura." His voice held hints of effort, as if he worked to force enough air from his lungs to be heard. He then nodded toward Bolt. "Errant Consto, it's been too long since you've graced us with your presence here in Cynestol."

Bolt shook his head. "You know why I don't go by that name anymore and why I don't come to Cynestol."

The Archbishop shrugged. "Yes." He sighed. "I do, but I so seldom meet a man of true humility. I think I can be forgiven if it throws me off balance."

"It had nothing to do with humility, and you know it," Bolt said.

Vyne nodded as he took in Gael and Rory with a glance that belied his years and I amended my original estimation. Archbishop Vyne, might be old, but he didn't miss much. "Well, I suppose we've satisfied the obligatory pleasantries. How did you get stuck with this duty, Lord Dura? Did you roll double ones or draw the short straw? I told Hradian to bring Pellin or Toria Deel."

I shrugged. "I more or less became Hradian's desperation choice. If you'd wanted one of the others, you should have sent him earlier. Pellin and Toria Deel had already left by the time he got to us." I cocked my head. "You don't seem very disappointed."

He nodded with a knowing look in his eyes. "I've found that an unexpected turn of events often leaves room for the will of Aer. I've been surprised more times than I can count when circumstances have turned out for the best precisely because events didn't follow my particular plan. Tell me, did the Eldest find something more important to do elsewhere?" Vyne moved past me to take a seat at the head of the polished red-tinted table. I watched his reflection in the wood, like an offering of blood, as he waved at the chairs. "Please, be seated."

I took the seat to his immediate left. Gael, Bolt, and Rory arrayed themselves along either side. "The Eldest keeps his own counsel, Archbishop," I said. "I noticed you sent striplings with Hradian. That seems to indicate a fear that there were dwimor operating in Cynestol. I'm told Queen Chora was hardly ancient and the crowds headed into and out of the city seem to indicate that she died before she could pass her gift on to her heir."

"The youth were for the protection of the Vigil, Lord Dura. As for the queen, people die from accidents every day," Vyne said. "Every great once in a while, those people are important. It would be a mistake to assume a probability equates to murder."

"Do you think she was murdered, Archbishop? Do you need my unique combination of gift and skills?"

Vyne sighed as if I'd failed some sort of test, and his black and gray eyebrows drew together over his aquiline nose. "You disappoint me, Lord Dura. After Chief Brid Teorian's reports, I expected to be witness to a more impressive display of investigative or intuitive acumen. Surely, your observations on the way to see me should indicate whether or not I believe your skills are needed."

"I won't know that until I gather a bit more information, Archbishop," I said. "I've seen too many strange occurrences lately."

His eyebrows lifted a fraction. "Really? Such as?"

"A suicide disguised as a murder."

He nodded. "Ah, the girl, Viona Ness. The Chief of Servants told me about her. Very well. You wish to investigate the queen's death. What do you offer in return?"

"What do you want, Archbishop?"

Vyne nodded. "Exactly what I would have required from Pellin, had he come here. The queen fell down a staircase to her death, and as you've conjectured, her gift has gone free. The most powerful throne on the northern continent is empty, and any number of men and women would do anything to fill it. I want you to use your gift to eliminate the pretenders."

That surprised me. "You don't want me to catch the killer?"

"Of course I do." He shook his head. "*If* there is a killer. But the possibility must be acknowledged that, if Chora was murdered, the killer has already fled the city. Let the dead bury the dead, as they say. It's far more important to find the one who holds the gift of kings and place them on the throne. We're at war, whether the populace in general is aware of it or not." The Archbishop tapped his lips with one finger. "But I'm afraid I'm going to require a bit more from you, Lord Dura."

Without moving, I braced myself. "And what would that be?"

He nodded his head. "No matter what you find, the queen's death must officially remain an accident."

On my left, Bolt grunted. "Not much has changed in Cynestol."

Instead of taking offense, the Archbishop merely nodded. "Nor will it, while I remain in power."

"You're asking me to lie," I said.

"Far from it," the Archbishop replied. "I'm asking you not to speak. Cynestol is a city of over three hundred thousand souls, most of whom are simple people who rely on the church and the crown to preserve order. If word should spread that Queen Chora was murdered, many more people will die in the panic."

"You already know she was murdered," I said. "She was a dancer. What are the chances someone who expressed their physical gift that way would fall down a set of stairs?"

He nodded. "That's better. I'm not proficient in the mathematicum, but I would say the chances are almost none. To the point, however, do I have your word, Lord Dura?"

I didn't like it, but I didn't have much choice. "Yes. I need to see her body."

"Out of the question. To give you or anyone else not a part of the royal household access to Queen Chora's body is as much as admitting she was murdered."

"Then how am I supposed to find her killer, Archbishop?"

He smiled. "I'm going to give you access to court, Lord Dura." He waved at all of us assembled around him. "You and all your friends. If there is a killer stupid enough to remain in the city, then he or she is probably there."

The Archbishop rose and walked with shuffling steps back to his desk, where he took parchment and ink and wrote two notes. "The first letter is to Queen Chora's chamberlain, instructing him to provide rooms and servants in the palace for your stay. You cannot view the body, but this will allow you to inspect the scene of her death. The second one is to the queen's seneschal. He'll introduce you at court." He nodded to Gael and Rory. "All of you. Now, if you'll excuse me, the queen's death has placed the temporal burdens of running the city onto the shoulders of the church, and there are thousands of details to tend to."

After we'd departed the Archbishop's chambers and were out of earshot of his secretary, Bolt held out his hand. "Let me see the notes."

He read through both of them, his face twisting in disgust. "I thought as much. I've always suspected Vyne of a mean streak."

"What did he do?" Gael asked.

"He's introduced me to the chamberlain and the seneschal as Tueri Consto. I never did like that name."

Chapter 14

Bishop Serius met us at the door to Cardinal Jactans's office to escort us out of the cathedral. He didn't speak, but every few steps I could see him looking at Bolt out of the corner of his eyes.

"You don't remember me, do you, Errant Consto?" he finally said as we came to the entrance leading out to the stables.

"Aer have mercy," Bolt growled. "It's bad enough that you and the Archbishop have saddled me with my name again, but now you're going to put my title in front of it as well? Did it never occur to any of you that I might have a job to do here?"

Flustered, Serius elected to ignore the question. "I was there the day the assassins came for Queen Chora."

"Everyone was there," Bolt said. "King Sylvest had just married her, and she was being coronated."

"No." He shook his head. "I mean, yes, but I was the Archbishop's page," Serius continued. "I saw you and the other Errants protect the queen." He shook his head, his amazement still fresh after forty years. "We knew you were all gifted, but I've never seen such a display." He turned to face the rest of us. "A hundred arrows . . ."

"Probably no more than a score and a half," Bolt muttered.

". . . came for the queen," Serius said as though Bolt hadn't spoken. "But the Errants pulled swords and shields and created a shell of protection over her. That's when the assassins, thirty of them . . ."

"More like ten," Bolt corrected.

". . . themselves gifted, came leaping out of the crowd. The

Errants—only four in number—set a hedge around Queen Chora to meet the attack, their blades appearing and disappearing as if by magic."

"That part's true enough"—Bolt shrugged—"but so did the blades of the attackers."

"The blows came too quick to follow," Serius said, his arms and eyes wide, "and blood flew everywhere, but at the last only three attackers and Errant Consto remained."

"Nonsense," Bolt said. "It was two. Those men had gifts that were very nearly as pure as ours. Three against one would have reduced me to chopped mutton."

"Placing himself between the attackers and the queen," Serius said, "the last Errant challenged them, his voice raining disdain."

"Aer have mercy," Bolt said rounding on our escort. "Serius, if you were there, you know I did no such thing. I was trying to save a frightened girl without getting cut to ribbons myself. I put myself in front of the queen because it forced the assassins to come at me one at a time." He put his hand against his left side. "Even so it was a close thing. I didn't have time or breath to make any silly challenges. I just wanted to make sure we both lived."

Disappointment clouded the bishop's face. "It sounds better the way I tell it."

"Except for the fact that it's not true," Bolt said.

"It's mostly true."

We claimed our horses from a shy-looking priest who didn't meet our gaze, and I wondered after Myle. Who would visit him now that Gael had left Bunard?

"The palace is on the other side of the city," Bolt said. "The people of Aille like to maintain the fiction that the church and the state are separate entities."

"Aren't they?" Gael asked.

Bolt shook his head. "Not really. The split of the church was more pronounced in the northern kingdoms. Here in Aille, and to a lesser extent, Caisel, not much changed. The edict of tolerance meant the other orders of the church could practice and proselytize, but the Merum church has remained dominant. The kings and queens of

Aille tread very lightly around the Merum order. Every ruler for the past thousand years has had a Merum priest as their chief advisor."

Gael rode next to me, and I caught her peering at the merchant women we passed, her gaze intent. I followed it and coughed, surprised by the amount of skin I could see. One woman had adorned her navel with an emerald, and her lightweight skirts had been sewn with slits that left most of her legs bare.

"Cloth must be more expensive here than in Collum," I said. "They seem to be running short of it."

Gael patted my cheek and laughed. "It's a different climate and a different culture, Willet. You can't expect people to follow northern customs under this sun."

Ahead of us, a merchant in a very low-cut dress dropped her ledger and bent to pick it up. I held my breath as she retrieved it, then sighed in relief as the expected disaster failed to materialize. "And they must have some grace or physical gift I'm unaware of," I quipped.

Gael laughed, and for a moment I forgot about vaults and assassins and all the rest of it.

The royal palace of Aille occupied a hill nearly as large as the one that sat beneath the cathedral. The design was the same—a perfect hexagon—but the height, width, and breadth had all been reduced, each dimension ever so slightly less than that of the cathedral.

"That's not by accident," Bolt said when he noticed me staring. "It's a constant reminder that the church holds primacy here in Cynestol."

We presented ourselves to the green-liveried guards at the gate, who snapped to when they saw the Archbishop's seal on our letter. A moment later, we were dispatched in the company of one of the palace pages, a girl roughly of an age with Rory, with dark hair, deep olive skin, and rich brown eyes typical of the southern part of Aille.

We walked in our usual formation, Rory out front with Gael, then me, and Bolt bringing up the rear.

"How old is he?" our page asked Gael as she nodded to Rory.

I saw the corner of Gael's mouth turn upward, but her voice remained neutral. "He's sixteen."

"He moves like one of the gifted," our page said. "My name is Charisse. Is he presently without betrothal?"

"Am I what?" Rory coughed.

The page looked him up and down, like a horse trader searching for flaws. "My father is a third son but has risen to the rank of second minister of security. Though I have no gift of my own, my family can number almost fifty generations within the court of Cynestol."

Rory stared at her, his mouth agape.

"Thank you, Charisse," Gael said. "May your father's house prosper and endure. Rory is serving as apprentice to Lord Dura's guard, and questions of his betrothal will have to wait."

Charisse received this polite refusal with equanimity and nodded. "Commitments should be honored—a rare and desirable trait in a husband."

"A what?" Rory gurgled.

We stopped at the door to the chamberlain's office, and Charisse bowed. "Please remember me if circumstances should change," she said to Gael. "I have mastered the fifth part of the mathematicum, and my mother has instructed me in the marriage arts."

Gael looked the rest of us over, her lower lip between her teeth in thought. "I'd almost forgotten about that part of court here in Cynestol."

I pointed to the retreating form of our page. "You mean everyone is like that?"

She nodded. "Alliances and weddings are the national pastime. Be careful of what you say, gentlemen, or you may find yourself with a wife."

"Wife?" Rory's voice squeaked.

Gael nodded. "Here in Cynestol, you're considered to be of marriageable age at fifteen. The courtiers will assume that since you're gifted, you're nobility." She pointed to Bolt. "And the fact that you're in the company of Tueri Consto, the last Errant, will only cement that in their minds."

I started laughing.

"What's so funny, growler?" Rory drawled in his fake accent. "You're in the same boat, yah?"

I shook my head. "I'm already betrothed." I stabbed my finger in the air at him and Bolt. "For once I can go into court and it's everybody with me who has to worry." I straightened. "I think I'm going to like it here in Cynestol."

"Let's get this over with," Bolt said as he pushed through the chamberlain's door. "With any luck Queen Chora died by accident and we'll find her heir tonight. I hate this place."

The chamberlain, Lord Unidia, a short fussy man with an ever-present glass of wine in one hand, took one look at our letter and our clothes and declared himself cursed by Aer.

"It can't be done," he despaired. "I can't have them ready for court tonight." He rounded on one of his assistants, a tall woman whose dress showed more than it covered. "Daicia, fetch the minister of court protocol. Perhaps he can shed some insight into this predicament." He rounded on us. "Regardless, you all smell like horses. Unless they've turned court into a stable, that won't do. Tressa"—he nodded to another woman, shorter and with luminous brown eyes—"show our guests to the baths, then bring them back here for clothes."

He quaffed the contents of his glass and waved it in the air. An attendant refilled it for him. "I haven't been to haeling in months." He sighed. "That's why Aer is doing this to me."

The bath turned out to be an open-air pool fed from an aqueduct. I looked into its depth, trying to see the bottom. Rory whooped and jumped in, splashing water on the rest of us.

"Relax," Bolt said as he walked down the steps into the water. He waded out into the middle of the pool, where the level stopped halfway up his stomach. "It's only a little over a pace deep." He shook his head. "You really need to learn how to swim, Willet."

I half listened to Rory splashing and talking about how he never wanted to leave Cynestol, but I kept the remainder of my thoughts focused on our introduction to the nobility. "What can you tell me about court here in Cynestol?" I asked Bolt.

He poured soap out of a pitcher and proceeded to lather his hair. "The one thing you can count on with Ailleans and their court is change. They become enamored with a new trend and it spreads like brushfire through court and lasts about as long." He dunked his head into the water. "I can't really tell you what to expect because the last time I was here was twenty years ago as Pellin's guard."

I scrubbed soap through my scalp. "Is what Gael said true?"

He nodded. "Their penchant for marriage and alliance? That seems to be the one constant of court life." One of his arms came out of the water to point at Rory. "We better keep him close at hand tonight. The women of Cynestol . . . well, you'll see."

A moment later, Tressa came storming through one of the arches, waving her arms. "What are you still doing in the bath? Hurry, or we'll never get you to court on time." She stood tapping one foot against the clay-tiled floor.

With a shrug, Bolt walked up the steps past her and draped himself with a towel. "Leave your clothes," he said to us. "If you put them back on, they'll just make you take another bath."

"Move!" the woman yelled.

Rory and I exchanged looks. We weren't moving toward the steps. In fact, both of us had edged toward the farther end of the pool.

"We'll be along shortly," I said.

Bolt, wrapped in a towel, tapped her on the shoulder. "What he means is that you're a woman and they're unused to being naked in front of women."

Her eyes widened. "Are they priests?"

"After a fashion," Bolt said.

She straightened. "Oh, well then, I'll leave you to guide them back."

A heartbeat after her shadow disappeared through the archway, I came out of the pool and wrapped a towel around my waist. Rory followed.

"Get used to it," Bolt said. "Hot-weather customs are very different. Follow me."

We returned to the chamberlain by the same route we'd taken and came into a room full of attendants surrounding him and another man who might have been his twin.

He came forward and grabbed Bolt by his chin, turning his face left, then right. I winced, waiting for my guard to knock him unconscious, but nothing happened.

"Hmmm. What's his rank?" he asked the chamberlain.

"Errant," Lord Unidia said.

He dropped his inspection to turn to the chamberlain with a smile. "Surely?" At Unidia's nod, he bowed. "My thanks, brother chamberlain. Court brings so few challenges." He turned back to Bolt. "Rest assured, honored Errant, I shall dress you in a fashion befitting your station."

Bolt sighed. "And so it begins."

Two hours and interminable changes of clothes later, the three of us stood just outside the entrance to court, the lilting strains of music drifting toward us along with the scents of strangely spiced food.

"Where's Lady Gael?" Rory asked.

"It's customary for women to arrive a few minutes after the men," Bolt said, "or at least it was the last time I was here."

A male attendant, broad-shouldered and muscled with chiseled looks even Duke Orlan might have envied, escorted Gael to us. I tried not to stare and failed miserably. Gael wore a floor-length dress that left both arms and one shoulder bare. Despite the short notice, the deep blue folds of her outfit appeared to have been tailored to her.

Exactly to her. A slit up the side exposed most of her left leg, and I had difficulty keeping my gaze above her shoulders.

"She is gorgeous, is she not?" the attendant asked, giving her an appreciative glance.

I didn't care for the way his gaze lingered on the exposed bits of my betrothed. "Go away," I said, my voice flat.

He bowed and turned on one heel.

Gael spun, and the shimmering fabric flared, showing both of her legs well above the knees. "Do you like it, Willet? I'm told it's a bit conservative for Cynestol, but can you imagine the uproar this dress would cause in Bunard?"

"Who was he?" I pointed at the retreating attendant.

Gael's throaty laugh mocked me. "Just a servant with muscles where his brains should be."

I retrieved the other letter of introduction, the one to the royal seneschal, and stepped forward to the guards posted at the door. After reading the letter, one of them slipped inside, and a moment later, a gray-haired man with deeply tanned skin stepped through, his eyes lighting as his gaze swept across us.

"Finally, something different," he said. "A lord and lady of the north and an Errant! Aer is kind." He pivoted, showing us his back without saying anything more. "Follow me."

He led us through a broad short hall to an archway where a trumpeter blew a fanfare. In a high, piercing tenor that only someone gifted could manage, the seneschal addressed the court.

"A rare treat is yours. From the farthest reaches of the north, from the city of Bunard in the distant kingdom of Collum, I present Lady

Gael Alainn and her betrothed, Lord Willet Dura, with their attendant, Lord Rory."

"Lord?" Rory snorted. "I'm a thief."

"So are most of the nobility," I said. "They're just better dressed."

The seneschal made shooing motions that sent us into the expansive court of Cynestol. "Isn't he going to announce Bolt?" Rory asked.

Gael nodded. "Oh yes, but he doesn't want anything or anyone to distract from his presentation."

"Because he's an Errant?"

"Because he's the *last* Errant," Gael said. "Their exploits are legendary."

Behind us, the seneschal proclaimed Bolt's presence in a voice that I imagined could be heard in Caisel's capital city of Vadras. "Nobility of the realm, I bring you an unexpected honor . . ."

I listened as he described Bolt in mythical terms for the next five minutes. By the time he finished, the music and entertainment had stopped and every eye was fastened expectantly on the entrance.

Bolt stepped through, dressed all in white, his face like granite.

As one, the crowd bowed to him according to their rank and station, and it was as if a wind had blown across a field of flowers. When the music and noise resumed I got my first glimpse of court in Cynestol.

CHAPTER 15

I made some offhand comment on the appearance of court that was out of my head as soon as it left my mouth, and Bolt shrugged with his response. "The court of kings isn't square or even close to it. The hall and the cathedral are both built to the same ratios, nine long, six wide, and four high."

The numbers of the Exordium. I took a deep breath. I had my own date with those numbers, a task hinted at by Ealdor that left me guessing most of the time. Gael nudged me forward into a maelstrom of color and noise and scent that left me reeling. Three times the size of Bunard's court, it wasn't just its extents that overwhelmed me—the walls and pillars, each four paces broad at the base, were clad in silver to a height of five paces and polished to a mirror finish. Every time someone moved, countless reflections moved with them.

"The court in Cynestol is designed to overwhelm visitors," Gael murmured in my ear.

"It's doing a great job," I said. "I think I'm going to be sick."

"Focus on a single point and concentrate on the sound of just one of the musicians, and the rest will become manageable."

I nodded and squinted, locking my gaze onto Bolt's back. No one else in the room had chosen to dress in white. I would have laughed if the contrast between Bunard's court and this one hadn't been so stark. People clustered around Bolt, drawing near but keeping a respectful distance, waiting.

Gael gestured to Rory and me. "Stay close together and keep watch while I circulate among the crowd. It's customary in Cynestol for visitors to greet as many of the nobility as possible."

I took a few quick steps toward Bolt, and Rory trailed me by half a dozen paces. A number of young women took the opportunity to come forward and make his acquaintance. Charisse was among them. I could have pitied our young thief.

When I stepped in at Bolt's side, the crowd looked at me as though I'd blasphemed and Aer might strike me dead at any moment.

"You would think that after a few decades, people would have more sense than to behave like this," he muttered.

"They look as if they're waiting for you to say something."

He grunted. "They are."

"Why?"

He sighed, and if I hadn't known better, I'd swear that my guard was on the verge of pouting. "I saved Queen Chora's life and they've built that piece of history up in their minds until they've turned me into some myth that has no resemblance to flesh and blood. They're waiting for me to make a pronouncement."

"What?"

He didn't get the chance to explain. A woman of perhaps thirty, wearing a gown that fired the imagination without requiring much of it, stepped forward and put her fingertips on Bolt's bare arm. "Errant Consto"—she curtsied without breaking contact—"when will you declare your regency?"

"What?!" I squawked like a bird before I could help myself.

Bolt grabbed my arm and hauled me two steps back. "This is why I didn't want to come back here, especially now," he whispered. "The Errants have a history in Cynestol going back twenty centuries. On those few occasions when the king or queen died without passing on their gift, one of the Errants would serve as regent until the new ruler was found."

I shook my head. "I've read the history books. The last time Aille had a regent was three hundred years ago."

He sighed. "Cynestol has been here for almost two thousand years. These people regard tradition with the same reverence as the people of Moorclaire hold the mathematicum."

"But there aren't any more Errants," I muttered. "You've been attached to the Vigil for decades." I searched through the memories of all my history lessons, wishing I'd paid more attention. "What happened to them? Why are you the last one?"

Something flickered across the background of his gaze, something hot. "The ones who fell with me were never replaced. The attack on Queen Chora was orchestrated by Bael Waerloga."

I nodded. "I think I remember that part."

"Ha!" Bolt laughed. "But likely not all of it. Bael was one of us, an Errant, but he was also cousin to the pretender."

"Do you have to serve?"

He looked out across the crowd, and I followed his gaze. Even the people who weren't looking at us directly had their bodies turned so they could watch us without seeming to. "No, but I'm going to have to offer them something in return."

A shadow fell across the space between us.

"Errant Consto?" the woman in the diaphanous dress called his attention, the tips of her fingers working their way up his arm toward his neck. "Are you currently unattached?"

I admired the way he managed to keep his gaze from drifting away from her face. He bowed, and I tried to remember if I'd ever seen him offer that gesture to anyone else before. "Duty precludes me from such sweet entanglements," he said in a voice that carried well past our circle. "I have spoken with the Archbishop, and we have decided it would be better if I declined the regency."

A buzz of collected mutters and whispers swept through the crowd like ripples on a pond. People no longer pretended to look elsewhere. Everyone faced my guard. "However, my companions and I have been asked by Archbishop Vyne to aid him in verifying the rightful heir, and it is a task we have accepted."

I watched the crowd with their innumerable reflections to see if any of them might betray themselves. I'd assumed it to be a scant hope. If any of them were scheming for the throne, they wouldn't be stupid enough to let their objection to Bolt's announcement show, but waves of displeasure washed over the crowd like clouds drifting in front of the sun. Mutters of disapproval built into an angry buzz that reflected from the walls with almost as much clarity as their likenesses and a few of the closest went so far as to show their backs to us.

I leaned toward my guard so that no one else could hear me. "I don't understand."

He shook his head. "By having me decline the regency while verifying the ascension, Vyne just removed the last fiction that the church and the throne were separate."

"That doesn't make any sense. In Bunard the priests always test for the gift of kings when the throne comes to another. I should know. I killed a man who'd stolen enough of the gifts to pass the test and take the throne."

Bolt nodded. "The Errants performed the same function here. The difference is that I just placed myself under Vyne's authority in that process." Disapproval had created an open circle of space around us, but he checked to make sure no one was within hearing anyway. "The Errants were much like the Vigil, birthed from the church, but autonomous. The crowd would have preferred me to say that I would use my power to ensure the selection is correct."

I nodded. "That way, you would have been seen as an outsider, there to make sure the church didn't place a pretender on the throne. Now, they think you're part of a plot." I thought about that for a moment. "Is Vyne so mistrusted, then?"

The last Errant shrugged. "Who in power isn't?"

"Lai—" I stopped. Laidir had been the best king I could imagine, but even so, nearly half his nobles had objected to his authority.

"Exactly," Bolt said.

"Why say it that way, then?" I asked as I waved my arm at the crowd. "They despise you now."

"Because if I hadn't, they'd keep pestering me to take the regency. This will make our job easier."

"Oh yes, the job is always easier when people hate you and are trying to kill you."

"Humph. You really should do something about that sarcastic streak."

"You're one to talk."

Gael emerged from a knot of nobles and their wavering reflections to step across the isolation and join us. "You certainly know how to charm a crowd."

Bolt's eyes narrowed. "'Better the wounds of a friend than the kisses of an enemy,'" he quoted. "They'll thank me later, when the rightful heir sits the throne."

Nice as that sounded, I'd seen enough of human nature to know it wasn't true. "No, they won't."

He nodded. "You're right, they won't, but it sounds good." He pivoted on one heel and made for the west end of the hall, where Queen Chora had held court. On a raised dais stood a throne of dark polished wood gilded with silver and gold. The jeweled headpiece, a gull perched on an oak branch, symbolized the sea and the land from which Aille drew its vast wealth. The throne sat empty, but the chairs flanking it weren't.

Two men more different would be hard to describe. One, perhaps a score and five, sat alone in the left-hand chair with the fixed scowl of a man wishing for an offense. Muscled, he could have passed for a soldier but for the silver and gold thread that adorned his tunic and hose of rich green.

Bolt sighed. "Prince Maenelic," he said. "Delve him if you can do it without being obvious," he muttered.

I couldn't see anything particularly menacing about the prince, other than the fact that he was a noble who outranked me and appeared to be in foul humor—a circumstance with which I had more than passing familiarity. "Why?" I asked.

"Because by now the entire nobility of Cynestol knows the gift of kings must have passed to someone else," Bolt said. "His presence here is a needless exercise in humiliation. It would be interesting to know what motivates him to endure it."

"Alright." I nodded to the other chair, where a Merum bishop sat surveying the crowd with scarcely concealed amusement. Four uniformed cosp stood watch, guarding him. The dichotomy between the bishop and the prince was stark, to say the least. "What about him?"

"Bishop Gehata," Bolt said. "He's the Merum advisor to the throne. The death of Queen Chora means he's Archbishop Vyne's fulcrum. That makes him the second most powerful man in Aille, just after the Archbishop."

Younger than I expected, the bishop surveyed the crowd, his lips curled in condescension. My elevation to the nobility in Collum had given me the opportunity to meet any number of men who'd been born into wealth. Most of them had learned very quickly how to carry themselves as if they deserved it. Gehata could have been the man who gave them lessons. "He makes Duke Orlan look almost humble."

"Lineage is far more complicated in Aille," Bolt said. "Their habit of getting divorced and remarried turns all the family trees into one giant hedge, but his sits very close to the top."

I trailed Bolt and copied his bow to Prince Maenelic, making sure to go a bit deeper on mine than he did, since he was the last Errant. Gael's curtsy showed enough skin to catch the prince's gaze.

"Your Highness," Bolt said, "may I offer my condolences on the death of your mother?"

Maenelic's expression never changed, but he did swap targets, bringing his scowl to bear on Bolt. "Why would I want them?" he spat, but he slurred his words, and random splashes of red marked the floor by his chair. "She died without passing her gift to me." He let his gaze sweep over the bishop and his guards. "Do I merit even a single guard any longer?" He waved a hand at the nobles before him. "Look at them, dancing with as much spring in their step as always. Do they have sense enough to wonder how a dancer could die by falling? Did they fast for her death? Should I?" He laughed a bitter sound, like a saw tearing through wood, and pointed at a random nobleman of considerable girth. "I think that fellow might have missed a snack. All continues as it has since the beginning. Kings and queens are like grass."

Bolt dipped his head but didn't respond. "We will do everything we can to find her killer, Your Highness."

Maenelic lurched to his feet, wavering. "You fool!" He gripped his wine glass like a club. "My place has been given to another! I don't care if she was killed. I don't care if you find her killer!" He cocked his arm and threw.

The goblet leapt from the prince's hand, but Bolt snatched it out of the air, his motions almost too quick to follow. I was surprised at first that he would put his gift on such broad display before I remembered every one of these people knew him as the last Errant. They would have expected no less of Tueri Consto.

He held the goblet out to the prince with a bow. "I crave your pardon, Your Highness. You seem to have dropped your glass."

The prince's anger, deprived of a target, drained from him, and with a glance around the throne room, he reseated himself.

"Well, that was unfortunate," Gehata said to Bolt. "We must remember to pray for poor Maenelic. The stress of his mother's death weighs more heavily upon him than we supposed." He spoke as if the prince was no longer present, and his expression never shifted as he wielded his amusement like a rapier. "It's just as well," he said. "Please, Errant Consto, join us."

His gaze sharpened a fraction when Bolt made no move. "Oh, I see. You have no place to sit. Come, Prince Maenelic. Errant Consto can hardly be expected to stand for the duration of court. Where are your manners? Give the last Errant your seat."

The prince locked gazes with Bishop Gehata, and rage mottled his face, but at last the bishop's disdain and the collective scrutiny of the court proved to be more than he could bear. With an oath owing its origin to the barracks rather than the palace, he left the hall. The nobles parted for him, but their expressions conveyed uniform contempt. Not one face in the entire hall spared Maenelic enough compassion to even pretend a show of sympathy.

Then I understood. Maenelic's behavior had unmasked them. In his grief, the prince had dispensed with cordial niceties and put the true nature of court on full display. He had stripped away their pretense, and that was unforgiveable.

"Well, that was amusing, if uncomfortable," Gehata said, his voice dropping to a purr. "I will have to ensure the prince does not return to court. Perhaps some time with Aille's forces will allow him some measure of healing." He laughed. "Or I might permit him to watch as you give his birthright to another. Of course, to do that you'll need to hear the petitions of those who wish to state a claim to the throne." The bishop's smile turned predatory. "As counselor to the throne, it will be my privilege to advise you. Please, Errant Consto"—Gehata's voice sharpened—"sit."

I'd seen men of all stripes kick a man who was down, both literally and figuratively, but I'd never seen anyone take as much pleasure in the act as Gehata. The bishop had just emasculated the prince in front of the entire court and had forced Bolt to take part. I'd been wrong when I thought I couldn't hate anyone more than Duke Orlan.

The buzz of the crowd grew behind us as Bolt approached Maenelic's seat. "They don't seem too pleased with the prospect of you sitting there," I said.

Bolt shook his head. "They're not. If I had declared myself regent, I would have had the right to it until the rightful heir was found. I'll need you to flank me."

"And why are we doing this?" I asked. "Other than to make ourselves targets in a room full of people you've just disappointed."

He almost smiled. "As the bishop said, to receive claimants to the
throne. Vyne wants to know who the next king or queen is going to
be. This is how we find them." He cut his eyes toward me. "I hope.
Any noble who wishes to make the claim to the gift of kings will have
to introduce themselves."

I almost stumbled. "You want me to delve them? Just in case you
needed reminding, I can't see gifts."

We turned to face the crowd and their myriad reflections. "You
won't have to," Bolt said. "If they hold the gift of kings, their memories will show it."

"This soon?" Gael asked. "It took the priests weeks to verify Cailin's
son held the gift after Laidir's passing."

"That's because Brod was a child. It's different with adults." Bolt
sat in the right-hand chair while Gael and I flanked him on either
side. "They know almost from the moment it comes upon them."

I looked out across the crowd, struck again by the lack of mourning
for Queen Chora and the sheer amount of naked ambition present
in the room. "And what do we do when each and every noble in here
claims to hold the gift of kings? I can't delve more than five or six
a day."

Bolt's shoulders, still thick with muscle after three score plus years,
shifted, shedding my concerns. "We exert the privilege to make them
wait until the next day or the one after that or next week or month."

"What?"

He shook his head. "What did you think, Willet? Cynestol boasts
a ponderous history. Nothing here moves quickly."

Strains of music drifted to us from the musicians stationed at
each of the corners of the throne room. Somehow through all the
tumult they had managed to stay in time with each other, and their
music reflected the mood of the court, their chords ascending first
into augmented mystery before dropping into a cascade of notes that
reflected the diminished hopes of the crowd. I wondered if they were
mocking us. Was it possible to make a mandolin sound sarcastic?

A woman stepped from the crowd, her dress so filmy it could have
doubled as a scarf. A deep red, it shifted and floated behind her as
she moved. Somehow it managed to stay in place, and I wondered

what sort of craft or sorcery managed the task. She approached the dais as if we were her subjects, wisps of her blond hair mimicking the dress she wore.

"I know this one," Gael murmured looking at Bolt, "at least by reputation. Duchess Lyllian Hungor. Does Willet have to delve her?"

He nodded. "If she claims to hold the gift of kings, he must."

She turned to me, shaking her head. "If even half the talk about the duchess is true, you're probably going to want to put her memories away as quickly as you can."

Closer, Hungor appeared to hold about two score years. Fine lines showed around her eyes and the beginning of smile lines lay on the sides of her mouth. Yet, age had managed to enhance her beauty instead of diminishing it, though most men would consider her features strong rather than comely.

"Errant Consto"—she curtsied—"allow me to welcome you back to the court of your homeland."

He inclined his head with enough grace to make any monarch or dancer envious. "Duchess Hungor, I thank you for your welcome, though anyone looking at me would know my birth lies elsewhere."

She nodded, smiling indulgently. "But Cynestol is your home, and you've earned the right to call it such."

"Do you wish to make a claim for the gulled throne?"

She dipped her head. "I do. The burden of our people rests heavily upon me, and I believe the gift of Aer does as well." A thread of uncertainty marred the serenity of those green eyes. "Naturally, I would reward all those who have served Aille so well in the past." Her glance darted to Gael, then me. "Or would do so in the future."

Bolt matched her gesture, his head lowering slightly. "Allow me to introduce my friends and advisors, Lady Gael Alainn and her betrothed, Lord Willet Dura."

The duchess extended her right hand, palm forward, which Gael matched with her left, each finger and thumb placed to touch their opposite. After a brief moment in which Gael's eyes widened visibly, they parted and the duchess turned to me, this time extending her left hand in the same manner.

I'd stripped off my gloves and raised my right hand to match hers. I knew what to expect, but in the instant before I fell into the delve, the heat of her touch still surprised me. The river of her memories flowed past me in a swirl of colored recollections. But where the colors of most people I'd met showed hues of startling clarity denoting both pleasure and pain, most of hers were muted.

I let them wash over me until I became Duchess Lyllian Hungor, a major power in the kingdom of Aille and as lost a soul as humanity or circumstance could contrive. I spent my days in quests for influence and pleasure, trying to fill a hole the death of my first husband had put in my soul. But each fleeting moment of pleasure carved out a bit more of my insides, until the hole became a cavern. At the last, nothing of pleasure remained in my liaisons, only a hunger that refused to be filled.

I blinked, finding myself in the throne room with my right hand a whisper away from her left and my face flaming. I jerked as if I'd been burned and tried to turn the motion into a bow that would hide my embarrassment. The duchess eyed me, suspicion engraved in her expression.

"Thank you, Duchess Hungor," Bolt said from his seat. "Your dedication to Aille is noted." At the tone of dismissal, Lyllian Hungor curtsied once more and withdrew, her dress and hair trailing after in the breeze of her departure.

"Willet?" Gael asked.

I swallowed, working to put the fresh set of memories away, but try as I might, there were vivid images that remained. "Well . . . that was an education."

Bolt laughed, his bark of amusement drawing the stares of court.

For a moment, I saw Gael's sculpted features flash a look I'd seen on other women, but never on her until that moment. Jealousy. I would have told her that the duchess was more to be pitied than censured, but the other chief nobles, emboldened by the encounter, queued up to present themselves as contenders for the throne.

An eternity of formality and half a dozen sets of memories later, Bolt withdrew from court, allowing me to trail in his wake. Not one of the nobles I had delved possessed the gift of kings or, more correctly, none of them were aware of having such a gift. The only monarch I'd ever delved was King Laidir, and that had been in the earliest days of my gift, before I even knew I had or understood it.

"Are you sure the one who has the gift will know?" I asked Bolt in the privacy of our rooms.

He nodded as if the question had already been asked and answered. To be fair, it had. "Imagine yourself suddenly skilled at every endeavor known to man. How could you not know?"

I shrugged. "What if it came to a drunkard? Some poor sot who's never sober enough to understand what he's feeling might completely miss the fact that he's supposed to be the next king."

His shoulders dropped as he turned my way. "Then I suppose we'll have to go through the city and round up all the drunks so we can sober one of them up enough to take the throne." He lifted a hand. "Do you always have to imagine the worst set of circumstances?"

I shrugged. "It usually saves time."

Bolt turned to Gael. "Are you sure you want to marry him? He's dour enough to be a Vigil guard."

She gave me a smile along with one of those smoldering looks from beneath her lashes. "I've never noticed that. Maybe it's the company he keeps."

"Never mind." He grew serious as he looked at me. "Are you ready to do your job?"

Queen Chora's death. "I wonder what it would be like to be a cobbler or musician, to be part of a profession that didn't have to deal in the worst humanity had to offer." But inside I could feel the beat of my heart quicken, and I nodded.

We left our quarters and began the long trek to the royal chambers, making slight turns that fell short of the expected right angles as we negotiated the six-sided palace one leg at a time, the thick carpet muffling the sound of our steps. On our right, floor-to-ceiling windows offered a view of Cynestol at night, a city so lit that it resembled a mass of light bugs hovering over a field. On our left, toward the interior of the palace, were short hallways filled with doors, an uncountable number. I nodded down the hallway. "Why are so many people still up?" I asked Bolt.

"Cynestol is huge. The bigger the city, the more people it takes to keep it running smoothly." His mouth pulled to one side. "Plus, there have been so many marriages among the nobility that nearly all of them work here in some capacity or another."

"Does the crown really need all these people?" Rory asked.

Bolt shrugged. "No, but it helps keep them out of trouble. There's a ministry for nearly everything, most of them incredibly insignificant. Except for the attempt on Chora that ended the time of the Errants, it's been hundreds of years since any of the major nobles did any serious plotting against the throne."

We came around to the east side of the palace after something closer to a hike than a walk. A quartet of guards stood sentry over a pair of double doors fifteen feet tall and wide enough for eight men to walk through abreast. The wood, light and nearly without grain, looked as if it had been freshly lacquered the week before. They probably had a minister for that.

One of the guards advanced, a captain's insignia on his shoulder. "No one is permitted into the royal chambers, by order of the bishop."

Bolt nodded. "Almost no one, and I think you mean the Archbishop." He reached inside his doublet and pulled the letter from Vyne.

The captain read the letter in increments, pausing to look at Bolt and the rest of us. He handed back the letter with a shake of his head. "No, Errant Consto. I mean the bishop. Bishop Gehata has forbidden access to the royal apartments until such time as the church can confirm a new king." He nodded toward the letter in Bolt's hand. "The Archbishop's letter grants you quarters in the palace, not access to Queen Chora's apartments."

Bolt gazed at the captain through narrowed eyes. "I suppose the bishop has the entrance guarded round the clock?"

At the captain's nod, we retreated the way we came, Rory leading with Bolt on my left, chewing the inside of his cheek the whole way.

"We're stuck," I said, more to dispel the silence than anything else.

"For the moment," Bolt said.

"Vyne never intended for us to investigate Chora's death," I said.

Bolt nodded. "The Vigil is the biggest secret the church has, Willet, but not its only secret. In Vyne's mind, Chora is dead and the risks associated with uncovering the facts of it outweigh the benefits."

Something mulishly stubborn flared to life in my chest. Bishop, Archbishop, or no, I was determined to find a way to investigate the queen's death. Bolt's soft laughter hit me like iced water dumped down my back. "What's so funny?"

"The Archbishop has played us perfectly," he said. "He can't forbid you from investigating the queen's death, but he can deny you access to the facts of it."

Rory turned from his survey of the hall ahead. "Is everyone in the nobility and the church a schemer? They make Fess and Mark look like choirboys."

"No," Bolt said. "Not all of them or anything close to it, but the ones in power don't get there by being stupid, no matter what their intentions are. You didn't really believe the urchins were the only ones who bluffed or conned people, did you?"

Rory stiffened. "Of course not," he said, but I could see a different perspective growing behind his eyes.

"Where does this leave us?" I asked.

Bolt took a deep breath. "For now, this leaves us in the throne room."

"Oh, good," I said. "That's just what I've always wanted, a chance to swim in the accumulated indulgences of the richest kingdom on earth. Lovely. When I'm done, I think I'll have a bath in the sewer."

"Stop complaining," Bolt growled. "It's a chance to see if any of those peacocks know anything that can help us."

CHAPTER 16

A week after sailing from Port City, Pellin sat on his bunk with Mark and Elieve seated before him. The gentle rocking of the ship beneath the blue canopy of the sky had served to lull the girl into a semblance of calm. Allta guarded the door. Mark's hands twitched every time his gaze fell on the blindfold Elieve wore. Pellin placed his hand on Elieve's arm, had just enough time to enjoy the infrequent sensation of touching another before the delve took him into her mind.

What he saw astounded him. His expectation, his hope, had been that Elieve would accumulate memories as swiftly as a newborn, but Mark's focused companionship had managed to create memories within the girl at an even faster rate. While Elieve's memories still constituted a stream rather than a river, there was no danger of the girl losing her way.

With a brief mental exertion, he lifted his hand from her skin and came out of her mind. "Well done, Mark. I think we can do more than just try to restore her vision; I think I'll be able to take away all of Cerena's memories."

He glanced at Allta, waited for his guard to acknowledge him before he continued. "Listen carefully. Here is how it must be done. When those with the gift of domere enter a person's mind, we see their memories as a river composed of colored strands. The color indicates the emotion attached to the particular memory. When I first entered Elieve's mind, every strand I saw was black with hatred. That was Cesla's doing."

He sighed against the coming fatigue. "Since all of those memories had to be destroyed, it was a fairly simple process. What I must do now is harder. I will have to sift through Elieve's memories until I have destroyed every remnant of Cerena's life. Within her mind, I will grasp each memory, one at a time, to determine its origin. If it is Elieve's, I will release it. If it is Cerena's, a mental twist, hardly more than the intention of destroying it, will serve to obliterate it. Delving runs at incomprehensible speed compared to the waking world, but even so, this will take a long time. Do you understand what I'm telling you, Mark?"

His apprentice—strange that the word carried more weight now—nodded.

"Good," Pellin said. "You must commit everything I tell you to memory. It's important."

Mark's answering nod was serious. "Yes, Eldest."

He put his hand back on Elieve's arm.

When he lifted it again, the ship still rocked, but the morning sky outside the porthole had turned to charcoal and a scarlet wash of clouds on the horizon showed that night was mere minutes away. The room spun in his vision, and he pitched toward the floor.

Strong hands caught him, helped him upright. Slowly, the room stabilized and Pellin pointed to a chair. Allta half carried him, but once sitting, his real senses reasserted themselves, and after a drink he found speech possible.

"I have done all I can to ensure she is well and truly Elieve. I think you can remove her blindfold now, Mark, though she may find even this dim light uncomfortable at first."

Mark reached up to untie his thief's blindfold from the girl.

"Be ready, Allta," Pellin said. "Her response is unpredictable."

The girl ducked her head, squinting against the light, then buried her face into the crook of Mark's shoulder.

"It's alright, Elieve," Mark said.

The sound of his voice pulled her head up, her eyes wide, but his nearness kept her from focusing on him, and blinking, she leaned away until almost a foot of space separated them.

"Elieve," Mark said again.

"Loved," she said.

"Yes." Mark nodded.

Pellin watched her gaze fix upon Mark's lips. "Keep talking to her, lad."

"You are loved," Mark said.

Elieve lifted her hands to Mark's face, feeling, poking him clumsily as he spoke to her, tracing the movements of his mouth. Her head lifted as her gaze traveled up from his lips, and wherever her sight landed her hands followed, touching. When she got to his eyes, a light blue that matched the color of the sky at noon, she stopped.

His shy grin showed teeth, and she reached out to touch them. "Greetings," Mark said.

She traced the movement with her hands and copied it in a husky voice. "G-gr-greetings."

This time when he smiled, she copied that as well.

Hesitantly, his moves gentle and slow, as though she was a fawn he didn't want to startle, Mark turned Elieve around so that she faced Pellin. "Look."

Her eyes. Her eyes were a light brown, tan, the color of weakest tea with cream, but they were colored. Not clear.

Tears stung his old man's gaze, and he drew a deep shuddering breath. How long had it been since he'd felt this, this sense of wonder, since he'd felt young? "It's a miracle."

Mark laughed softly, his posture mirroring the fatigue wrought by Elieve's constant care. Smudges of exhaustion beneath his eyes testified to the price he'd paid to bring Elieve's mind back from oblivion. "Do all miracles take so much work? I thought they were supposed to be like magic."

Pellin sighed. Despite the tone of jesting, Mark's question carried hints of earnestness that shouldn't be ignored. "I think so, though I haven't seen enough to claim any expertise. Perhaps a miracle must carry a cost, but most of the time we just don't see it."

Mark nodded. "That makes sense. Someone should put that in the liturgy."

"It's in there," Pellin said, "for the really important ones anyway."

"Ma-ark," Elieve said, putting her hand to his chest.

Mark's smile lit the room. "That's right, Elieve. That's right." He turned. "What do I do now, Eldest?"

Pellin shook his head as he smiled. "You're asking me? I've never brought anyone back from such emptiness. What I have to do and what you have to do from this point are very different." He let all the pride he felt at Mark's accomplishment blaze in his smile. "I'm going to record everything you've done in the most minute detail so that those who follow us will know how to rescue such lost souls. Aer be praised, lad! Do you know what you've done?" Without waiting for an answer, he turned to Allta. "She's coming with us to see the southern Vigil. What's most important?"

Allta nodded. "She needs to be able to tend to her own ablutions, to dress and feed herself, to be able to ride, and to speak."

Mark's face stilled. "Elieve's like a newborn. That will take years."

Pellin shook his head. "I think not, lad. She knows her name and yours already. The nature of memory holds more mystery than we can divine. We spoke of the inseparable nature of the mind and the body and the spirit. In her spirit, she knows all these things already, even if they've been temporarily erased from her mind. I believe, based on what you've accomplished already, that her mind and body will relearn the rest with amazing speed." He lifted his hands, palm up. "But in any case, the most important thing is for you to teach her to tend to herself without constant supervision. We won't have time for you to bathe her every day."

For the next two days Pellin watched, amazed, as Mark tended to Elieve. The boy had been committed before, but with Elieve's mind now her own, Mark had been afforded the opportunity to obtain regular sleep and rest. He taught Elieve with an intensity belied by his playful demeanor. Each morning he would talk her through breakfast, insisting that she feed herself, describing the utensils, the food, even the taste. When Elieve's attention flagged, he would cease that particular lesson and adjourn to the deck.

Hand in hand they would walk around the ship, and Mark would take Elieve's fingertips and rub it across the surfaces, describing each in turn, or point to objects that shared the same color to call them out. It was during one of these moments that Elieve rediscovered her sense of humor.

"Blue," Mark said, pointing to the waters of the southern sea. Then he pointed to the sky and repeated the word.

Elieve shook her head. "Red."

"No." Mark shook his head and pointed to his tongue. "Red."

Then he pointed to the sea and sky again. "What color are they, Elieve?"

She nodded confidently, her light-brown-eyed gaze dancing. "Red."

"No," Mark huffed in exasperation. "They're blue." He pointed again. "Tell me the color."

"Red," Elieve said, smiling.

"No, no, no," Mark said and pointed to his tongue again. "Red. See my tongue. It's red. Now look at the sea and sky and tell me the color."

Laughing, Elieve put her hand to Mark's face. "Red."

Mark slumped in defeat before turning to Pellin. "If you laugh with her, Eldest, you'll just encourage her to do it again."

Pellin nodded. "Good. There's little enough joy in the world, Mark. Allow her to experience as much of it as she can."

After nightfall and supper that evening, Mark took Elieve to their cabin and under Pellin's discreetly watchful eye, he continued teaching Elieve how to bathe and dress herself, a situation made more difficult by the fact that Elieve's rediscovered sense of humor had yet to be tempered by a sense of propriety.

Making Mark blush seemed to be her favorite pastime, and the instruction on bathing and dressing offered innumerable opportunities. After another series of lessons in which Elieve managed to set Mark's face aflame with her unselfconsciousness and playful attempts to undress him, Pellin intervened.

"I think you should leave off teaching her how to bathe herself, lad."

"Eldest?"

"Elieve is more than in love with you, Mark. The lessons on dressing and bathing are an opportunity for her to approach you in an intimate way."

"How can that be, Eldest? She still has the mind of a child."

"True," Pellin nodded, "but her body and spirit are that of a young woman. Before Cesla took her and transformed her into an assassin, Elieve might have been anything, lad. She might have been a maid or a servant with a husband, or even a courtesan or night woman."

"You don't trust me with her, Eldest?"

Pellin laughed and shook his head. "Far from it, Mark. Given her playful advances, I've been meaning to ask you how you've managed to resist returning her affection."

Mark didn't mirror his smile. In fact, he grew more somber. "Do you know about justice in the urchins, Eldest?"

When Pellin shook his head, Mark turned, pacing the cabin. Elieve, dressed now after her bath watched him as she always did, her fingers combing through her wet hair. "Rory inherited the urchins after Ilroy died. Usually, when someone new takes over the urchins, they make changes to the rules, about how much we're allowed to steal and who from."

"But one of the permanent codes we follow in the urchins is we never, ever, take advantage of another urchin." He turned to face Pellin. "In any way. Would it surprise you to know that urchins will often marry each other as soon as they've gone through the change?"

He shook his head. "So soon?"

"Life on the streets is short, Eldest. Within the urchins, at fourteen or fifteen—I don't really know which—I'm of marriageable age." He looked at Elieve. "It seems Elieve is a year or two older than I am."

Pellin believed he already knew the answer to his next question, and he had no intention to tempt his apprentice, but certain facets of Mark's character would have to be stronger than steel to survive being in the Vigil. "Why haven't you returned her affection, lad? I'm old, but even at seven hundred years I can appreciate beauty, and Elieve has more than her fair share of it."

Mark shook his head, and something of anger showed in his eyes. "Right now she's still a child, Eldest. Justice in the urchins is very swift. Any boy or girl caught taking advantage of an urchin whose mind is less than whole is killed. We usually throw them from a rooftop or push them under a passing carriage. The city watch doesn't interfere. They're not interested in investigating the death of a throwaway."

A weight settled in Pellin's stomach at the thought of children meting out such punishment. "Harsh."

Mark shook his head. "Necessary. Most of the children in the urchins come to us as castoffs without the power to defend themselves or resist those who prey on them. Central to our code, Eldest, is that we will not do that to each other. However short life in the urchins may be, it is to be safe." He shrugged. "Or as safe as we can make it."

Mark's answer amazed him, and again he marveled at how such harsh conditions could create such a tempered character as Mark possessed. "She's not an urchin," Pellin pressed. "Her mind is that of a child, but her body and spirit obviously regard you as more than her teacher. Do you love her?"

Mark laughed. "How can I not? I've spent every moment since I captured her taking care of her every need, but it's more the love a parent has for their child."

"Do you think you might want her as your wife someday?" Pellin asked. "Marriage in the Vigil is exceedingly rare. We live too long."

Mark shrugged, the gravity of his expression belonging to an older man. "She may not want me as her husband. There are a lot of men in the world, and I am just a thief, after all."

"Hardly that, my boy," Pellin said. "Hardly that."

CHAPTER 17

Toria reined in her horse outside of Hylowold, a city half the size of Bunard that sat on the bend of the Sorrow River, where it looped to the east halfway between Cynestol and the Darkwater Forest. She dismounted and put her hands into the thick ruff of fur surrounding Wag's neck.

Mistress! Do we hunt?

In a way. Keep close while in the city. We don't wish to alert our prey.

His tongue flopped out of the side of his mouth. *I will keep close.* He turned to push his muzzle against Toria's neck, and she pushed back.

When it became obvious that she meant to enter Hylowold with the sentinel in tow, Fess raised the expected objection. "Should we not skirt the city, Lady Deel?"

"Perhaps," she conceded, "but it is well after noon, and Hylowold offers the most immediate access to the west side of the Sorrow River." Memories of her capture at Treflow driving her, she clenched her hands inside her gloves until she heard her knuckles pop.

"Surely there are ferries that can be hired upstream," Fess said.

She pulled a pair of deep breaths and let them out in a protracted exhale until her heart calmed. "It is customary to scout the enemy before a battle, Fess."

"And you believe that our enemy is within the walls of Hylowold?"

"Yes," she said, "and in every other village and town within earshot of rumors about the forest."

"By that you mean everywhere."

"Yes. To fight, Cesla needs men. He has no forces of his own to draw upon, so he lures the unsuspecting to the forest."

He sighed, but she didn't know whether it was in surrender or agreement.

They crossed the main bridge west into the city proper and settled on an inn in the northwest quarter, where the majority of craftsmen and merchants kept their shops. The cost of the stablehand's silence in allowing Wag to stay with their horses lightened her purse of a fair amount of silver. She would have to exchange the gold in it once they gained Treflow.

Together, she and Fess stepped off the broad porch of the inn and into the bustle of the streets. "We have two hours until dark," Fess observed. "Too little to search out the entire city."

"But more than enough to accomplish the pair of tasks I have in mind," she said. "We need to make our way to Criers' Square."

His brows rose. "They have one of those here in Aille?"

She smiled around a soft laugh. "You've adapted so quickly to being a member of the Vigil and a guard," she said with a small catch of grief in her voice, "that I often forget you haven't traveled the continent. There is no Criers' square in Cynestol, or Vadras, for that matter. The Merum still hold nearly absolute sway in the southern part of the continent, but as we move north you will find all four orders represented—nominally, at any rate." She rolled her shoulders. "I wish to see if the Clast still operates after Jorgen's death. If we make haste, we will still make the afternoon reading of the office."

"You will leave any delving of them to me, Toria Deel," Fess said.

A flash of indignation, a spark of displeasure, flared and heated her face, but when she turned to correct his presumption, the planes of his face matched the steel in his voice, and she nodded stiffly. "Agreed."

"And what is our second task?" he asked.

"A trip to the ironmongers," she said. "Those who wish to mine the forest for gold will need tools."

They turned east to catch the main road through the city—a winding affair that paralleled the river—until they came to a juncture of the north-south road and the east-west road leading to the main bridge. A prominent cathedral boasting six sides filled the southwest corner, dwarfing the buildings of the Servants, Absold, and Vanguard that occupied the compass points opposite.

"Modest," Fess observed.

Toria shrugged, and a fresh bead of sweat trickled down her back. "This is Aille. The Merum have been the dominant order in this country since the split with the One Church on the southern continent. Many in the order still see the Merum's split into four parts as a temporary inconvenience."

They threaded their way through the crowd to the sound of bells coming from a tower attached to one of the Merum cathedral's six walls. On cue, four robed clerics ascended their stands, prepared to offer their admonition or interpretation of the liturgy. Toria tapped Fess's shoulder and pointed to a man dressed in the nondescript clothing of a lower craftsman, wearing an apron in which she spied awls and a light hammer, the tools of a cobbler. He stood near a none-too-steady pile of crates and pallets, eyeing the clerics beneath brows heavy with disdain.

"There," she said.

Fess nodded. "I see him. What sort of cobbler wears his apron and tools into the street? I could lift everything except the hammer off of him in one pass."

He melted from her side before she could protest, threading his way through the crowd as the Merum priest mounted the steps to take his place behind his rostrum. "The first commandment is this," he intoned in a clear tenor. "You shall not delve the deep places of the earth, for in the day you do, you shall surely die."

"The fool," Toria whispered. "He couldn't have devised a greater temptation to lure men to the forest if he had tried."

The crowd milled, clearly uncomfortable, many choosing that moment to look anywhere but at the speaker. Undeterred, he raised his voice. "And what does this mean to 'delve the deep places of the earth'? What snare is Aer warning of?"

Across the street, Fess approached the cobbler, pulling the boot from his left foot as he neared. Two men on either side of the cobbler, pretending to be disinterested onlookers moved toward Fess to intercept him, but he stumbled, twisting as he fell, and slipped through their grasp. She moved closer to hear, but she needn't have bothered. Fess pitched his voice to carry.

"Just the man I'm looking for," Fess said as he tottered on one foot. "See this?" He waved the boot under the cobbler's nose, as if the man might somehow fail to notice. Fess's other hand gripped the top of the cobbler's shoulder for balance. "Cursed thing is going to pinch my toes to porridge if I don't get the leather stretched."

"Get off me, you stupid drunk," the cobbler snarled. He moved to push Fess away but failed to get a firm hold on him.

"Nonsense," Fess said. He pivoted as one of the cobbler's men attempted to grab him by the arm, "inadvertently" hitting the man in the chin with his elbow.

"Sorry, my mistake." Fess blinked at the man, then returned his attention to his original target. "Look at your tools, man. You're a cobbler. Surely you can fix my boot."

"Get this fool off me," the cobbler said with a furtive glance toward the Merum cleric. The crowd nearest him had ceased to listen to the office, choosing instead to observe the spectacle of an obviously drunken Fess trying to cajole the cobbler into fixing his boot.

"How can we honor Aer if we do not keep the first commandment?" The priest's voice rose to a shriek in a vain attempt to compete with the crowd's laughter.

The cobbler's other guard came charging in, opting to tackle Fess.

"Heavens!" Fess roared at the man. "I just want my boot fixed!"

He shifted toward the cobbler, and the guard changed direction to follow. Too late, he realized his error. His momentum, too great to be checked, took him crashing into Fess and the cobbler. All three men went down in a pile of flailing limbs, shouted curses, and Fess's cries.

"Where's my boot? My boot!" Fess thrust his left hand toward the heavens in appeal.

The cleric, unable to compete with the spectacle being played out on the street and gutter before him, ceased his imprecations.

The guards began to rain blows on Fess, who curled into a protective ball, his arms covering his face. Twice he managed to catch the guards with an elbow to the chin as he spun away from their fists. The sound of breaking teeth carried to Toria. Fess reached from his protective posture to retrieve his discarded boot and began to rain blows on the guards with the substantial heel.

The guards, wobbly from their exertions and unexpected blows, chose to withdraw, dragging the cobbler with them. Fess waved his boot at their backs. "You lousy excuse for a cobbler! You still haven't fixed my boot!"

He turned away and with studied indifference, pulled his boot back on. He straightened in surprise, wiggling his foot. "Well, there's a surprise, right enough." Turning, he cupped his hands to his mouth. "My thanks, cobbler. Well done."

The crier for the Absold mounted her podium for the afternoon exhortation, but most of the crowd dispersed. Fess made a show of straightening his clothes and then sketched an unsteady path to return to Toria's side. The smell of spirits arrived a moment before he did.

"You smell like a distillery," Toria said when they were out of earshot of others once more. "How did you manage it?"

For an instant, genuine mirth might have danced behind his eyes before his grief quenched it. "It's an idea the Mark and I picked up from the healers in Bunard. You wouldn't see any of them on the streets without a bag of essential medicines and implements. In the same way we carry oddments we can use at need for a bluff." He appeared to consider for a moment before continuing. "Though Mark seldom used his. A con should be planned well enough not to require gimmickry."

She put her gloved hand on his arm. "Regardless of the inspiration, that was masterfully done, Fess."

He continued to scan the street but reached up to grasp her hand in his. Something passed between them, and she took a moment to check the street before ducking into an alley. There in her hand lay a lump of blue-tinged gold.

Toria shook her head. "How? I watched you the whole time."

By way of answer, he jerked and pointed at the entrance to the alley, but when Toria checked, only an empty expanse of street greeted her. "Ah, when you fell and put your other hand in the air."

His voice dropped. "We learned long ago in the urchins that men and women, no matter their station or breeding, are attuned to threats above all else. Everyone in the crowd followed the motion of my free hand, looking for danger. That's all any man is, Lady Deel, a collection of fears and hatreds. Nothing more." He turned to lead her back out onto the main thoroughfare.

She walked beside him in silence. Whatever crisis of faith or belief he suffered, his reticence precluded her response. He turned right at the next intersection. In the distance, she heard the sounds of smithies, the dull impact of the hammer followed by the ping of ringing iron.

The smell of spirits clung to him, but his steps were deliberate. "There's a smith in particular we wish to find, a man named Isenbend," he said leaning close. "The cobbler held a memory of him close to the surface."

She put aside the deeper question of why he had delved the cobbler. "Did you see why?" she asked.

"I touched him by accident," he said, "and relieving him of his gold seemed the greater priority." He stopped in front of a shed open on two sides, where a squad of shirtless young men worked the bellows while an older man, wearing a heavy leather apron spotted with soot and scars in equal measure called for more fire.

"Here," Fess said.

They watched the smith as he peered into an egg-shaped vessel on his hearth, adding alloys with the care and precision of an alchemist. Satisfied, he tipped the vessel on its hinges until molten metal poured out, filling channels of dense green casting sand before filling the smith's mold.

Toria watched, working to exercise patience as the process continued. The ironmonger's art had never interested her, but she knew better than to interrupt the smith at his work. Fess stood rapt at her side, almost entranced.

"What do you see?" she murmured.

"Something new." Both the laughing youth and the stoic guard in his demeanor were absent now, stripped away as Fess watched the smith with singular intensity. "Look there."

Minutes passed and the glow of molten metal died, fading so that Toria could see the shape of the smith's cast. Pickaxes. The smith waited until the red glow of the castings had faded, though shimmers of heat still rose from the sand. With a long-handled pair of tongs he pulled each of the tools free and set them on a heavy table covered with brick.

When the smith showed no signs of doing anything further with the castings, Fess led her to a cooper's stall across the street. The smell of oak filled the air, and barrels in various stages of production filled the aisles. "Isenbend and his work were uppermost in the cobbler's mind. Have you ever seen a smith work that way before?"

"No," she said, "but little of the ironworker's art is known to me."

He almost smiled. "A boy without a home or apprenticeship has a lot of time between thefts. I used to watch the craftsmen work in Bunard." He frowned. "I thought that if I could show them how much I knew they might apprentice me out of the urchins." He pointed. "No smith I've ever seen works that way."

"It's different?" she asked.

"It's not just that it's different, Lady Deel. It's a complete diversion from the traditional way. He's made a casting of the pick heads instead of forging them. Then, when he was done, he didn't quench them, but left them to cool in the air. I've never seen the alloying elements he used—chorum and magnetite—spent on a common pickaxe. It's far cheaper to replace the tool if it breaks."

"Those elements aren't found in the mines of Aille," she said. "Caisel is the source." Perhaps it was nothing more than an unexpected draft of cool air that raised gooseflesh on her neck. "A gifted smith might have the insight to attempt such."

Fess turned to give her an unblinking stare. "Would a gifted smith time his work so that he would have to test it during the night? It will be dark before the pick heads will be cool enough to handle."

The acrid smoke that hung in the air stung her eyes, and the scent of rust and scorched oil abraded her throat. Across the street, Isenbend closed the broad barn doors to his shop, the sound of the bar dropping into place to secure them clear in the late afternoon. "Your experience in the urchins will serve us well, Fess," she said. "Find us a place we can hide and observe our innovative smith."

CHAPTER 18

Toria crouched next to Fess, watching the smith's shop from behind the closed doors of a competitor next door. A generous quantity of silver along with Fess's urgings had been insufficient to persuade the man to lend them the use of his business as a watch point. In the end, she'd resorted to the use of her power to confuse him. She allowed herself a sigh of regret and condemnation. Her touch had been unexpectedly clumsy, and the man's wife, fearing he had suffered a stroke, had taken him to the healer. She had no doubt the healer would wish to observe him for several hours. It would take at least that long for his memories to heal.

An hour after midnight, lantern light floated into Isenbend's shop, but the smith kept the doors closed.

"Stay here, Lady Deel," Fess directed.

Before he could leave, she caught him by the arm, a pointless gesture if he wished to pull away. "What do you mean to do?"

"I heard voices. If I am discovered, it will be a simple matter for me to escape." He pulled the hood of his cloak over his blond hair and ghosted off into the darkness, slipping through the door without a sound.

She waited, catching hints of movement and conversation from Isenbend's smithy but unable to take the pieces of sight and sound and assemble them into clarity and meaning. She stood in the dark, gnawing her worries, as a voice—Isenbend's or another's—rose in pitch, the staccato cadence of command obvious in the clipped delivery. Then a low hum drifted from his shop followed by the shriek of metal.

The strike of flint gave her the only warning that the owner of the shop had returned. Ducking, she hid behind the bellows, but she bumped the heavy leather, and soot drifted in the air.

"You see, love," a woman said. "There's no one here. Now come in. The healer says you need to rest."

Toria squeezed her eyes shut and tried to swallow the soot that clogged her throat, but the black dust refused to budge. She needed to cough or sneeze. The lamp light came no closer, but neither did it recede. Tears tracked their way down her cheeks and spots swam in her eyes with the need to breathe.

"Come in, Corwian. The shop's closed, see?"

Toria ducked her head and retched, burying her face in her cloak, working to muffle the sound. Bile and vomit cleared the soot, but rough hands grabbed her and hauled her to her feet.

"What have we here? What might you be doing, sneaking around my shop?" A charcoal-stained face leered at her, the prominent nose running askew from the rest of the features. "You see, Willa? I told you there was someone in my shop."

Toria listened, praying to hear the sound of grinding from the smithy. "Please," she said. "I just needed a place to spend the night. I didn't mean any harm." Her eyes wide with fear, she looked to the smith's wife in pleading and breathed a sigh of relief when the woman drew almost near enough to touch.

Corwian's brows drew together over the wreck of his nose. His hands dug into her arms, pinning them to her side "I've seen you before, haven't I?" A portion of the fog clouding his gaze lifted. "You were here offering me—"

Toria twisted in his grasp, working to bring her fingers to up to his wrists. There. She dropped into his mind and struck. An instant later she stood, Corwian dropping toward her. "Help me." She worked to catch his weight, but the man weighed more than twice what she did. His bulk bore her down to the earthen floor of the shop.

She scrambled from beneath him to see Willa edging toward her with the lamp held forward, a poker in the other hand. "What did you do to him?"

Toria backed away, but the smith's wife followed. "Your husband is fine."

Willa charged, the poker swinging in a wide arc toward her head.

Toria darted back out of range of the blow. Snarling her rage, the smith's wife followed, reaching farther with each swing.

Toria waited, her hands shaking for the next strike. The poker came for her, whistling as Willa strived to reach her. She ducked, her hair ruffling with the displaced air and leapt, her hands extended.

Caught unaware, Willa stood flat-footed as Toria crashed into her, her hands closing on her head. In that instant she struck, disrupting the flow of memories that lay before her, but when she released the delve, pain lanced through her temple. Righting the fallen lamp, she reached up to finger the knot on her head. No blood stained her fingers, but the room swam as if it had been *her* memories that had been muddled.

Setting the fallen lamp on the table, she put it out and made for the door to the street.

The sound of grinding, punctuated by brief silences, still came from Isenbend's shop. Of Fess, there was no sign. She circled around to come from the other side, where she might be able to see through the slits in the broad doors.

A hand grabbed her and she spun, her fingers groping.

"Quiet," Fess said. "He's nearly done grinding."

"The smith came back and surprised me," she said in the barest whisper.

He led her around to the north side of the shed, where a hole almost the size of her fist offered an unobstructed view of Isenbend and the fake cobbler, who watched his art. Several wraps of cloth covered his eyes. The grinding sounds had ceased, replaced by the sibilant buzz of steel against the polishing belt.

"He'll see us," Toria whispered.

Fess shook his head. "Don't put your face against the hole. Leave space so that the light from his shop doesn't fall across your skin. Even so, it's unlikely he'll look this way."

Curiosity tugged at her. "Why?"

Amusement colored his response. "It's something we learned in the urchins. Isenbend is right-handed and we're standing on his left. Like most people, he searches for threats toward his dominant hand."

Isenbend polished the blade and the point for a bit longer before setting the handle through the eye of the tool head. Without flourish or conversation, he handed it to the cobbler.

"Have you succeeded?" the cobbler asked as he hefted the tool. "My master is impatient."

The smith flexed hands as big as hams. "If your master had any sense, he could have used the money I spent on alloying agents to buy a dozen picks."

The cobbler's expression closed. "It's as I told you, a normal tool won't do. The rock is too hard." He moved to the one side, the pick-axe gripped for an overhead blow. Instead of stopping him, Isenbend stepped back, wary. With a grunt of effort, the cobbler swung, bringing the sharpened pick of the tool down in a furious blow against the anvil. The ring that echoed through the smith's shop brought a smile to the cobbler as he inspected the tool. "That's one," he said, rubbing his hand along a deep gouge in the anvil. "And it's still sharp."

He swung for a second time, and the ringing sound filled the shop once more. But this time it carried a note of complaint, an unintended dissonance that erased the cobbler's smile. Yet the tool showed no flaws Toria could see. "That's two. Once more."

The cobbler adjusted the veil covering his eyes, set his feet, and swung. Instead of the ringing sound heard before, the retort of breaking metal shattered the air. Four inches broke from the end of the pick and went flying. The cobbler filled the air with curses as he spun and threw the broken pickaxe against the far wall, where it hit a rack of tools and sent them cascading to the floor.

Isenbend stood his ground. "You owe me payment."

"I owe you nothing," the cobbler spat. "It broke! After three swings against mere iron, it broke."

"I care nothing for that," Isenbend said. "Your master provided the instructions for which alloying agents to use. I told you they had to come from Vadras. If the tool broke, it is your fault, not mine."

The cobbler spewed invective, his expression beneath his veil wild. "You failed, Isenbend. Don't try to blame your lack of skill on the powders."

The smith threw a string of curses at the cobbler. "I told you. The alloying agents had to be pure, absolutely pure."

"The powders were as pure as the alchemist could make them," the cobbler said.

The smith clenched his fists. "You're a fool if you think one alchemist is the same as another. I said they had to come from Vadras, from the shop of Helioma." He took a step forward. "I want my payment now, or I will cease to provide you any tools at all."

"My master pays for results," the cobbler said. "Succeed and you will be paid more handsomely than you can imagine." He shrugged. "However, so that you will know my master is merciful, I will replenish the funds you need to make another attempt." He reached into his tunic, searching, his mouth gaping as he grooped his clothes.

The smith's hands shot out to grab the cobbler by his throat. His shoulders bunching, he lifted the smaller man into the air. "Swindler! I cannot succeed without money to buy supplies."

Toria turned, reaching, but Fess had melted into the darkness.

Grimacing, the cobbler's fists blurred as he hammered them into the smith's forearms. Twin cracks, the breaking of bone, mixed with the smith's cry of pain as he dropped to his knees. The cobbler smiled. "It seems you will be unable to make another attempt after all."

Fess entered the smith's shop, closing the door behind him. "Ah, master cobbler. About that boot." Smiling, he held the blue-tinged lump of gold aloft.

The cobbler gathered his legs beneath him and leapt toward her apprentice, his fingers curled into claws. Fess appeared to shift to one side without transition, his hands moving more quickly than she could follow to rip the protective cloth from the cobbler's eyes. Tools scattered and fell as the cobbler crashed into a broad worktable. He lay stunned, his arm thrown protectively across his face.

Toria darted to the broad door of the smithy, but by the time she entered Fess had lifted the cobbler from the floor and forced his arms away from his eyes. The cobbler's struggles weakened, but he filled the air with threats of violence. With no more emotion than he might spare an insect, Fess put his bare hand on the cobbler's neck.

Toria stepped over to where the smith lay on his side, his arms curled protectively across his chest. "How many more like the cobbler are there?" she asked. Then she touched him and dove into his stream of memories, swimming through those closest to the surface, but there were no images other than those of the man with them.

She destroyed all the threads of recollection connected to the cobbler and the new process for casting Isenbend had learned from him. When she released the delve, the smith had passed out, and Fess stood by her side, his eyes devoid of anger, pity, or even triumph. The cobbler lay forgotten on the floor, his unfocused gaze staring at her, a mute accusation. Only the shallow rise and fall of his chest showed that he lived.

When Fess stepped around her toward the door, she clutched at his tunic. "The mercy stroke."

He turned to regard her, his eyes coolly thoughtful, before he demurred. "He's beyond any succor or mercy we can render, Toria Deel. He passed beyond such aid when I destroyed his vault. If we kill him, the masses may lift him up as a martyr, but if they see him with his mind broken, they will be fearful of sharing his fate.

He stepped past her. "The people of Bunard had a saying about those of us in the urchins, Lady Deel. 'Nothing in life is ever wasted. It can always be used as a bad example.' I'd say the cobbler qualifies on that account." At the door, he paused. "There are others besides the cobbler," he said.

"There would almost have to be," she replied. "When we get back to the inn, I'll apprise the Chief of Servants of what we found here. She can inform regent Cailin and the rest of the monarchs to keep an eye on the smiths."

Fess glanced at the broken pickaxe where it lay on Isenband's table. "Let's hope they all met with similar success."

CHAPTER 19

I spent a succession of days in Cynestol in a procession of delves interspersed with the savage niceties practiced by court. The overpowering luster of their throne room had ceased to impress. The nobles of Cynestol were no more substantial than their images the polished silver threw at me, and I had enough of their memories to prove it. My time in the collective psyche of Cynestol's nobility had taught me to hate the city.

Then the entertainers changed. Cynestol, like every other court on the continent boasted any number of permanent musicians, acrobats, and the like, but there were more than a few itinerant court entertainers present as well. The niches in the wall were filled with men and women possessing a physical gift and the preponderance of some talent that enabled them to make a better-than-decent living putting on a show for others.

I recognized one of them. Heedless of Rory trailing me or Bolt's stare, I sought the juggler who kept a weave of daggers in perpetual motion while he stood on top of a ball. Every now and then he would pretend to slip, but the knives betrayed his intent. Each throw and spin remained perfect. He saw me, and recognition dawned in eyes so dark they were almost black. The knives disappeared one by one until the air had emptied and he dismounted.

"My apologies, master juggler." I bowed. "I did not mean to interrupt your performance."

He bowed in return. I was, after all, a visiting lord, a guest of the kingdom, and the advisor to the last Errant. None of that accounted for the depth of his bow or the smile that accompanied it. "It is good to see you again, master reeve, or should I say, Lord Dura. The last I'd heard, you'd killed a count in Laidir's throne room. I have to confess that I'm surprised to see you alive."

My smile mirrored his. "Thanks in part to you, master juggler." I looked around. Not one of the nobles paid us any mind. "I would have thought the gold I put in your hands would have freed you from entertaining those who take your abilities for granted."

He shrugged. "I enjoy the work, and they pay me well enough, even if the coin is more to prove they can command my skills at their convenience rather than any real appreciation of my art." He sighed. "As for the gold, well, money has wings, as they say, especially if a man has a gift for picking the wrong wagers."

"Too true." I nodded. "You have sharp eyes and ears, master juggler. I'd be willing to pay for useful information."

The smile fled from his face. "Cynestol is my home, Lord Dura. I find I no longer have the desire to travel the other kingdoms. If the politics of Bunard are murky, here in Cynestol they're downright opaque." He turned his back to me and remounted the large wooden ball. A moment later his knives filled the air and he'd adopted the fixed stare of a juggler working his craft.

I made my way to Bolt's side, reflecting on the twists and turns that had brought me to Cynestol. A woman in a filmy blue dress that managed to float like a feather on the wind even as it clung to the curves of her body approached the throne, her movements as fluid as water. Nothing in her open, even friendly, expression hinted at the thoughts that lurked behind her deep brown eyes. Nothing in the expressions of the other nobles I'd delved had either.

"I hate this place," I murmured.

From his seat to one side of the queen's empty throne, Bolt nodded. "Of course you do. You spend all your time seeing the worst parts of it."

The noblewoman was still ten paces away. "You mean the inside of everyone's head?" I asked.

He nodded. "From what Pellin told me, it's the same everywhere. Courts are defined by hierarchy and utterly ruthless competition. That tends to bring out the worst in people."

I sighed. "And I get to wallow in their ambition."

Bolt grunted. "I noticed you've been taking a lot more baths." He stood as the woman in blue stopped and curtsied.

I took a deep breath and pulled the gloves from my hands. "I can't seem to get clean," I whispered, but if Bolt heard me, he gave no sign.

The conversation between Bolt and the woman proceeded along the same line as all the others had. After a few moments, Bolt turned to me. "Duchess Leogan, may I present my advisor, Lord Dura of Bunard."

She curtsied and I bowed and we stepped toward each other to engage in the customary greeting. She extended her right palm as I held out my left so that our fingers matched, and I fell into her thoughts.

Delving nobles day after day had honed my ability to don the identity of the one I delved while simultaneously holding on to my own. As quickly as I could, I checked for any knowledge or demonstration that Duchess Leogan held the gift of kings. After sifting through a few dozen of the most recent recollections and tracing them to their origin, I prepared to surrender the link, but a particularly bright thread caught my attention. There in the river of Leogan's memories was a gold-colored thread that shone like the sun. Curious, I reached for it.

A moment later, I stepped back from the duchess, bowing to a depth that surprised her. "Duchess Leogan, you honor us," I said.

Her brows, beautiful but not as exquisite as Gael's, drew together for a moment, curious. "The pleasure is mine, Lord Dura." She turned to Bolt. "I hope you will remember me, Errant Consto, in your deliberations."

Bolt dipped his head. "Alas, Duchess, the only criterion for the throne I may consider is the gift of kings."

She nodded and with a swirl of cloth and hair returned to the riot of color and sound that defined court.

I leaned over. "I have what we need."

Hours later, well before midnight, we approached the guards standing watch at the entrance to the queen's expansive apartments. The captain came forward, his mouth ready with denials. "Errant Consto, you may not enter without Bishop Gehata's permission."

Bolt gestured me forward. "I believe Lord Dura has acquired the documents necessary for entrance, Captain."

I put the parchment into his hand and held my breath, watching as the captain's eyes widened and then narrowed as he read. With quick, sharp gestures, he refolded the parchment, checking the soldiers behind him.

"You may pass," he said, but fury burned behind his eyes. With a nod, the guards opened the doors to the queen's apartments. The vaulted space beyond was pitch-black. Not one lamp or candle burned to relieve the darkness.

"Where's Prince Maenelic?" I asked.

The captain eyed me as if unsure whether he should or had to answer me. He opted for silence until Bolt repeated the question.

"Bishop Gehata thought it best to remove the prince from the environs of his mother's untimely death. He felt such proximity was weighing unduly upon the prince's mind. The prince has been sent north to help command our forces in the battle against the Darkwater."

Of a wonder, no one in our group made the obvious remark. Bolt retreated a few steps to pull a pair of lamps from the wall and we entered, the sound of the doors closing behind us hollow, like a cell door closing.

Gael tugged at my sleeve. "The captain had the look of a man who wanted to kill you."

"Nothing unusual about that, yah?" Rory said.

"He had reason," I said. "That letter wasn't permission from Bishop Gehata, it was a threat to expose his affair with Duchess Leogan."

Rory shook his head. "Marriage here is a sport. Why would anyone care?"

"The nobles here don't like it when people secretly change teams," Gael said.

I pointed into the darkness. "We'll need more light—as much as possible." I moved around the entrance hall, lighting each of the lamps that hung from silver sconces until argent illumination filled the space. And what a space it was. We stood in a greeting room big enough to serve as a throne room in a lesser kingdom. Toward the east a wide set of stairs swept upward, spiraling toward the next level.

"The royal quarters are upstairs, but this is where Queen Chora died," Bolt said, pointing to the staircase. The stairs, naked of any adornment except the natural veins of the stone and a mirror polish ascended away from me. They were steeper than I expected.

"How many steps are there?"

"Thirty-six," Bolt said.

I wasn't from Moorclaire, where they lived the mathematicum, but I'd had enough education to recognize the numbers from the Exordium, either the four by nine sides of the rectangle or the six square. I stopped to wonder what mysteries the Exordium held and whether Ealdor and his Fayit brethren had anything to do with it.

I walked toward the steps with my eyes on the floor. A lighter spot at the foot of the staircase indicated an area that had been cleaned, a whiter shade than the surrounding stone. I pulled my gloves and lifted a prayer to Aer that months with the gift could give me a portion of what had taken long years for Bronwyn to learn. I bent to the spot and closed my eyes, hardly daring to breathe for fear of missing what I might see.

Ghosts of images flickered across my awareness, and I reached for them, trying to pull them to me. One of those images, the owner of the blood on the floor, would have to be stronger than the others, but it defied me. Unbidden, Bronwyn's admonition came to me. *Relax. You can't force it.*

I exhaled and let my breathing slow. There, hovering at the edge of perception I caught the hint of a woman, gifted. "She died here."

With a glance to Bolt, I grabbed one of the lamps and moved up the stairs, searching for spots where the stone had been cleansed of Chora's blood. I found another, smaller, spot about a third of the way up, but I searched for something more telling. At the top near the heavy marble rail, I found a bleached circle a pair of hands wide. I stooped, and laid my hands on the mark, pressing my skin against cool marble.

I rose after a moment and surveyed the floor in both directions, walking and counting my paces until I hit thirty, but I found no more. Retreating back to the top of the stairs, I called to Bolt. "I found Queen Chora's blood in three places. At the bottom, a third of the way up"—I caught Bolt's gaze—"and here at the top."

He blinked. "You're sure—absolutely sure?"

"It's hers."

His chest rose and fell. "And it's recent?"

I nodded. "They all are."

Bolt knelt and ran his sword hand along the bleached spot on the stone. "It's smaller than I expected."

Gareth, my partner reeve in Bunard, knew more about how a man

144

could bleed out than anyone living, and he'd managed to teach me a few things in our time together. "There are too many things we still don't know."

He looked at me, his face as cold as the mountains in winter. "But there are some we do."

Gael and Rory ascended the stairs, their expressions questioning. "What did you find?" Gael asked.

I scuffed the bleached spot on the floor with my foot. "A mystery."

She looked from me to Bolt and back again. "She didn't die from the fall?"

"It's possible," I said, "but I think she had help. I found evidence of a pool of her blood here . . . at the top of the stairs."

"So the dwimor got to her after all," Rory said.

I pulled a breath. "I'm not sure."

Bolt looked as if he could chew rocks and ask for seconds. "The Archbishop lied to us. That's the sort of thing that puts me in a bad mood."

"He might not have lied," I said. "The knife stroke at the top of the stairs might not have killed her."

"I don't bother trying to distinguish between lying and deceiving by omission," Bolt said. "Vyne left out a few details." He looked at me. "I think we've been played, Willet. You were able to pull the memory of Chora's presence from a trio of bleached smudges on the floor. You shouldn't have been able to do that."

With their experience, Pellin and Toria would have little difficulty doing what I had done. "Would Vyne have known that?"

"Probably," Bolt said. "He may have waited for Pellin and Toria Deel to slip away."

I sighed. "I don't think there's anything more we can do here. Where's the body? I need to see it."

Gael reached out to touch my arm. "Why? We know she was killed by a dwimor."

"Too many things are out of place," I said. "We need to be sure." A familiar tickle in my mind put me on my guard. Something important nagged at me.

Bolt shook his head at me. "She's lying in state in the cathedral, Willet. Archbishop Vyne has already denied us permission to view the body."

I nodded. "I wasn't actually thinking of asking again. Do they leave the body in the sanctuary around the clock?"

He'd already opened his mouth in denial, but my last question stopped him. "No. It's removed each night so the gravesmen can tend to her."

Rory frowned. "And do what?"

Gael put a hand on his shoulder in a protective gesture. "The queen will lie in state for two weeks. At the end of each day the gravesmen tend to her to make sure she's suitable for viewing, especially toward the end."

"Silly custom," Rory said. "I don't want a bunch of people gawking at me after I die. Just put me in a coracle and send me downstream. With any luck I'll pass over the western sea and my spirit will see what's out there."

I stifled a sigh. Those who chose the coracle instead of burial or cremation clung to the old beliefs, a faith that hardly recognized Aer, Iosa, and Gaoithe at all. I knew the reasons behind Rory's disbelief, but it still grieved me.

"Can we get in to see her?"

Bolt gave me a slow nod. "Possibly, but there's no way to hide the visit from Vyne."

I flexed a hand. "Yes there is, if we can keep from being seen by too many people."

Bolt looked like he wanted to argue, but something he saw in my expression must have made him reconsider. "At least we have most of the night to get this done. We'll need it. The cathedral is on the other side of Cynestol."

We worked our way down and out of the royal compound and finally came to the stables. I didn't know if the hands recognized Bolt, but they gave us four horses without question and we set a canter east toward the cathedral.

The six-sided church, the mother of the faith here on the northern continent, loomed over us in the dark like an omen of judgment for our sacrilege. The fact that I rode in the company of three gifted somehow failed to encourage me. If we were discovered, Archbishop Vyne would summon Hradian and the rest of the cosp and overwhelm us by numbers.

Four hours before dawn we dismounted in the stable yard of an inn two streets away from the basilica and surrendered the reins of our horses to a sleepy attendant who made a halfhearted attempt to peer beneath the hoods of our cloaks. When Bolt added another half-crown to the fee, the attendant bowed and kept his gaze on his feet.

"I take it we're not going through the front door," Gael said.

I shook my head. "There will be priests awake, even at this forsaken hour, brothers and postulants in the process of taking their orders. It's traditional for them to fast and go without sleep before they recite their final vows."

In the dark, the six sides of the cathedral blended, their demarcation points nearly indistinct so that the huge construct appeared almost circular. "Which entrance is least likely to have traffic at this hour?" I asked Bolt.

"The entrances facing northeast and northwest are the least used, even during the daytime."

It took us thirty minutes to circle around as we avoided the occasional member of the watch. I tried to ignore the disapproving way the church loomed over me, as if I'd brought evil intentions here from the cold, dark north of my home. "Get us in," I told Rory. "We'll wait for you here."

He slipped out of his cloak. His shirt and breeches were dark, blending with the shadows. "Are the doors barred from the inside?" he asked Bolt.

At Bolt's nod, he stepped back, eyeing the distance to the first parapet. "That's too bad. I'd rather pick a lock than climb. Still, it's a church. There's lots of ornamentation."

He moved to the left, toward the spot where two of the walls came together at one of those odd, obtuse angles and set his hands on the staggered outcroppings of stone. Within a minute he was twenty feet above us. Ten minutes later the door opened.

Chapter 20

Rory stood outlined in the gloom of the cathedral entrance, the light of the moon casting his eyes into shadow. How could a place of worship seem so forbidding? "Where is the queen kept?" I whispered.

Bolt shook his head. "It's not like the rulers of Aille drop dead on a regular basis. Let's start with the rooms closest to the sanctuary."

With Rory in the lead, we ascended a set of stairs that spiraled up into darkness. Halfway up, he froze. I stood on the balls of my feet, waiting while my heart thundered in my chest, my ears straining to hear whatever had brought Rory to a stop. A moment later, we continued on, moving in darkness without the benefit of a torch to guide us. By the time we reached the top of the stairs, we were far enough above the base of the cathedral that a fall would have killed a man.

Rory stared out into the broad hallway without moving. Slowly, to avoid even the sound of cloth against cloth, I removed my gloves, closed my eyes, and put my hand on his neck.

His vision replaced the darkness behind my lids, and the world came to me in muted shades of charcoal. A distant light illuminated two figures from behind, passing the intersection of our hallway and another, larger, one. Rory's sense of smell couldn't begin to compare with Wag's, but with his physical gift I caught the barest hint of the gravesman's art. The smell drifted to me from beyond the intersection.

The men passed. "She's on this floor," I whispered.

Rory didn't move after the men passed, standing instead at attention, a throwing knife in each hand. Then I saw the outline of another pair of figures, passing in the same direction. Familiarity tugged at me as I watched them until they left my field of vision.

I lifted my hand, and the world sprang back to normal with an abruptness that made my eyes hurt. I stepped back into the shelter of the stairwell, motioning for my companions to join me.

"There are regular patrols," I said. "About half a minute apart."

"That's going to make it difficult," Gael said.

"There's more."

"Of course there is," Bolt whispered in disgust. "What?"

"They're cosp. I recognized a couple of the men who came for us at Edring. What would be so important about keeping anyone from examining the queen's body that Vyne would ring it with physically gifted in the dead of night?"

I heard Bolt's sigh. "Why does everything have to be difficult?" he asked.

Gael gave an amused little laugh. "We're sneaking around the cathedral at night so that we can examine the queen's body. What did you expect?"

"This, pretty much," he said, "but once, just once, I'd like for something to go unexpectedly easy."

"We have to get past the intersection," I said. "The queen is somewhere on the far side. The problem is, the guards are patrolling a circuit, and if they're all in sight of each other, it'll be impossible to get through without being seen."

Bolt and Rory exchanged a quick glance before Rory shed his shoes, pulled the hood of his cloak to his face, and before going ten steps disappeared into the shadows of the hallway.

"What do we do if the patrols are too tightly bunched to get through?" I asked.

Bolt shook his head. "Haven't we had this conversation before? Why do you insist on borrowing trouble?"

Instead of responding, I put my hand on Gael's neck to watch Rory sneak down the hallway. Even knowing he was there, I had trouble spotting him. He kept to the wall, flitting from doorway to doorway, disappearing into spaces that shouldn't have been large enough to conceal him.

Two men walked past, and Rory darted on silent feet to the intersection, his head cocked for a split second before peeking around the corner. I knew he must be counting, but I couldn't help but mark the time with the beats of my heart.

I hadn't gotten to three before he jerked backward without a sound and merged with the shadow of the nearest doorway once more. He waited, and then repeated the process until the same pair of guards made the circuit. When he rejoined us, I had to fight the temptation to borrow some of Jeb's vocabulary.

"It's going to be tight," Rory said. He didn't have to look at me for everyone to know what he meant. I was the only one of our group who wasn't physically gifted. Everyone else would have no trouble darting across the hallway in silence before they could be seen. But me? If the spaces between the guards should close, or I make just a hint too much noise, they would be on us.

Bolt shook his head. "The risk is too great, Willet. We need to withdraw. My first duty is to safeguard you. Do I need to remind you that you're one of four people on the entire continent who can fight the Darkwater?"

"We can't," I said. "If it wasn't plain before, it is now. We *have* to see the queen."

"They're going to hear you, Willet," Gael said. "You can't move quietly or quickly enough."

I pulled a deep breath into my shaking lungs. "Maybe I can. How wide is the hallway, Rory?"

"Maybe fifty feet."

Twenty paces. I had perhaps three seconds to get across twenty paces without making a sound.

That physically gifted guards wouldn't hear.

Sure.

I opened my mouth to admit defeat—to tell Bolt we were headed back to the palace—when Rory tugged on my sleeve. "I can show you how to be quick and silent, like a thief."

"You can do that?"

I could barely see his smile in the gloom as he tapped his head. "I've been training thieves for years."

Bolt and Gael were still shaking their heads. I knew why. Even with Rory's knowledge, I would still have to be quick, very quick, across the gap.

"Alright." I nodded and put my hand on his arm and let the memories he offered flood through me. Instead of storing them, I let them combine with my own so that his instructions to a horde of boys and girls less than half my age filled my mind. When I lifted my hand, I knew how to be silent, but I still didn't know how to be fast enough.

Bolt looked at me, shaking his head. "You mean to do this, don't you."

I nodded. "There's something here that's more than just a little wrong."

"Yeah, I figured. In that case, you'll go first. If they don't catch you, they won't catch the rest of us."

"And if they do?" Gael asked.

He sighed. "Then we'll have to put as many of them down as it takes for us to get loose from the cathedral." He gave me a steady look. "You know we'll have to leave the city then, don't you? There's no way Vyne will ever believe this wasn't our doing."

I took a deep breath, concentrating on stilling my heart. "It's a single toss of the bones."

Rory laughed quietly in the dark. "I thought you said being part of the Vigil was mostly boredom."

Bolt's growl might have come from Wag. "It's supposed to be."

Copying Rory and the rest, I took off my boots and stockings, the smooth polished stones of the cathedral tacky beneath the soles of my feet. Then I reached up to undo the clasp of my cloak and handed it to Gael, who brushed my cheek with her lips. "Be quick. Be safe."

I glued myself to the wall and crept toward the intersection and the soft wash of light, rolling my gait from the outside of my foot to the inside. I breathed slowly and deeply through my nose and focused on keeping my pulse as steady as possible. Each time I came to a doorway, I pressed myself into the shadows and listened.

I went slower than Rory had. Delving him might have given me the advice and lessons he'd given to the urchins, but it couldn't give me his muscle memory. The movements of a thief were unfamiliar to me. Even so, I arrived at the intersection of the two hallways far sooner than I wanted.

A pair of cosp walked by me, not close enough to touch, but a normal breath would have alerted them. As soon as they were beyond the point of being able to see me with their peripheral vision, I dared to poke my head out far enough to look back up the hallway they'd just come from.

I started counting, and at three I saw a man's foot come into view. I ducked back into shadow and stood there, my mouth going dry as I waited for them to pass, but when the time came for me to run, I froze.

The next pair of guards went by. And the next. My heart raced, and the only thing I could hear was the rush of blood through my veins. I chided myself for a fool. If I could willingly lead men into the Darkwater, I could run twenty paces in the dark.

I tried not to listen to the voice in my head that recited a litany of all the stupid decisions I'd ever made, along with the consequences and scars I still bore. I tried, but I failed. That voice in my head—my fearful self—continued, but it went too far. The list lost its immediacy, its ability to incapacitate. Yes, I'd made some incredibly stupid decisions, but I didn't bother trying to argue this wasn't one of them. I chose a different approach.

What was one more?

A pair of guards went by, and I crouched. The moment they could no longer see me at the edge of their sight, I darted from my hiding place and ran on the balls of my feet across the light of the hallway to the shadows beyond. I never made a sound, and it was all I could do to keep from laughing the whole way.

The retreating guards stopped, one turning toward his right, to the place I'd been. He shrugged and they continued on their route.

A few minutes later Rory relieved my solitude, his grin matching mine. Then Gael and Bolt joined us, and we followed the scent of embalming fluid.

We stopped before a heavy door of polished wood, and Bolt whispered in the darkness. "We're directly behind the sanctuary. Priests will be holding their vigil and some of them might be in this room."

I looked at the bottom of the door, saw a soft glow of steady light from beneath.

"We should have brought Fess," Rory whispered. "He makes a great priest."

I nodded. And with his gift he could incapacitate anyone in the room before they had a chance to cry out.

"Well," Bolt said, "there's nothing for it but to attempt this insanity." He opened the door and slipped through the barest crack, his dagger clutched so that he could strike with the pommel.

I waited for a pair of heartbeats for the expected commotion, but nothing came.

Then the door opened wider and Bolt beckoned us inside. After he closed it behind us, he pointed to a gilded coffin illuminated by a single large candle on a table behind it. "Whatever you mean to do, Willet, do it quickly. We've burned most of the night getting here, and there are going to be priests crawling all over the cathedral soon. "Rory, guard the door."

I grabbed the candle, used it to light another one, and then handed both of them to Gael. "Hold them high so that I can see her."

When I flipped open the casket, though death had begun its work, I saw a woman in her fifties whose face still held most of the beauty men would have ascribed to her youth. As quickly as I could, trying without success to stifle the feelings of sacrilege my actions roused in me, I removed Queen Chora's burial dress.

"This alone could get you executed, Vigil or no," Gael said.

I nodded, silently apologizing to the body within the coffin. "I know. All the more reason to hurry." I felt along Chora's neck, from the top of her back going upward. At the top, I no longer felt the expected jut of each vertebra. Instead, I heard and felt the grinding of splinters of bone. "Vyne told the truth about her broken neck at any rate."

There were bruises on her face, and it appeared that the fall had broken her nose, but I couldn't find any evidence of a wound that would have left the telltale pools of blood. I looked at Bolt. "I can't find the wound."

"Was Vyne telling the truth?"

I shook my head. "Why was her blood at the top of the stairs? Dwimor or not, I know it was hers. Help me turn her over."

We put our hands beneath the queen's body and rolled until she lay facedown in her own coffin. I tried to still the voice in my head that cited the old superstition—the one about burying people upside down to keep their souls trapped on earth. I looked down at the back of Queen Chora's body, the back and legs still strong and muscled, the body of a dancer.

"*Kreppa*," I breathed.

CHAPTER 21

"We've got to get out of here now!" Bolt said. Without pausing for decorum or respect, he flipped the queen's body back over. As quickly as we could, we dressed Chora and closed the coffin.

Rory turned away from his position by the door. "Why?"

I blew out the extra candle we'd lit, praying that no one would notice the difference when they came to retrieve the queen's body. "Because she wasn't killed by a dwimor, and she didn't accidentally fall down the stairs."

"How—"

"Later," Bolt growled.

We closed the door behind us and retraced our footsteps to the circuit where the cosp guards continued their patrol. "I have to go last," I said.

Gael shook her head in the darkness, but Bolt nodded. "I'll go first, then Gael, then Rory."

"Why?" Gael's angry whisper sounded like a sword stroke through the air.

"Because he's the last Errant," I said. "This is his responsibility. Whatever happens, he has to get free so that he can demand an examination of the queen's body."

"Why can't I go after you?" she persisted. I could have kissed her.

"Because as soon as you get free, you're going to keep going without waiting for me," I said. "If they raise the alarm, they're going to bottle up the entire cathedral. If any of you are seen with me, you're as good as dead."

She tried to argue, but in the end necessity won out and I was right back where I'd been an hour earlier, staring across a hallway, trying to convince my feet that what I was telling them to do wasn't an act of insanity.

I watched a pair of guards pass in front of me, waited until they were just past the point where they would see me out of their peripheral vision. And ran.

For a moment, I thought that Rory's memories and instruction had managed to see me safely back across the gap, despite my ineptitude. Then the guards stopped and turned at the whisper the soles of my feet made on the stone floor. Without a sound, their steps more silent than mine, they came in pursuit, closing the gap between us with the speed only the physically gifted could muster.

I stopped. Somewhere in the darkness ahead of me, my friends should have been making their way down the stairs to freedom. Despite Bolt's assertion that they would, I had no doubt they were watching me from the shadows. My guard and my betrothed would no doubt be arguing about whether to kill the guards. Knocking them unconscious would only delay our imprisonment or death. As soon as they identified us and took the information to Archbishop Vyne, we would have no choice but to flee the city.

My heart threatened to break free from its prison behind my ribs as I peeled my gloves off and turned to face my captors. They hadn't raised an alarm. I had a chance, an achingly slim chance, to get free. The guards came forward with their swords drawn, and I thrust my hands behind my back as though hiding some stolen trinket, keeping my head down.

"Show us your hands," one of the guards said.

Closer. I needed them to come closer. I put my hands out in front of me, my fists still clenched. *Please,* I begged Aer, *let them be curious.*

One of the guards reached toward my fists with his free hand, turning it palm up. I let the fingers of my right hand uncurl and touched the guard's wrist with the tips.

The hall of the cathedral fled from me as I dropped into his thoughts and saw the familiar river. I grabbed the thoughts that flowed past me, his memories of the current moment, and slashed at them as if I were breaking a vault. A gap in the river appeared. Before it could close, I came out of the delve and struck him with my fist.

The other guard grappled with my left hand as the first guard fell, and I prayed that the desire to capture me alive would outweigh his sense of danger.

It didn't happen.

His sword streaked toward me as I reached to make contact with his skin. It was only a foot from me when I dropped into the delve and struck. Outside his mind, I felt an impact against my side, the pain a flare of red in my mind. I hurled the sensation into the guard, and shock flooded through the bond I shared with him. I opened my eyes to see his eyes clenched against the pain of a wound he didn't have.

I landed a blow to his temple that sent him to the floor next to the first guard and ran toward the stairs. The clatter of swords couldn't have been missed, but I hoped the bodies of the two guards would cause enough of a delay to allow my escape.

I took the stairs two at a time with my arm clamped against my side. The pain made me want to vomit, and my tunic felt wet against my skin. Halfway down the stairs my vision narrowed to a pinpoint as boots and voices sounded above me.

I focused on putting one step in front of the other and staying quiet. If I got very lucky, the cosp upstairs would delay their search until the other guards regained consciousness. The stairs at my feet wavered, as if I saw them through a sheet of running water.

The world went black.

Pain jolted me awake. I found myself on horseback with the thunder of hooves around me. I struggled, and hands, a woman's, kept me from pitching off the horse.

"You're safe, Willet," Gael said.

"I'm bleeding."

"I know," her voice caught. "We're taking you to a healer."

"Not the palace," I croaked. "They'll know they marked someone." I felt air across my naked feet and panic gripped me. "My boots!"

"We have them," Gael said. "Stay quiet."

I didn't have any trouble with that last part. I passed out again.

When I woke once more, I found myself in a unfamiliar room, lamps lit against the darkness that still showed outside. Gael's right hand was behind my head, and with the other she pressed a glass against my lips. "Drink this. The healer says it will help with the blood loss."

When the cup was empty, she refilled it and I drank again. The room still swam in my vision, but my side no longer hurt. It just felt numb. "What happened?" My voice sounded far enough away to belong to someone else.

"We caught you halfway down the stairs." She shook her head, and her black hair waved with the motion. "I've never seen Bolt so unsure. We were already at the bottom, sure you'd gotten clear—we hadn't heard anything—when he turned around and headed back up the stairs. That's when the noise started."

That almost made sense, but not quite. "How did you buy enough time to get me out?"

Her lips curved upward in a way that made me wish I was hale and whole enough to thank her properly. "Rory stayed behind and threw daggers in the dark. He didn't kill anyone but it kept them from charging down the stairs until we could get you clear."

The lights in the room turned to liquid, and I pulled a breath that felt as if a draft horse was sitting on my chest. "We have to get back to the palace."

I didn't see Bolt in the room with us, but I heard his voice. "You can't, Willet."

Another breath pulled me closer to sleep. "Why not?"

His face appeared above mine, shimmering through tears and exhaustion. "You've lost too much blood. If we move you, you'll die. The healer says it will be days before you're able to stand."

I shook my head, or would have if it hadn't been so heavy. "If we're not in the palace by morning, that will be as good as confessing we broke into the cathedral. We didn't put everything back the way we found it, you know." Aer have mercy. I'd never trained as a healer, but I knew why I felt so cold. "Help me up," I said to Gael. The room spun. Stupid room. "Do we have any chiccor root syrup?" I asked Bolt.

Instead of answering, he looked at Gael. "See? I told you. Alright, Willet, have it your way." He moved out of my vision and returned a moment later with a small stoppered vial. The cork made a soft popping sound, and he tilted the bottle so I could drink.

The taste was wrong. In the space of five heartbeats my vision narrowed to pinpoint. "That wasn't chiccor root."

Bolt's face and the room faded as the drug pulled my lids closed.

"No," he said. "It wasn't. Rest and heal, Willet."

CHAPTER 22

After almost two weeks at sea, they made port under cloudy skies at the northernmost tip of the southern continent. Standing at the rail next to Pellin, Allta was the first to notice the squadrons of men on the piers.

Pellin looked across the shortening distance to the dock and reached out with both arms to pull Mark and Allta closer. "The gauntlet to the southern Vigil is not easily run, gentlemen. Guard your words, and whenever possible, allow me to speak for the group."

He gave Mark's arm a gentle squeeze. "From this moment on, Elieve will be your sister, one whom Aer favored with beauty, if not intelligence."

At the questioning look from his apprentice, he continued. "The mark of the forest is on her. If they discover she has a vault, even one that doesn't seem inclined to open, they'll kill her with hardly a thought."

Anger closed Mark's expression, but his question, when it came, surprised him. "Why haven't we?"

Pellin nodded. "What you've done would have been considered impossible less than a month ago. There is something in my heart that tells me that somewhere in the girl's redemption lies the secret for defeating the Darkwater. Elieve is important." He sighed. "Though I cannot tell you exactly why."

A soft bump and the calls to make fast preceded a terse exchange between the captain and the dockmaster as well as a pair of guards. Once it was completed, Captain Onen came up to Pellin, his expression unchanged, but his shoulders curled as if unseen blows might land on his back at any moment. "Aye, this explains the traffic into port, it does."

Pellin took a moment to examine the broad sweep of the harbor, a huge natural arc that opened just enough to permit vessels out to sea. Everywhere along its length he saw ships bobbing gently against their piers. In the entirety of his extended life, he'd never seen so many craft in one place.

"I don't understand, Captain," Pellin said, "the port looks full to overflowing."

"Aye." Onen ground the word like a curse. "That's because transport inland from Erimos has been pinched until it's almost stopped. You can have a full cask, you can, but if you can't open the spigot, ye'll have a hard time serving yourself a drink."

Pellin's intuition told him the answer to his next question before he asked it. The religious and political structure of society on the southern continent held less complication than it did on the northern one. "What's happened, Captain?"

"The churchmen have their dander up about something," the captain said, "but neither the soldiers nor the dockmaster are saying. When I asked why, you would have thought they'd taken lessons from clams about being close-mouthed. They've got scores of ships stuck here while their factors wait for permission to transport their goods to the interior, Master Pellin. You'll be a very long time waiting to get through." He gave Pellin a look that surprisingly contained no graft or greed within it. "I'm only here to deliver my cargo. There's no need to pay me for the return trip. I can't wait that long for you."

Pellin dug into the purse at his waist, pulling enough silver to double the previously agreed upon fee, and extended his palm. "How much time will this buy, Captain Onen?"

Onen hefted the metal on his palm, and for a moment he swayed like a mast at sea, refusal writ within his expression. "Time-and-a-half," he said nodding. "Money's better in the hand than across the sea, as we say."

Pellin nodded his thanks. "I hope to Aer I get to sail with you again, Captain, but if I don't, fair winds and blue waters to you for the rest of your days."

Onen gave him a puzzled look. "My da's da used to say that. Ye must be older than ye look."

Pellin allowed himself a smile. "We'll gather our things and take our leave."

Allta stepped in beside him with Mark and Elieve trailing. Mark pointed to buildings and objects that would be strange to her, naming them in a soft murmur. Elieve's mimicked responses still carried the joyful pitch of discovery, common to children and those who loved learning.

"Eldest," Allta said, "your protection is in my care. I can only think of two reasons for the church's behavior."

Pellin nodded. In truth, he'd been able to hypothesize four possibilities, all variations on a theme. Perhaps his guard had seen more clearly than he. "What might those be?"

Allta's voice dipped, though for the moment no one stood near them on the pier. "That the Vigil here on the southern continent means to quarantine themselves from the north. No one is allowed into the interior unless they've first been delved and found free of the Darkwater's poison. They're checking each traveler for a vault."

He nodded. His own thoughts ran in that direction, though he'd included possible complications with the Merum order's upheaval. "What is your other theory?"

Allta waited for a passerby who would have had no chance at overhearing their conversation unless they were gifted to wander away. It might have been Pellin's imagination or the angle of the southern sun, but in that moment Allta appeared wan, almost colorless. When he made the sign of the intersecting arcs on his forehead, Pellin gaped.

"Speak, Allta."

His guard came to a stop. Pellin stood with him, waiting.

"My time with the Vigil dates back only a decade, Eldest," Allta said.

"I know that," Pellin responded, his voice sharper than he wished.

Something of discipline or habit reasserted itself, and Allta's stoic demeanor returned. "I don't know how well Cesla knows the southern continent."

As if someone had opened the veins on his legs, Pellin felt his blood draining away from his face and the world spun, but this was a familiar fear.

"Eldest, did you tell them Cesla was alive?"

Like an errant bolt from a crossbow that magically finds a single chink in the armor, Allta's question pierced him, but this too was known to him. "Without the scrying stones, I had to send word by messenger out of Cynestol. I sent a flock of colm messenger birds as well. I don't think Cesla has come here."

"Eldest, the forest and the desert are common, both are guarded by the Vigil. Even if Cesla didn't come himself—"

"He could have sent dwimor." Pellin held up his hands. "Yes, I know. There is nothing for it but to get to the Vigil here and submit ourselves to inspection." He stopped to address Mark. "From this point on, you and Elieve must stay as close to me and Allta as possible. Do not leave our sides for an instant. If the Vigil here should delve her before they delve the rest of us, she'll be put to death before we're afforded the opportunity to explain why she might be important."

Mark nodded. "Yes, Eldest, but wouldn't we notice them?"

Pellin shook his head. "The relationship between the southern Vigil and the church here is more formalized than ours, but they still operate in secret. If merchants are being vetted before they're allowed onto the caravan routes, they won't know why. An incidental brush is enough to delve them and check for a vault."

"How do we find them?" Mark asked. "This city is about to explode."

"Most of them are known to me, as I am known to them," Pellin said. "My presence will be noted, especially now." He reached into his pocket and withdrew the emblem that signified his standing within the Merum order, the only order formally recognized by the church on the southern continent. "This should suffice to get their attention. Then we need only wait until I am recognized."

They threaded their way through the streets of Erimos, working toward the wall that enclosed it, isolating merchants and travelers alike from the rest of the continent. Everywhere he looked, he saw the effects of the quarantine. Pellin lifted a silent prayer that the crowd would be free of dwimor. In the congestion, one of the assassins could kill all of them with ease.

He shook his head at the foolishness that surrounded him. Everywhere his gaze fell, Pellin could see evidence of a city fit to burst. Tempers flared more than once in the heat, and daggers flashed, providing a temporary space for combatants that lasted only until one of them withdrew or died.

"Join hands," Pellin yelled above the din. "Allta, lead us!"

His guard pulled the four of them through the crowd by main strength, his gift forcing others aside as the breadth of his shoulders cleared a momentary gap through which Pellin, Mark, and Elieve followed. A thousand yards later, Pellin caught sight of the gates that separated Erimos from the overland trade routes.

A hundred yards shy of the gates, the traffic and press of people had been cut off as if it had never been. A double cordon of guards separated the crowd from the area around the gate, and church functionaries stood at the apex of the arc, directing those caravan masters forward who'd been permitted to pass through. Armed guards searched each cart and wagon as if hunting for the emperor's killer, even going so far as to draw swords and stab through goods and produce to the anger and angst of the factors standing by.

"Him." Pellin pointed to one of the church functionaries dressed in the blue of deep water under sunlight. "That's the man we need to see."

Allta nodded, but Mark shook his head. "How can you tell, Eldest?"

He pointed to the hem of the man's vestments. "The One Church, as they call it, follows a different liturgical calendar than the Merum. Their colors are different as well. See the three horizontal black bands on his hem? They signify him as an interpreter of the liturgy. One band means the wearer is a patera, equivalent to a priest in the Merum tradition. Two bands denote a cardinalio. The three bands on that man's hem means he has the authority to interpret the liturgy according to the time in which they live. In the southern church, only those with four bands, those referred to as revelators, carry a higher rank."

"Why do they wear the rank on the hem?" Mark asked him. "It's pretty easy to miss."

"Not if that's where your gaze is directed," Pellin said. "The southern church never split, lad. Their hold on the continent is absolute, and they brook no insolence to the faith. The emperor serves at the pleasure of the council of the twelve."

They shouldered their way closer. When Pellin could make out the face of the man with the banded hem, he reached into his tunic for the badge that signified his rank as a bishop in the Merum church. Mark's tug at his sleeve brought him up short, and Pellin had to strain to hear him.

"Will he know that you're in the Vigil?"

"No. Even within the monolith of the southern continent, we are kept secret from all except the emperor and the council of revelators." He nodded to Elieve. "Say nothing and keep anyone from touching her."

Mark looked around, his expression disbelieving. "In this crowd?"

"Put her between you and Allta. There is a member of the southern Vigil here, and they must touch one of us first."

Pellin left Allta's protection and stepped toward the concentric arcs of soldiers, his right hand gripping the heavy silver badge of a Merum bishop. Unlike the Servant's emblem of a foot resting in an open hand, this was simpler. It showed the two intersecting arcs with their common endpoint on the left and overlapping tails on the right. In the years that Pellin had carried the sigil, it had tarnished and been polished so many times that the metal no longer wore a uniform thickness, but that it was made from purest silver would be obvious to anyone with a passing knowledge of the metal.

A glint of reflected light from the emblem caught the interpreter's eye as Pellin stepped forward, and he halted his conversation with a burly wagon master to point in Pellin's direction, snapping a command. A squad of four soldiers peeled off the inner arc and came toward him in formation.

Turning to Allta, he waved the rest of the group forward to join him. The soldiers advanced until the space between them narrowed to a yard. Then one of them in the middle, a man with jet black hair and a single circle emblazoned on each side of his tunic, edged closer until his face was hardly more than a handsbreadth from Pellin's.

"You and your company are permitted forward."

The guards closed around them, each pair of hands resting on the hilt of their sword and dagger. "They have a pretty funny version of permission here in the south," Mark muttered.

"Funny!" Elieve said laughing, but when Mark didn't respond, she returned to her quiet inspection of the strange world around her.

The interpreter watched them come, his dark skin and fine features similar to the people from Elania, but where blue eyes bred true for Toria Deel and her countrymen, the interpreter's eyes were the vivid green of seawater close to the shore, striking, but not friendly at the moment. Taller than their Elanian cousins, the interpreter overtopped Pellin by a few inches, though Allta still dwarfed him and most of the guards surrounding them.

Pellin lowered his eyes to the man's hem. "Interpreter, this is an unexpected honor."

"I am Arcadial." He paused as if expecting the name to be recognized. When it wasn't, his tone sharpened. "Is it?" he asked.

Pellin shook his head, raising it to meet that gaze. "I don't understand your question." The interpreter's skin held the unbroken smoothness of youth, but his hair was shot with gray.

"Is it all of those things, Bishop? Unexpected? An honor?"

Pellin's answering nod didn't mollify him.

"What business does a bishop of the Merum have on the southern continent?"

He bowed, using the opportunity to check the soldiers. They all possessed the bearing of military men, and none of them had moved their hands from their weapons, but that told him little. The interpreter's attitude told him more. He wore the demeanor of a man unused to taking orders who'd just been given one he didn't like.

One of the soldiers surrounding them coughed, and the interpreter's eye twitched. "You and your party will accompany us through the gate, Bishop."

Pellin nodded, his gaze returning to the interpreter's hem in a show of respect, but Arcadial had already turned away, raising puffs of dust where his heels smote the ground. Another four soldiers joined the original quartet and they progressed through the open gates.

No tradesmen or foreigners trafficked the southern half of the city. As a result, the streets of this part of Erimos seemed empty compared to the concentration they'd just left. A market of sorts, remnants from a time before the quarantine, still stood ready to do business with the few permanent residents of the city, but the men and women who manned the stalls wore the expressions of those who'd surrendered hope.

"They'll have to relocate to the other side of the gates if they want customers," Mark said. "They should have seen this coming."

Pellin kept his eyes on their escort, still ready to intervene if one of them tried to touch Elieve, but Mark's observation piqued his interest. "Seen what, exactly?"

"That the bottleneck created by the church would create a whole host of desperate sellers on the far side of the gate. With a bit of coin and a little time, any citizen of Erimos could set themselves up as a merchant."

164

"The *meirikio* is perceptive," Arcadial said without turning. "Indeed, a number of the citizens of the city have contrived to do just that."

"*Meirikio* is the southern word for *lad*," Pellin said to Mark.

"Or *apprentice*," one of the soldiers, the one who coughed, amended.

Mark nodded. "Whether they can succeed as a merchant when that advantage disappears would be interesting to see."

"Truly." The soldier nodded.

Pellin came to a turn where the street narrowed between market stalls and their column narrowed, forcing them to walk three abreast until they reached the end of the turn. *Here.* If one of the soldiers accompanying them was in reality a member of the Vigil, he or she would attempt a delve as they jostled past one another. *It's what he would do.*

Darting a glance behind, Pellin saw one of the soldiers stumble as if the man after him had accidentally kicked his feet. Flailing, the soldier's hand darted toward the nearest figure.

Directly toward Elieve.

CHAPTER 23

Pellin thrust his arm backward so that the man's hand was forced to touch him instead. In his mind he locked away every recollection of Elieve and her vault. Then he waited for the presence of the soldier to appear, though the stumbling man was unfamiliar to him. The instant their skin touched, the man's image appeared in his sanctuary, the projection a few years younger than the man himself.

"If you will allow it"—Pellin bowed within his mind—"I would like to explain our presence in Erimos in the traditional way."

The soldier's hand left his, and they continued walking. Nothing more was said until they reached the southernmost tip of the city, where another wall and pair of gates stood vigil. The soldier coughed twice, and like a horse on a leading rein, Arcadial swerved toward a building composed of two long wings, intersecting in the middle with a red-tiled roof. High arches that reached almost to the ceiling ran through each room. Pellin stood at the entrance and found he could see completely through the building's length.

"The summers here are intense," he explained to Mark. "The archways capture and magnify the breezes, keeping the interior cool."

"This way," Arcadial ordered in clipped tones, leading them toward the center of the building, where the two wings intersected. At his command the four doors of the room were closed and barred. Without the cooling breezes, the air turned stifling. A pair of soldiers posted up on the far side of each door until only Arcadial and the soldier who had attempted to delve Elieve remained with Pellin and his company.

166

Pellin bowed to the soldier. "The north sends greetings to our honored brethren in the south."

Instead of returning his bow, the soldier's gaze cut to Arcadial, whose mouth had tightened so that the skin around his lips blanched.

"Is it not enough," Arcadial demanded, "that the twelve have asserted their authority over me by proxy? Must you also make it so obvious that even untutored norlanders can see it?"

The guard sighed. "Interpreter Arcadial, as I've said before, the twelve mean you no disrespect, but circumstances—"

"Circumstances they refuse to share!" Arcadial spat the words as if they had the power to wound. "What good is the One Church if we harbor the same divisions internally that the uncouth orders of the north parade externally?"

Pellin blinked and the soldier stiffened. "Interpreter Arcadial," the soldier said, enunciating each syllable formally, "you go too far. The bishop and his party are guests here in the south, and your words and tone are offensive. I think it would be better if I spoke to them alone."

Arcadial turned apoplectic. A crooked vein throbbed on the side of his forehead. "*You* are dismissing *me*? Do you think the twelve will tolerate this behavior out of one of their messengers, Dukasti?"

The soldier pointed to the door, his face devoid of any emotion. "I suggest you excuse yourself to some locale where you may scry any of the twelve of your choice and state your grievance. But Arcadial," Dukasti added as the interpreter stomped away, "I suggest you do it in private, just in case the conversation doesn't go as you intend. I know how zealous you are concerning your position and the dignity of the church."

He waited until the door closed behind the interpreter before turning to Pellin, but his demeanor didn't change. "I offer apologies for Interpreter Arcadial. He is young to be an interpreter and thinks to compensate by donning gravity as other men would a tunic. I offer you greetings, Eldest Pellin, from your kinsman of the gift here in the south."

Pellin nodded, but a knot in his chest remained even after the welcome. "I have no memory of you, watchful one, though I thank you for your recognition. How old are you in the gift?"

Dukasti smiled. "In some quarters, the abruptness of your question would be considered coarse." He shrugged. "I have held the gift for fifteen years."

Rings showed under his eyes and his voice held the brittle timber of forced equanimity.

"Does Igesia still lead the southern Vigil, Dukasti?" At the man's nod, he inched forward. "I need to see him."

Dukasti's dark brows lowered until his eyes glittered at Pellin from the depths. "When I touched you, Eldest, I noted many things that disturbed me." He nodded toward Elieve. "We'll leave the question of why your memories of her were locked behind the doors of your sanctuary for later. I noticed that you were not wholly surprised by circumstances here in Erimos." His face darkened further. "Do you not wish to know the specifics that require one of the southern Vigil to delve every merchant before allowing them to go inland?"

"Since you touched me, Dukasti, then you know I have suspicions." He inclined his head in apology. "And that the northern Vigil holds the blame for your circumstances. I would ask your forgiveness."

A hint of a smile that held no humor might have touched Dukasti's face. "You know our theology differs from yours in the north. We do not hold with the idea of blaming the group for an individual's wrong."

Unexpected tears burned his eyes. "Cesla . . ." He stopped, then restarted. "I knew something had changed within my brother. He grew restive at the end with his duty to guard and judge. He wanted victory." A pair of tears, one for each lost brother tracked their way down his cheeks. He would have wiped them away and pretended they had never been, but the culture of the southern continent frowned upon such gestures.

Dukasti straightened. "You should have deposed him."

Bitter laughter burst from him. "And have us be led by who? Elwin? He worshipped the ground Cesla walked on. Me? I was the youngest of us and least suited to leadership. I am Eldest now by virtue of attrition."

"Forgive me for saying so, Eldest," Dukasti emphasized the title, "but you've yet to make a case for why I should grant you passage to see Igesia."

"The north is falling, Dukasti," Pellin said. "I need whatever information I can get from Igesia to help me stop it."

Dukasti shook his head. "No, Eldest. The north *has* fallen. When Cesla delved the forest, he loosed evil upon you. You and what survives of the northern Vigil will be welcomed here, but we will not risk ourselves."

Before Pellin could respond, Mark's laughter interrupted their conversation. Elieve, unable to understand the exchange, joined in anyway.

"You surprise me, Eldest," Dukasti said. "I would have thought an apprentice of yours would be more politically astute than to laugh at such an inopportune moment. It is difficult to wring concessions from those who have been mocked."

Pellin turned, anger and embarrassment heating his face. "Mark, you will apologize."

Mark blinked, then turned toward their host. "My apologies for laughing at the crudity of your bluff, watchful one."

Dukasti spluttered. "Do you not know, child, that it is within my power to expel or imprison you?"

Mark nodded. "I assumed as much. I also know that if you're like most of the Vigil, you've been trained as a priest. Yes?" At Dukasti's sharp nod, he continued. "Then you know the nature of evil. If the north falls, you cannot hope to keep it from your shores."

Dukasti, taller than Mark by several inches, looked down upon him. "And how would a youth of ten and five know this?"

Mark smiled. "My education is more informal than yours, watchful one, but no less thorough. Evil is a hunger that consumes those who practice it. I know this because I've seen it in practice countless times. I've watched men and women sample the alchemist's potions, consuming more and more of their art. I've seen men give themselves to their basest desires with night women until no amount of traffic or feigned intimacy could satisfy them. Evil is a fire, watchful one, that consumes all. When it has devoured the north, it will come for your continent, and you cannot win."

Dukasti gazed at him, his expression no longer dismissive. "And are you a captain as well as a theologian, that you should know this? We can defend our shores."

Mark shook his head. "No, you can't, because you have no margin of error. You must win every time, but the evil of the Darkwater needs only to win once and all is lost."

"There your logic defeats itself," Dukasti said. "If that is the case then all is already lost."

"Not so," Pellin said, drawing Dukasti's attention back to him. "There is a chance that we can kill Cesla and restore the north. I have something to offer the southern Vigil in exchange for your aid— information Igesia will want very badly." He held out his arm and brought all his collected memories of the Fayit out of the depths of the sanctuary within his mind where he'd kept them locked away—his last bargaining chip. "Touch me once more."

Dukasti's delve was abrupt. Pellin didn't bother to greet him as he had before. There was no need. When he withdrew, Dukasti's eyes had widened until white became visible all around the blue. "Is this true?"

Pellin nodded. "It is. I wouldn't risk a phantom memory here. Not now."

His eyes narrowed. "You must get to the interior quickly. Igesia is old and his time approaches. He doesn't travel anymore."

Dukasti's tone said plainly there was more he wasn't saying, and Pellin asked for it.

"We don't speak ill of the dying, Eldest," Dukasti said. "Igesia hasn't left the village of Oasi in years, and his habits have become strange. He spends much of his time gazing into the desert at night, speaking to his memories."

A desperate fear wormed through Pellin's mind, but he kept himself from voicing it. Dukasti's aid held a tenuous air that one wrong word or comment might destroy. "Do the sentinels still patrol the outskirts?"

At Dukasti's nod, Pellin's fear eased, but then the southern Vigil member stepped toward the rest of Pellin's company with his hand outstretched. "I am bound to delve everyone who passes through the gate, Eldest. Without exception."

Pellin couldn't protest without surrendering what he'd come to Erimos to accomplish. But he couldn't allow Dukasti unfettered access to Elieve's mind either—her importance to their mission couldn't be sacrificed. He stepped in front of the girl while he delved Allta and Mark.

Dukasti rounded on him, his face livid. "You would knowingly bring this pestilence here?"

Pellin jerked his head at Mark and Allta. "Get her out of earshot." When they were gone, he stepped forward to meet his counterpart's anger with his own. "Don't you understand what you've seen, Dukasti?" He pointed toward the door his companions had exited. "She lives."

"And she shouldn't!" Dukasti yelled. "She's a creation, spawn of a war that should never have been. You took the gifts of domere and devotion and turned them into an abomination."

"I know! Don't you think I know?" He clenched his fists, but brought his voice under control. "But she's more than that now. Willet Dura is the first man to come into the gift of domere who has a vault, and the Fayit told me there is knowledge within it that we must have to defeat Cesla." He pointed toward his hidden companions once more. "She's more than a creation, Dukasti. Elieve is the third person I know who's survived a vault, but more, she's the first dwimor ever who's been restored." He clutched at Dukasti's arm. "You've seen her. As far as that girl's mind is concerned, she's been raised from the dead."

Pellin watched a hundred different responses chase across Dukasti's expression without finding voice. At the last, he shook his head. "No. This burden is yours, Eldest. My responsibility is to *my* people. I cannot grant you passage to the desert if she goes with you. There are no guarantees you can give that once out of my sight she will not kill you and yours and wreak havoc."

"Then come with us," Pellin said.

Dukasti's eyes bulged, showing white above dark smudges of fatigue. "Has she poisoned you already, Eldest? You're actually suggesting I shut down the merchant traffic in Erimos?"

He shook his head. "You will have to at any rate, my friend." He pointed to a mirror that lay on a table by the entrance. "Have you seen yourself?"

Dukasti massaged his eyes as if he could rub his weariness away. "I know what I look like, but 'what must be done, can be borne.'"

Instead of answering his objection, Pellin chose to assume his agreement. "How long would it take us to reach Igesia?"

His counterpart shook his head in denial even as he spoke. "The edge of the desert is over a week with a constant change of horses." He barked a laugh. "You think I look bad now? I ride poorly, Eldest, and the desert is merciless beyond description. Your solution sounds like undeserved penance."

Pellin lifted his hand, gesturing toward the sea. "The traffic is so slow through the gate now it might as well be stopped already. The Fayit, Dukasti! Think of it! The oldest questions we have lie within Ealdor's knowledge. Where do we come from? What was the world like before men came? We could have answers to questions we've scarcely dared to dream."

"Are we supposed to have them, Eldest?" Dukasti asked. "Did knowledge of the Darkwater bring peace or power to your brother? He's a slave to the evil he tried to understand, all because he broke the first commandment." He turned away from Pellin and started toward the door.

What would they do now? What could they do except take ship back to the north and pray for some other solution?

"Come, Eldest," Dukasti called from the entrance. "I will make arrangements for those merchants we've already delved to provide the traffic needed to keep the port open." He shrugged. "They will scream as if I've taken their firstborn, but they are nothing if not resilient."

"We're going to see Igesia?" Pellin asked, not sure if he heard or understood correctly.

Dukasti nodded. His gaze, blue like the sea, still wore the fatigue of too many uses of his gift, but something else burned in the depths now as well. "I am as guilty as you. The knowledge of the Fayit is too tempting to forego. I pray to Aer in three that I have not brought ruin on my homeland."

CHAPTER 24

Three days out from Hylowold, the incessant trot they used to eat up the ground had turned Toria's saddle into an instrument of torture. Yet she hated dismounting, because it meant she would have to walk, and her legs refused to bear her weight. When they came to Treflow another four days later, the city she'd visited beyond counting had been transformed. Carpenters worked to install heavy scaffolding, makeshift parapets, inside the walls while river boats and carts delivered food and armaments before departing empty.

But it was the people who told her war had come again. They moved with the stiff posture and ground-focused gaze of those who lived under constant threat. The sound of smiths' hammers merged with the commands and acknowledgments of soldiers, and the smell of burning sulfur and quenching oil mixed with the more normal scent of roasted meat.

The preparation for war provided one unintended benefit. Few of the soldiers and fewer of the civilians took the time to note the sentinel walking next to their horses. "Why don't they just leave?" Fess asked.

She followed his gaze to the market, where a lieutenant in the Aille army organized the stalls and products with frequent references to a sheaf of parchments. "Most of them will."

He frowned at her. "I don't understand."

The air carried too many scents that she associated with warfare and dying. "Unfortunately, I do. Treflow is the largest defensible city close to the forest. King Rymark is fortifying it in case he has to retreat."

She followed his gaze as he took in the walls, high enough to offer a decent defense, but nowhere close to the impregnability of the tor in Bunard. He turned to face northwest, where one of the interminable branches of the river that bore the name of the forest flowed into the city beneath the wall. Soldiers and engineers manned heavy winches, working to lower a black iron grate into the water. Then he shifted, looking toward the interior once more.

Toria watched him, reading his thoughts, though her gloved hands held only each other. Wherever his gaze fell, he stilled for a time, studying the preparations before him, but in the end his response was always the same. He would give a small shake of his head before turning to inspect some other facet of the city's preparations. "Hylowold would offer better defenses, Bunard and Cynestol even more so."

"True," she said, "but those cities are farther from the forest. King Rymark understands the nature and strategy of war better than any captain on the continent. He cannot allow Cesla the space to grow his forces. The farther he withdraws from the forest, the more porous his blockade of it becomes. By the time he retreats to Hylowold—"

"He's already lost," Fess said. He took a deep breath. "I see."

They made their way to Treflow's north gate, where a squad of soldiers blocked the exit with stern glances for any who ventured too close. Massive beams of dark wood barred the heavy-timbered gates. "No traffic north of the city," the lieutenant in charge said as they approached.

"I've come from Cynestol," she said. "My colleague and I are on our way to see King Rymark." Even before she finished, she could tell her claim had no effect on the guard.

"I don't care if you've come from Aer himself," he said. "No one is allowed north of Treflow except by the command of King Rymark."

She bent forward to speak to him more closely "Use your brains and take a close look at the animal accompanying us, Lieutenant. Have you ever seen a dog that big?"

His face paled as he stared at Wag. Something in the sentinel's gray-eyed gaze held him transfixed. "Is that—"

She reached out to squeeze his arm, interrupting him. "Precisely. Now open the gate."

He straightened, licking his lips. "I'm sorry, my lady. Not without the proper orders." He drew back, as if he expected her to command Wag to eat him.

Fess dismounted and waved to the lieutenant. "A moment, if you please, Lieutenant," he said, stepping a few paces away from the rest of the guards.

Fess's back blocked her view, but a moment later the lieutenant stiffened and turned toward her. "I'm sorry to have impeded you, my lady. I am Lieutenant Anbroce. You may journey north tomorrow morning when I take the next set of dispatches to the king. "

As they retreated to the center of the city to find lodgings, Toria tried not to grind her teeth at the delay. "How did you persuade him to let us through?"

"I showed him my scrying stone and offered to let him speak with King Rymark directly," Fess said. "I might have mentioned that the king's not the most patient man when he's interrupted."

"Clever," Toria said, "but the scrying stones don't connect us to Rymark, only each other in the Vigil and Brid Teorian. I don't think the lieutenant would have been as impressed talking to the Chief of Servants."

He shrugged. "I doubt whether the king and queens bother to tell their subjects about who holds which set of scrying stones."

The next morning, the lieutenant joined them, mounted on a serviceable black horse and carrying a pack stuffed with reports for the king. Two pennants, the top one red and the lower one green fluttered on a slender pole seated into his left stirrup. Seeing their question the lieutenant nodded. "The patrols have orders to shoot anyone north of here without the colors of the day. King Rymark's orders."

It took eight guards to lift the beam that secured the gate and two more to move it on its massive black hinges, but within minutes she and Fess and the sentinel stood with the lieutenant outside the walls of Treflow. The gates banged shut with a hollow boom that sounded too much like the knell of an iron bell.

A day and a half north of Treflow, Wag went still, his nose pointed into the headwind and the thick fur on his neck bristling. Toria dismounted and put her bare hand on his head, closing her eyes to avoid the vertigo that came with the sudden shift in perception. "What do you smell?" she asked. But by the time the question left her lips, Wag's answer was no longer necessary. She was already in the delve.

Heavy on the wind came the smell of death, not the scent of a decaying animal, but the heavy cloying odor of men, unburied and left in the open to rot.

She remounted and they continued north, but they encountered their first patrol before they came across any bodies. A squad of soldiers in green and white in the distance spotted them when they crested a hill and came thundering toward them at a gallop. Fess pulled his sword and palmed a dagger with the other hand. "You should place yourself behind me, Lady Deel."

With a glance toward the lieutenant, she shook her head. "If you're going to be part of our company, Fess, you're going to have to learn how to deal with others without drawing your sword." She waited as the pounding of hooves grew more distinct, but he didn't reply.

The soldiers reined in and came to a stop twenty paces away, the five of them spreading so that they covered a broad arc. The lieutenant stepped forward, interposing himself between Toria and the squad. "What's the meaning of this? Can you not see the flag?"

The soldier in the center, dark-haired to match his countenance, nodded. "Aye, but security has been doubled." His stare took in Fess, searching, before he looked at Toria, his gaze doing a slow pan from boots to hair, pausing at various times. Men had looked at her that way before, and she met the soldier's stare with her own, cold and implacable.

"Why?" she demanded, her voice cracking in the early morning air. Caught off guard, he blinked. "Why what?"

She let enough of her frustration show on her face to make him lean back in his saddle. "Why have the patrols been doubled?" she grated.

Instead of answering, he turned to Lieutenant Anbroce. "You will deliver your reports to me and return to Treflow." He glanced at Toria. "And take them with you."

"We must see King Rymark," Toria said.

The squad leader snapped his fingers and the men on either side of him drew their swords. "On the contrary, you must do as you're told."

Anger flooded through her like a tidal wave, turning her vision red. At her side, Fess drew his sword, already leaning forward in his saddle, a preface to attack. She managed to reach out and put one restraining hand on his arm. Taking a deep breath, she spoke a single word. "Wag."

The sentinel exploded into motion. Blurring as he took half a dozen strides in less than a heartbeat, he leapt with jaws wide, taking the squad leader in the throat, bearing him to the ground, where he struggled to pull his dagger. Wag's jaws closed a fraction, and the squad leader quieted, hardly daring to breathe.

"Don't move, Captain," Toria said. "It would be unfortunate if Wag misinterpreted your struggles as a threat."

"Release me," he said, his eyes burning. "Or I'll order my men to kill you."

"Don't be an idiot, Captain. Wag isn't a dog, in case you haven't noticed. He could dispatch you and the rest of your men before they came within sword reach. Now use your brains, if Aer has seen fit to give you any. If I have one of the sentinels, wouldn't it be a good idea if I were permitted to get to the front where he could be useful?"

"All the sentinels are dead," the captain said in a strained whisper.

Toria allowed herself a thin smile that she shared with the captain and the rest of his men. "Obviously not, or do you wish to report to King Rymark that you and your men were incapacitated by an ordinary dog? Our conversation has become tedious. I'm going to tell Wag to release you, and you're going to escort my companions and me to the king. Wag will be following. Be careful how you move. As a sentinel, Wag is worth far more to the defense of the forest than a mere captain. Your death would be nothing more than a regrettable footnote. Understood?"

At the captain's nod, she called Wag back to her side. "How far is it to Rymark's camp?"

The captain rubbed his neck, his expression sullen. "Most of the day. If we push the horses, we'll make it before nightfall."

She kept her expression neutral, just. "He's farther south than I expected," she said to Fess. "You will accompany us alone, Captain. I'm sure your men are needed on their assigned patrol."

The sun had sunk to two hands above the horizon when they crested a hill and came within sight of Rymark's encampment. A double palisade of sharpened stakes framed an area large enough to hold several thousand men and hundreds of horses. To the south, outside the camp, dozens of mules had been staked on a picket line near innumerable carts. More tents had been set up outside the walls to the east and west, and men moved between them, their motions brisk, almost urgent. Rymark's headquarters bustled with the activity of a small city, but there were no cries of hawkers or sellers. Only the occasional bark of an order, given to men training in the center of the yard, broke the silence.

"It's quiet," Fess remarked.

She nodded. Memories of other silent encampments, all prefacing the clamor of battle and dying cascaded through her, but this would be different. "Night is coming," she said.

They proceeded through the gates on the captain's authority, but when she asked to see King Rymark, a ring of soldiers surrounded them, refusing to let them advance or withdraw while a runner sprinted away toward the center of the camp. Moments later she saw the king's diminutive figure emerge, flanked by a tall, bulky man on his right with a heavy beard that defied traditional attempts of grooming. On Rymark's left, but two paces back and outside the ring of guards, a man with the dark olive skin and coloring of Aille strode, leaning forward as if he were walking into a gale.

"That explains the extra men outside the walls," she said to Fess. "The man on Rymark's right is King Ellias of Moorclaire. The other is a surprise. That's Prince Maenelic. Queen Chora's son." She looked down at the sentinel by her side. "Wag, keep close." His tongue came lolling out of his mouth in a grin.

CHAPTER 25

"Welcome, Lady Deel," Rymark said. He spared a glance for Fess before his gaze landed on Wag. "You've come with an unexpected gift."

His command tent, a perfect square, could have held nearly a hundred officers, far more than just the four of them and the sentinel. The abundance of so much covered space after days of riding in the open air made Toria feel oddly confined, as if she should be able to see the sun or trees in the distance, but couldn't. At her request, the traditional guards had been dismissed. More than one, unaware of her identity or station, had communicated their silent displeasure to her on their way out, with glowers that had intensified when they landed on Fess.

Rymark and Ellias wielded the gift of kings for their respective kingdoms, Owmead and Moorclaire. Each held the same gift, yet two more different men would have been difficult to find. Short and clean-shaven, Rymark dominated the space within the tent with his intensity. Quick gestures and a darting gaze created the impression of a man whose slight stature barely contained the force of the personality within it.

While Rymark stalked about the tent as if searching for some hidden enemy or slight, Ellias stood to one side like a plinth of granite, tall and broad-shouldered as a blacksmith. His demeanor and gaze testified to a temperament of thoughtfulness or observation rather than the passion that ruled Rymark. Yet for all their differences, the two kings seemed at ease with each other.

The third man, Prince Maenelic, stood a space apart, careful to observe a polite distance between himself and the kings, but he watched with the focused attention of a surgeon. Circles of fatigue or grief beneath his eyes testified to his physical state, and Toria flexed her hands, resolved to delve the prince to learn what had happened in Cynestol.

"You're farther south than expected, Your Majesty," Toria said. "We didn't expect to see you for another day,"

Rymark nodded, disgust written on his face. "You have King Ellias to thank for that." He shook his head. "Thankfully, the move was preemptive. If our greater distance from the forest means it takes us longer to fight, then it also provides us with a measure of safety." Rymark's jaws clenched over and again, chewing words he didn't want to say. "The boundaries of the forest have become unpredictable, and the attacks are . . ." He faltered before nodding toward King Ellias. "He'll have to explain it."

Instead of responding directly, Ellias strode to the tent flap and beckoned. A moment later a captain in the red and green of Moorclaire strode through the entrance carrying several rolls of parchment and laid them on the rude trestle table that dominated the tent. But when they were unrolled, only one of them showed a map. The others were filled with the arcane symbols of the mathematicum.

Fess bent at her side to peer first at the map, then at the other papers. "What is all this?"

Toria sighed. Members of the Vigil rotated among the kingdoms, changing location every ten years to keep their prolonged lives from being noticed. Twice, she'd served within the demesne of Moorclaire, ranging from the chief city of Loklallin to the eastern border of the Darkwater Forest. The kingdom's passion for the mathematicum was well known.

"It's the national passion of Moorclaire," she said. "Pellin is more suited to it than I."

Ellias chuckled. "The other kingdoms often jest that our pursuit of the arcane beauty of the mathematicum has addled our minds. It's just possible they might be right." At Toria's start, he stroked his chin. "Are you surprised, Toria Deel, to find that I own a sense of humor?"

Before she could help herself, she nodded, but Ellias only chuckled again.

"Well, you're not alone."

"Yes, yes," Rymark cut in. "Monarchs have souls. Any number of my subjects would be surprised as well, but to the point, Ellias?"

"Ah." He nodded. "We cannot hold the cordon around the forest."

His pronouncement hit her all the harder for the offhand way in which he said it. Rymark grunted at her reaction. "Disturbing, isn't it, Lady Deel?" he asked. "The way he talks about the end of the northern continent as if he were wondering whether or not to have mutton for supper."

"Explain, please," Toria said.

Rymark gestured at the map of the forest and its surroundings, one thick finger tracing the edge. "The cordon we've set up surrounds the Darkwater on three sides, beginning at the northern end in Frayel and running south through the western edge of Moorclaire, where it turns to run west through the northern tips of Aille and Caisel. From there it turns north through Owmead and Collum before it stops again at the mountains of the northern waste." He straightened, working to bring his gaze level with hers. "We cannot surround the forest completely, understand. There simply aren't enough soldiers. Instead we've established five central camps." He glanced around the tent. "You're in one of them. The others are located in Collum, Owmead, Moorclaire, and Frayel. In between the central camps are operational camps, each a third of the size of this one, where we stage men and supplies. There's an operational camp every twelve to fifteen miles. Between the operational camps are outposts. Their number and placement vary, but they house enough men to ride patrol on the forest during the day."

His description allowed her to ask the question at the forefront of her mind. "Why are you and King Ellias here in the central command in northern Aille?"

Rymark nodded and the hint of a smile tugged at one corner of his mouth. "When His Majesty, King Ellias, asked to meet with me, it seemed the logical choice. This command center is centrally located between those of Owmead and Moorclaire." He might have shrugged. "It has the additional advantage of separating me from my own troops, a fact that seems to bring the other kings and queens a degree of comfort." He turned to Maenelic. "The prince was kind enough to welcome us to Aille's command post."

Maenelic bowed from the waist. "We are honored to welcome you and your men here," he said, but he offered nothing further.

"That you willingly left your troops is impressive for a man of your reputation, King Rymark," she said.

Rymark's expression soured. "Meaning it's a surprise that I haven't been more opportunistic? Ha, it would be more impressive if we were winning." He threw up his hands. "Or even if I could tell you how long we could hold. This isn't warfare I've ever seen or even read of, Lady Deel. You have my congratulations. Tell Pellin that the fight against the Darkwater has managed to do what he and his brothers failed to accomplish for decades. I am now a religious man."

"We've seen little sign of battle or casualties, Your Majesty," Fess said. "Why can't you win?"

Rymark and Ellias turned to regard her apprentice. "So young . . . Is he one of You?" Rymark asked. "I assumed he was your guard."

She nodded. "This is Fess. He received Bronwyn's gift. With the death of my guard, he is temporarily acting in that guise as well. It affords us a measure of security and access we might not otherwise have," she said, skirting the subject of physical gifts.

The king of Owmead nodded in approval. "He's more plainspoken than the last dandy the Vigil took for an apprentice."

She forced a tight smile, but the memory of Peret Volsk stung, a wound Rymark had just poured salt on. "We've noticed that as well."

Rymark looked to where King Ellias stood regarding the parchments. "I'm going to defer your question to my brother king. I barely understand his answers myself."

"The Darkwater Forest covers too much territory to quarantine effectively, Lord Fess," King Ellias said.

Her apprentice jerked and his mouth twitched. "Lord Fess?"

The king of Moorclaire rolled his shoulders. "If that title is insufficient, I will use another."

"Title?"

Confused, Ellias turned toward her.

"Fess is, as yet, unaccustomed to certain political facets of being in our company," she said.

"What Lady Deel means to say," Fess cut in, "is that I was an urchin."

Ellias mouthed the word, testing it.

"King Ellias . . ." Fess bowed. "Before I joined Toria Deel, I was a beggar and thief living on the streets of Bunard. I spent my days running bluffs to trick merchants and priests out of their coin. I am unused to polite society."

Rymark snorted. "That he thinks nobles are polite shows just how little he knows. You've been lax in his education, Lady Deel."

She nodded in acknowledgment. "No doubt. We've been rather busy."

"Well," King Ellias said, "to his question, then. King Rymark's assertion that this is no ordinary war is the fulcrum of our problem. Given our current positions and tactics, it is mathematically impossible to keep those who desire to enter the Darkwater in check. The traditional mathematicum calculations of warfare don't apply."

Rymark had already turned his attention back to the arcane writing on the parchments. "It took Ellias some time to convince me, but our losses are like a plague." He shook his head. "Explain, Ellias. I'm more comfortable with tactics and strategy." He shook his head. "As if we had any."

Toria stifled her surprise at Rymark's rare show of humility. Ellias sorted through the stack of parchments, his expression thoughtful, until he found one more smudged and yellowed than the rest. "I think this would be the best place to start."

He pointed to a section of the parchment that contained two horizontal lines with a sinuous curve that joined them at the lower left and ran to the upper right.

"This is a model of the Darkwater's contagion, according to the mathematicum," he said. He put his finger on the curve between the second and third vertical lines. "This is where we're at now."

Toria had undertaken some rudimentary studies of the mathematicum a few decades ago when she was last placed in Moorclaire, but her talents ran toward others rather than logic and space. Even so, she recognized the curve. "I'm familiar with it," she said. "It's called the plague curve, though it goes by other names."

Fess pointed to the first half of the graph, where the curve grew progressively steeper from left to right. "I've heard healers talk about this. They called it the kingdom killer."

Ellias nodded his approval. "Perceptive and correct. The left-hand side of the curve describes what happens at the start of a plague, but to grasp the whole it will help to think of a hypothetical kingdom on a remote island. No one comes and no one can leave. Now, introduce a perfectly deadly plague." He shrugged. "It doesn't really matter which one."

"Everyone would fall ill sooner or later," Fess said.

"Exactly." Ellias nodded. "At first the number of sick would be fairly small, but they would grow quickly. A healer might have two patients the first week and four the week after, but by the third week he would have eight and then sixteen by the fourth week."

Ellias caught her eye. She knew what would come next. "The healer, if he's new to his craft, might not suspect what shape the graph of the contagion must take. He might suppose the rate would continue as before, doubling every week."

Fess pointed to the right-hand side of the graph. "Sooner or later, most of the kingdom has already been infected. The rate can't double because over half the people have already caught the disease."

Ellias nodded. "The young healer, seeing the rate of disease start to slow, becomes encouraged. He doesn't realize his death sentence and that of everyone on the island has already been written."

Fess looked back at the curve, and Toria saw his face grow pale. "You're saying the evil of the Darkwater is like that?"

Ellias nodded. "Exactly. The northern continent is the island. It's early, very early yet, but we're locked in a battle that's going badly."

She leaned against the table. "I refuse to accept that defeat is inevitable. It isn't."

Rymark cocked his head at her. "There is a note of confidence in your voice, Lady Deel, in defiance of our explanation."

Unwilling to explain or commit to Ealdor's instruction, she turned away. "The assembled might and gifts of the entire north are bent to this task, Your Majesties. Surely you don't think victory is impossible."

Rymark and Ellias exchanged a glance, and both men sighed. "The issue is still in doubt, Lady Deel," Rymark said. "We are still in the early part of the curve and have yet to reach the point of no return."

Fess pointed to the exact middle of the diagram, where a point on the curve lay halfway between the two horizontal lines. "Is that here?"

Rymark's voice rasped within the tent. "I wish it were."

Ellias shook his head. "By that time, half our forces are infected and it's too late. No. To defeat the forest, the poison's momentum must be halted well before that." He pulled an artist's charcoal stick that had been sharpened to a fine point and drew a line that touched the curve near the left end, where it turned up to grow steeper. "If we reach this point, the war is lost. The momentum behind the forest will be too great to stop."

"Then we must find a way to stop it," Toria said.

Rymark shook his head. "Bravely spoken, but my men can't see in the dark, Lady Deel, and the enemy can. It's not just that we can't fight what we can't see, we can't stop it either. At some point our forces will be too thin to reliably quarantine the forest."

Fess pointed to the map. "Then have your patrols pull back from the forest."

"That means they have to cover more ground," Rymark said. "Not less."

Fess nodded. "If you widen the ring around the forest enough, those who slip by the outer patrols won't be able to make it to the boundary of the Darkwater before sunrise."

"If we maintained an inner cordon as well, we would catch those heading for the forest during the daylight."

"Your Majesty," Maenelic said. "Is it a good idea to split your forces?"

"Not usually, no, but we're in a most unusual war." Rymark pursed his lips before turning to the king of Moorclaire. "You're better at the numbers than I am, Ellias. Do we have enough men?"

He nodded. "For now, but it's going to mean short rest and no reserves."

Rymark turned to Fess. "It's an unorthodox approach, but I find I'm more inclined to listen to new ideas of late."

"'Nothing gets a man's attention,'" Fess murmured.

Rymark laughed, harsh, loud. "'Like the prospect of death,'" he finished.

Toria nodded even as she managed to stifle a sigh. "Do those who venture into the forest strike singly, or do they coordinate their attacks?"

"Their strikes are random, Toria Deel," Ellias said. "And there are fewer attacks than I would have thought."

"Those who do strike are like an alchemist's experiment gone wrong," Rymark growled. "They move like gifted, creating explosions of violence and killing a squad or more before they can be put down. Some of the attackers are soldiers, Toria Deel, men or women who've gone to the forest. The deaths are bad," Rymark growled, "but the impact on morale is worse. Soldiers must trust those they fight alongside to be effective. That trust is waning. When it's gone entirely, we're going to have mass desertions on our hands."

CHAPTER 26

Toria leaned over the table, gesturing. "Show me where you've had the heaviest fighting." At her side Wag peered at the map, his ears perked in the canine equivalent of curiosity.

Rymark started to ask a question, then shook his head. "If you can call it fighting. Our men no longer call the waning of day sunset. They call it the dying time."

He bent over the map, pointing to markers in red that had been placed to show the worst confrontations with the forest. By the time he was halfway through, she knew the purpose behind the attacks.

"Cesla is trying to gain access to the towns beyond," she said. "He needs tools."

"Aye," Ellias said. "We received your message, Lady Deel. Anticipating that Cesla would be targeting the towns beyond the forest with the strongest ironworkers guilds, King Rymark shifted our forces."

"And that's when we entered into battle proper," Rymark said. He paused to look around the tent, though they had been alone and were still. "We must find a way to turn this tide, Lady Deel."

"Are your losses so great, then?" she asked.

"Not taken as a whole, no." Rymark shook his head. "But the enemy doesn't just kill, my lady. They take a casualty, sometimes two, and they deliver the bodies to the next outpost or camp." He licked his lips. "Lady Deel, an army is made of men and women who can face death with courage despite the fear that works to undermine them. The bodies—"

She held up a hand. "I understand, Your Majesty. Most men talk of evil without ever encountering the depth of its reality." A region on the map struck her as odd, and she put her finger on it. "Why is this marked?"

Rymark glanced at the king of Moorclaire. "The casualties there are half what they have been at any other outpost," he said. "I thought it was nothing, but Ellias tells me the difference is . . ." He searched for the right word.

"Significant," King Ellias said.

"That's it." Rymark nodded. "I've asked for a report, but the increased skirmishes have disrupted communications." He looked at her and Fess. "The outpost is close enough that I have considered going myself."

"Ridiculous notion," she said before she could stop herself. "I mean no disrespect, Your Majesty, but it's two days away, and you command the armies of the north. You can't be spared for this. Fess and I will go."

"Your argument is sound," Ellias said. "But can the two of *you* be spared, Toria Deel?"

"The Vigil has never been an instrument of war, Your Majesty. We have always exerted our influence through more personal engagements." She glanced outside. "We'll leave in the morning."

Rymark nodded with a glance at Wag. "I'll have quarters arranged for you and your companions inside the compound."

Screams jolted Toria awake, and she jerked from slumber to wakefulness without transition. Quick as she might have been, Fess stood over her, weapons in hand. The beat of her heart rocked her back and forth like a pendulum. Outside the tent, the glow of light lit the compound. White light.

"Come," she said as she jerked on her boots. She fumbled in the gloom for her weapon. "Wag!"

Thrusting aside the flap, she burst out of their shared tent to chaos. Men and women raced to the walls, climbing makeshift scaffolding. Soldiers crowded the towers at each corner of the camp, filling broad platforms at the top, most armed with short bows. In the center of each platform a brazier of solas powder burned, banishing the dark-

PATRICK W. CARR

ness in white-hot balls of sunlight, while on either side of the flame, men or women aimed mirrors out into the darkness.

Massive guards came charging out of the tent next to hers, hemming in the king of Owmead. Rymark screamed orders to a series of runners who dashed up and just as quickly dashed away. Over the din of screaming, she heard thumps against timbered walls of the compound.

"Your Majesty! King Rymark!" She screamed, but the king of Owmead ignored her calls, issuing commands for light and torches.

Toria threaded her way through his guard, clutching. "What can we do?"

He turned to her, his gaze desperate before it landed on the sentinel. "We've got men camped outside the gate. We'll lose them all."

She jerked a nod, breaking into a run. "Wag, Fess, with me." She raced across the compound, willing her legs to go faster. The gates were fashioned from huge logs. On the far side men and women beat at them, begging admittance against the sound of slaughter.

"Open them!" Toria yelled at the soldiers. "By order of King Rymark."

As the men worked to throw the massive beams, she knelt, put her hands on Wag's thick ruff and sank into the delve.

Hunt! she ordered. *But only those with the scent of the forest on them, and you must live!* A flood of impressions came across the link, the smell of blood, its taste, salty and hot on her tongue, the crunch of bone.

Wag raced through the opening, and a mix of screams filled the night air as men and women in the colors of Moorclaire flooded through, frantic to escape. A veiled man wearing the clothes of a merchant came leaping out of the darkness toward the gates. Just before he reached the opening, hundreds of pounds of fur and muscle hit him from the side and powerful jaws snapped his neck. The gates closed.

"We have to get back to Rymark." Fess took her hand and ran, half pulling her back to the king, who stood gazing at the northwest tower, a stream of sulfurous language spilling from him.

"Protect her!" he ordered his guards, pointing, but none of the guards moved to obey.

She followed the line of his point, saw a woman standing on the tower, light from the burning solas powder framing her like a halo.

A soldier at her side followed her prompts, aiming his mirror into the darkness.

"Who is she?" Toria asked.

"Timbriend," Rymark said. "The best mathematical mind in her generation."

She stepped to the king. "What is she doing?"

King Ellias came lumbering out of the darkness with his personal guard. "She's counting," he said "working to calculate the number involved in the attack."

An arrow streaked out of the darkness to take the soldier working with Timbriend in the chest, and he crumpled. A heartbeat later, an arm, pasty with the pallor of a maggot, appeared over the edge of the wall. Fear etched her face, but she stepped in to take the mirror, turning its focus on the attacker. A diminishing roar of frustration accompanied his fall.

Rymark's head swiveled, searching for his captains. Another shaft came arcing toward the light, its passage close enough to make Timbriend flinch. Still, she worked the mirror, counting.

More attackers with veils covering their eyes appeared atop the wall. A pair of arrows struck one in the leg and arm. With a snarl, he yanked them free and moved toward the light adjacent to Timbriend's. The soldiers defending the brazier went down beneath strokes Toria never saw. A moment later the attackers pushed the burning fire from the platform, its light winking out as the flaming powder drifted to the ground.

Around the perimeter of the wall, hands appeared, grappling for the top. Rymark's soldiers fired volleys, but the attackers shrugged off their wounds. On the north wall, a pair of men in ragged clothes turned to attack the soldiers defending Timbriend's light.

Fess burst from Toria's side at a run, his feet blurring into motion, hardly touching the ground. King Rymark watched him depart, his expression inscrutable, but Ellias turned to her, frowning. "He holds two gifts. That's forbidden."

"Not for Aer," she said. "The gift of domere came to him freely after he received the physical one."

She turned to see Rymark screaming at his runners. "Light the circles! However you have to do it, get them lit!"

Fess gathered and launched himself into space with a leap that carried him halfway up Timbriend's platform. He clutched at the ladder, swinging his body around so that his feet found purchase. They'd hardly touched the rough wood before they were moving again, taking the rungs two at a time. The soldiers had gathered around Timbriend, forming a tight wedge with their swords toward the attackers as if they wielded pikes.

The attackers closed the distance, dodging clumsy thrusts from the crowded soldiers. Timbriend's defenders collapsed in a wave. Only the press of bodies kept them from the brazier, but they were advancing. Timbriend and her light were mere feet away.

Fess gained the top of the platform behind her as the last four defenders closed ranks. A soldier went down, taken through the chest. Another died from a slash to the throat, crimson staining the air. Fess charged past Timbriend as the last of the soldiers on the tower died. Steel clashed with a ring, and Fess lunged, cutting through the veils that shielded them from the light with sword strokes Toria never saw. With a cry of agony the attackers covered their unprotected eyes. Moments later their bodies hit the ground beneath the tower.

A man's scream of warning and death sounded behind Toria, and she wheeled to see a wave of attackers dropping from the parapet of the south wall. Their heads lifted, seeking, scenting through the thin cloth of their veils. Then as one they charged.

Toward her.

Soldiers veered in to meet the new attack and died. On open ground, the attackers moved with fluid grace, leaving dead in their wake. Fess jumped from the tower, rolled, and came for Toria, racing faster than a hound.

Rymark's personal guard formed up around him and began a retreat toward the north towers. Ellias's guards pulled him south.

Horror brought bile to Toria's throat and she fought to pull her sword. Fess reached her side and pulled her toward the east, away from Rymark and Ellias. The attackers split into two groups without slowing, targeting the kings.

Toria stood in a circle of calm, the swords and daggers of the enemy leaving a trail of blood as they strove to reach the kings. Screams filled the air—of men dying, of Rymark calling orders. Drowned by the cacophony, the king of Owmead's voice was lost. Fess moved to join the fight, stopped, then retreated to stand by her once more.

More attackers gained the wall. Rymark, surrounded by his guard, caught her gaze and screamed, pointing. The cords of his neck stood in stark relief as he tried to make himself heard. His hand stabbed the air, pointing to the towers. She grabbed Fess. "What is he saying?"

He watched the king, followed his motion. "Fire the circles." He shook his head. "I don't know what he means." Attackers, taking grievous wounds, fell at last, but more were gaining the walls.

Intuition exploded through her. "The towers," she yelled. "The men on the towers had fire and naptha. Rymark would have planned for this. Go."

Still, they stood in calm as the camp mustered to protect the kings. Bodies covered the ground, preventing retreat or advance.

"I can't leave you," Fess yelled.

She drew breath to argue, surrendered. "Then I'll go with you." And she started at a run toward the northeast tower where Timbriend still stood. Fess caught Toria's arm in a grip that brought flares of red to her vision. He shifted his grip, his arm around her waist and raced up the ladders three rungs at a time.

In seconds they gained the top. "There are too many," Timbriend said. Her eyes stared, unblinking, into the compound below, and she wavered on her feet.

Fess grabbed a bow and set fire to arrows that arced, flaming, into the night sky to land beyond the fort. The glow of fire leapt, and by its light Toria could see concentric rings of wood surrounding the camp flare into life. The cries of attackers beyond the wall scaled upward, turning into shrieks of hatred and pain.

Deprived of reinforcements, the tide of the attack inside the camp turned. Outside, attackers, disoriented and trapped by the rings of fire, fell to a rain of arrows as more of Rymark's soldiers gained the parapet.

Even after the last scream died away, Toria remained atop the tower with Fess and Timbriend as she completed her count. Then they descended the ladder, with Fess leading, his face and clothes covered in spatters of blood.

Rymark issued orders, and the gates were opened. "See to the wounded," he ordered a captain, "and organize a detail to bury the dead." His dark brows hooded his eyes in the firelight, promising retribution. "Have the men separate the attackers from ours and count the bodies."

Wag, covered with blood and panting, came trotting up to her. She put her hands on him. *Well done, Wag.*

Thank you, Mistress. His tongue lolled to one side, but thankfully, he didn't lick her. *The forest men outside the second fire got away.* An undercurrent of sorrow accompanied this.

How many escaped? Within his mind rose the image of a great pack, easily fifty or more. She rose, slipping her gloves back on. "Thank you, Wag."

Rymark and Ellias, still tightly ringed by their personal guard stood waiting for her. Toria bowed her respect. "The rings of fire were well conceived," she said. "What made you think to do it?"

He nodded in acknowledgment. "The art of war is to adapt, Lady Deel. When Lord Fess put forth his idea to ring the forest twice to keep people from entering, it occurred to me to use something similar for our defense. We put oil-soaked wood in two perimeters outside the camp, far enough away to keep from endangering ourselves."

Toria nodded. "But within bowshot."

"Well, Timbriend?" Ellias asked.

Her face held the pallor of death, but she bore no sign of injury. Her hands shook as she pulled a charcoal writing stick and parchment from her cloak. Rymark closed the distance, his expression thunderous. "What possessed you to ascend the tower during the attack? My men could have counted for you."

She shook her head. "It had to be accurate. Even so, I have no estimate for how many escaped."

"At least fifty," Toria said. She didn't attempt to explain her insight.

Timbriend sighed. "I'll have to revise my calculations."

She looked at Ellias. "The numbers are wrong. There shouldn't have been so many. I need to get to my tent." Timbriend took a step, but the trembling in her hands shifted to her legs, betraying her. When she pitched forward, Fess caught her and helped her find her balance, and Rymark ordered two of his men to help her away.

"What did she mean there were too many?" Toria said to Ellias before he could leave.

Ellias, big enough to match his guards, grew somber. "Timbriend is one of the brightest minds in Moorclaire. She has only to show mastery of the tenth part of the mathematicum to be considered a master."

"The tenth part of the mathematicum?" Fess asked. "What is that?"

Toria bit her lip in frustration, not wanting to divert Ellias from her question. "A student wishing to attain master must explore a new field for the applications of the mathematicum."

"Exactly," Ellias said. "Timbriend chose to apply the mathematicum to the exercise of warfare in a new way. Even I have a difficult time understanding much of what she attempts."

"What did she mean, there were too many?" Toria pressed.

The king's lungs filled like a bellows before he answered. "The answer is at once both obvious and unknown. She meant the number of attackers sent against us shouldn't have been possible, but I'm afraid we will have to leave deeper interpretations for dawn." Rejoining his guards, he left.

CHAPTER 27

Toria came to with a start, jolting upright on her cot before she realized quiet still filled the camp.

"We've been summoned," Fess said.

The lamp in his hand brought tears to her eyes, and she scrubbed at them in an effort to see. "How long have I been asleep?"

"They've only changed the guard once, so no more than four hours. Here."

She nodded, bit a piece of the chiccor root he offered, and stood, still fully clothed and booted. Wag lifted his head, blinking. "Stay here," she commanded.

They emerged from their tent into the cool of morning, but it wasn't the weather that made her shiver. Bodies still littered the ground, and members of Ellias's retinue moved to each, looking for whatever information they might use. She could have told them what they would find, of course. Bas-solas had taught her. Those who had come from the forest would show horrible bruising, the effect of mindlessly pushing their muscles past the breaking point. Instead, she searched the faces of the dead, looking for those she might know.

They passed through a cluster of guards and into Rymark's tent, where the kings of Owmead and Moorclaire waited for them along with Timbriend, all of them a study in fatigue. Dark circles wreathed their eyes, and Rymark's rod-straight posture had left him, his back curved beneath the burden of command.

"Where's Prince Maenelic?" Toria asked.

Ellias shook his head. When he spoke his voice rumbled with anger.

"The prince was outside the gates seeing to my men when the attack came. He took a couple of nasty strokes during the fight. The healers are seeing to him."

"I'll send my personal surgeon," Rymark said. "The prince has been instrumental in the cooperation of Aille's forces." He turned to her. "When I returned to my tent, I used my scrying stone to call the other monarchs and warn them." He nodded to Toria and Fess. "Doubtless you noticed that the attackers focused their assault on Ellias and me. I thought it best to warn the rest, though none of them were attacked."

He went on. "Cesla knows what Ellias and I look like, Toria Deel, but he also knows your visage—and probably you, Lord Fess. Why would he choose to focus his attack on us?"

She shook her head. "I don't know, but it seems axiomatic that he will strike at his biggest threat. Queen Chora died as we left Edring. We heard the bells as they swept north from Cynestol." She turned to Timbriend. "You said last night that there were too many attackers. Why?"

Timbriend took a deep breath and pointed at the map. "I was able to estimate the number that came against us." She looked up. "It was a concentrated force of well over two hundred, Lady Deel. The vast majority of the attackers never made it inside the walls. Such a force entering the Darkwater would have drawn the attention of the patrols. The fact that never took place meant that the force was gathered inside the Darkwater and then sent under cover of night to attack us here."

Rymark pointed at his map. Splotches of red marked their encampment now. "There's an outpost directly north of here. They were untouched last night. The implications of that are why I asked you here, Lady Deel."

She pulled her gloves. In hundreds upon hundreds of square miles of farmland, the enemy had found them and attacked. "You think you have a traitor in your midst."

He nodded. "It's a possibility I must acknowledge. We have to assume they know where we are and how we defeated them last night. If there is a traitor among us, I must know. Lady Deel, I want you to delve each of us. Once you have determined that we are free from the forest's influence, I will show you where I intend to move the camp, but no one outside this room will know before being delved."

196

She tucked her gloves away and stepped quickly around the room, delving Rymark, Ellias, and Timbriend in turn, her touch thorough enough to determine each person's innocence. Beside Fess once more, she nodded. "You're safe, Your Majesty, at least so far as the people in this room are concerned."

Timbriend spoke into the pause. "King Ellias has informed me of your unique gift, Lady Deel. Why not delve the entire camp?"

Rymark answered for her. "We have thousands of men and women here," he said. "The use of the gift is tiring. While it may come to what you suggest, even with Lord Fess joining her, the process would take weeks, perhaps months, to complete."

Ellias dipped his head in agreement. "Come, Timbriend. We are done here, and I wish to see your analysis of last night's engagement as soon as possible." The tent flap fluttered at their departure.

Toria gestured at the map. "Where will you place your camp, Your Majesty? I should know that before we depart."

"You're still leaving?"

She nodded. "Nothing has changed. Despite your losses here, Cesla's losses were worse. He gambled a sizable force on the attack and lost much of it, but you still need weapons, and the camp to the west has fewer casualties than any other—we must find out why."

"Our losses may be greater than you know, Lady Deel," he said, nodding to Fess. "Your suggestion of placing twin rings around the forest requires a great deal of men and perfect discipline. We have the first, provided we don't suffer many more attacks like last night's, but the second is impossible, or nearly so." He shook his head. "We already have more conscripts than I'd prefer. Men who've joined the army at the point of a sword have a way of disappearing."

"All the more reason Fess and I should investigate the lower casualty rate at your outpost," she said. "Whatever they're doing is working."

Rymark sighed. "Very well." He pointed to a spot thirty leagues from their current position. "I'll be moving the camp here." His finger landed on the Darkwater River, ten leagues north of Treflow.

Her heart might have skipped a beat as the implications of his choice became clear. "You're planning lines of retreat, Your Majesty?"

His eyes, somber and hooded with lack of sleep, betrayed him for an instant. "I've developed an intuition about battle, Lady Deel, which has seldom betrayed me. I will use every tool and suggestion that I can put my hand to, even using the arcane knowledge of the mathematicum. But my intuition tells me this is a war I cannot win."

She kept herself from nodding, unwilling to confirm his fears. "Hold as long as you can. If men and weapons cannot win the war, then we will find another way. If Aer is willing."

"You'll need uniforms and letters of authorization," Rymark said. "They'll help you move among the outposts, and you'll be able to commandeer whatever you require."

They reached the first outpost later that morning, the men already working to split weapons and supplies, with the majority moving farther from the forest. Toria reined in her horse, sighing. Wag sat on her left, waiting patiently.

"Lady Deel?" Fess asked.

"It's time that you shouldered your burden as a member of the Vigil, Fess. We'll delve a sampling of the soldiers and check for vaults." When his face tightened, she went on, her tone sharpening. "Bronwyn didn't pass her gift to you. It went free and came to you by Aer's intent."

The fingers of his hand twitched, an attempt to brush her assertion away. "Chance."

Her tone became withering. "Don't be childish. You know better. Bronwyn chose you to be her apprentice and then died, purposely without passing it on to you. Aer stepped in and brought the gift to you anyway. You would never have received it by mere chance. When we see Timbriend again, I can ask her to calculate the probability of such an event, if you wish. I have no feel for the mathematicum, but I know an impossibility when I see it. Aer chose you."

"I didn't want it."

"No one does!" She clenched her teeth. "Some of us only think we do. Then we discover exactly what you have. Do you think you're the first to be disappointed by what you've seen in your fellow man? You wanted to believe they're good. You should have known better."

Struck, he tried to retreat into his stoicism. "Do you have any other commands, Lady Deel?" His voice imbued her title with mockery.

She chose to ignore it. "Yes. Give me your hand. I'm going to show you something I've hidden behind my walls for decades. I haven't let anyone see this, but you will."

He didn't move. "Why?"

She shrugged. "I could give you any number of reasons. Why not? We're nothing more than animated dust with burdens to be shared. I'm tired of dragging a secret around with me. I have more cheap justifications, if you want to hear them."

"Why do I feel like none of those are the real reason?" he asked.

"Because you're insightful," she said. "The truth is I'm tired of you wallowing in your self-pity and depriving me and the rest of the world of the hope you brought to us. The gift didn't make you precious, Fess. You already were, just the way Aer made you. Imagine it, a boy who grew up in the urchins who managed to find joy in everything. You have no right to let your self-pity deprive others of such a gift. Yes, I said gift."

He laughed at her, but the sound carried no joy, only breath. "Do you think I want to be like this?"

She nodded. "You are choosing this. It might not seem that way to you, but you are. You've wallowed in your grief until the tears dried and there was nothing left but self-pity."

Her words struck him like axe blows against a sapling, shaking him until his expression crumpled. "I don't know how to get back," he cried.

"Oh, Fess," she said, enfolding him in her arms and putting her head on his chest. "You were like a breath of wind that captured our hearts. Let us love you."

"Bronwyn loved me and she died."

She reached out for his hand. "We all die. Here, let me show you something sad and foolish and funny." She took his wrist and guided his hand to her cheek. Then she opened the locked door where she'd stored the memories she'd collected, recollections she'd prized above all others and taken care to keep secret.

She didn't see the pupils of his eyes dilate as the gift took him, but he grew so still he might have become one of the surrounding trees. When he came out of the delve, he held her, his embrace willing and voluntary. She thought she might cry, but he needed more than that. She let his warmth cover her, a welcome hearth fire on a cold night.

Then she laughed. "Ridiculous, isn't it?"

He chuckled. It sounded ghastly, like a man who'd never made the sound before, but it loosened after a moment. "That is funny to you?"

"Elanians are possessed with an ironic and rather tragic sense of humor compared to those of the other kingdoms," she said, knowing Fess had to realize that wasn't the whole truth. He'd delved her. He couldn't help but know the shame she attached to those memories.

"Bronwyn taught me that the church holds the rite of confession as sacrosanct," he said. "There's little privacy in the urchins. Our lives are too crowded and desperate for it. I'm not a priest, but I will honor your confession. I don't know what a priest would say, but I think courage comes in many guises."

Then the tears did come and she clutched at him until she could laugh again. Pushing away, she started for the guards at the perimeter of the outpost, leading Fess and the sentinel toward the gate. "Come. We have much to do on our ride west."

Wag padded at her side, but after half a dozen strides, he stopped, his legs stiff and the ruff of his neck standing on end. A rumble of promised violence throbbed deep in his throat, and he scented the air, his nose twitching.

"Stop," Toria called to Fess. Quickly, before they could draw the attention of the soldiers manning the gate, she put her hand on Wag's head. "What do you smell?"

The forest, Mistress. There are men here who reek of it.

For Fess's benefit she spoke out loud. "You can smell evil?"

No, Mistress. There are men here who smell like those who attacked the man-pack.

"We have to be sure, Wag," she said. "Do you know what you're smelling?"

Mud.

Realization and fear coursed through her. She licked her lips, fearing the answer to her next question. "Were there any men left in the man-camp who smelled of this mud?"

None living, Mistress.

She pulled a shuddering breath into her lungs, let her fear drift away with it as she exhaled. "Fess, have your weapons ready. There are men here who have gone to the forest."

200

PATRICK W. CARR

Without seeming to move, a dagger appeared in his free hand, hidden behind his forearm. "How many, Lady Deel?"

She stopped, horrified at her unwitting mistake. "How many in this camp have the smell of the forest on them?"

Wag's nose twitched before he answered. *Half the pack, Mistress.*

CHAPTER 28

I marked the passage of time by the intervals of light and darkness outside the small window of my room. Maybe five days had gone by. I couldn't be sure. My healer, a short stump of a man with prominent eyebrows, didn't talk much except to tell me how stupid I'd been.

"I'd say you're lucky you didn't bleed to death," he groused, "except it wasn't luck at all. It was my skill, and even at that, it was a close thing. It's just plain stupidity, going out in the city at night."

During my stay, I'd learned not to argue. "Thank you," I said.

The healer glowered at me, his eyebrows trembling with suppressed indignation, but he could find nothing in my gratitude with which to take exception. "Humph. Stay out of trouble, Lord Dura. There are two things I don't enjoy—repeating myself and restitching wounds."

I knew the first to be a lie. Master Gieman loved to repeat himself, especially where comments on my stupidity were concerned. "That sounds as though I'm being discharged from your care," I said.

He nodded. "Evidently, you're needed at court. Your guard and the lady are waiting for you outside."

Fifteen minutes later I stepped into the noise of Cynestol, a current of sound I'd been unaware of during my time at the healer's. Scents of meat and smoke washed over me, and in the distance I heard honest laughter, but the buildings waved in my vision as though the earth and heavens had become untethered from their moorings.

Gael caught me before I could fall. "Can you ride?"

I nodded. "I think so."

She and Rory helped me into the saddle, and after a few blocks of

202

walking through Cynestol's working-class quarter, my head cleared enough to worry. "Won't the healer talk?"

"No." Gael shook her head. "He's an old friend of Bolt's." She must have seen something in my pallor or expression that worried her. "Come, Willet, just a little farther."

Her tone made me wonder just how bad I looked. True to her word, we were only a mile from the palace. Even so, the distance stretched into an agony where I felt each step of my mount in my injured side and the slightest misstep of my horse sent the moon and stars spinning.

When we got to the palace stable, I slid out of the saddle into Gael's arms, as if my bones had turned to wax. I heard more than saw the clink of heavy silver coins she used to buy the hostler's silence.

I felt as if I could have slept for days more. "How long until court opens?" I croaked.

"Not for twelve hours or so," Gael said.

We threaded our way through the halls, and the rooms set aside for our use, a short journey that carried its own misery. Every time we came across a servant or functionary, I had to surrender Gael's support and pretend to be a healthy man in possession of his requisite amount of blood.

When we made it to the privacy of our chambers, I fell into bed and plummeted into slumber.

Sunlight streamed through the west-facing window in a bar of light that spilled across the rich blue-patterned carpet in the room, up the bed, and onto my face. I didn't understand at first, but a moment later my heart, already beating faster with the loss of blood, accelerated with my panic. I jerked awake, then put a hand to the stitches in my side.

"Court," I gaped.

"It's alright, Willet," Gael said, "Bolt is there and he's made excuses for us, as he has for days. His excuses would have fallen apart in Bunard, but in Cynestol's court they have worked to perfection." She couldn't quite suppress the smile that made me want to cover her mouth with mine.

"What would those be?" I croaked as I reached to make use of the water pitcher by the nightstand. Stripped to the waist, I had a better idea of the damages. I'd taken a sword stroke to the side, and judging by the padding beneath the linen binding the wound, it had been significant, but the wound had lost most of its heat. I wouldn't die because it fouled.

"He and Rory are letting everyone in court know that you've noticed my wandering eye here in Cynestol, specifically for a certain male servant, and you're taking the luxury and the time to remind me just why I chose you to be my future husband."

I didn't have my full allotment of blood, but some of it made it to my face anyway. "They're saying that?"

She nodded, this time showing more teeth as she smiled. "Or something even more suggestive."

"You know what everyone will think," I said.

Now she laughed. "Willet, my love, if I cared what people thought I would never have agreed to bind myself to 'Laidir's Jackal' in the first place." She shrugged. "It's a different culture here. The nobles in Cynestol are far less concerned with the timing of the consummation of a betrothal and far more concerned with honoring the vow while the marriage is in force, however short that may be." She took a deep breath and slid her hands around my neck. "However, if you're worried about Bolt and Rory being truthful . . ."

Our lips parted a moment later and she smiled at me. "There. You just reminded me why I chose you. Come, those excuses will wear thin even here. We need to make some kind of appearance."

I took a step toward the massive wardrobe at the other end of the room and wobbled. "I'm still unsteady on my feet," I said. "People will notice."

Gael laughed, a deep seductive sound. "I'll just remind them that I am physically gifted."

She laughed harder when I gaped at her. "You're not concerned with your reputation?" I asked.

"When we could die any day from dwimor, insane people from the Darkwater, or power-mad clergy within the church?" She shook her head. "I think you're asking the wrong question, my heart. The real question is why do *you* care what people think?"

She had a certain logic to her arguments. After that, I stopped worrying about the opinions of strangers. In truth, I usually didn't. I'd carried any number of names in the past year or so. Jackal, assassin, and peasant-lord were just a few I could repeat in polite company. If the court of Cynestol wanted to label me a deflowerer of women, they would do it with or without my objections.

Better that than have Archbishop Vyne discover us.

Gael helped me dress, and we left our room to make our way back to court—where the assembled frippery of Cynestol nobility waited to press their case for rule to the last Errant. My mind was in better shape than my body, but not by any great amount. I hoped I would be able to delve enough of the nobility to sustain our ruse.

Outside our door, Rory waited, lounging against the far wall in a way that would make anyone think life in Cynestol bored him to death. He fell in beside me after a quick scan up and down the hallway. For the moment, it stood empty.

"What was it about the queen's body that upset you and Bolt?" he asked.

The image of the queen, unclothed and facedown in her coffin rose in my mind. "She broke her neck, but it wasn't any dwimor's doing." I briefly wondered why neither Gael nor Bolt had spoke of this to him, but I couldn't think of any reason he should be left in the dark.

"How could you know that?" Rory pressed.

It took me a moment to remember he'd been guarding the door. He hadn't seen Chora's body. "She had identical cuts above the back of each knee. Deep."

Rory had never shouldered the burden of serving Collum in its wars against Owmead, but he'd picked up a lot of experience on the streets of Bunard. "The killer hamstrung her? Why?"

"That's what I'd like to know," I said, "but I don't think a dwimor would bother with trying to disguise the queen's death as an accident."

Rory shook his head. "But that doesn't make any sense either. For that to work, someone would have had to plan her death ahead of time."

"Possibly," I said. "Or they'd have to possess the resources to improvise on the spot. That means they'd have to remove the queen's body before anyone could see her."

"And then guard the body with the cosp so no one might see how she really died," Gael added, her voice hard.

Rory checked the hall around us, though his physically gifted hearing would have picked up on anyone following. "The Archbishop," he said.

I stopped. "Possibly not." I turned to Gael. "He wasn't close enough to so quickly arrange her death, but the queen's advisor was. He never left her side."

Her eyes narrowed. "Bishop Gehata. But he could be working for Vyne."

I nodded, holding up my hand. "Aer have mercy, I'm tired, but I have to find a way to touch him."

A few moments later, we arrived at court, Rory preceding us to scan the crowd for any who might not be visible to others. We stepped into the silvered hall and the kaleidoscope it produced. Gael put her hand on my arm. "Speak of evil . . ." she murmured.

I looked up to see Bishop Gehata moving toward us through the crowd, attended by a half-dozen cosp.

"And it appears," I finished.

CHAPTER 29

Bishop Gehata and his attendants came through the crowd, the assembled nobility parting for them like the waves coming off the prow of a ship. The bishop's eyes flicked to Bolt before they resumed inspection of their intended target. Me.

"This can't be good," I said.

I tried to assume a relaxed pose, but the linen binding my wound kept me from taking a deep breath, and the strain of remaining upright made me sweat. Chances were the bishop wouldn't be taken in by any stories of dalliance between Gael and me.

At five paces, I copied the genuflections the rest of the nobility offered him, careful to match them exactly. When I straightened he stood before me, almost close enough to touch, but not quite.

"Greetings, Lord Dura," the bishop said. "Lord Rory. Lady Gael," he nodded.

"Bishop Gehata." Gael curtsied with enough grace to make the movements of the cosp look awkward.

The bishop turned a slow circle, catching the eye of the nobles leaning in around us. "I wonder, Lord Dura," he said without looking my way, "if I might have a word with you—privately, of course."

The nobles around us melted away, each finding some reason to be engaged elsewhere. I recognized the expressions they wore—fear, followed by relief—had seen them any number of times in Bunard when Duke Orlan or his wife threatened me.

The bishop's guards encircled us, ostensibly to ensure our privacy in the middle of the throne room, but the space between my

207

shoulder blades started to itch. On the dais, Bolt watched us as he observed court, trapped there by a line of nobles claiming to hold the gift of kings. With the queen's death, Gehata held temporal power in Cynestol, and Errant or no, throne room or not, everyone else submitted to him.

"To what do we owe the honor and pleasure?" Gael said, sliding her arm through mine, a motion that might have been intended to convey protection.

The bishop smiled. "The Archbishop is too ill to attend court. He sends his regrets."

I kept myself from gaping while my heart struggled to free itself from my chest. "The Archbishop is ill? Is it serious?"

Gehata tempered his ever-present smirk. "The Archbishop is old. Every illness is serious." He surveyed the throne room. Most of the nobility shied from his gaze. "How goes the search for the heir?"

Around us, the cosp tightened their ring, edging closer.

If I'd noticed it, Gael couldn't have possibly missed it, but she kept her gaze on Gehata. "I wouldn't know, Your Eminence." She nodded toward the dais. "I will be happy to ask Errant Consto, if you wish." Her arm loosened in mine, but instead of moving away, she shifted her weight to the balls of her feet. No one inside the circle of the bishop's guards could possibly have misinterpreted her stance.

"Hardly necessary," the bishop said. He turned to survey the nobles with amused disdain. "It's doubtful in the extreme he will find the heir here. If one of the nobles present held the gift of kings, I'm sure they would have presented themselves before now. Few of them realize that the last Errant is not the sort of man whose favor can be purchased with a few blandishments and empty promises. They lack the character to comprehend men of absolutes." His gaze landed on me. "Do you know the liturgy, Lord Dura?"

I nodded. "I was one week from taking my orders when the call from my king came to muster for war," I said. "Once I'd spilled blood, the priesthood was denied me."

Gehata shook his head, his smile of condescension plain. "You've been misinformed, Lord Dura. There is no proscription against a man joining the priesthood if he's spilled blood."

I gave the bishop as direct a look as I dared. "Oh, I don't doubt the priesthood has its share of murderers." I paused until the bishop's eyes widened at my affront before I continued. "It was the burden in my heart at killing, Eminence, that kept me from the priesthood. I felt unclean."

He nodded in pretend sympathy, forced from my insult by the frank admission. "It doesn't sound as though you were entering the Absold, Lord Dura.

"No. I never desired any order but the Merum."

"So you do know the liturgy," he pressed.

I bowed my head in admission. "I'm more than passingly familiar with it."

He smiled, but his eyes held all the glittering malice of a viper. "Then you've heard it said not to seek the living among the dead."

I nodded.

He stepped closer, almost close enough for me to touch. "The opposite advice could prove wise as well."

I turned the proverb over in my mind, but shook my head, feigning ignorance in case I was mistaken. "Your Eminence?"

All expression fell from his face. "Don't seek the dead."

The bishop's gaze darted over my left shoulder for the barest fraction of an instant before he plastered his smile back on his face. "Where are my manners?" he said. "I haven't introduced you to my cohort." He nodded toward the man on his right. "This is Lord Forwaithe."

We exchanged handshakes and I felt the strength of his grip through my glove, grinding my knuckles into butter.

"And this is his betrothed," the bishop said with a dip of his head. "Lady Mirren."

She extended her hand toward me, her long delicate fingers reaching. A weight hit me from the side, not hard enough to knock me down, but I was propelled away from the bishop and through his ring of guards.

"Begging your pardon, Eminence," Rory called as he pushed me toward the dais and Bolt, "but Errant Consto demands Lord Dura's immediate presence." Without waiting for a reply, the scrawny little thief pushed me toward my guard so hard I almost fell. Gael had no choice but to follow.

"When we get to the dais," Rory muttered in my ear, "talk to Bolt as if you're being reprimanded."

"What?" I asked. "Why?"

"Brilliant, yah?" Rory hissed. "I'll explain later."

I gave up on trying to resist and instead walked ahead of Rory fast enough to keep him from shoving me. More than a few nobles were laughing at the sight of a skinny adolescent pushing a grown man around. Stopping to insist he explain wouldn't have helped much.

We joined Bolt on the dais, where he sat listening to the petition of a woman clothed in a revealing orange dress. She looked like a half-peeled piece of fruit. I kept my gaze in place, just.

"Lord Dura," Bolt said, "may I present the most recent supplicant to the throne of Cynestol? This is Duchess Naranha."

I reached out to take the proffered hand as Rory slid into view over the Duchess's shoulder, his gaze intent on mine. A moment later I fell through Naranha's light brown-eyed gaze and into her thoughts. Reaching into the stream of memories, I lived the most recent parts of her life, tracing each event back in time until just before Queen Chora had been murdered. Other than a divorce and marriage within the last week, neither of which created memories of strong color, nothing in her mind suggested the duchess had come into the gift of kings.

"It's my honor to meet you, Duchess Naranha," I said after I let go of her hand.

"The pleasure is mine," the duchess said. Turning to Bolt, she nodded. "I trust you will do what is best for Aille, Errant Consto."

"No matter the cost," Bolt said. The edge to his voice caught the duchess's attention for a moment, but when he didn't bother to elaborate, she turned on one heel and rejoined the crowd.

"Boy," Bolt said to Rory in a voice that sounded like rocks breaking. "What in the name of all that's holy would make you show your backside to Bishop Gehata? You've just made a very powerful enemy."

Rory leaned in to whisper his answer, his hands cupped on both sides of his mouth.

"Can you hear them?" I asked Gael.

"No." She shook her head. "I think that's the point."

Bolt's squint, his usual expression, departed for a moment before I saw him force it back into place.

"*Kreppa*," he whispered. He stood to address the rest of the court. "Friends, I hope you'll excuse me until this evening. There are matters I must attend to."

Instead of leaving by the main entrance, he guided us out the back, through the kitchens, taking turns at random in the hallways beyond until we found our way to the outer wall. We circled around, back to our quarters. By the time we got there, spots of fatigue danced in front of my eyes. Once we were inside, I collapsed into a chair as Bolt threw the bar on the door.

"Here, Willet," Gael said handing me a glass of wine and a water-skin. "You need a drink. The loss of blood is making you weak."

"Among other reasons." I looked at Bolt and Rory. "Things are worse than I know, aren't they?"

They both nodded.

"The Archbishop isn't just sick," Bolt said. "Rory overheard Gehata speaking to someone before he headed to you. Vyne had a stroke, and he's not waking up."

I held out the empty wine glass to Gael. "I think I'm going to need a refill. I can tell by the way they're looking at me that there's more."

"Tell him," Bolt said to Rory.

"When Gehata came into court, he had six of the cosp with him."

"I noticed," I said. "It was kind of hard to miss since the bishop seemed intent on letting everyone know he could ring me with steel if he wanted." I shook my head. "Bullies are the same everywhere."

"I don't think that was why he did that," Rory said. "One of them wasn't right."

"What do you mean?"

"Only five of those guards were physically gifted," Rory said. "The one standing to your left was just an ordinary woman. I could tell by the way she moved."

"Lady Mirren?"

"Yah. Twice, when the guards closed in, she came within a hair's breadth of touching you. Then, when the bishop introduced her, you were wearing your gloves, but she extended her fingers so that she would have touched your skin."

I replayed the scene in my mind, as closely and exactly as my memory would allow. "Did you see her touch anyone else?"

Rory nodded. "When the servant brought Gehata wine, she made a point of sipping from his glass before giving it to him. She made sure to touch the servant."

"Nobody suspects foul play so quickly as the guilty," Bolt muttered.

"That's why you were watching me delving Duchess Naranha," I said.

Rory nodded. "You're better at it than she is, but whenever you delve someone the blacks of your eyes get bigger for an instant. Mirren's eyes got bigger than yours when she touched the servant."

I took a deep breath. "Do we have any way of getting word to Pellin or Toria Deel?"

Bolt shook his head. "Not without a scrying stone, and the Archbishop surrendered his."

I tried not to get angry, again, that the Chief of Servants had kept her scrying stone at Pellin's behest instead of surrendering it to me. I failed. Now, their suspicion had put us in danger. "Maybe there's another way," I said. "What about Chora's? If we can get to her stone, we might be able to get word to the rest of the Vigil."

He sighed. "We can ask the chamberlain. He should have it safeguarded, but that will only put us in touch with the other monarchs."

"We need to contact them anyway," I said. "The threat of the dwimor against the monarchs is real, even if that's not exactly what happened here."

"How can you be certain?" Rory asked.

"Fair question," I nodded. "And I wasn't until tonight. The bishop favored me with a twisted quote from the liturgy to threaten me, something along the lines of 'Why seek the living among the dead.' That, coupled with the soldiers guarding the queen's body, paints a picture."

"So there never was a dwimor?"

I shook my head. "No, I think there was, but I think it was spotted, perhaps killed. Then I think Gehata used the presence of the dwimor as a cover to kill Chora. Knowing Vyne's health was failing, the opportunity to take control of the Merum church and Aille was probably irresistible." I shrugged. "It's a theory anyway."

"What do you want us to do, Willet?" Bolt asked.

I checked his expression for signs of sarcasm, but he seemed in earnest. "Me? You're the last Errant."

"But I don't hold the gift of domere. You do. Whoever Lady Mirren really is, she holds the gift—Laewan's or Jorgen's. This takes precedence over the search for the heir, and she's your responsibility. You have to train her." He shook his head at the look on my face. "There's no one else."

"You're assuming we can get to her," I said. "If you think Gehata is guarding Chora's body closely, what's he going to do with someone who can see into the mind of his enemies?"

My guard shrugged. "I didn't say it would be easy."

"Easy?!" My voice scaled up an octave. "It's going to be difficult enough to make getting to Chora look like a child's game in comparison. We were too late to keep Cesla from killing Queen Chora—so that's off the table. Our most important priority is to find the heir." I stopped without bothering to say I still didn't know why Cesla had wanted to kill the queen. Her death wouldn't guarantee a fight for the throne or a disruption in the fight for the Darkwater.

"Has he always been like this?" Bolt asked Gael.

She smiled. "Perhaps you should ask Rory. I've only known him for a little over a year."

Rory took the exchange literally. "No. He used to be a lot calmer before he got involved with the Vigil, yah?"

"You all know I'm standing right here, don't you?" I said. But Bolt was right. It didn't matter that we already had one impossible task on our plate. Now that I'd had the chance to think about it, we had to bring Mirren into the Vigil. "Do you think Bishop Gehata is still in the throne room?"

"Doubtful," Bolt said. "'Once you've won the battle it's time to quit the field.'"

It wasn't one of his best. "Rory, I want you to follow the bishop and Lady Mirren. See where they go."

"No," Bolt said. "He's your guard against the dwimor, or do I need to remind you that I can't see them?"

I spread my hands. "You just told me I have to bring her in. How did you think we were going to find out where Gehata is keeping her? Our resources here are pretty limited."

I was happy to see him look at me in disgust. That's how I knew I'd won the argument. "Go," he said to Rory. "No unnecessary risks."

"Me?" Rory asked.

"You. This time use my definition of risk, not yours."

The little thief slipped out of the room, careful to close the door behind him.

CHAPTER 30

Bolt sighed. "The nobles will be expecting us back in the throne room for the evening meal." He looked at Gael. "You'll have to lead the way. With Rory gone, you have a better chance of spotting an assassin than Willet or I."

Rory gone. Those two words made me feel naked and I almost laughed out loud at the insanity of a world where I depended on the eyes and knives of an erstwhile thief for safety. I looked at Bolt and Gael. "We need an ally."

My guard snorted. "An ally?" he asked. "As in only one?"

I nodded. "If he's the right one, that's all we'll need."

Bolt pointed at my face. "You've got that look again, the one that says you're considering something foolish." He turned to Gael. "One of the reasons I agreed to let you help me guard him was because I thought you'd be able to curb impulses like this. You're a disappointment. Aer have mercy, these ideas of his make my stomach hurt."

Gael smiled and lifted one eyebrow. "You thought that? I'm a woman, not a miracle worker."

"You haven't even heard my idea yet," I said.

"I don't have to hear it," he shot back. "You've got that look on your face that says you're about to take a very large risk and you'll want our help with it."

"If he's going to do it," Gael said, "it's probably better for you to know what 'it' is."

"What are the odds Rory is going to track Mirren right back to the cathedral?" I asked.

Bolt shrugged. "Better than half."

"To put it conservatively," I added. "And once he gets there, that's all he'll learn. All we'll know is that Gehata has her somewhere under his thumb and so well-guarded we won't be able to get anywhere near her."

Bolt nodded, his gaze speculative. "All true. You still haven't gotten to the part that's going to give me the flux."

"We need someone who can walk the halls, all of the halls, of the cathedral with impunity." I ignored the look on Bolt's face. "That gives us two choices," I said. "Bishop Serius or Lieutenant Hradian."

"Serius," Gael said. "He practically worships the last Errant."

"He might already know where Mirren is kept," I said, rubbing my chin. "All we would have to do is get her out."

Bolt looked at me with disgust. "When you rub your chin like that it creates the illusion you've thought this through. Gehata knows Mirren holds the gift of domere, and he probably learned that from Archbishop Vyne." He pointed one of his stubby fingers at my chest. "That makes it a pretty safe roll of the bones that he knows you hold the gift as well." He shook his head. "If we were smart we'd leave Cynestol and let Gehata rule."

"You jest," Gael said.

My guard shook his head. "The history of the north covers a long and lurid day, girl. A bad person doesn't necessarily make a bad king just like a good person won't necessarily make a good one." He looked at me. "None of those people in the throne room hold the gift of kings. Court has become a waste of time."

I nodded, finding fault in nothing he'd said. "Do you think Gehata already knows the person possessing the crown of Aille and is holding them prisoner?"

"It's a better than good possibility," Bolt said. "A dwimor didn't kill Chora. Someone hamstrung her to make her fall. For all we know she might have survived long enough to pass her gift before they finished her off to make it look good. Gehata might have arranged as much."

Gael took a breath. "She might not have had time to pass on the gift."

"Even if she didn't," I said, "the rightful heir is out there somewhere and you want to run?" I asked Bolt.

He shook his head. "Gehata has the city sewn up tight. He's got the church and the cosp and the gift of domere under his thumb."

I nodded. "You're right. We should leave." I ignored Gael's look of disbelief and the subtle shift in Bolt's countenance that suggested hope. "The only problem is that we can't."

"Why not?"

"Because whether the dwimor was successful or not, Cesla *was* trying to kill Chora. Ealdor said we would know how to stop him by what he attacked. What was it about Chora that threatened him?"

"You mean besides commanding the largest army of the northern continent?" Bolt asked.

"Yes, besides that," I said. "Vyne is the real power here. You said so yourself and Cesla would have known that. He'd already agreed to send the army north." I waved my arm at what I hoped was a northerly direction. "Their forces were already gone when Chora was attacked. Stopping it couldn't have been Cesla's goal."

"So," Bolt asked, "what was?"

I sat down. "I don't know. Something else."

"If we stay here, sooner or later Bishop Gehata is going to scoop us up in his net and make us disappear," Bolt said. "The fact that I'm the last Errant won't save me. If he knows you're with the Vigil, you're his biggest threat. Searching for that 'something else' sounds like a good way to end up dead."

"What about finding the rightful heir?" I asked.

"Not my problem anymore," Bolt said. "My loyalty to the Vigil precedes that request. My job is to keep you alive."

I nodded. "And what's my job?"

He opened his mouth to speak, though I already knew what he was about to say. "Curse you," he muttered. "It's like you planned the whole conversation to force me to say it. Alright, confound your stupid, stubborn hide, I'll say it. Your job is to fight the Darkwater."

"And to do that, we need as many Vigil members as we can get."

"You can't do that job if you're dead!"

"Then let's persuade Serius to get us into the cathedral," Gael said.

"You're supposed to be my apprentice," Bolt said to her, "not his. You're picking up bad habits."

She nodded. "Inevitable, I suppose."

We returned to court and took our place on the dais next to the empty throne we were trying to fill. For hours we listened to the pleas, impassioned or logical, of nobles vying for Bolt's blessing to take the throne, and I swam in the thoughts and memories of each, but my own thoughts were west, in the cathedral with Rory. Bolt adjourned court at midnight, and we returned to our rooms.

Rory was waiting for us. "I came here instead of court," the thief said.

"Why?" I asked.

He smiled at my ignorance. "One way to make sure people notice you've been missing is to show up late."

"Well?" Bolt asked.

Rory shrugged. "Mostly what you expected. Gehata and his soldiers took a carriage back to the cathedral. I followed on foot." He laughed. "There's so much traffic in this city, I could tail anyone and they'd never see me. I don't think I had to break into a run more than half a dozen times."

"That's it?" Bolt asked.

Rory nodded. "I tracked them around to the south side of the cathedral where they left the carriage and entered through an entrance guarded by a dozen of the cosp. I couldn't follow, so I came back here."

"The south side?" Bolt asked. "You're sure?"

Rory nodded. "Gehata and everyone from his entourage entered, and all the cosp guarding it followed them inside."

"You saw this?" Bolt asked. "The whole time?"

"I said so, yah?"

Bolt turned to me. "Delve him. It'll be quicker."

Rory shrugged and held out his arm. I'd already been through half a dozen sets of memories, and the mental fatigue coupled with my injury made me long for bed, but Bolt's curiosity fired my own.

I dropped through his eyes and into the memories of his run through the streets of Cynestol, moving forward in time until I came to the point where Gehata's carriage stopped in front of a pair of heavy double doors at the base of the cathedral and disembarked before entering. Three of the guards, swords bare, hopped down from the top and sides of the carriage, while the other three and the bishop disembarked. I knew what I was seeing, but I traced Rory's memory back and forth twice, searching for details.

The doors on the south side of the cathedral were heavy, insanely thick, and horizontally banded with iron in half a dozen places. I'd seen their kind before, but not on churches and certainly not on the entrance we'd used upon coming into the city. It seemed a prison more than a place of worship.

I came out of his mind. "Mirren rode in the carriage with Gehata, not on the outside."

Bolt squinted at me. "What happened when the carriage stopped? Tell me exactly what the guards did."

"They formed up around Gehata and escorted him inside," I said.

"Rory?" Bolt asked.

He nodded.

"If Gehata was concerned about her escape," Bolt said, "wouldn't they have formed up around her?"

I nodded as I searched Rory's memories again. "She still had her weapon. Even if she's not gifted, Gehata wouldn't have allowed it unless he was sure of her."

"Which brings us to the question," Bolt said with a sigh.

"Who is Gehata holding prisoner?" Gael asked.

"It appears we'll be staying in Cynestol after all," Bolt said. "Tomorrow, before court opens, we'll approach Serius and petition him for his aid."

"Only after I delve him," I said. "I have no intention of blindly trusting anyone outside of this room."

Gael favored Bolt with her most winsome smile. "You see. He's learning discretion already."

"Humph. Let's see if it sticks. You know what they say—'Good habits are hard to keep and bad ones are hard to break.'"

CHAPTER 31

I woke at the first ray of dawn, sweat drenched and gasping from exertion. I reached up, felt Bolt's arms pinning me against the sheets. I muttered something uncomplimentary, but the curse wasn't for Bolt and he knew it. He moved away to stand by the bed.

"It's a big city, Willet. "There's bound to be a murder some nights."

I was winded, but I didn't feel the bone-numbing exhaustion that came with most of my night-walks. "When did I try to leave?"

"About an hour ago."

A weight settled into my soul, or maybe I just became aware again of a burden that never left. "I wonder who died," I said. "What did they find waiting for them on the other side of eternity?"

"I hope we never know," Bolt said.

When I looked at him in surprise, he held up a hand. "I only meant that I hope it's a stranger who's been killed—unrelated to our investigation. We have enough on our plate."

The door to Gael's room was still closed, as was Rory's. I tried to force a measure of levity into my voice. "What shall we do today, Errant Consto?"

He looked at me with all the warmth he might spare for a weevil in his porridge, only southerners didn't really eat porridge. Perhaps the squint of mild disgust would have been for a fly in his wine.

I didn't have the opportunity to ask. From the direction of the cathedral across the city, I heard the tolling sound of heavy iron bells. The color drained from Bolt's face but his reserve never deserted him.

Dread hollowed me out from the inside. I knew what the bells meant. "Archbishop Vyne is dead."

A nod. "Bound to happen. He was old, and old men don't usually recover from a stroke."

He didn't say what we both had to be thinking. "It could be a coincidence," I said. "In a city this size, it's almost certain to happen that a murder would happen on any given night. It doesn't prove someone killed the Archbishop."

Bolt looked at me without blinking. "I can't get this picture out of my head of someone—Gehata or one of his cosp—holding a pillow over that poor man's head. The bishop doesn't strike me as a patient sort of man."

I sighed. "They will assemble all of the Merum bishops so the council can choose the next Archbishop. The trip south from Collum and Frayel will take weeks."

Bolt nodded. "How many of the Archbishops have come from Cynestol?"

He couldn't help but know, but I answered him anyway. "Most," I said. "That's all the more reason to get to Bishop Serius and put an end to this."

Something that had been bothering me about the events in the throne room the previous evening clicked into place—at least I thought so. I turned to Gael. With her practiced eye, she would have noticed. "Mirren," I said.

"What about her?" Gael asked.

"Tell me everything you noticed about her in the throne room."

Gael closed her eyes, and I saw Bolt looking at me with that squint of his that might mean anything from curiosity to irritation. After a moment my betrothed opened her eyes and looked at me with a shrug. "I don't think I noticed anything that you wouldn't have."

I nodded, more confident in my suspicion. "Tell me anyway."

"Alright," Gael said as she started to pace the room. "She's young, older than a decade and a half, but less than a score. She's pretty, but not remarkably so, with a steady gaze and a self-assurance that older women might envy." Gael lifted her hands, conceding. "I don't know what you're looking for, Willet."

"That's alright." I waved. "You've already said it."

Rory lounged near the door, watching our discussion as he spun a dagger on the back of his hand, making it look easy. "How many times did Mirren delve people in the throne room, Rory?"

His shoulders made the trip to his ears and back. "Twice that I saw, but she tried to hit you a couple of times before I got you away."

I shot a glance at Bolt. He was looking at me in expectation.

"How long did each of her delves last?" As much as I wanted to, I didn't add any qualifiers to the question. I didn't want to prejudice his answer.

"About as long as yours, maybe just a bit longer, but she was pretty deft with her touch so it was hard to tell."

I looked at Bolt. "Fess has Bronwyn's gift," I said. "He has to. It came to him as soon as she died."

He nodded. "And we now know Cesla's gift didn't go free. That traitor is still running around with it."

"That leaves only two possibilities," I said. "Either Mirren came into Laewan's gift after Bas-solas, or she came into Jorgen's gift when Fess killed him."

Bolt gave me one solemn nod. "I still need to thank him for that."

"I hope you get the opportunity," I said, "but either way, Mirren is too good."

"What do you mean, Willet?" Gael asked.

Bolt answered for me in a voice raspy enough to peel the bark off a tree. "He means that she could never have learned how to use the gift that well on her own in such a short amount of time." He looked at me with murder in his gaze. "I'm going to kill him this time—mark my words. I should have done it already."

"Kill who?" Rory asked. "Stop talking around the answer and just say it, yah?"

"Volsk," I said. "He's the only one who could have given Mirren the training she needed to keep from breaking her own mind."

"There's another possibility," Gael said. "If Mirren has one of the two missing gifts, couldn't the holder of the other one be her trainer?"

I shook my head. "That just forces the problem back a generation. Who would have trained that person?"

"Maybe Cesla," Rory answered.

"If she were working for Cesla," I said, "she wouldn't be walking around in the daylight."

"Maybe she doesn't have a vault," Bolt said.

"Either way I think I need to have a look inside Mirren's mind."

Bolt's expression turned even more stony than usual. "What are the chances that you'll be able to do that without Mirren or Gehata knowing you've done it?"

"Virtually nil," I said.

He nodded. "Then as soon as you do, you've signed your death warrant. Gehata won't rest until you're dead. What he's done is punishable by death. He's taken the gift of domere and turned it into a tool to exercise his power. If Pellin or Toria Deel were here, they'd put their hands on him and snap his mind like a dry twig. So should you."

He shook his head as if struggling to refocus. "We have to get into the cathedral and persuade Bishop Serius to aid us." He cocked an ear, listening to the bells outside. "The nobles will be gathering at the cathedral to mourn. We should be—"

A thumping at the door that began close to the top and dropped toward the floor interrupted him.

"A servant?" Gael asked.

I moved to rise as Bolt and Rory pulled weapons. "Only if they decided to fall against the door instead of knocking on it," Bolt said. He motioned to Rory. "You stay between me and Willet."

He unbarred the door and opened it just enough to peer through the crack before opening it wide. Hradian lay on the floor, his arms and legs moving as if each of them belonged to a different person.

"Rory!" Bolt snapped. "Is anyone else in the hallway?"

Our thief peered out the open doorway, a knife in each hand before he stepped over the lieutenant's twitching form to check the length of the corridor. He pointed to the left and stepped back as if preparing to run. "I hear someone running."

"Stand!" Bolt said. "They're too far away by now." He motioned Rory back into our quarters as he grabbed one of the lieutenant's arms and dragged him inside.

Hradian peered up at Bolt, his face knotted in confusion. "Errant Consto?"

Bolt lifted the lieutenant and put him on one of the couches. "Delve him."

I was already moving, peeling the gloves from my hands. I placed my fingertips on his brow and tunneled through his brown eyes and into his thoughts, expecting the river of multihued threads that comprised the lieutenant's memories. His current flowed before me, eddying and swirling, agitated. Instead of the distinct colors I'd come to expect when delving, his stream of consciousness held the singular hue of mud. I reached into it for one of the threads that constituted Hradian's most recent memories. Nothing but disconnected impressions came to me, sounds without meaning, smells without context, flashes of multicolored light instead of vision.

Vertigo took me, and I slipped deeper into Hradian's mind, carried along on the tide of memory. A recollection floated past, whole and green like a promise of spring, and I grabbed it. I, Hradian, stood in a line of similarly attired men, all of us gifted, but it was my name that had been called. I stepped forward in response, called to be a successor to the Errants. I would be one of the cosp.

With an effort, I came out of the delve, the room pitching sideways as I straightened. Gael caught me, her face etched with concern, and set me upright. She didn't let go until I nodded.

Hradian still lay on the couch, blinking in puzzlement.

I pointed at his head. "His most recent memories have been scrambled."

"What does his mind look like?" Bolt asked.

"Like a creek that someone stirred from the bottom."

"Will he be alright?"

"He's fine now," I said, "just a little disoriented. He doesn't remember how he got here, so everything seems more than passing strange to him."

Bolt shook his head in resigned disgust. "I guess there's no point in asking who did this. The question is why was Hradian coming to see us?" He turned to me. "Is it possible for you to piece his memories back together?"

I stared at my guard. "Could Pellin do it?"

Bolt shrugged and favored me with a noncommittal nod. "Probably."

I shook my head. "I don't have seven hundred years of experience. I wouldn't even know where to begin." I started for the door. "But as a reeve, I'd find out exactly who came here with him. We're in the queen's palace. You can't cross the hall without bumping into a guard or servant."

We left our rooms and made for the nearest entrance, the south one, where a pair of ceremonial guards with sparkling swords that never needed sharpening stood like tailor's dummies. I nudged Bolt and pointed in their direction. "I think the last Errant has a better chance of getting the truth out of those two than a minor lord from a northern backwater."

I stepped across the grand entrance to a pair of servants who were busy polishing the brass of the candelabra along the wall. I stepped to the side, pretending to focus my attention on the brilliantly colored tapestry to their right. I reached into my purse and dropped a silver half crown on the floor, the quiet ring of the metal pure and sweet against the polished stone.

I bent to retrieve it, but instead of picking it up, I flicked it toward the servants. One of them glanced at me before dropping her polishing cloth over the coin. She made no move to return it to me, but both women had their heads cocked in my direction.

"Beautiful," I gestured toward the tapestry. "A visitor to Cynestol would be so caught up in its detail they might not notice the comings and goings in this very hall."

One of the women, short with close-cropped brown hair, nodded without looking my way. "Aye, Cynestol is full of sights that might distract a visitor."

"But everything becomes commonplace when you're around it long enough," the other woman said. She was thin, with sandy blond hair and hazel eyes.

"True enough," the first woman said, pretending to work a spot on the metal. "They're just things after all. People are more interesting."

I leaned forward to peer at the depiction of a man on horseback, but I jingled my purse with the other hand. "A member of the cosp came to my room," I said. "It would be important to me to know if he passed through this room."

"How important?" the blond-haired woman asked.

I let another half crown drop to the floor and nudged it with my foot, sliding it her way. Without missing a stroke with her cleaning rag she stepped on it while it was still moving.

"Hradian," the woman said. "Hard to miss, that one. Looks like one of the queen's racing hounds, he does."

I nodded. "Was he alone?"

The women said nothing until I relieved my purse of some more of its weight. "No," the shorter one said. "There was a woman with him, young."

I stepped back, letting my gaze run the length of the tapestry and pretended to notice the women at their work for the first time. Before they could respond, I stepped their way, nodding at the mirror-bright candelabra. "You missed a spot." I pointed, letting my finger touch the hand of the shorter woman, the one who'd spoken first.

The room receded as I entered into her memories. I had no need to determine guilt or innocence, just the truth of what she'd told me, but her memory of working in the palace held the tenor of the unfamiliar. As time passed in the delve, faster than the blink of an eye, the merest fraction between heartbeats, I found the memories that confirmed my suspicion. Mirren had been with Hradian.

I searched for the answer to my next question within her mind, but the knowledge wasn't there. Disappointed and unwilling to put her at risk, I turned away, bending to check my boots and pulled a full crown from my purse. I put the coin on the floor next to the brassy metal of the candelabra. "I don't talk to servants," I said.

"True enough, my lord, but thank you." The crown disappeared beneath the cloth and I moved away.

CHAPTER 32

We gathered Hradian and left the palace for the cathedral, hoping to meet with Bishop Serius. The lieutenant retained enough sense to sit a horse, but he rode through the streets of Cynestol with the befuddled look of a man who'd expected it to be night exiting a house at noon.

By the time we arrived at the six-sided monolith that commanded the most dominant order on the continent, his eyes had cleared enough so that he rode his mount with familiarity, if not confidence.

"Hradian," Bolt called as we dismounted in front of the cathedral. "Can you take us to see Bishop Serius?"

His brows furrowed over his long nose, and he nodded, but I could see the makings of a question in his eyes that he couldn't frame. "Why am I doing that?" he asked.

"You came to my quarters," Bolt said. "Do you know what purpose brought you there?"

The lieutenant shook his head. "I remember being in your apartment." He looked at Gael, Rory, and me in turn. "And all of you were there." His gaze rested on me for a moment longer before he turned back to Bolt. "I don't remember how I got there."

Bolt nodded. "What's the last thing you remember before you found yourself on my couch?"

He looked at the cathedral and the sun in confusion. "It was night and I was on my way . . ." His face clenched with the effort of remembering. "I was on my way . . ." He shook his head. "I was on my way somewhere, somewhere important." He tapped his chest. "I can feel it here."

226

"Can you take us to Bishop Serius?" Bolt asked again. "I think he might know."

Hradian nodded, but lines etched his face as he struggled to piece the memory of his purpose together. "This way," he said, his voice hollow with abstraction. "The offices of the bishops occupy the eastern wall so that they can watch the sunrise each morning."

He led us through an entrance imposing enough to make a full squad of soldiers feel small, and we walked an open-air corridor constructed of archways that surrounded most of the cathedral. We came to a set of doors at the middle of the east-facing wall and traversed a broad hallway that connected to another corridor running from north to south.

"These are the offices of the leaders of the Merum church," Hradian said. He pointed to the office immediately to our left. "That's the Archbishop's office. He . . ." Hradian stopped. "No, that's not right. The Archbishop is dead." He squeezed his eyes shut—"I knew that"—and shook his head, trying to clear it. "Come." He set off at a crisp walk. "Bishop Serius's office is only a few doors down.

We entered the anteroom of the bishop's office, a high-vaulted space apparently designed to impress upon its occupant their insignificance in the grand scheme of Aer and the church. If so, it succeeded. In the center of the room sat a man of more than middle years dressed in the red of the Merum order, writing. The scratching noise of his quill reached us despite the distance.

Bolt stepped forward to the edge of the table and waited. Gael, Rory, and I stood behind him while Lieutenant Hradian walked the perimeter of the room, his eyes hooded and confused. After another moment, the man raised his head, showing no recognition of the last Errant.

"Yes?"

Bolt bowed from the waist until his torso paralleled the floor, a gesture I'd never seen him make before. "Errant Consto seeks an audience with Bishop Serius."

The man rose and nodded. "I will see if the bishop is accepting visitors." He disappeared through the door behind his desk, only to reappear a moment later.

"The bishop will be with you shortly, Errant Consto," the secretary said. "If you will excuse me, I have an errand to attend to." Without a glance for the rest of us, he departed, closing the door behind him.

Rory was the first of us to speak. "Have you ever felt someone *not* looking at you?"

Gael nodded. "He had his eyes locked on the door the moment he came out from the office."

Behind me, I heard Hradian muttering. "Was I here? Is this where I was?"

Bolt growled an oath and crossed to the exit. "Locked from the other side," he growled. "Quickly," he ordered, "into Serius's office. They'll be coming for us."

We darted the length of the room and into the bishop's expansive quarters. Bookshelves of rich, silver-gilded wood lined each of the four walls, their contents filled with books and scrolls of every imaginable description. In front of a pair of arched windows stood a solitary desk, three paces wide and a pace deep, with a heavily padded chair in red behind it.

Where Serius sat staring blankly at us.

"Rory, lock the door and find some way to wedge it closed," I said.

I didn't bother to wait for Bolt's encouragement or permission but crossed over to the bishop and entered his mind, touching him just long enough to see the disruption to his memories. Less than a heartbeat later, I came out. "Mud," I said, "just like I saw in Hradian's mind. Mirren's been a busy girl."

"You've got to put his memories back together," Bolt ordered. "With Vyne dead, this man is our best chance for stability in the Merum order."

I shook my head. "I can't do what I don't know how to do. You've been with me the entire time I've held the gift. You know I can't do this."

"Mirren's newer to the gift than you are," Bolt said, "and she managed to destroy them."

"What's easier, breaking a bone or healing it?" I asked.

The sound of men flooding into the room beyond, curtailed whatever answer he might have made.

Rory crossed over to the window casement and swung the lever that opened the windows. "This way," he said.

Bolt nodded. "Go."

I caught a glimpse of Rory's fluttering cloak as he dropped out of sight. The sound of a key turning in the lock behind us accompanied his departure. Gael crossed over to the casement and looked down. "It's too high," she said. "Willet can't make the jump."

Bolt shook his head. "He can if we catch him. Now go!"

The fall lifted her hair, giving the impression that she didn't jump so much as flew. Then she was gone. The chair Rory had used to block the door shifted and cracked as the men on the other side hit it with their weight. Bolt crossed over to the window and leaned out of it, but instead of jumping, he closed the casement.

"What are you doing?"

"It's too far. When you're as old as I am, your bones can snap like dried twigs."

I didn't bother to look out the window. I knew he was lying to me. A pair of thumps sounded from the far side of the door and the frame of the chair wedged beneath the lever cracked. "If you leave, the three of you will have a better chance of rescuing me."

His shoulders shifted beneath his tunic, but he didn't make any move to draw his sword. "I don't break my vows."

With the cracking sound of a drumstick in the jaws of a hound, the chair gave way and cosp filled the room, but when they saw Hradian standing there, they stopped, momentarily confused.

Bishop Gehata, standing behind a row of gifted soldiers, snapped his fingers in our direction. "Take them, all of them." He pointed at me. "Take care with that one. Don't harm him, but don't allow him to touch you."

"Arms up," one of the soldiers in front gestured with his weapon.

Hradian shook himself like a dog coming up out of the water. "I came here." He nodded. "Something had happened to . . ." He turned to Bishop Gehata. "You did something."

"Take the lieutenant as well." Gehata pointed at Hradian. "His mind has been corrupted somehow. Perhaps we can heal him."

Rough hands relieved me of my sword and daggers, even the one I kept hidden in my boot. I tried to think of some way of getting my hands onto one of Gehata's men, but the bishop kept his gaze fixed on them, as if they might turn into vipers any second. One of the guards unbuckled Bolt's sword and pulled a foot and a half of the steel from the scabbard, his gaze appreciative.

Bolt leaned forward, his expression flat. "Be mindful of that. I'm going to want it back."

Gehata nodded. "Who knows, Errant? Perhaps you will find yourself in a position to use it again." He backed toward the door. "I think it would be better if we continued this discussion in a more private location." He spared a glance for Bishop Serius, still at his desk staring blankly at the scene before him in incomprehension. "We wouldn't want to disturb the bishop from his contemplations."

I sucked air to make a retort, but Bolt stepped on my foot and shook his head. The cosp took us to a set of stairs at the southern end of the cathedral. They must have sent runners ahead to clear the way, because we didn't see a soul on the way down.

We descended until we were below ground level, the passageways growing progressively damper with each descent. Lieutenant Hradian was the first to be interred, and then we descended down another level and the guards stopped in front of a cell. Gehata pointed at me, and a quartet of sword points came to rest against my chest.

"I have far too much respect for your abilities, Errant Consto, to allow you any heroics." He nodded toward the cell. "In you go."

I saw my friend consider for a moment, and I knew he would be calculating speed and distance for each man he would need to kill and how much damage he could take to himself and still succeed. At the last, with a small indifferent shrug, he entered the cell, but his gaze held threats and promises for Gehata.

We resumed our trek, descending yet another flight of stairs into the bowels of the cathedral. "May I lower my arms?" I asked. "My shoulders are getting tired."

Gehata laughed. "How very civil of you, Lord Dura." He gave me a fluttering wave, and the guards put a circle of naked steel around me. "And here I'd been led to believe you were brash, ruthless, and defiant, even to your own detriment."

I gestured to the halls of monolithic stone surrounding us. "Putting each of us on a different level of the cathedral prison seems a bit extreme."

Gehata shrugged, but in the flickering torchlight I could see his self-indulgent smile. "There's no point in allowing you to confer if I can prevent it. I'm a cautious man. The cathedral contains nine levels to serve as places of interment for those the church considered dangerous, a holdover from the Order Wars."

"Am I dangerous, then?"

Gehata smiled, but his eyes no longer held the pleasure of a moment before. "Immeasurably so, Lord Dura. You surely must realize by now that I'm aware of your gift."

I nodded. "It seems strange that you would take me prisoner, given the church's tradition of allowing autonomy for us."

His smile grew until it became predatory. "The church has made many mistakes concerning your kind, as well as in other matters— mistakes that I intend to rectify."

At his signal we stopped at the threshold of a cell with a puddle on the floor in front of its door. "My mistake," I said. "I thought you were ambitious. Now I discover you're insane."

He laughed at me with something akin to genuine mirth. "Me? You accuse me of being insane? Why, Lord Dura, you've found a jest to lighten my heart. Almost I'm tempted to spare you and keep you by my side to ease the burden of rule."

One of the cosp unlocked the door, and the sword points around me shifted position to force me into the empty cell. "Lovely accommodations," I said, "but you forgot the rats."

Evidently, Bishop Gehata's need for conversation had run dry. The heavy timbers with their barred window slammed shut with the booming echo of a drum. Gehata's light receded until the cell and the corridor turned to pitch. I waited for my eyes to adjust, but the Merum prison was utterly lightless.

I walked my cell, too far below any food source to harbor rats or spiders or other vermin, and obviously beneath some portion of Cynestol's water table. Over half my steps created a soft splash. The farthest corner from the door must have been slightly elevated. While not dry, it didn't hold water the way the rest of the cell did. I huddled to preserve my warmth and gave myself to contemplation of Gehata's threat.

He'd mentioned sparing me, but the context said plainly that he had no intention of doing so. I laughed softly. Even a village idiot could have figured out what Gehata intended. It might not work. I didn't know enough about the seventh gift, the gift of domere, to know whether it would pass on to whomever was closest at my death or whether it would ignore them and go free.

I hoped it would be the latter. The prospect of living in a world where Aer allowed the wicked a free hand in corrupting His plan bothered me more than a little. From somewhere in my past, before

I'd been diminished by war and the duties of a reeve, came a prayer for the lost. I recited it even as questions of its intention swirled in my mind. Just who was I praying for? Myself? The Vigil? Serius or Gehata? In the end, I couldn't decide. It occurred to me that any of us met the requirements.

I stood, my hand tracing its way up the damp stone of my prison. Since I had no intention of trying to measure my cell as precisely as Volsk had done in Bunard—I was weak in the mathematicum anyway—I gave myself to thoughts of escape.

Gael and Rory had fled, and it was barely possible that they might find a way to sneak into the prisons of the cathedral and free me. Possible, but unlikely in the extreme. My best chance of escape lay along one of two different paths, both only slightly less unlikely. First, I could try to deceive Gehata into believing I was more valuable alive. Chuckles welled up in me at the thought. In my entire life I'd been able to deliver a successful lie less than a handful of times. I was that bad at it. Even if I told Gehata the truth of how the gift of domere had come to me, of how Elwin had refused Iselle's touch so that he could give the gift to me, I doubted I would be believed.

My other option lay in attacking him from an unexpected direction. Bishop Gehata meant to kill me slowly enough to allow my gift to pass into him or one of his choosing, but the bishop would almost surely have Mirren delve me first. He'd already tried, and his hunger for power implied an equally voracious appetite for knowledge.

After Elwin had been killed, I'd managed to deceive Laewan into thinking my mind was empty by locking my memories away. It had been a gamble I probably should have lost, and I'd survived by the slimmest of margins. Attempting the same ruse here would only get me killed that much quicker. If Gehata thought my mind was empty, he would open an artery in my arm or leg or throat and wait for the gift to flee my dying body.

I needed another way. In my mind I replayed the steps I'd taken to my captivity and tried to determine in which direction the Everwood Forest lay. It probably didn't matter, but I turned a slow circle with my eyes closed, hoping to feel some tug within me when I faced it. After a moment, I stopped.

"Ealdor," I called. "I need you." A moment passed, and I had the opportunity to compare the cadence of my heartbeat to the dripping of water in my cell. "Please. No one's here to teach me." I looked around. Perhaps with enough imagination my cell would transform itself into a church. It shouldn't be too hard. It was dark, and Gehata had entombed me in the bottom of the Merum cathedral.

I lifted my hands and began the Exordium.

CHAPTER 33

As I finished the Exordium I waited . . . in silence.

"Gehata means to kill me, Ealdor. Please."

Desperation sharpened my voice to an edge. "You're fairly capricious about when you choose to honor your vows." But even as I said it I knew I wasn't being fair. He had come to me several times when it wasn't within the rules. Doing so had resulted in his diminishment. He no longer inhabited the physical world. My friend had been reduced to nothing more than a wounded shadow.

Grief snuffed my anger like a chill wind extinguishing a candle. "Forgive me, my friend," I said to no one, "for asking for more than you could give."

I made my way to the door of my cell, my feet splashing the puddle of water, and peered through the bars. Not the slightest hint of light intruded upon the darkness. I concentrated on blinking a few times to ensure my eyes were open. In the silence of my cell it occurred to me that I had seen Ealdor for the last time, either by his death or mine.

A fresh tide of mourning, with its brackish taste, poured through me. Desperate, I almost laughed. Hope had died, and I would probably follow in short order. Here at the end, like those I'd accompanied in the house of passing, I would beg Aer for my life.

I raised my hands and began the antidon, the words familiar through long practice. "Aer, Iosa, and Gaoithe, we commend your servant, Willet Dura—me—into your care, and pray that you would bring him into the company of those that have passed before. From darkness, let him pass into light. From death, let him pass into life."

I stopped, the rest of the prayer turning to ashes on my lips. Aer knew the antidon better than I possibly could. He'd heard it more times than I could reckon. "Aer, I need to live. Help me to find a way to beat Gehata and the forest. Please."

I can't say I felt joy, but an odd reassurance stole over me. I had done what I could. My life and that of my friends and countrymen were in the hands of all-powerful Aer, but He had given me the mind of a reeve so that I could have some hand in the fight.

In the tales, the heroes never have to sit around and wait for very long. My story should have swept to its thrilling conclusion, the hero fighting and winning against insurmountable odds. Water dripped behind me, the plop of each little splash mocking my imprisonment.

"Stupid fables," I said, but it was just as well I had to wait. I needed a way to survive. I bowed my head and relived every conversation I'd ever had about the gift of domere, searching.

Gehata's men would enter my cell with their sword points out front, while one of them bound and covered my hands. Then Mirren would delve me for whatever information Gehata might find useful.

After Mirren delved me, one of the guards, or perhaps Gehata himself, would open me with a dagger and let me bleed to death, allowing time for my gift to find its way to a new owner.

After Mirren delved me.

There had to be something I could do, some way to fight.

When I had delved Barl, one of the lost souls who'd gone to the forest, black threads had leapt for me within his mind, pinning me, making me, the delver, powerless. If I could do the same to Mirren, I could trap her mind within mine. Before I released her, I could force her will to my own, turning her against Gehata.

I smiled, a lost gesture in the darkness of my cell, but the expression evaporated. The knowledge of how to take Mirren's mind captive might have been written somewhere within the Vigil library, but Custos had disappeared. There were no rats in my cell, but desperation ate at me just as effectively. Without knowledge or intuition on how to fight Mirren's gift, I had no recourse except to hide the knowledge Gehata wanted.

Retreating within my mind, I entered the sanctum of the Merum library in Bunard once more and prepared a door behind which I would place every memory from the last year. Before Mirren entered my mind, I would lock the memories away, denying their knowledge to Bishop Gehata. I knew the gesture to be a feeble one. It wouldn't keep me alive, but I had nothing else I could do.

My imminent death clarified my desires. I stood and lifted my arms in benison, and I appealed directly to Aer. "'The six charisms of Aer are these: for the body, beauty and craft; for the soul, sum and parts; for the spirit, helps and devotion. The nine talents of man are these: language, logic, space, rhythm, motion, nature, self, others, and all. The four temperaments of creation are these: impulse, passion, observation, and thought. Within them all and the gift of domere are found knowledge and wisdom. Know and learn.'"

I finished the liturgy of the rite of haeling and sat, resigned, if not exactly peaceful. In the end, the battle was Aer's. If I could have carried the burden of saving our world from the poison of the Darkwater, then Aer, Iosa, and Gaoithe wouldn't have needed to touch the world they'd made.

Did I believe that?

In the dark with doubt gnawing at my spirit, I couldn't say. Any number of points within the proverbs of the liturgy proclaimed His control, and churchmen recited it every day to console or congratulate those souls who'd been denied or received a gift.

How far was I willing to go in those beliefs? Would I be able to surrender my will to survive?

I don't know how long I pondered those questions, wavering between certainty and disbelief, but at some point in my deliberation I heard the irregular footsteps of men in the distance. A moment later, I saw the yellow bobbing of lantern light coming toward my cell. I genuflected and made the sign of the intersecting arcs on my forehead.

Did I believe?

Keys rattled in the lock and the door swung open. I would have laughed at how prescient I'd been in my imaginings had I not been about to die. A half-dozen guards with their weapons leveled at my chest squeezed into the confines of my cell, their sword points a hairsbreadth from my tunic or touching it. I tried not to breathe too deeply. One of the guards came forward with a thick leather bag and a length of stout cord.

I didn't bother to argue or fight. Instead, I extended my hands in front of me and watched as the guard covered and bound them, removing the only weapon I had. Bishop Gehata and Mirren stood outside in the hallway, illuminated by a pair of lanterns on either side. I watched as Mirren stripped the gloves from her hands.

"You've returned sooner than I expected," I said to Gehata.

"Sooner?" He smiled. "It's the sixth hour of the night."

I shrugged. "You know what's written in the proverbs as well as I. 'A thousand days is as a breath.'"

He laughed. "And 'the coming of Aer catches fools unaware.'"

I met his gaze with my own, for once deadly serious. "So it does."

His smile wilted a bit at the corners, turning to a sneer of disdain. "Find what you can, Mirren, and then break his mind."

I had hoped she might refuse, that such cold-blooded murder would be the line she refused to cross, but she stepped forward, her hand cupped and raised to my face as if she meant to offer me a caress.

I closed my eyes before she made contact. Panic prowled through my mind like a wounded animal in a trap, desperate for escape. I felt the touch of her skin, and reflexively I retreated into the depths of my construct. Powerless.

I stood in the sanctum of the Merum library in Bunard, somewhat surprised at Custos's absence. The trestle table stood in the middle of the room with a broad taper on it that gave light, but the shelves and nooks were devoid of books or parchments. In my panic, I must have put them away.

A woman, hardly more than a girl, stood before me, gazing around the room in surprise. Her eyes were a deep green, not quite olive, but more akin to the color of the sea beneath clouds. She'd pulled her ash-blond hair back in the style of the cosp, but she wore no sword.

No sword. In her mind, she didn't see herself as a soldier of the cosp.

"Greetings, Mirren."

Her eyes widened. "You can talk to me?"

I nodded. "If one is aware of the gift and expecting it, they can converse. I have a good friend who showed me how."

She shook her head. "Where are your memories?"

I gestured to the walls of the sanctum, lined with doors. "Locked away."

Her mouth pursed. "Do you think that will save you from me? From him?"

"No," I said. "He means to have my gift. It may be as close to him as a dagger thrust, or not, but even if he is denied, he still means to see me dead."

She stepped toward me, and I felt pressure within my mind.

"Do you know why you have the gift?" I asked.

Mirren nodded. "Aer willed it."

"Yes. Why do I have it?"

Her face darkened. "Most of those memories were denied to me, but I learned enough. You have it because you took it from a dying man."

She looked at me as if she expected me to deny it. "True enough, but I never wanted it, Mirren. I never desired to be able to see into the minds of others. How many times has it brought you joy to look into the hearts of those around you?"

She didn't answer, but her brows knotted.

"Has Bishop Gehata allowed you to touch him?" I asked.

"It's forbidden."

I didn't laugh. The pressure on my mind reminded me that despite being in my construct, Mirren could destroy me. "I don't recall reading that in the liturgy anywhere as an acolyte."

"You're a priest?" Her eyes widened enough to lighten their dark green.

I nodded. "Most of the Vigil are—though I was a week from taking my vows when my king conscripted me into the war."

Instead of mollifying her anger, my answer intensified it. She stepped toward me. "Betrayers of the faith! The bishop told me what you've done, corrupting your gift for power."

The pressure on my mind increased until it became a stabbing pain, and the doors within my sanctum rippled as if they were nothing more than cloth in the wind. "Stop."

Her fury escalated. "So you can continue to manipulate and lie and kill? Your secrets betray you, Lord Dura. If I cannot bring your deeds to light before I break your mind, you will have to justify yourself to Aer."

"Aer? Is that whom you serve?" She didn't answer. A part of my mind cracked and my thoughts blurred. What did I believe?

I held up a hand in surrender. The pressure didn't ease, but it didn't increase either. "It's yours."

"What's mine?" she asked, pointing at the doors. "You've locked them all away."

238

"The gift," I said. "It came to you freely. It's yours." I either believed what I believed or I didn't. With a mental wrench of effort, I opened all the doors of my sanctum. Light flashed as a lifetime of memories came into existence in the room in the form of books and scrolls, some dusty, others with the ink still wet.

But the pressure on my mind remained. "This won't save you," Mirren said.

"Probably not," I agreed. "But before Gehata kills me, you should know the truth of the man you're condemning." I gestured at the walls. "This is my life. All of it."

Pain lanced through my head. "Do you take me for a fool, Lord Dura?" she snarled. "I can't absorb your entire life without breaking my mind. I know that."

I nodded in spite of the lights exploding in my head. "Time outside the delve passes far more slowly than it does here." I pointed to a shelf. "My knowledge and memories of the Vigil are there. It only encompasses a few months, but there are connections to my past that you will need for context."

She moved to the indicated case and touched a book, her expression plainly speaking doubt. A flash of light that made my head hurt lit the sanctum, and the book flared with light as Mirren absorbed the memories. I stood too far away to see which one it had been and the organization of my mind couldn't begin to rival Custos's, but she didn't appear impressed.

Mirren moved to the next scroll and showed it to me, her expression grim. I recognized it as the set of memories from my capture by the Vigil and my visit to the prison cells beneath the king's tor in Bunard.

"I was a reeve," I told her. "You won't like what you find in there."

"Tricks," she said shaking her head, but when the scroll flashed, she doubled over, retching.

The pressure vanished, and I walked over to her, bent and clutching her stomach by the case. "I'm sorry, Mirren."

She straightened. "You grieve for me?"

I nodded. "The gift came to you—though it might be as accurate to say that it came *for* you." I pulled another book from the shelf, the next set of memories of my life after the ones she'd just absorbed.

"No." Her blond hair rippled with her refusal.

She could have denied me. I was the one being delved, but when

I held the book out to her, she took it. A flare of memory-light later the book had closed again. I reached for another, but she held up her hand. "It's too much."

"Put them away," I said. "Only keep in your mind what you need. Lock the rest behind doors. You can't absorb my life, but this is only a few months. Even at that, most of my memories are insignificant and can be ignored."

She took the book from my hands with the air of a woman accepting her death.

Inside the delve, half a day might have passed by the time Mirren emptied the shelf. She slumped on the floor, her back against the wall and her knees curled protectively against her body, shaking her head.

"Gehata will see me killed, Mirren. You have to find a way to summon Ealdor," I said.

She gaped at me as if I'd asked her to shoulder the weight of the moon and parade around the cathedral with it. "He doesn't even know me."

I lifted my hands. "It's difficult to determine what the Fayit know. He might. It doesn't matter. Gehata means to have my gift." What did I believe? "I don't think it will go to him, but that will make little difference to me." I pointed at her head. "You have to get my memories and thoughts to the rest of the Vigil." I paused. "I'd like to say they'll know what to do, but they might not."

Mirren looked at me, her head moving slowly from side to side. Then her eyes grew wide. "I've been here too long. Someone is shaking me." Standing, she gave me an inscrutable look that might have held pity or judgment or both. "Put it away." She pointed at the rest of my life lining the walls. "All of it. Leave the barest portion of yourself here," she ordered. "Just the last few moments of your imprisonment."

I tried to smile. I knew what she meant to do. "That won't stop him."

The anger I'd seen in her at the first, returned. "We'll see, Lord Dura."

Pressure, sharp and intense, built against my mind until my thoughts broke and broke again. Darkness grew at the edge of my vision, swallowing the walls of the sanctum, growing until it consumed the shelves, the trestle table, and the candle upon it. And me.

CHAPTER 34

I woke to cold and damp. My hands groped and found stone, wet with the same chill that tightened my legs into cramps. Gehata and Mirren would be coming for me. I tried to play the scene in my head, but my thoughts wouldn't cooperate. They moved, sluggish as a stick floating on the Rinwash.

The bishop would come for me. I nodded. Yes, that felt right, but his men would enter my cell first. They'd come with their sword points out front. Gehata wouldn't take the chance that I might touch one of them and turn him.

Had I?

I shook my head, and my thoughts oozed with the motion, muddy and thick. Had? Was I remembering?

One of them would cover my hands. Then they bound them.

Hints of visions haunted me. No. Gehata hadn't been here yet. I cast further back, remembering my imprisoned isolation in perfect clarity. I needed to live, and for that I needed a plan.

Mirren would delve me for whatever information Gehata might find useful. What would that be? What had Gehata wanted?

I shook my head, but I couldn't reconcile conjectures that felt like memories.

Power. Gehata wanted power.

He wanted the rest of the Vigil. If one of us remained outside of his control, his position as head of the Merum church was precarious at best. It wouldn't take much to convince the rulers to gather their armies and march on Cynestol. And the Darkwater would be left undefended. Thousands upon thousands would venture into the forest like a deluge bringing ruin to the north.

After Mirren delved me, one of the guards, or perhaps Gehata himself, would open me with a dagger and let me bleed to death allowing plenty of time for my gift to find its way to—

I stopped as the barest hint of light shone outside my cell, without no sound. Gehata was coming, but where were his men? The light grew, and I withdrew into the corner of my cell as if I could find some escape there. Fear bubbled through the ruin of my thoughts.

Fight, I told myself. If I couldn't hear the sound of boots, they weren't coming for me in strength. A key turned in the lock.

Only Mirren stood in the hall. I threw up a hand to shield my eyes from the light of her torch, but I didn't attack. Despite the fact that she showed no weapon, fear held me, and I wanted to cower in the corner and beg her to go away. I struggled to think as hints of nightmares and reality blended.

"The fear will fade," she said, "but we have to get out of here. Dawn is less than an hour away."

She held out a gloved hand. I didn't take it, but I managed to step toward her. "We have to get Bolt," I said. I tried to ignore the way my voice quavered.

"And the rest," Mirren added. "The guards will change any minute. If they discover the keys gone, the cosp will fall on us like an avalanche."

"Bolt first," I said. We went up one level, my legs as confident as a newborn colt's, and down the long hallway until we found his cell.

He blinked once in the lantern light and with that simple motion appeared to shed any indisposition of his captivity. "I don't suppose you brought my sword."

"That would have raised questions I couldn't answer," Mirren said. "We have to go back to the lower levels."

I shook my head. My thoughts still wouldn't cooperate. "Why?"

"I told you," Mirren said. "We have to get the others."

Instead of following, Bolt lashed out, grabbing Mirren by the arm. Her mouth opened in a silent cry of pain. She struggled to bring her other hand to bear, striving to touch him, but he caught her by the wrist and a mewing cry whispered from her.

"What did you do to him?" Bolt asked.

"I muddled his thoughts," Mirren said. "Let's go. We don't have time for this."

My guard shook his head. "Where did you learn how to do this?"

"From the man Bishop Gehata took."

"Volsk."

Bolt released Mirren's arm, shoving her toward the stairs. "Run, girl."

We went down the dark rock steps, splashing accumulated water with every other stride, passing the level where I'd been held to the one beneath. In the light of Mirren's lamp it was indistinguishable from the others, but it held the sense of occupation, a hint of warmth or breath that belied the initial impression of emptiness.

Mirren took a dozen steps and opened the door on her right, raising the lamp, but no one ventured forth. "He's weak," she said.

We stepped into the cell and drew in a collective breath. Bolt reached down and lifted Volsk as easily as I would a young child, but his head lolled as if his neck were broken. "He's not weak," Bolt said. "He's dying."

For a moment Peret Volsk's eyes roamed over us, plainly trying to make sense of what he saw. His gaze had been dark to match his hair during his time as apprentice to the Vigil. Now it matched the color of obsidian, set by lurid bruises on his face. Blood discolored his mouth.

I shook my head, confused. "Why would they bother to beat him?"

A coughing sound filled the cell, and Volsk bent with the effort as fresh droplets of crimson stained his lips. No. Not coughing. Laughing.

"Lord Dura," Volsk wheezed, "we seem to have a penchant for meeting in prisons. This cell is slightly larger than the one I occupied in Bunard. I managed to solve the measurement problem. Would you like to know how I did it?"

Bolt and Mirren looked at me, and with effort I pulled a memory out of my past. "He's not from Moorclaire, but he enjoys the mathematicum just the same."

"What did you do to him?" Bolt asked. Mirren took a step back at the threat in the question, but Volsk waved him off.

"Not her," he said.

For some reason I couldn't identify, Volsk's appearance roused a protective anger in me. This, for the man who'd tried to arrange my death so that he could inherit the gift of domere. The idiocy of that struck me. Would there be some set of circumstances that would lead me to pity Bishop Gehata? And if so, what would those be?

"Fool men," Mirren said, "talking when you should be moving. Save your questions until we're safe."

Bolt moved to lift Volsk from the floor. "Stop," Volsk said. "If you move me I'll die that much sooner." He coughed again, weaker this time. "I made a mistake."

"Only one?" I asked.

A bit of his former arrogance flared in his eyes before it turned to ash. "I mocked the bishop one time too many," he said. "I thought I would be a healer, once. My ribs are broken. My lungs are bleeding."

"We can't stay here," Mirren said.

Bolt rose, his movements unexpectedly gentle as he rested Volsk on the floor. The traitorous Vigil apprentice closed his eyes, his breathing quick and shallow, but a moment later his hand twitched, hardly more than a flutter.

Instinctively, I knew what he wanted. Reaching out, I laid a hand on his head and fell into the dying ruin of his mind. He wasn't there to greet me. The dim color to his thoughts bore witness to his passing, but there was a book floating before me. With the barest touch of thought it flared into light, and Volsk's most precious memories became my own. Darkness descended within his mind and I broke contact.

The Vigil's apprentice lay dead. I created a door within my mind and interred his memories within the room beyond. Then I marked it with Toria Deel's name and sealed it shut. I might never have the chance to give them to her, and I wondered if she would want them.

We left the cell after Bolt closed Volsk's eyes.

I'd expected Mirren to take us to the next level beneath, but instead she led us thirty paces down the hall and stopped to open a door on the left. I darted in, my mind conjuring images and revenge. In the light, Custos blinked at me. Though he looked wan and hungry, he didn't carry the mass of bruises Volsk did.

"Hello, Willet." His voice rasped with disuse.

"Let's leave the joyful reunions for later," Bolt said. "I don't fancy trying to fight off any of the cosp without a sword. 'Long odds make for bad outcomes.'"

I nodded as we made what speed we could up the stairs toward freedom. "I like that one."

He snorted, and I could see the grimace on his stony face as we turned on one of the landings. "That's a surprise, coming from you. You don't hope for miracles—you rely on them."

We released Hradian from his cell and soon came to the top. I could feel a difference in the stone. Even though I suspected dawn had yet to break, I sensed I was once again in the presence of sun-warmed rock. The guards at the entrance to the prisons stood facing away from us, blinking and swaying on their feet.

Mirren held out a hand, then raised a finger to her lips. We waited as she went forward, her steps almost too light to hear. Almost.

The guards turned, their motions sluggish, and made to draw, but when they saw her they faltered. Mirren extended her bare hand, first to one and then the other, and the stares of the guards became as glass.

"She's good at that," I said.

Bolt nodded. "She's had a bit of practice."

Mirren pointed. "That's the closest way out."

Thoughts still churned in my head, like silt stirred from the river bottom, but I knew enough to ask Custos for confirmation. It was only after he nodded that it occurred to me that Mirren would only point out the closest avenue of escape if she didn't mean to come with us.

"It's been hours since I touched Gehata," she said. "If I don't return, his memories will settle and he'll know what I've done."

"What did you see in Gehata's mind?"

She shook her head. "I didn't take the time to delve him."

"We're going with you," Bolt said. "Lieutenant, you must find Bishop Serius and bring him to Gehata's quarters."

Hradian nodded, relieved one of the guards of his sword, and strode down the passageway. As he turned a corner, Mirren hissed, "I didn't go to the trouble of getting you out of prison just so you could put yourself back."

Bolt gave her a quick nod before relieving the other guard of his weapon. "We won't be going back."

Mirren's expression matched her laughter, but she didn't get the chance to put voice to her objection.

"I think it's better than fives that Bishop Gehata already knows who holds the gift of kings and that he's taken them prisoner," Bolt said. Since it had more possible combinations than any other number, five was the most common roll in bones. The combinations of a pair of four-sided bones ranged from two to eight, but a quarter of all throws would come up five, if the dice were fair.

"I've played," Mirren said. "That's still three times out of four that he doesn't know. What was it you said about long odds?"

The duration of their argument set my skin itching. "Custos, take me to Gehata's office."

He smiled, but my heart quailed at how pale he was. Even so, he turned and started down the hallway to the right, away from our escape.

Mirren and Bolt fell in behind us. Except for the occasional priest in red who eyed our strange company with curious suspicion, the hallways were empty.

"Why is the cathedral so empty?" I asked.

"It's still a few minutes to sunrise," Mirren said. "Everyone needs sleep."

"That's the truth of it," I said.

Mirren cut her gaze my way, suddenly uncomfortable. After delving me, she knew of my peculiar affliction. We came to Gehata's quarters, where a pair of cosp were posted outside the door. At the sight of Bolt, one of them sprinted away from us.

"Cosp! Guards!" His voice faded with the speed of his departure, but his screams continued.

The other moved to block our way, and we stopped. Bolt drew and advanced, his sword point down in a way that might have been intended to be less threatening. The guard didn't seem to take it that way. He coiled, waiting for the last Errant.

"I've sworn not to kill any of the church," Bolt said to the guard. "That's a vow I'd prefer to keep if I can."

The guard, a rangy fellow with a thin face, licked his lips. He was outmatched and knew it. "Then put away your sword."

"Hmmm," Bolt said, still closing. "If I do that, your bishop will put me back in prison."

I didn't see him move so much as I sensed it. The air exploded with violence as Bolt launched at the guard, his sword coming up in an attack on the high line.

Right at his head.

The guard was good, and he probably had enough fear coursing through him to fuel a whole company of soldiers. He parried Bolt's first strike. The air whined in complaint as Bolt riposted toward the opposite side, and the guard managed to block that strike just short of his skull.

The third landed, and the guard crumpled, blood coming from the split in his scalp. I didn't want to look, but I knew his gaze might tell me something, however unlikely, as he died. Only . . . he didn't. The cut on his head hadn't broken through the bone. I looked at my guard.

"I took him with the flat," Bolt said.

Custos nodded. "Interesting. That would explain why your strikes were so noisy. I've read about that, of course, but I've never seen it before."

The sound of boots, lots of them, sounded in the distance. Mirren bent to the guard. "Don't bother," I said. "One more or less won't make a difference now. We have to get to Gehata."

We locked the heavy door behind us, Bolt and Mirren disappearing into the interior. I tried not to stare at the opulence of Gehata's quarters, but there was enough gilt in his rooms to cover a wall. "He's an unassuming sort of fellow, isn't he?"

"These rooms are nearly a thousand years old, and the wealth is held by the church," Custos said. "Over that period of time, even incremental decoration accumulates."

"You're defending him?"

He shrugged. "I'm sure Bishop Gehata is as venal a man as you'll find, but most of this wealth predates him." He looked around. "I prefer figs, myself."

Bolt and Mirren came running out of separate rooms, their faces wearing different versions of the same emotion. "He's not here," they said in unison.

The boom of impact and the splintering of wood filled the air.

"They have us now," Bolt said. As slowly as a normal man, he drew his sword. "You were right about those long odds."

CHAPTER 35

The door didn't last through the next blow. Whoever had trapped us in the bishop's quarters had planned ahead—they'd brought a battering ram. Cosp filled the room, but they didn't strike, only set themselves with their swords and waited.

Bolt crouched, but a moment later he shook his head and tossed the sword onto the table in the middle of the room. "'If there's a choice between dying now and dying later . . .'" he murmured.

"'Choose later,'" I finished. I'd first heard that saying from the southern mercenaries who entered the Darkwater with me ten years ago. It didn't seem like a good omen.

A wall of cosp surrounded us and spilled out into the hall, cutting off any hope of escape. Bishop Gehata threaded his way through the soldiers, wearing that same smile of superiority that made me want to punch his face, but I noticed his eyes held a bit of the unbalance that probably still showed in mine.

"How?" Mirren asked.

The bishop's smile grew. "You were a calculated risk, Mirren—one that I was almost unwilling to take. Letting you inside Lord Dura's mind was a gamble, but necessary. I told my guards to watch me for any behavior that seemed out of place." He turned to me. "After I've disposed of your friends, Lord Dura, I'll be relieving you of your gift." He looked around. "I'll have to have my quarters cleansed, of course, but as we say, the growth of the church is watered by blood."

If there was a means to redeem Gehata from his ambition, it eluded me. I looked at the guards around him, as stoic and uncaring of his blasphemy as stone. "Do none of you care that he's going to destroy you all?"

The bishop's laughter mocked me. "Like you, Lord Dura, I prize loyalty, and I've gone to great lengths to ensure it." He sighed, almost purring his pleasure. Then he pointed at Custos. "I think I'd like that one to die first—the librarian. Kill him. Now."

Bolt moved to intercept, weaponless, but a half-dozen swords swung his way, and their owners positioned themselves so they each had a clean line of attack.

Before the guards could get to Custos, I stepped in front and pulled my gloves. "I won't stand idle while you kill him. I don't expect to win, but if this goes badly, I will die before you can take the gift. Your apothecary is not here."

A sharp retort of sound echoed in the room, and I saw Bishop Gehata applauding. "This is better than a play." He pointed to Custos. "Isn't it ironic that as the curtain goes up on the next act, it's actually coming down on his life?"

Bolt shifted closer to me, and the cosp closest withdrew a step, nervous. For months he'd been my constant companion, the purity of his gift an illustration of just how far humanity had fallen. But in all that time, even during the fight with Duke Orlan's pet killer, I had never seen the focused intensity, the capacity for explosive violence that I saw now.

The last Errant stood beside me.

Instead of being chagrined or angry at the prospect of more than a little violence in his quarters, Bishop Gehata looked pleased. He held the tip of his tongue against his upper lip as if in anticipation of some delicate morsel he'd never tasted before, and the pupils of his eyes had dilated like a lover's.

"Excellent," he said. He raised his hand, pointing at Bolt. "Let us see what the Errant—"

A clatter from the hallway interrupted him, the shock of a single sword rebounding from the stones of the corridor like a clarion. Its ring hung in the air—a repudiation—before being joined by another and then more. The cosp filling Gehata's quarters thinned as they moved to investigate. Then I saw them dropping weapons and kicking them away.

The six cosp closest to Gehata closed in, forming a ring around him, tense, as the rest moved away. I still couldn't see the reason for the surrender, but the clatter of dropping weapons continued to sound.

"Bishop Gehata," a voice rang from the hallway, "you are commanded to surrender yourself to the authority of the Merum church."

Bolt straightened from his crouch. "Serius."

"I *am* the church now, you fool," Gehata snarled.

A crowd of soldiers moved into view, filling the doorway, each one of them leveling a loaded crossbow at the bishop and his remaining men. Bolt pulled me and Custos out of the line of fire. The remaining cosp surrendered, their swords hitting the carpet with muffled rings. One by one they were manacled and led away, stripping Gehata of his protection. When one of the guards signaled Mirren to step forward, I held up a hand.

"Not her," I said. "She freed us."

Serius entered the room, his eyes clear, lucid. "My thoughts and reason have returned to me, Bishop Gehata."

Gehata laughed. "Do you expect me to grovel, Serius? You're a fool, like Vyne before you, wasting an opportunity for the true church to take control of the north and erase the errors of the past."

Serius didn't bother to answer but turned from Gehata as he would an object that held little significance. "Are you well, Errant Consto?"

Bolt nodded as he stepped forward with his eyes on the floor, examining the swords. He stooped, selecting one and then fastening it to his belt. "This will do until I find Robin's." Turning, he pointed through the floor. "There's at least one man dead by Gehata's order in the prison cells below us."

I searched Bolt's face for some satisfaction or regret over Peret Volsk's death, but he'd always been hard to read, and now was no exception.

Serius nodded. "I grieve your loss."

Bolt's expression didn't change, but his chin dropped toward his chest, and his eyes narrowed momentarily. "Do I?" he whispered too softly for any to hear. Except me.

"What will you do with him?" I asked Serius as I pointed at Gehata.

Serius mused for a moment before answering. "With your aid, Lord Dura, we will question him to determine just how far his influence has spread."

I noted that he'd addressed me, not Bolt. He knew about my gift.

Confirming my suspicion, I heard Rory's voice coming from the press of soldiers in the hallway.

"It's over, you stupid *kreppa*. Let us through."

A moment later he and Gael shouldered their way into the room. In the tales, whenever a woman discovers her beloved has survived, she falls into his arms. I wouldn't have minded that, but the writers of those tales had obviously never met Gael. She noted Gehata, her blue eyes darkening to the shade of an overcast sky, and took my hand, the bare one.

Divining her intent, I let myself fall into her mind, where I became one with her memories and emotions. In an instant, I knew what she and Rory had done, how they had retrieved Bishop Serius and, after his muddled mind had settled, convinced him of the danger Gehata represented. Emotions swirled among her memories, anger, and enough fear to cripple anyone, but Gael had channeled all of them into action.

Just before I surrendered our communion, one last thread of emotion washed over me. I blinked and found myself looking at my beloved in the midst of a sea of armed men and women. "You wouldn't really want me to do that," I said. "Not here and now."

No one outside of the two of us would have any context for the remark, but Gael only favored me with a smile and a lift of her brows. I tried to maintain some measure of reserve, but I must have failed.

"Bonkers," Rory snorted. "You'd think they'd been apart from each other for a lifetime instead of a few hours."

His amused disgust sobered me. Before I left that room, I knew what I needed to do. Stepping around the table we'd used as our puny defense, I approached Gehata where a handful of soldiers held him. "With your permission, Bishop Serius, I would like to ask a question of the man who killed my friend." The description I used for Peret Volsk stopped me for an instant. Had he been my friend?

Serius bowed his assent, but I saw his gaze turn intense. He knew what I meant to do. Gehata recoiled, but the guards held him fast. Perhaps I enjoyed his fear, taking it as some measure of recompense for what he'd done and had intended to do. I slowed my approach.

"Who holds the gift of kings for Aille, and where are they?" I asked. The question was mostly a ruse to satisfy the demands of the scene we played, but I hoped it served to bring the information closer to the surface of Gehata's mind.

He didn't answer, of course, but that only made my part easier to play. I stepped forward, my hands outstretched, my fingers tense, grasping. I didn't have to pretend to anger, but I walled it away. I needed as much information as I could pull from Gehata's mind, and finding the heir was only the beginning.

The bishop shook his head as he pressed himself back against his guards. With a savage wrench that belied his soft bulk, he freed an arm. His hand flashed to his opposite sleeve and steel glinted in the light.

Somewhere behind me, I sensed as much as heard my friends exploding into motion, but they were too slow. In a cool detached part of my mind, I noted that Gehata must have acquired some portion of a physical gift.

I stood within his reach. Recoiling and knowing it was useless, I watched in horrified fascination as the edge of his knife swept a glinting arc through the air. Blood fountained from his neck as his eyes filled with triumph.

The fading light in his gaze leapt at me as I put my bloodstained hands on his throat. I tunneled through his eyes and into his thoughts, racing through his memories in my panic. The knowledge was here. It had to be!

I filled myself with his life while all around me the color of his memories faded to black. Gehata was dying fast. His last memory flickered and his fleeing spirit trapped at me like an undertow. I'd stayed too long in his mind. My vision receded to a point as I raced toward eternity. With my last conscious thought I willed myself to let go of Gehata's neck.

Nothing happened. I hurtled away from the ruin of Gehata's body, but I couldn't sense anything beyond that numbing speed. No sight or sound or intuition intruded upon my flight. I worked to move my hands, but I couldn't feel. I tried to blink, but my sight and senses had been severed. Only the rushing sensation remained, but no destination revealed itself.

In the onward rush, I sensed a presence that might have been Aer or Ealder and a voice that warmed me like an answered prayer. *You have work left to do.*

The headlong rush slowed until I hung suspended.

I blinked against torchlight that hurt, my arms and legs twitching as if I had no concept of how to control them. Hands held me and a buzz of noise resolved into Bolt's growl and Gael's weeping.

Memory returned.

Gehata's body lay before me, blood everywhere. The bishop's suicide had managed to keep many of his most important memories from me, including the location of the heir, but not all. "That's wrong," I said out loud before I could keep from speaking. Blinking, I found myself the center of attention.

Bishop Serius spoke into the crowded silence. "Place the cosp who worked with Gehata in the lower cells."

I cleared my throat. "I think the bishop had a hold on many of them to ensure their loyalty."

Serius nodded. "Captain, please inter Gehata's men into separate cells until we can make some determination as to their fate. Errant Consto, would you and your friends accompany me to my quarters? There is much we need to discuss."

Chapter 36

Coming again to the quarters allotted to Bishop Serius, I noted the resemblance to those of Gehata. But there were subtle differences in the atmosphere that I could only attribute to the attitude of the men who occupied them. Serius's quarters held an air of gratitude and acknowledgment, whereas Gehata's had held those same gifts as rightful acknowledgment.

Bishop Serius—I hoped he would be the next Archbishop—waved us to chairs and, without asking, served us wine, including Rory. For some inexplicable reason, watching the bishop drain his glass and refill it before speaking comforted me. "I think you should begin, Lord Dura. I'm especially keen to know what sort of information you found floating in the detritus of that contemptible little man's mind."

Bolt nodded his approval of the insult, but what I'd seen in Gehata's mind disturbed me for reasons that had nothing to do with the man himself. "The dwimor who came for the queen," I said. "It doesn't make sense."

"Dwimor?" Serius asked. "Are you telling me a phantom tried to kill Queen Chora?"

"The dwimor are assassins who can't be seen except by children," Bolt said, "fashioned by people who share Lord Dura's gift. It requires a gift of devotion." He turned to me. "What about it?"

"He was huge," I said recalling the testimonies given to Gehata. "According to the witnesses who saw him, he was built like a black-

254

smith." The bishop started to shake his head but stopped almost immediately, and my estimation of him rose a notch, perhaps two.

"That seems at cross purposes with creating an assassin who can't be seen," he said.

Possibilities swirled in my mind, and I cursed my ignorance. I needed to get to the witnesses who'd seen the attempt on Queen Chora. Fortunately, I didn't have to depend on my intuition. Gehata's memories told me he had sent them both to a farm outside the city, ostensibly to do penance, but the girls had never been part of the church. The sun had risen enough to light Serius's stained-glass windows, and though the thoughts in my mind still flowed like mud and my eyes burned with the need for sleep, I wanted to get to the farm.

"Thank you for your aid," I said to the bishop.

Serius pursed his lips. "That sounds as though you're taking your leave, Lord Dura." He held up a hand in forbidding. "What of the heir? Who holds the gift of kings for Aille?"

"If I am successful, Your Eminence, the throne will be filled." I bowed. "I hope you will come to rule the Merum order. You seem to me to be a man who would do the job well."

"If the council of bishops wills it," he said.

I smiled. "Even if they do not, anyone will be an improvement over Gehata. Sometimes we have to settle for avoiding the worst choice instead of making the best."

Bolt cocked his head. "With a little bit of work I could use that."

We left the cathedral, and I resisted the urge to look behind me every few steps to check if we were being followed. If Serius had insisted on sending a company of soldiers to escort us, I would have been hard-pressed to come up with a plausible reason for refusing.

"What's going on in that mind of yours, Willet?" Gael asked after we'd procured horses.

It felt good to be a whole company again, or mostly whole—though I had difficulty sorting through Volsk's death. Mirren accompanied us in his place. There were things I needed to tell Mirren, or possibly Gael, in case I never got to Toria. She would want to know. I thought so anyway.

"The throne room," I said. "You tried to touch me. Why?"

"Gehata told me to scramble your memories." She swallowed. "He was going to insist on having his healer tend you."

"You weren't trying to delve me?"

She shook her head. "He said it was too dangerous, that if I stayed in your mind too long, it would leave me open to attack."

"It doesn't work quite that way," I said. "I'm going to have to train you—as much as I can, anyway. Volsk misled Gehata and you regarding the use of our gift. It was brilliant. That's how we managed to escape."

She shook her head, and I had to remind myself that Gehata had found her by chance, his habit of intercepting the Archbishop's correspondence leading him to her. She didn't know anything of her ability, except for the half-truths that had been beaten out of Peret Volsk. "Gehata didn't want to let you delve anyone within the Vigil," I told her, "until he was ready to take the gift himself."

"It would have exposed the lies he'd fed me," she said, but without anger. Instead, her eyes held cold calculation. I would have placed a large wager that at least one of her talents tended toward logic, and her temperaments toward observation and thought. The newest member of the Vigil didn't appear interested in wasting her time on meaningless vengeance.

"Gehata didn't have a clue as to how skillfully he'd been played. He decided the best way to get you the skills he needed for your gift was to torture it out of Volsk and Custos. He started with Volsk, of course. He'd been the Vigil's apprentice for years." I stopped for a moment, forced myself to replay each scene where members of the cosp beat Volsk for the truth.

"Each time they appeared on the verge of giving up and torturing Custos instead, he pretended to crack—not so much as to make them suspicious, but enough to keep them occupied." I smiled. "I think Fess and Mark would have appreciated his artistry. What he told you," I said to Mirren, "was almost true, but he changed it. He had you muddle the memories of those you touched instead of destroying them."

Her eyes widened. "You . . . I . . . can do that?"

"Yes," I said. "For something so destructive, it's ridiculously simple. What Volsk taught you created confusion within the minds of those you touched. You put your hand into the river of their thoughts and stirred them, mixing the threads the way a fisherman's clumsy steps stir mud from the bottom of a stream, but their memories weren't destroyed. Like the stream, the memories and emotions settled and cleared after a time."

"He kept Gehata pinned," she said, "occupied with the same task over and over again."

I nodded. "Volsk counted on the hope that sooner or later you wouldn't be able to keep everyone's memories muddled, and that we would prevail before you realized the truth of your gift."

Custos nodded, the sun glinting off the bald dome of his head. "I wondered why no one came to question me."

Gael reined her horse closer to mine. "You didn't tell Serius where we're going or why," she said.

"No," I replied. "As much as I want to trust him, as much as I believe he's a good man, we might find ourselves at cross-purposes very soon. As a matter of fact, I can probably guarantee it."

Bolt grimaced, which from anyone else would be the equivalent of screaming in terror. "Aer have mercy," he growled. "What are you planning now?"

CHAPTER 37

Two days after they'd cleansed the outpost infiltrated by Cesla's men, breaking the vaults and minds of all who'd been to the forest, Toria and Fess arrived at their destination—a camp situated on a hillock offering a clear view to all points of the compass. She nodded her approval. "It's defensible, at least in the customary sense."

Fess pursed his lips in thought. "Would that alone account for their success?"

"No," she said. "Any squad leader with a thimble's worth of experience would situate his camp thus. Wag, do you smell the forest here?"

No, Mistress, only men and females. He chuffed. *Their scent is very strong.*

She smiled, turning to Fess. "The camp is clean, but Wag says some of the soldiers need a bath."

They entered the camp, the guards at the gate snapping to when they spotted their rank. A runner sprinted off to the center of the stockade, and moments later, the ranking officer, wearing lieutenant's bars, emerged. Most of his uniform had been replaced with black clothing, and his buttons and buckles had been smeared with lamp-black. The color of his hair was impossible to determine, smeared with mud as it was. Even the pores of his skin showed its residue. "How may I serve you?" His voice carried the sharp edge of fatigue.

She nodded. "I'm looking for information, Lieutenant. Your command has suffered fewer casualties than any other and not by a small amount. King Rymark wants to know why."

Fess called her name and pointed around the camp. "Lady Deel, there's almost no one here, yet there are enough cook fires burning to feed five times the men I see."

She turned back to the officer. "Where are the rest of your men, Lieutenant?"

"I assure you all my men are accounted for. They're sleeping."

Fess touched her on the elbow before she could respond. "Look there."

Her apprentice pointed to a tent in the middle of camp. At first, she noticed nothing odd about it other than its larger size, but the breeze that ruffled the other canvas tents around the compound seemed oddly muted. It was then that she noticed the color and the coating of mud.

"Why would . . ." she began, then noticed Fess nodding in appreciation.

"Clever," he said, "but I doubt the lieutenant is the source of the inspiration. How long has it been since your men have seen daylight?"

"It varies," he said, nervous.

Then she understood. "You keep them in perpetual dark so they can see at night."

He nodded, but his expression still lacked the pride in the accomplishment she would have expected. "Our night vision isn't as good as theirs, but you may tell the king that our outpost will hold."

"Will it, Lieutenant?" she asked. "You've accomplished what no other outpost in the defense of the forest has, and yet you receive praises as if they were condemnations."

He licked his lips. "Even we have suffered losses, Lady Deel. I must have reinforcements."

She shook her head. "Have your superiors not sent them to you?"

Instead of answering, his gaze darted to the tent. "You have the authority," he hissed. "You could order her back to the main camp. Tell her the king wants her to teach the other camps how to fight them." His words spilled out of him in a rush, his tongue struggling to keep pace with his fear.

Her. A stab of premonition cut across Toria's chest. "Shall I go talk to the soldiers in your tent?"

His head jerked. "No."

"When will they come out?"

He fought to pull a breath. "Just before sunset. There's a window of time at dusk we use to get them in position."

Fess glanced at the sun. "Two hours, maybe a bit less."

"Unless you have something more to tell me, Lieutenant, we'll wait," Toria said.

He swallowed. "She doesn't like strangers."

"Your point is taken," she said, "but I'm not sure we are strangers. Please have one of your men tend our horses."

Toria seated herself on a nearby bench and settled herself to wait, Fess standing guard over her and Wag lying at her feet. She closed her eyes and entered the construct in her mind—a copy of the vast library in Cynestol. As the weight of a thousand different memories manifested, a sigh ghosted from her, insubstantial because it wasn't real. At the speed of quickest thought, she checked the doors, found them all secure, and then placed herself before the one she sought.

She opened it and memories spilled out.

"Go ahead," Bronwyn said as she dabbed at her cheeks with a damp cloth in an effort to mitigate the heat of Cynestol's summer. "The paverin sap will keep him calm."

Toria reached, leaning to make contact so she could dart back if he woke, her fingers coming to rest on the man's hand. She plunged down into his memories, the memories of a murderer. New to the gift, less than a year, she had just begun to fathom the depth of her ignorance. Colored strands raced past her in a rush as the condemned man's memories ran their circuit.

She plunged beneath them, searching at Bronwyn's instruction until she found it—a scroll, not black but gray—that had been leached of any hint of color. It was closed, tightly curled to protect its secrets. With a shudder of revulsion, a spasm that she felt in her stomach as well as her mind, she reached out to destroy the vault.

And stopped. That wasn't her purpose. Swallowing her distaste, she examined it instead, searching for entrance or writing that would give her a clue as to its origin or purpose. After an indeterminate amount of time she gave up.

"What did you see?" Bronwyn asked her.

"A vault," Toria said, "but it was gray and without writing. Why did you order me not to destroy it?"

Bronwyn's eyebrows rose, a gesture of both questioning and displeasure. "That is not our purpose, Toria Deel. We fight the Darkwater and dispense justice where needed. That man is a murderer."

She shook her head. "Surely not," she said. "There was nothing of violence in his memories. Did I misread him?"

Bronwyn shook her head. "No. Had I delved him, I would have seen no more than you. There are two men before you. A second man is contained within that vault. Violent. Savage. A tavern full of patrons saw him stab another man to death—a man they say resembled his father."

She swallowed. From the first day, the instruction of the Vigil had taken her to depths that frightened her, had taught her the fragility of the mind. "Would not destroying the vault restore this man?"

Bronwyn gazed at her, her green eyes placid. "A good question, but think on what you've learned, and ask again."

She stared at the man, the silence growing until it loomed over her, a fourth person in the room. "It's been tried, and more than once." She met Bronwyn's gaze. "That we have not taken it upon ourselves to intervene in that way says each attempt was unsuccessful."

Bronwyn nodded. "Better. Continue."

Toria followed her train of logic until she came to a split and found herself considering two possibilities. "Either the destruction of their vaults destroyed them, or they re-created them later. Which was it?"

"They each occurred, depending on the person," Bronwyn said. "We never found a pattern we could use to determine which would happen. In the end, it hardly mattered. Our gift is insufficient for the task."

Sorrow filled Toria and despite her revulsion, she reached out to lay a hand on the sleeping man's chest. "Is there nothing that can be done for such as these?"

Bronwyn nodded her approval. "There is no healing to be found within the use of our gift, but there are some who have recovered from such brokenness. It takes time and love—and an abundance of both."

Toria nodded. "What of him? Will anyone be able to heal him?"

Bronwyn's expression closed. "He has already been tried and convicted, Toria Deel. This man's fate has been determined. It's not our place to interfere."

"His name is Eofot."

Anger brought heat to her skin until she burned with it, at the waste of life, at her own inability to heal it, but most of all at whatever circumstance had taken Eofot and broken him.

Toria replayed the memory and a hundred more like it, searching for some knowledge or lore that might help her. A touch brought her out of her mind, and she opened her eyes to see the horizon swallowing the light of the sun.

In the midst of the small rectangle that defined their camp, men and women, dressed in black, their faces smeared with lampblack or mud came stumbling into the waning day, their eyes covered in heavy swaths of cloth.

"Tell me, Lieutenant," Toria said. "Has she killed any besides those who have come from the forest?"

The lieutenant shook his head in a way that told Toria she'd asked the wrong question. "No."

On her left, Fess might have sighed in relief.

"How many of those who come from the forest are women?" Toria asked.

The lieutenant's face tightened. "Nearly half."

She pointed at a figure emerging from the blackened tent, a figure owning a heart-shaped face, visible despite the cloth and mud. "How many women from the forest has she killed?"

The lieutenant stiffened. "None. She has left them for the others."

"Come, Fess, and bring Wag with you. Let us renew our acquaintance. Lelwin is waiting for us."

"Lelwin?" The lieutenant's mouth twisted around the word, giving it an unfamiliar sound. "You mean Brekana?"

Sorrow, but not surprise, washed through her. She forced a nod. "Yes. I mean her."

CHAPTER 38

A little over a week out from Erimos, Dukasti held up his hand and they pulled to a stop, the horses champing and huffing. The sun still stood well above the horizon. Pellin had long since stopped bothering to mop his brow. The cloth allotted for the purpose was sodden past the point of usefulness.

Dukasti dismounted with a signal, and a score of southern warriors followed suit, their crescents—the half-moon blade affixed to a bar of iron—clanking at their side. "We will rest here, Eldest," he said. "Tomorrow, or perhaps the day after, we will endeavor to make the journey to the border of the true desert, the Maveth, where Igesia awaits."

"Can we not journey a bit more today?" Mark asked. "We still have hours of daylight left."

Dukasti smiled. During their journey Pellin had watched his counterpart develop an affinity for the urchin, not only for his insights, but for the unwavering commitment he exhibited for Elieve's care. "Igesia dwells in Oasi," he said. "It is one of the few spots of respite on the border of the corruption, but there are no more between here and there. The ride can be accomplished with twelve hours of hard riding, no less. The desert is not a place to spend the night, unless you wish to freeze to death."

"Freeze?" Mark laughed. "I feel like butter that's been left next to the oven."

Dukasti nodded. "Oasi lies beyond a stretch of tens of miles of nothing but sand. No river or stream, no plants or animals, make their home there. The air cannot hold the heat, and when the sun goes down, any who are caught unaware succumb to the dry and cold." He beckoned. "Come. The hospitality of the sandmen is proverbial here, and my brother Karam will be expecting us. I sent a bird ahead."

They surrendered their horses, and Dukasti led them to a long low building in the shape of a cross. Arched hallways tapered toward the center of the roof and focused the breeze, but even so, the force of the southern sun struck Pellin like a physical blow. They passed through a doorway into a room whose roof was latticed to provide shade and permit air to circulate.

Instead of chairs, large cushions surrounded low tables, but few merchants or traders were in attendance. A southerner, his azure eyes bright against the deep charcoal of his skin appeared out of a side room and made for Dukasti. "Brother! It is good to see you."

Dukasti's lips parted into a rare smile. "Karam, it is good to see you as well."

Karam's smile deepened, but he shrugged. "Yes and no. The only time I see you is when you are on your way to Oasi, and that only happens when there is trouble."

Dukasti's expression turned stricken. "I came to visit you on your naming day, did I not?"

This earned him a shake of the head. "That was five years ago, brother." Turning serious, he eyed Pellin and the rest of their company. "I have a hard time believing dire circumstances could arise from such as these. Surely the light of Aer shines upon them." His eyes narrowed when he noticed Elieve. "Though this one carries a tale worth hearing."

Dukasti shook his head. "Some tales are for the bearer only." To Pellin he said, "My brother Karam holds a unique blend of talents that provide insights that others cannot see. Even he doesn't know how he does it. He's probably a sorcerer."

"Nonsense," Karam said, "I merely watch and listen. The heart speaks what the spirit yearns to utter, even if the mind and mouth do not partake."

Pellin nodded. "I know of one such—a reeve, as chance would have it."

Karam tapped Dukasti on the chest with the back of his hand. "There, you see? There is no need for magic. Come, make yourselves comfortable, and I will have Tanvi bring you date wine and figs for your refreshment while we prepare dinner."

A moment later a girl entered, eyes wide, carrying a broad tray with a pitcher of wine, cups, and figs. As she passed by, Elieve reached out and touched the shimmering half-sleeved shirt and wrapping cloth the girl wore. "Pretty," she breathed.

The girl smiled, showing her resemblance to her father. "Do you like it?"

Elieve nodded, her eyes wide and earnest.

"This is the sari my father gave me on my seventeenth naming day," Tanvi said.

"It's beautiful," Elieve nodded, touching the shimmering cloth again.

Tanvi straightened and eyed Elieve with a speculative look. "Dinner will be some time coming. Among my people it is traditional to dress for the meal as a way to honor guests. Would you like to wear a sari for your dinner?"

Elieve's eyes went wide and she nodded.

Tanvi laughed. "Come. I seldom get the chance to spend time with girls my own age."

Elieve stood, but when Mark released her hand, her face turned stricken and she hesitated. "Go," Mark smiled. "Tanvi is a friend."

Hesitantly—with stops and starts like a child taking their first steps, and looking back over her shoulder for reassurance—Elieve moved away. But she gained confidence as she went, and by the time she left the room, she and Tanvi were running as they held hands and laughter trailed behind them.

"An important moment?" Dukasti asked as he watched Mark.

"I think so," Pellin said. "This is the first time Elieve has been out of Mark's sight since we found her."

"Tanvi is the only daughter of my brother," Dukasti said.

Pellin nodded. Dukasti's implication was painfully clear. "Elieve's vault has yet to open, and it is still three hours until sunset. Both of the girls are safe. However, I can send Allta to watch over them, if you wish."

"No. As Tanvi has hinted, without girls of her own age around, living on the edge of the desert has been hard for her."

Pellin leaned forward. "Tell me, Dukasti, have any of the southern

Vigil ever succeeded in breaking a vault without also breaking its bearer?" A desperate hope flared in his chest.

But his guide shook his head. "I am new to the Vigil, but nothing I've read in our library hints at such, and very few attempt the desert. From what Igesia and the rest of our Vigil have told me, the northern Vigil contends with far more incidents of the evil than we." Pellin assumed he'd done a poor job of hiding his dismay, because Dukasti amended his assessment. "But Igesia is far older and wiser than I, Eldest, and he says things from the depths of his contemplation that are hard for me to understand."

They talked of inconsequential matters for perhaps another hour, during which time Mark grew progressively restless. As he made to rise from the cushions, Tanvi and Elieve finally entered.

"I'm sorry for taking so long," Tanvi said, "but I thought it would be rude not to offer Elieve the opportunity to bathe. The crossing to our oasis is a grim undertaking." She laughed a sparkling sound and stepped aside to give the men an unobstructed view of Elieve.

Her rich brown hair had been pulled back with a brooch to expose the delicate curve of her neck, and twin gaersum stones rested on her forehead and in the hollow of her throat. A sari of deep shimmering blue caught a half-sleeved shirt of the same color at her waist, and a skirt the color of night flared to show sandals decorated with polished stones.

Pellin smiled. "I've lived for a very long time, Tanvi, but I don't think I've ever seen two young women more beautiful."

At his side, Mark didn't speak. He gazed at Elieve, drinking in the sight of her, a young man in the desert desperate to quench his thirst.

"You like it?" Elieve asked him.

He nodded, and she came forward to take his hand.

Dukasti rose, a smile on his face and held his hands out to both Tanvi and Elieve. "You are rare flowers in the desert, startling in your beauty."

Both girls laughed and reached out to take his hands. Mark bolted upright, his protest plain on his face, but Pellin waved him back and watched as Dukasti's eyes dilated, the smile on his face never wavering. An instant later he released Tanvi's hand to hold Elieve's for a moment longer. He stepped back, beaming. "Perhaps, Tanvi, you have something within your chests that would be suitable for Elieve to wear for the crossing tomorrow. The sari is not suited for the harshness of the desert."

After the girls departed, he turned to Pellin. "I meant no offense, Eldest, but thought it best to verify the girl's state before we made the journey." Turning to Mark, he bowed until his torso ran parallel to the ground. "It is rare to see such strength of commitment in any, but especially in one so young. Tell me, Eldest," he said turning back to Pellin, "have you had him tested for the gift of devotion?"

Mark's laughter filled the room. "Gifted? Me? I don't think so, watchful one. If you've truly delved me, then you know I am an urchin. The streets have been my home for as long as I can remember, and if anyone had bothered to put their hand on me in blessing, I doubt I would have lived there."

Dukasti nodded, pursing his lips. "But blessing is not the only means by which a gift may be passed." He pointed to the door the girls had used to exit the room. "The gift of devotion is the most difficult to test, but it often calls to its own."

Pellin knew this, had known it for centuries, but it took Mark a moment to catch Dukasti's inference. "You mean my gift is the reason I've taken care of Elieve?" His mouth tightened in disapproval. "I didn't have any choice in the matter?"

Mark's anger deepened with Dukasti's chuckle, but the southern Vigil member held up a hand. "Far from it, apprentice. You chose, and then your gift of devotion came to your aid, strengthening your will to undertake a difficult task." He pointed to Pellin. "I have delved your Eldest as well. I saw how you ran back into danger when you were pursued by those the forest had claimed. You were armed with nothing more than a torch and your wits. You pride yourself on knowing when a bluff or con might succeed and when the odds are too great. Tell me, young Mark, what would make you undertake such a foolish gamble? You should have died."

"I . . ." His eyes narrowed. "I don't know."

Dukasti smiled. "I do, and I am humbled by your strength of commitment."

"But it's not really me," Mark said. "It's the gift doing the work."

Pellin smiled, raising his hand for their attention. "Mark, my treasured apprentice, the gift doesn't decide; it only enables the bearer to do what the bearer wishes. It provides the strength of the spirit to allow the mind and body to go beyond what they would normally do."

They set out for Oasi the next morning, before the sun had cleared the horizon, but the soldiers did not accompany them. "Igesia permits no one to come any closer to the Maveth Desert unless their circumstances require it. The soldiers will stay here to prevent others from following." He exhaled a deep breath that misted in the morning air. "We must ride quickly. If we cover enough ground while the horses are fresh then our trip will succeed."

"And if we do not?" Allta asked. "The Eldest's safety is in my care."

Dukasti shrugged. "If the Eldest wishes to meet with Igesia, then we must brave the crossing. Igesia will not leave his contemplation of the desert."

They rode the horses at a fast trot that ate up the miles, following Dukasti on his trail through the sand. The sun rose throughout the ride, and Pellin removed the layers of clothing that had kept him warm until only his long-sleeved shirt and linen breeches remained. "How do you know our route?" he asked during one of their stops to water the horses.

The southerner nodded. "In truth, Eldest, one can only know the approximate direction. Oasi lies almost due south of my brother's hospitality. I correct as we go, based on our elapsed time and the position of the sun."

"Wouldn't it be easier to map a trail or place signs?" Mark asked.

Dukasti nodded. "I've often wished for as much, but the sandstorms have the power to change the landscape, and we desire to keep Oasi as isolated from those who would challenge the desert as possible."

Pellin nodded his agreement. "But Oasi is surely small enough to miss, even if you have plotted your course well."

Dukasti pointed to the extra horse tied behind his own, the one that carried water for them all. "The pack horse carries tar-soaked wood. When we have traveled the correct time and distance, we will stop and light a signal fire. The properties of the desert that so often kill can be used to guide us to Igesia. As the desert grows hotter, the air becomes more still, until the only wind will be that of our passage. The thick black smoke of our fire will rise straight to the heavens. As one of the Vigil, I have a scrying stone that is twin to Igesia's. He will guide us in to the last oasis."

"I see a wall," Elieve said behind them.

Pellin smiled in preparation for laughter. The girl's childlike observations throughout their ride had served to distract him from the heat, but Dukasti didn't laugh. He spun, scattering sand around his feet to stare in the direction of Elieve's point. Horror etched his face.

"Ride!" he screamed, running toward his horse. "We must make Oasi before the storm."

Hands clamped Pellin's shoulders, and the world pitched as Allta threw him into his saddle before doing the same with Elieve. Dukasti had already thundered off to the south, plumes rising from the hooves of his horse. Pellin turned in his saddle and gaped.

A wall of swirling brown malevolence a thousand feet high came at them from the northwest, still distant, but even now Pellin could see billows within the storm, ugly swells as it ate up the ground. In panic, he dug his heels into the sides of his horse, too sharply. His mount reared, threatening to pitch him from the saddle. His cloak fluttered with the motion, and a glint of green caught the light as his scrying stone tumbled free to drop end over end to the ground.

Then the world pitched as his horse shied. Pellin slid from its back, searching. Dukasti, looking back and seeing him, screamed. "We must ride, Eldest!"

"The stone," he screamed in panic. Nothing but sand and rock showed beneath his feet. "I dropped the stone."

They circled, searching as the wind blew grit across his vision. "What color is it?" Dukasti asked.

"Green," he said, "like the palest sea." He looked up. "Aer, have mercy. How long will it take the storm to reach us?"

Dukasti turned to face the menacing wall, shaking his head. "I'm a child of the coast, Eldest. I don't know. But if we cannot make the protection of Oasi before the storm hits, the sand will flay the skin from our hides."

CHAPTER 39

Fear put a hand around Pellin's chest and squeezed, keeping him from drawing a breath, as though the storm had already hit. Dared he leave the stone?

"Pretty," Elieve said, slipping out of her saddle, wandering from Mark to Pellin's side.

Growling, he spun, but his remonstrance died on his lips. Elieve pointed to a stretch of soft sand and thrust her hand toward its surface. When she raised it, she held a shard of light green in her fist.

Pellin took the stone. "Aer be praised," he said, blessing and prayer and relief mingling together. "Thank you, Elieve." He looked at the wall, still distant but looming, growing. "Hurry."

Dukasti mounted and rode, his own scrying stone, blue, held against his ear, working desperately to guide his horse with one hand. The initial burst of fear that had propelled the horses as they galloped across the dunes had begun to fade. Already they were showing signs of tiring. Pellin darted a glance back at the oncoming storm.

The wall raced toward them, looming over their party as it came boiling out of the northwest. Bits of grit and dirt filled the air, and he coughed. Dukasti stopped, reining in his horse with a curse and screaming above the sound of the storm. "I can barely hear him, Eldest." He flung an arm in the direction they'd been riding. "Igesia sees the storm in the distance, but the smoke from any fire he lights will be lost."

"Why?" Mark asked.

Dukasti spat an oath in a different language. "It's going to be dark as nightfall in a few moments."

"Then we must find shelter," Allta said.

Dukasti shook his head as if Pellin's guard had gone mad. "There is no shelter here. There is nothing between us and Igesia except the dunes. When the storm hits, the wind will turn the sand into carpenter's cloth." He swallowed and coughed, turning to face east as he drew the intersecting arcs on his forehead. "I'm sorry, Eldest. Will you pray with me?" He darted a look at the storm. "We don't have much time."

Allta's hand lashed out, grabbing the southerner by his arm. "How close are we to Igesia?"

"It doesn't matter."

Pellin's guard shook him like doll. "How close, curse you?"

Dukasti shook his head, his expression dark. "We're going to die, you fool northerner. Let me say my prayers!"

Allta thrust Dukasti away. Gathering the reins of all their horses, he pulled his sword. At the last, he turned to Mark. "She shouldn't see this. Keep her head down."

Mark pulled Elieve into his embrace, sheltering her eyes and ears. The wind rose to a whine that swept all other sounds before it. Already, Pellin could barely see past the length of his arm. With strokes too fast to follow, Allta put the horses down, their screams merging with the wind. Straining with effort, Pellin's guard worked to stack the bodies into position, creating a barrier to the wind.

The desert sun shrank to a pinpoint of white and disappeared.

Pellin fell toward the shelter, felt hands move him toward the bodies of the horses and cover him with a cloak. Someone—Mark, he thought—pressed against him on his left. Hands moved behind him, working to protect him.

Allta's voice, right by his ear, sounded in the darkness. "How long will the storm last, Dukasti?"

When he answered, his voice held a hint of wonder. "They vary. Some only a few minutes—others may last for hours or even days. You've given me cause to wonder and hope, good Allta. It may be that Aer will see fit to deliver us from the storm."

Their heads were no more than a couple of hands apart, and Pellin could smell their breakfast on Dukasti's breath. Someone moved beneath the confines of their cloaks, and for a moment a bit of wind and sand swirled among them.

"Mark," Allta said with grit in his voice, "be still."

The boy quieted, but a moment later, a soft glow appeared in their midst, though it lacked the strength to illuminate. Indeed, Pellin could only make out the outline of Mark's hand by it, but it cheered him, and darkness retreated from it, however slightly.

Pellin nodded in the darkness, but the gesture was for himself. "Thank you, Mark. Even a soft bit of light is welcome."

"And I bid you welcome as well," Elieve's voice came to them from the darkness. "Welcome to my demesne."

"Hold her!" Pellin's voice rasped beneath their covering. The wind howled as Allta surged forward to bring Elieve into the circle of his arms. Flying sand stung Pellin's skin as the storm howled and screamed.

"I have her," Allta yelled over the sound of the storm. "Mark, anchor the blanket back over us."

A semblance of order returned to their makeshift shelter and a portion of quiet as well once the thick blanket covered them again. Harsh breathing filled the space, and Pellin struggled to quiet the thunder of his heart. "Mark, check to ensure Elieve holds no weapon. Dukasti and I cannot risk touching her."

"Risk?" Dukasti asked. "We've strayed into the Maveth. We have to leave!"

"You said yourself, the storm means death," Allta said.

"Better death than the Maveth," Dukasti said.

Mark's voice, disembodied by the darkness, came to him. "She's unarmed, Eldest." He paused. "What's happened to her?"

Pellin ignored the question—it would be answered soon enough. He tried to wet his lips, but dust caked them. "Can you hold her, Allta?"

"Yes, Eldest, but if she lashes out with her feet, she could injure or kill you before I have a chance to stop her."

"I assure you, such precautions are unnecessary," Elieve said.

Despite the heat, gooseflesh pebbled Pellin's skin. While the voice was undeniably Elieve's, the cadence and diction of the words were alien, had never had a part of the girl's experience.

"Who are you?"

"So young." Elieve's voice carried a smile with it. "And so ignorant."

"Are you the curse of the Maveth?" Dukasti asked.

Soft laughter, breathy and mocking, came from Elieve's mouth. "So, your race is equipped with some knowledge after all. Over the centuries, the few who've stumbled into my domain have exhibited no awareness of me other than a child's fear of the dark." More laughter. "Tell me, what else do you know?"

Pellin considered not answering. The risks were unknown, but no less great for that. A chasm loomed at his feet. In the end, that same measure of risk demanded he seek guidance from the southern Vigil.

"Dukasti, has anyone ever returned from the Maveth and spoken with the Vigil?" he asked.

A stir shifted the blanket, as if Dukasti had shaken his head. "No, not in my experience or any of our writings."

Pellin mused while the storm raged. The voice that had spoken through Elieve seemed content to wait. In the end, even with seven hundred years of experience, he was too short-lived to foresee the consequences of his decision. Even if Elieve's vault offered access to the southern evil, Allta should be more than a physical match for the girl, but what the evil might learn of them and how it could be used were impossible to know.

What would Cesla have done? Pellin laughed, struck by the absurdity of the idea, and he rejected it.

What should I do? Guide me, Aer.

"You have been imprisoned for a very long time," Pellin said finally, "with nothing but the rhythm of the desert to keep you company and the occasional stray man or woman to offer you an outlet for your vengeance."

"Well laid," the voice replied. "But perhaps that stroke landed by chance. Come, human, give me some token that you hold wisdom."

"To what end?" Pellin asked. "What can a prisoner without hope of freedom or redemption have to offer me in exchange?"

Laughter wore the trappings of Elieve's voice, coarse as the sand beneath them. "Perhaps our conversation is nothing more than the longing of the lonely seeking to relieve his solitude?"

"Then you could surely have engaged in such with the few who have wandered into your domain," Pellin said, "instead of breaking their minds."

"Would you deny the condemned interludes of distraction from their eternal imprisonment?"

Now, the voice from Elieve's mouth spoke of itself in plural terms. How many prisoners were there? "Distraction?" Pellin asked quickly to cover his shock. "That is how you regard the images of Aer?"

Laughter shook their makeshift tent. "Images of Aer?" Elieve's voice scaled upward in its mirth. "I thank you. By bringing this vessel to me, you offer a greater amusement than the simple breaking of—as you put it—images? You poor insects. You've lived with your fallen state for so long you no longer realize the height from which you descended."

Pellin's heart thundered within his chest with fear and the thrill of discovery. Beside him, Dukasti sat as still as if he'd become part of the desert. Pellin prayed his intuition was correct. If not, his next question might serve to end the conversation. "Were the Fayit so very lofty, then?"

"You are nothing," Elieve answered. Pellin kept himself from exhaling in relief. "You grub like ants in the dirt, believing your hills of rock and stone to be accomplishments, all the while ignorant of the ones who preceded you. Fools!" The voice turned angry. "We were gods. The heavens and the engines of creation itself were within our grasp."

"Until iniquity was found in your hearts," Dukasti said.

Elieve jerked as if she'd been struck. "Do you think your definitions or constraints could possibly apply to us?"

"Do they not?" Pellin asked, desperate to keep Elieve talking. "Even the Fayit must have lived by moral precepts—else how did you come to find yourself imprisoned?" He took a breath and exhaled it slowly, striving to seem casual. "What transgression placed you in your prison of aurium?"

Instead of responding in anger, the being using Elieve's voice evinced a measure of surprise. "Ah? You come to me with words of power on your tongue, little one, though we knew it under a different name. I sense in you some measure of intelligence, something higher and nobler than those few pitiful gnats whose minds I've broken over the long centuries of my imprisonment. Your mind is inquisitive, and though it lacks the perfection of the Fayit, there is much I could teach you. The knowledge of the Fayit could be yours."

Deep within Pellin a part of him leapt, frantic at the offer. Before Cesla had undertaken to break the first commandment, before his brother had delved the Darkwater, Pellin had spent his time in the libraries of the world, but here was an offer of knowledge beyond expectation or imagining. The air, thick within the closeness of their space, became even more difficult to breathe.

He was not young, but he had avoided the profligate use of his gift that had aged Elwin to the point of death in the last ten years. If he husbanded his efforts, he would live for another two or three hundred years. What might he learn in that time? What wonders could he glimpse? He leaned forward.

"Merchants always put the best side of the melons forward," Mark said softly.

The spell broke, and the temptation passed, but Pellin grieved the emptiness it left behind. Still, the conversation had to be played out. "In our diminishment," he said, "we have a saying that 'knowledge is grief, but wisdom is power.' What price would you exact for this gift?"

Elieve laughed once more, but within the confines of their improvised tent, it sounded forced, desperate. "None," she said. "You have only to come to me here, with this one or one like her. As recompense for relieving my solitude, I will tell you whatever you wish to know."

Again, temptation clutched at Pellin, but he knew himself too well. Then the sound of the storm faded, and he felt himself freed. "Perhaps we will talk again," Pellin said. With one hand, he whipped the blanket away and a shock of sunlight blinded them. Elieve wailed where she sat enclosed within the grip of Allta's arms, her voice keening the loss of darkness until it faded entirely.

"It's bright," she said in her own voice. She covered her eyes with her hands.

"Thank Aer for that," Pellin said. He put his hand on her head in blessing.

Dukasti nodded, standing against the weight of sand that had accumulated around them during the storm. "Perhaps, if Aer wills it, we will survive the march to Igesia." The sun, no longer blocked by the sand and dust, beat at them with the force of a smith's hammer.

CHAPTER 40

Thick smoke ascended from Dukasti's pitch-covered torch to paint a black smear against the sky, like a forewarning of disease. Collectively, they scanned the horizon in all directions, searching for Igesia's response.

"The longer it takes him to see our signal, the farther away the sanctuary of Oasi is," Dukasti said.

Pellin nodded. What Dukasti hadn't said was what they would do if they were still too distant from Oasi for Igesia to see their signal at all. There was no need to say it, of course. If they couldn't attain Oasi in what remained of the day, they would die.

"I see dust," Elieve said, pointing.

"That's good," Mark encouraged, "but we're looking for smoke."

"Dust?" Dukasti asked. "The storm should have scoured the air."

"There," Elieve said.

Pellin shifted to look, scattering droplets of sweat into the sand at his feet. Dukasti sighted along her arm, squinting against the glare. "It's faint."

Allta nodded. "And it's headed our way. Horses."

The plume continued to approach and a few moments later two riders crested the dune to the southwest of them—leading a train of horses. "I know these men," Dukasti said. "They are the yaqiza, the guards for the Honored One."

"Were they expecting us?" Pellin asked.

"No," Dukasti shook his head. "I mean, yes, they knew we were coming to Oasi, but that doesn't explain the horses." He looked at Pellin, his expression inscrutable. "There are too many."

Within minutes the guards had covered the distance and stood before them. "Greetings, friends and strangers alike," the man in front said. Except for his coloring, he could have been Allta's twin. "We are commanded to see you to Igesia." The guard nodded toward the mounts. "With haste."

They mounted and headed back over the dunes. The other guard, only slightly less imposing than the leader, rode close to Pellin, offering water. Pellin unstopped the leather skin and poured, though the bouncing stride of his horse caused him to spill half of it down his shirt. The spots of fatigue swimming at the edges of his vision receded.

"Thank you," he said.

The guard accepted the skin with a smile. "The desert is a beautiful, but cruel companion, even for those accustomed to the southern sun."

Pellin nodded. "Sometimes such a companion is necessary company for a time. In the far north, they say the same of the bitter snows of winter."

The guard's eyes, an azure that spoke of water rather than the sky, widened. "Truly? I have heard of such a thing, though it is difficult to credit." He smiled. "I am Rafiq, Eldest One."

They crested a dune that stood a bit higher than the rest and came in sight of Oasi. It was smaller than Pellin had expected, but in its midst, he could see a thick clump of palm trees that signaled the presence of water. He could just make out a small building shrouded by their foliage, its walls as white as effort could make them. Men, dressed in clothes that matched those of their guards, worked to remove thick hides from the grates covering the windows.

They descended, the horses quickening their pace at the sight of water and rest. When they dismounted, Igesia's guards posted at their sides, weapons drawn.

"What is the meaning of this?" Dukasti asked. "Do you not recognize me, Rafiq?"

He nodded from his place beside Pellin, but the weapon remained in his hand with the point still tilted toward Pellin's midsection. "Of a surety, Watchful One. The Honored One will explain."

In the aftermath of the storm, a breeze wafted through the main room of the building. The center of the floor cradled a man whose appearance served to make Pellin seem almost young by comparison. Wrinkles and fissures had contrived to turn his face into a living parody of withered fruit, and bits of stubble, white as snow, littered the creases of his chin, struggling into view from beneath the thick cloth that served as his head covering.

But his voice cackled with glee when Pellin entered, and he motioned them all forward with a trembling wave of his hand. "Come. Come, my friend. You have tidings for me—yes?"

Pellin nodded and took a place on the carpet opposite Igesia. "And questions, Honored One."

"Ah," Igesia laughed. "And you've brought my heir with you," he said with a nod toward Dukasti.

"Me?" Dukasti shook his head in denial. "I am the youngest of us, Honored One."

"Yes, yes, and still impetuous," Igesia said, "but Aer and circumstance do not bow to the traditions or dictates of men." Without bothering to explain further, he motioned for Mark and Elieve to sit next to Pellin. "Let me look at you, young ones. Ha. The fig desires to view the apples." He smiled. "This one is a bit green yet," he said as he looked at Mark. He turned to Elieve, growing serious though his voice remained light. "And this one has a spot."

The guards moved toward Elieve with the blurring speed of the gifted, and thin cries came from her as she clutched Mark's arm.

"Did I tell any of you to move?" Igesia snapped in his old man's cackle. "Withdraw. Now!"

"Honored One," Rafiq demurred, "your life and safety are in our care."

"If you think so," Igesia said, "then you know nothing of Aer. Perhaps He does not *want* me to be safe, Rafiq." His head shook on the end of his neck. "Look outside if you still doubt. There is still an hour of light left to us. You're frightening the girl."

When they withdrew, he motioned to Elieve. "Come, my child. Come here."

Pellin thought she might refuse. Frightened, she would hardly concede to leave the protective circle of Mark's arms, but with hesitant movements she inched forward until she came within Igesia's reach. Gently, as though she might bound away, he brought her into his embrace, his hands resting upon her head.

278

Pellin leaned forward in expectation. Igesia's delving would only take a few seconds. Most of Elieve's memories had been destroyed twice over, and the black scroll of her vault lay near the surface of her mind. But a minute went by with Igesia making no move to break the embrace, and Elieve seemed as content in his arms as in Mark's.

Finally, at the moment alarm dictated that Pellin order Allta to pull her loose, Igesia's hands slid from her head to rest on the cloth of her shirt, breaking the delve. "Such a story deserves to be heard more than once," he said.

"Go to your companion," he told her, "before he becomes jealous of an old man." He bussed Elieve on the cheek with a cackle and shooed her away. "Her presence explains much, but not all, my friend. In my contemplation of the desert I have seen hints of the evil power entombed there, the corruption beneath the sand and wind that takes any who let darkness fall upon them. There is knowledge to be gleaned from the absence of life, and my reveries have allowed me to find the edge of its virulence. For years, it has not shifted by so much as a grain of sand. Yet during the storm I beheld a change, like the tiger coiling for the kill, as if the evil in the desert had cause to hope." He nodded toward Elieve. "There are traces of it in her mind, a suggestion of the deep places of the desert a woman of the north should not have."

Pellin paused to drink from the waterskin Dukasti had given him and edged toward Igesia. "If you will permit it, Honored One, I would trade awareness with you. There is much you need to know, so much that I'm not confident I could speak it all."

"And you wish to know what I have discovered of the forbidden desert." Igesia smiled. "For time out of mind, we have intuitively understood the connection between the Maveth Desert and the Dark-water Forest, even if we have not known the cause." He lifted his weathered arm, palm forward. Pellin grasped Igesia's hand in his own.

The Honored One's eyes leapt toward him and disappeared, and Pellin found himself confronted with the largest river of memories he'd ever seen. Only those of the rest of the Vigil and Custos could compare, but a mind less like the librarian's would be hard to imagine. Whereas Custos had organized his memories as thoroughly as the library in Bunard, Igesia's mind scarcely owned any organization at all. As Pellin watched, eddies appeared in the river to cut across the current and then actually ran backward against the flow.

How would he find anything?

"Come, friend," Igesia's voice sounded, and Pellin started. "Have you not heard that the children of Aer are like the wind? If you do not learn what you wish to know, it may be that you will learn something better." The hint of the old man's cackle surrounded him. With a sigh, Pellin plunged into the river.

The current swept his awareness away as he became Igesia.

He stood on the edge of the forsaken desert, the youngest of the southern Vigil. "It's beautiful in its desolation," he said. Qadim, the Honored One, stood at his side and nodded.

"You see well for one so young in the gift. To what would you compare the sword of the desert, Igesia?"

The encompassing sweep of his arm traced a path from horizon to horizon. "Not a sword, Honored One," he said, "but the headsman's axe. To let night fall on you in the desert is to place your head on the block."

"And is that all you see?"

Igesia bowed. "Yes, Honored One. Should I see more?"

By way of response, Qadim placed parchment and charcoal in Igesia's hands. "There is always more, my son. Draw and learn."

Time skipped and he stood within a prison on the far eastern edge of the desert, sweating despite the chill of early morning. The man inside the prison no longer raved, but Igesia paused even so. Sana stood at his side, older in the gift by three hundred years. "Your opportunity awaits, Igesia, and I pray you will never have another."

He swallowed dust. A hundred years in the gift had allowed him to see exactly five instances of those who had slipped through the marauding net of sentinels and spent a night within the borders of the desert. He'd never delved one before. Now he had been deemed experienced enough.

"Come," Sana said. "The Honored One commands us to take the next step in your education. Touch him as you would any other."

With a nod he beckoned the condemned man forward to the bars and placed his hand upon the dirt and grime of his wrist. As instructed, he plunged through the man's memories and emotions, of crimes and kindnesses both real and imagined, until he found the vault. Within the man's mind it appeared as a scroll written in a language he had never seen.

He paused, remaining in the delve to examine the writing at length. Elongated loops and whorls created a design that might have been written by wind. It tugged at him even as it mocked his ignorance, but his time studying the desolation of the waste had in no way prepared him for this. Foolishly, he had expected some insight into the nature of the vault, but nothing came. Still, the practice of patient observation was too ingrained to forsake. He remained in the delve until Sana, concerned at last, shook him loose.

The prison vanished, and now he stood on the edge of the desert, old and wrinkled as the thirteen bowed to his authority even as they objected to his decision. "Igesia, even the Honored One requires some measure of companionship," Sadiq said.

"And when I do, Aer will bring you to me. The wind will whisper my need upon your heart even before I've felt it, and you will come. Besides, my guards will remain against the last need." He turned to stare across the sand as a breeze lifted a puff of dust from a faraway dune. A sign? He didn't know. "Calm yourselves, brothers. It was for this that Qadim chose me. It may be that my contemplations will yield some morsel of knowledge about our ancient task."

"And if not?" one of the thirteen asked.

He shrugged. "Then not. Aer will decide."

Events shifted within the delve again, and Pellin skipped along Igesia's countless memories of days spent in observation of the Maveth Desert, its borders mapped so accurately he could almost pick the exact grains of sand that marked the boundary.

Pellin came out of the delve, shaking his head, prepared to speak, but Igesia still held his wrist and seemed in no hurry to leave his mind. Observation. Inwardly he sighed. His temperament ran more toward thought, but perhaps in this, Igesia saw more clearly than he. He placed his hand on the wrinkled skin once more.

A woman stood before him in the failing light of day. Despite her diminutive size, massive ropes as thick as hawsers bound her chest and limbs. At his side, three of the southern Vigil stood ready. Almawt, almost as old in the gift as he, stepped forward with the aid of the other two, his face a portrait in suffering.

"Are you convinced of the necessity of this?" Fatalan asked.

She hadn't directed her question to any of them in particular, and though he occupied the position of Honored One, it wasn't his place to answer, so he waited for Almawt to summon energy and composure enough to respond. "Necessity?" His pain turned the word into a growl. "I'm too old to pretend to such wisdom. Just as well to ask the desert. But whatever end comes to me will be a relief."

"Would not a draught of paverin help you in your task?" Fatalan persisted.

Almawt managed a smile, though his eyes continued to speak of torment. "The wasting disease is almost done with me, sister. I do not wish my last memories to be clouded by the drug." He stumped forward until he was within arm's reach of the tightly bound girl—and he waited.

At the last, the light fled and the shadows jumped. The girl's eyes dilated until the blue of her irises had all but disappeared. She blinked once and threw herself against her restraints, her lips pulled back from her teeth as she worked to attack Igesia's dying friend.

He worked his way around her and placed one bare hand on her neck and jerked, the reflex curve of his old man's back bending the wrong way. Igesia watched his eyes, but no sign showed his experience. Almawt's body continued to jerk, flinching as though he fought physical attacks within the girl's mind.

Without warning, he dropped, his hand falling away from the girl to clutch at his chest. Igesia leapt forward to come within their circle and reached for his friend, desperate to know his last thoughts. Warning cries surrounded him. It was death to be caught within the delve of the dying, and Almawt had obviously breathed his last, but his gaze shifted, struggling to focus. There were still fractions of a moment left before his light fled. Igesia's hand brushed the skin of Almawt's face.

He found Almawt waiting for him within his mind. "Words," he said. Around them, thousands upon thousands of memories accumulated over a life of hundreds of years flooded out from behind their doors to flare and die. "There are words within the words." An image of black writing appeared before him, a flash of utter blackness against the encroaching night of death.

Igesia broke the delve as Almawt's last memories flared into nothingness. When he looked down, his friend's eyes stared fixedly at a point beyond the horizon. The girl still struggled to free herself from her bonds, but her target had shifted. She no longer attempted to reach Almawt, but sought Igesia.

Pellin released his delve with Igesia once more, but this time he found the leader of the southern Vigil waiting for him, composed, but smiling as if he'd just shared his favorite jest. "Words within words," Pellin echoed. "Almawt's memories of the writing are different, but what does it mean?"

"I have often wondered as much my friend," Igesia said. Pellin watched Igesia's mirth drop away. "The writing seen from outside the scroll is different than from inside." He nodded toward Mark and Elieve. "And the writing on the exterior of her scroll different still, though the markings appear to be the same language." The leader of the southern Vigil worked himself to a standing position on his frail, skinny legs and turned to face Mark. Slowly, as though acknowledging an equal, he bowed. "Do you know what you have made possible, young Mark?"

When Mark shook his head, Igesia smiled. "Here on the southern continent we have a saying that the subtlety of Aer is beyond reckoning. You have redeemed Elieve from the death that had claimed her, but what is more, she holds within her a black scroll."

"She has been touched by the Darkwater," Pellin said, "but we have seen many in the north with such."

Igesia, reseated, leaned forward, his old man's eyes avid. "And how does the writing on their scroll appear?"

Pellin's heart quickened as he replayed the memories of every scroll he'd seen. "The same," he whispered. "It's always the same." His exhilaration faded. "But we can't read it. We're no better off than we were before."

Igesia shook his head. "No, my friend. There is something different at work here. Never has the desert spoken before, nor the forest, if your memories are true." He looked at Dukasti. "Prepare yourself, my young heir. Tonight I will attempt what Almawt attempted before me."

CHAPTER 41

"Must you do this?" Pellin asked. "You could summon another to delve her."

Igesia cackled as if Pellin had made a particularly apt jest. "Of course I could, old friend, but I am as Almawt was before me, used up and on the threshold of death. Perhaps we can wring some use out of these old bones of mine before I depart."

"Is your time so close, then?" Dukasti asked.

Igesia nodded. "I am tired, son of my heart. Would you deny an old man his rest?"

Outside, the sand stretching away to the horizon flared as the setting sun painted it in streaks of shadow and orange. Pellin sighed. If the voice of the desert spoke through Elieve again, the death of the day would have Igesia's passing to accompany it. "What must we do?"

"The border of the desert's evil lies a few hundred paces from here," Igesia said. "I placed a marker there." The gaps in his joyful smile accentuated his mirth. "Let us see what wonders Aer will reveal to us this night."

Mark stiffened, but Igesia shuffled over on his spindly legs to buss Elieve on the forehead. "Such a lovely girl," he said.

Elieve smiled, and Pellin remarked how within the last week, the quality of her expression had changed from that of a child to that of a young woman.

"Thank you," she said.

Even her voice had matured, settling into a lower register, as if she'd grown older physically as well as mentally.

Igesia leaned to one side to speak to Mark. "I will keep her as safe as I can, young Mark."

Mark's face clouded. No doubt he caught the ambiguity in Igesia's reassurance. "That's not quite a promise."

Igesia's expression sobered. "Such guarantees are evil, young Mark. They are beyond the scope of men. But I will do not only my utmost to guard her but also to provide healing, if I see a way."

They left the shelter of Igesia's home and walked west, toward the dying sun, with Igesia leading. Pellin looked back to see his guard searching the rolling dunes for threats, but each time his gaze passed over Elieve, it sharpened.

Though undoubtedly the oldest man in the world, Igesia still set a pace that had Pellin breathing hard. They climbed the shadowed side of a low dune and crested it in time to see the sun deepen from orange to red. "There," Igesia pointed. A few dozen paces away at the bottom of the dune a ragged bit of yellow cloth clung to a short pole. "That's the border."

"How do you know that the sands haven't shifted, Honored One?" Mark asked.

Igesia nodded. "The pole is quite long. It's anchored to the bedrock beneath the sand. That was a worthy question, though. I can see why Pellin apprenticed you."

Mark laughed. "He didn't have a whole lot of choices at the time, Honored One."

Igesia nodded as though Mark had uttered some deep wisdom. "Then allow me to restate, young Mark. I can see why Aer chose you. I have noticed that Aer often brings us to extreme circumstances to give us the opportunity to make the choice we should."

"What happens when we don't?" Mark asked.

Igesia sighed. "History is replete with the answer."

"I haven't had the opportunity to read much history, Honored One."

Igesia's voice lost its usual singsong, turning serious. "You should remedy that."

"I will," Mark said. At a look from the Honored One, he amended his answer. "If Aer wills."

They arrived at the marker, the cloth hanging limply in the dead air. "A pace or two beyond should suffice," Igesia said. "Allta, will you take Elieve in your arms? A wise man prepares for the unexpected and often receives a joyful surprise." He shuffled around the big guard so that he was shielded from Elieve's vision. "Be ready for anything, my friend."

They stood watching as the last ruddy light faded from the desert sky and stars to the east winked into view.

"You've returned already," Elieve said in a voice that carried no hint of youth or innocence.

Pellin nodded, as much for Igesia as for the thing that spoke using Elieve's voice. "I have. You promised knowledge. What do you have to offer?"

"Much," the voice said, "but first tell me of your world."

By the first light of the moon, Pellin saw Igesia nod, urging him to continue. "We are peoples of two continents," Pellin said.

"Only two?" the voice asked. "Still, the possibility cannot be ruled out. What of your rulers or governors?"

Caution filled Pellin at the question. He sensed pitfalls, but surely the intelligence in the desert would have learned of the gift of kings from those few unfortunate souls it had corrupted in the past, just as it must have known of the two continents peopled by man. "We are governed by those Aer has gifted to rule, though we are not immune to envy and strife and the wars that accompany them."

"It is as I said so long ago," Elieve said in that other voice.

Pellin assayed a question in the pause that followed. "Who are you?"

"I have many names," the voice said, laughing at some hidden jest. "As many as I could gather." Elieve's laughter scaled upward, and Mark's hand tightened on his dagger.

"I don't understand," Pellin said. He kept his gaze fixed on Elieve, but in his peripheral vision, he saw Igesia reach forward to touch her.

The Honored One's eyes widened at the contact, and Elieve jerked in Allta's grip. "You think to try me at last, stripling?" Elieve howled with laughter. "Long you have teased me at the edge of my power. Come then."

Elieve offered no struggle, but tension in Allta's arms and legs showed he expected violence any moment. Mark, his face stricken, held one of her hands and put his mouth to her ear. In the silence, Pellin could hear him whispering over and over. "You are loved. I love you."

Time lengthened and stretched, and the space between Pellin's heartbeats became an eternity as Igesia and Elieve stilled until they might have been nothing more than statues of themselves. All the while Mark held Elieve's hand and whispered his devotion into the night.

The moon rose, separating itself from the horizon to shine on Igesia, but there was no hint of the old man's internal struggle.

"Eldest," Allta called to him an hour after sunset, "what do we do?"

Inside, Pellin railed against his ignorance and helplessness. "Nothing. Until we have some means of relieving our ignorance, we will have to wait."

"If the corruption of the desert takes Igesia, Eldest, I will be hard-pressed to protect you all."

Dukasti stepped forward, drawing the long curved dagger from his waist and handing a shorter one to Pellin. "We will protect ourselves as we can, Allta," he said. "I think the Honored One might have foreseen these circumstances. He is too old and frail to constitute a threat to you, even if the desert takes him."

They waited as the moon rose. Shadows fell across the faces of those locked in combat in their strange tableau, Igesia, older than any living and Elieve, harboring an intelligence far older still. Mark's encouragement never wavered.

Pain, a sliver of glass in Pellin's heart, stabbed him. Almost certainly, Elieve's mind would be extinguished during Igesia's fight. She would lose the memories, her own this time, which she had gathered. If she lost all of them, which was likely, there would be no rebuilding her. The sweet girl that Mark's love had created would be gone. Pellin wept.

Hours later, Igesia's strained whisper broke the silence. "Touch her."

Allta spoke before Pellin could move. "Eldest, there's no way to know who speaks."

Dukasti nodded his agreement, his dark hair catching the moonlight. "Allow me, Eldest. The Vigil cannot afford to lose both the Honored One and the Eldest at the same time."

Pellin caught Dukasti's arm as he reached for Igesia. "Nor can the south afford to lose both Igesia and his heir. Consider, during the hours of his delving, Igesia has offered no word or hint of his struggle. Now he does. Only three conclusions are possible."

Dukasti shifted in the moonlight. "He has won or lost his struggle with the desert, or the issue has yet to be decided."

"Yes," Pellin whispered, "but regardless, he fought the evil to a standstill within Elieve's mind for hours." At that moment he was certain of what needed to be done. "Your strength and mine may be the margin of victory."

Dukasti gasped. "If it's not, we will carry the poison. The twin evils of the forest and the desert will be loosed on the world."

"Do you refuse?" Pellin asked.

Dukasti shook his head. "No. Together, then."

"Allta," Pellin said, "you must stand ready to administer the mercy stroke if we are taken." When his guard nodded, he reached out, his movements twin to Dukasti's, and put his hand on Elieve's head.

The desert, moon, and stars vanished as he plummeted into the delve, but the river of thought and the cavern of consciousness he'd been expecting were absent. Battle raged within Elieve's mind. Noise that he'd never before encountered testified to the conflict, but of Igesia, there was no sign.

Without warning, threads of black-forked lightning erupted from the vault beneath Elieve's river, racing unerringly toward him and Dukasti along a jagged path. With dual screams, the two of them slashed at the threads with their gift, and they disappeared. More came immediately, searching for them with the sentience of the desert. Again they struck at the same time duplicating their effort. "We must coordinate," Pellin screamed.

By unspoken agreement they divided the fight into two spheres of conflict, destroying threads that came at them from the dark. "What do we do?" Dukasti yelled.

Pellin turned his head to make himself heard, even as he slashed at a trio of threads that attacked from the darkness. "Find Igesia!"

"He's not here." Panic and loss broke Dukasti's voice.

"He is!" Pellin screamed. "Look." He pointed toward the vault.

Dukasti slashed a pair of threads that came for his legs, then gaped at the scroll. "It's monstrous."

Pellin nodded. Confused by the battle at first, they hadn't noticed that the black scroll that comprised the vault within Elieve's mind had grown huge, making it appear far closer than it was. "He's there, fighting with us."

"How do you know?" Dukasti asked.

"The threads would be more numerous if he were not."

Dukasti gaped, his face stricken. "More?"

"Yes." Pellin reached out to squeeze the southerner's shoulder. "Your gift is more powerful than you know. We must go to him."

Fear made Dukasti's face go slack for an instant before some reservoir of courage or resolve took hold and he nodded. Like men walking into a gale, they plowed forward, their power to destroy memories flashing at the threads of poison that came for them.

The evil within Elieve's mind must have sensed their intent. After they'd taken no more than three steps, a flurry of threads erupted from the scroll, the attacks coming so quickly that Pellin and Dukasti were forced to a standstill.

But like men who'd found the capacity to bear blows regardless of cost, they refused to retreat, standing their ground as the air erupted around them. An ululating cry erupted from Dukasti's lips as he tore through a handful of threads. "For Igesia!" he screamed.

Love, fierce and savage, broke loose from Pellin's heart and he thrust his hands forward, turning a dozen threads into wisps. "For Elieve!" Space opened unexpectedly before them, the attacks dwindling to almost nothing.

Intuition burst into Pellin's mind, as though a dam had burst. "Hurry! The desert seeks to end Igesia now."

They surged forward toward the scroll, flying across the distance with the speed of thought, stopping as they reached the vault. Swollen and grotesque, it loomed above them. Black writing covered it, but the glyphs made no more sense to Pellin than they ever had. The surface of the vault writhed, testimony to the battle that raged within it, but there was still no sign of Igesia.

"Where is he?"

Pellin swallowed against the sudden fear of a child who knows better than to enter the dark. "Inside."

Dukasti took his arm. "Together. Again."

With the strength of their gift, they tore a hole in the surface of the vault and passed through.

Pellin found himself on the inside of a sphere. Threads came for them, striking like vipers, but he and Dukasti slashed at them with their gift. They forged a path to the center and found Igesia.

The Honored One sat in repose, but fatigue had etched new furrows on his visage until he appeared on the point of death. His lungs worked to draw air, the tendons of his neck straining with effort. "Sit," he groaned in time with his exhale. He and Dukasti positioned themselves on either side, and with the motion of a man trying to lift boulders, Igesia held out his hands.

Pellin and Dukasti reached out. On impulse, Pellin reached for Dukasti with his free hand and the three of them joined within the depth of Elieve's mind.

Shocks buffeted him as Igesia's and Dukasti's thoughts flooded into his with the force of a tidal wave. He grappled with the waters, but the forces were too strong.

"Flow with them," Igesia's mind whispered into his.

Pellin's mind rebelled, working to maintain his sense of self, fearful of losing his identity. But Igesia's and Dukasti's hands still held his. Letting go of his thoughts, he focused instead on the feeling of their mental touch. The tidal wave didn't calm, but he swam with it instead of fighting it.

Presently, he found himself.

"Words within words," Igesia said. "Help me, my brothers. I haven't been able to see it all." With the merest nod, Igesia indicated the walls of Elieve's vault. Writing covered its interior, teasing Pellin with words he could almost understand, but threads formed and leapt from the surface.

Realization exploded in his mind. The evil in Elieve's mind was attacking them to keep Igesia from seeing the writing. Even now, threads gathered to obscure their vision inside the vault.

Coordinating their gift, Pellin and Dukasti fought the threads that came for them while Igesia burned them from the surface. Slowly, sections appeared and though the script defied comprehension, Pellin committed each glimpse to memory.

Igesia moaned, his body shuddering.

"Honored One," Dukasti yelled. "What's wrong?"

"The evil of the forest," Igesia panted. "It's trying to withdraw."

"Help him read the writing!" Pellin said. "I will fight the threads."

Dukasti withdrew his defense. Pellin felt him drop away. Threads leapt at them from everywhere, working to overwhelm them as the evil sought to escape.

Pellin paused, expecting the unslaught to lessen, but attacks still came from the walls, striking to get past their defenses. Exhaustion ached within his mind, a burden he could neither shed nor shoulder. "We need to withdraw," he begged.

"Yes," Dukasti pleaded.

"A little more my brothers," Igesia groaned. "Only a little more."

They fought on as the attacks grew more desperate, more frantic. Dukasti pitched forward, his gift flaring and guttering until it ceased and his presence disappeared. Pellin redoubled his efforts, but his counterattacks were slowing.

A score of threads came for them. He would never be able to destroy them all.

Inches away they stopped.

Light flared within Elieve's mind. Awareness ceased.

CHAPTER 42

Pellin woke to sunlight in his eyes and the grit of sand beneath his hands. Mark held Elieve, crooning to her, his words too soft to hear, his tone begging. Beside him, Igesia lay staring unblinking at the morning sun, a smile fixed on his face, but the rise and fall of his chest had ceased, and no pulse disturbed the withered flesh of his neck. Beyond him, Dukasti lay with his eyes closed, but after a moment, he shifted, drawing breath.

Then Pellin slept.

It was dark when he woke again. Someone had taken him back to Igesia's house. Lamps burned all around. Allta sat by his bed, his sword naked in his lap.

"Dukasti?" Pellin asked. He knew better than to ask after Igesia. The memory was real. The Honored One had died.

"Sleeping, Eldest," Allta said.

"It's night," Pellin said, then shook his head at the observation. "Brilliant," he muttered.

"Yes, Eldest," Allta said. "I would have bound Elieve to be safe, but there seems to be no need." Something broke for the barest instant in Allta's expression, an unmasking of the thoughts that lay behind it that Pellin had never seen before. "Eldest . . ." The word barely made it past his lips. "Eldest, she won't wake up. Mark's grief will break him. I asked him to give me his knives, but he refused."

Pellin needed to sleep in a way he hadn't felt in centuries, but Allta's news placed demands on him he couldn't ignore. "Take me to them," he ordered.

"Eldest, I've never seen that depth of mourning," Allta said.

He nodded. "Ordinarily I would tell you to let Mark's grief run its course, but I have learned the value of impatience. Carry me if you have to." He worked to get his hands beneath his chest and roll from the bed, but his arms might have been weighted with lead for all the success he had.

"Eldest?"

He struggled for a moment more. "I think you'll have to."

Allta set aside his sword, then bent to scoop him up and cradle him in his arms like a child. When he turned for the door, Pellin caught sight of Dukasti on a makeshift pallet, his skin pale. In the main room, with enough candles blazing to banish the specter of the desert, Mark sat like a statue, if a work of marble could have matched his hopeless expression—unmoving, uncaring of the heat, his gaze fixed on Elieve.

Allta set Pellin on an empty chair. When Pellin reached out, his guard grabbed his wrist. "Eldest, you cannot. You almost died."

Pellin sighed. Even now he could feel his gift guttering like a candle in the wind, but he had to know. He pulled back his hand. "Bring me wine or spirits," he said to Allta. "Anything you can find."

As soon as his guard left the room, Pellin extended one trembling arm to brush Elieve with his fingertips. His gift took him, and he felt his mind begin to snap, cracking like a board under too much weight.

Then it passed, the room and Elieve visible once more, though his vision had narrowed to a pinpoint. Someone put a cup in his hand, and he drank, the sweet syrup of date wine washing the grit of the desert from his throat.

"Gone," he whispered.

A sound broke from Mark, soft weeping that neither diminished nor scaled upward, a wellspring of grief that might last forever. The effort it took to reach for Mark made the room spin, threatened to pitch Pellin from his chair, and he grasped his apprentice's tunic as much to keep himself from falling as to get the boy's attention. "No," he whispered. "Her vault. It's gone. She's herself."

Mark turned to stare at him as if Pellin had assayed some cruel joke. "Her memories?"

Even smiling made the room tilt in his vision. "She has them. I must speak with Dukasti." He took another drink of date wine, and the pinpoint of light narrowed some more. "When I wake." His last sensation was of falling from the chair.

When Pellin woke again, Dukasti sat by his side. Circles darker than bruises lined the man's red-rimmed eyes, mute testimony to the extremity of his effort. "Greetings, Honored One," Pellin breathed.

To his credit, Dukasti didn't waste time on rebuttals, only nodded in acknowledgment. Yet the solemnity of the gesture carried awareness of the burden he bore. "Greetings, Eldest. Your guard and apprentice tell me you have delved the girl and found her vault to be gone." Dukasti's eyes widened at this, as if his own words held the power to amaze him. "Is this true?"

Pellin nodded. "Have you not delved her?"

His counterpart gave a brief shake of his head. "I am far younger in the gift than you, Eldest. It will be some days before I can exercise it again. Even the thought of using my gift makes my stomach roil."

Pellin stared at the ceiling. "Did you see it, there at the end?"

"No, Eldest," Dukasti said. "I lost consciousness. How is it Elieve has emerged from the night without her vault?"

"Igesia," Pellin said. "Some intuition or insight of Aer must have told him."

Dukasti nodded his agreement. "I think he would have said the extremity of our circumstances allowed Aer to show us what we needed to know."

Pellin smiled. "Amazing. We passed to the inside of Elieve's vault, and Igesia used his gift to keep the evil of the Darkwater from withdrawing. When the morning sun hit Elieve with her vault open, it destroyed it."

Dukasti nodded. "It took everything we had to manage it. We're fortunate beyond reckoning that the corruption didn't take us as well."

Pellin nodded. "Indeed, but if the Vigil were at full strength, I believe it could be done with less risk." His heartbeat increased in pace and intensity. "We have a way to break Willet Dura's vault without destroying him." A thought struck him. "Aer have mercy on me. We've killed hundreds. We could have saved them."

"You are not Aer," Dukasti admonished him. "There was no writing or lore to tell you how to save those who dared the forest."

Pellin swallowed. "We didn't think to ask."

Dukasti said. "Do not fault yourself for what you couldn't have known. You are not Aer. What of the writing in Elieve's mind? Why did the evil work so hard to keep us from seeing what we couldn't possibly read?"

"I don't know yet," Pellin said, "but I believe Lord Dura can summon those who can." He took a moment to compare memories. "The writing inside Elieve's mind is different than the writing I saw in Almawt's memories."

"Perhaps every vault is unique," Dukasti said, "tied in some way to its owner."

Pellin nodded. "Perhaps. Regardless, we will find our answers on the northern continent. There are none in the south who are infected with the poison of the desert."

"Thank Aer for that," Dukasti breathed.

"Yes," Pellin agreed, "unfortunately, we have enough people with a vault in the north to test any number of theories."

"I am the Honored One now, Pellin," Dukasti said. "I could send some of the southern Vigil with you."

His heart leapt at the offer, but after a moment, he demurred. "The ancients divided those with a gift for a reason. If we strip the defenses of the desert, we will find ourselves fighting a two-front war." He looked outside. The deep night revealed hints of moonlight that bathed the sands in argent ghost light. He couldn't see the stars, but in the sky overhead there would be scattered grains of light, testifying to the power of the Creator.

His bones ached with age and fatigue, and he wondered, idly, what it would be like to surrender his gift to Mark and sleep.

"I'm glad it's night," he said at last. "I need sleep. Tomorrow we leave for the northern continent." He looked at Dukasti. "We will need whatever speed your authority and wealth can provide."

The new Honored One assented with a small bow. "I will ride with you and ensure you have whatever you require."

Pellin offered his thanks. "I must contact Toria Deel and the Chief of Servants and let them know of our success and my return." He turned to Allta. "Would you bring my scrying stone?"

As he waited, Pellin thought of all that had occurred in the last day. For the first time in history, they had healed someone of their vault. He retreated into the sanctuary in his mind and floated past each door—so many—where he'd sequestered the memories of those he'd broken.

One by one, by name and visage, he apologized to their memory and pled Aer's forgiveness. When he opened his eyes, he found Allta and Dukasti staring at him, their expectation plain. "I found myself in need of absolution," he said. "Now, let us share the news of our victory with those who fight the battle with us."

Allta placed the perfect shard of green diamond in Pellin's hands, but when he called into the stone, no one answered.

Allta's voice intruded. "Eldest."

Pellin lifted a hand, asking for silence, then called again, but still no one responded. "I don't understand."

"Eldest," Allta called again. "Look." He pointed.

There on the topmost edge of the stone, a nick, hardly more than the width of a hair, marred the diamond's perfection. A new fear gripped Pellin, and he clutched at Allta's arm. "The evil of the Darkwater has tasted defeat for the first time. It will become desperate now." The nick in the scrying stone might have been etched on his heart. "I have no way to warn them."

CHAPTER 43

A half hour before sunrise, Fess awakened Toria. "They're returning, Lady Deel."

Three days had passed since they'd been reunited with Lelwin. In that time the girl had had refused all contact and conversation except what was absolutely necessary for battle. After Toria's persistent questioning, Lelwin finally assured her that Branna had arrived safely to the healers in Elbas. She refused, however, to explain why she, too, was not with them.

Pulling her thoughts back to the conflict at hand, Toria looked to Fess. "Wag?"

"He's with them and unhurt."

She sighed. "Praise Aer for that, anyway. And the soldiers?"

"They've suffered heavy losses, Lady Deel, again."

She stood, stamping her feet to settle them into her boots. "The same as the other camps," she said. "Rymark's inner ring is crumbling. We'll have to fall back."

"Lelwin won't agree," Fess said.

"Perhaps not, but let's see if she refuses before we argue against it."

They exited the tent to the charcoal-colored sky of predawn. A group of twenty men and women, many bearing wounds, entered the camp, their eyes already veiled against the light. "That's all?" Her voice broke with the question.

"Heavy losses," Fess repeated. "The forest is fighting back."

"Enough," she said. Striding quickly across the camp, she positioned herself in front of the tent where Lelwin and the rest would

297

spend the day, hiding from the sun. "Stop," she commanded. "You cannot continue to fight in this way." Wag, his coat spattered with blood, trotted around to stand beside her, his ears pointed forward.

Lelwin stood at the forefront of her men, waving her away. "We need rest and food, Toria Deel, and you're keeping us from both."

"This is finished," Toria said. "You lost half of what remained of your command this night. You must retreat." Lelwin's mouth set in a line, her refusal plain.

Before she could speak, Toria stepped to the side to address the veiled men and women who waited to enter the tent's darkness. "I'm going to give you two reasons why you must retreat."

She circled the group, working to her right toward the embers of one of the few fires in the camp. "First, from this minute forward, you will no longer have the sentinel to fight with you." A buzz of angry mutters rose from the camp, from those veiled and unveiled, until Fess appeared at her side, his sword drawn.

Lelwin shrugged her indifference. "We held the outpost before the sentinel's arrival, Toria Deel. We can hold it again."

Toria leaned forward, pretending surprise. "Can you? With no reinforcements?" She continued to circle toward the fire. "How many more nights like this last can you endure?"

"If we must, we will reduce the area we patrol around our camp," Lelwin said. "We will hold, Toria Deel, and if we do not, we will strike a blow against the evil of the forest that you would not." Beneath her veil, Lelwin smiled. "I will not abandon those with me to evil, as you did."

Toria stifled her reply. Defending herself against Lelwin's accusations would avail her nothing. "A military campaign runs according to a chain of command," she said. "While you are in command of this outpost—in fact, if not in name—I have been given authority by King Rymark to command this and every other outpost."

Lelwin laughed. "I will not obey your orders, Toria Deel, nor will any of those who fight with me."

Toria dipped her head. "Perhaps, but there is another reason you must retreat." She bent, pulling a half-burned branch from the dying fire and threw. Spinning, the branch soared toward the heavy canvas tent, the air bringing the ember to life. It fell atop the heavy fabric, and the tent erupted in flames.

Lelwin wheeled on her, screaming. "You dare! Do you know what you've done?"

She nodded, working to keep her face placid. "Yes. Like any good commander, I've ensured that my orders will be followed."

Her face mottled with rage, Lelwin yanked a dagger from her belt and threw in a single motion. Toria watched the blade streak toward her chest, striving to move and knowing she would fail.

The ring of steel pierced the air, and Lelwin's knife fell to the ground, knocked aside by Fess's sword. Toria stared, disbelieving as Lelwin moved to throw again.

But Fess, gifted and unsurprised, was quicker. "Wag!"

A blur of muscle and fur streaked across her vision, and Lelwin was down, Wag's jaws around her throat. "Hold her," Toria ordered. "The rest of you, take off your veils. It's time you reacquainted yourselves with the light."

"And if we refuse?" a man behind Lelwin asked.

Toria nodded toward Fess. "Then you've rejected a direct order from a superior, and my guard will kill you where you stand."

Slowly, starting with the men and women in back, the soldiers removed their heavy veils, squinting against the predawn light that Toria found barely sufficient. Behind her, the crackle of fire grew.

"No!" Lelwin screamed within Wag's grip. "We must fight."

Toria's heart wrenched within her with the need to fold Lelwin in her arms, but she pushed the impulse aside. "Wag, bring her to me."

With Lelwin screaming the entire way, the sentinel dragged her across the ground. At the last, Lelwin lay before Toria, her hands covering her veil, striving to keep it in place. Toria bent to rip the cloth loose."

The first hint of sunlight broke above the horizon as the veil tore and fell away. Lelwin's brokenhearted wail filled the camp, breaking the dawn into splinters of jagged sound. She screamed until her breath died, then curled into a ball, her head tucked between her knees. Toria slipped a hand free and delved her for less than the space of a heartbeat, just long enough to confirm the suspicion she'd held for the past three days.

Toria called to the man who had stood silent, paces away, through the entire exchange. "Lieutenant, get your men moving south. You can't hold your outpost any longer."

The lieutenant eyed the men and women who stood staring at Lelwin, still curled on the ground. "You're not coming with us?" He stepped closer. "What if they refuse to follow?"

Toria shrugged. "Then leave them or kill them. The decision is yours." She nodded toward the picket line, where the horses snorted, nervous. "You have a number of spare mounts now. I'll need one."

"Are you going to kill her?" the lieutenant asked.

"Kill who?" Threads of emotions she couldn't identify were woven into the question, but she had no desire to explain her guilt.

"Brekana," he said. Then after a pause, "Lelwin."

"One, hopefully not the other," she said.

Fess lifted Lelwin into the saddle and forced her legs to straighten enough to place her feet in the stirrups, but his attempts to force her to hold the reins proved futile. She simply let them fall. In the end, he tied the reins to his saddle. "I'll have to lead her, Lady Deel."

She nodded. "Watch her. We'll be in the saddle most of the day."

"Where are we going?" Fess asked.

"Back to King Rymark, but first I want to see how the other outposts have fared."

Eight hours later Toria gazed on the fourth outpost they'd checked that day. Smoke drifted upward from portions of the stockade, where fire and embers still burned, their glow hidden by the harsh light of the sun. The same could not be said of the tents. All that remained were bits of charred canvas and rope.

And bodies.

"Like the others," Fess said. "Completely overwhelmed."

As before, she sent Wag to search the surrounding area before she spoke to Fess. "Check for survivors."

He dismounted, moving toward the gate where men and women lay dead and scattered, the extremity of their defense obvious even at a distance. Toria contemplated suspicions and actions she preferred to ignore. "I could have been a sculptor's apprentice," she said to Lelwin, but the girl hadn't stirred on the ride to the outposts, and she didn't move now. "I could have lived a simple life. I could have loved and married and had children and died a score of years ago."

With a mental shrug, she pushed those thoughts aside. She would have to delay any attempt to heal Lelwin until later. For the moment the girl's illness served the Vigil better. Toria ignored the voice in her head that accused her. There would be time later for her to wallow in her revulsions. Reaching out, she touched Lelwin's bare arm, dropped into the girl's mind just long enough to confirm that the vault—gray but not black—lay still and closed beneath the river of thoughts that rushed like a torrent through her, a river composed almost entirely of darkest hues.

Fess returned, but she didn't need to see his expression to know none of the defenders of the outpost had survived. The fact that his arms were empty, told her as much. "I need you to make a veil."

His face stiffened. "And then protect you?"

Toria closed herself to his unspoken condemnations. She had too many of her own. "Yes."

He stood unmoving. "You told me that I should let the Vigil love me. Is this how you show that love to others?"

Stung, she wheeled on him. "Delve her! Look in her mind and tell me what you see, apprentice!"

He met her passion with the rock-like stoicism of any Vigil guard, but he peeled a glove and touched the curled figure on horseback. "She has a vault."

"Brilliant," Toria said. "You still know how to use your gift. What color was it?"

"Gray."

"Excellent," she drawled. "Now tell me, what does such color in a vault signify?" When he didn't answer, she continued, lashing at him with her voice. "Come now, surely Bronwyn told you what it meant."

He shook his head. "She did not."

She let her eyes go wide in feigned surprise. "Do you mean you don't know? Perhaps an apprentice to the Vigil should accompany his accusations with knowledge."

"That stroke was well laid," he said. "How well did you know Willet Dura when you tried to kill him?"

The fire of her anger disappeared as if Fess had dumped ice on it. "That's unfair."

Breath burst from him. "Unfair? What about any of this is fair?"

"None of it," she said, then gestured at Lelwin. "What was done

301

to her, least of all. You noticed her vault wasn't black. Did you also note the lack of writing on it?"

"I did," he said, his voice neutral once more.

"If you were to go back to Bunard with your gift, you would doubtless find any number of vaults such as Lelwin's among the urchins," she said. "It's the mind's last defense against memories that cannot be suffered any longer."

Fess's expression turned stricken. "Because she never made it to the healers."

"Or refused to stay," Toria answered. "Regardless, at some point she wrapped herself in darkness and ceased to be Lelwin, becoming Brekana. We need to know as much as we can about Cesla's plans. Brekana fought him to a standstill until last night, Fess. Any knowledge we can give Rymark will help him. Lelwin doesn't know anything of the battle."

"But Brekana does," Fess said. He left her then, returning a moment later with a blanket that had escaped the ravages of the fire mostly unscathed. Methodically, he began ripping it into long, wide strips. "If we open Lelwin's vault, will we be able to close it again?"

"I believe so, but if I guaranteed it, I'd be lying," she said. "The mind is at once stronger and more fragile than we know. Of a certainty, it is far more complex than we can imagine."

He lifted Lelwin's curled body from the back of her horse and laid her on the ground, his motions gentle. Then he searched her, his hands probing, thorough, until every hiding place for a weapon had been emptied. With long pauses in between, he wrapped the strips of blanket around Lelwin's eyes.

After the third, she jerked, taking her weight from Fess's arms to sit on her own. "Where are we?"

"Four outposts east of yours, Brekana," Toria said.

Brekana smiled, wolfish, beneath her veil. "So you've decided to call me by my name." Her hands shifted. "But you've taken my weapons."

Toria nodded. "I thought it best, since you tried to kill me."

She inched closer, but Lelwin stood and moved back. "What do you want?"

"The same thing as you, to fight those that come from the Darkwater," Toria said.

Brekana laughed. "You think that's what I want? So old and so ignorant. I don't want to just fight, I want to bathe in the blood of men until I can paint the world with it."

Toria had expected no less. "All men? What of Fess or Mark or Rory?"

"Boys," Brekana said. "It would be a mercy to kill them before time and opportunity turn them into men."

There would be no reasoning with Brekana, and every moment they allowed her personality ascendancy, Lelwin suffered. "What happened last night?" Toria asked.

But Lelwin shook her head. "If you want knowledge, Toria Deel, you must be prepared to pay for it."

Toria took a step closer, but Lelwin retreated, maintaining their distance. "Every moment you are free is by my sufferance, Brekana."

"You let them have me," Brekana snarled. "They forced themselves on me, and you gave me useless mind tricks. When I close my eyes, I can hear them. I can smell them." She lifted her hands toward her veil. "The men of the forest are coming for you, Toria Deel, as they did for me. I would rather return Lelwin to you than help you."

Brekana paused, her smile of triumph still baring her teeth.

"Now, Fess."

Brekana lifted her hands to remove her veil, but Fess closed the distance, moving so quickly from one moment to the next that he seemed to disappear then reappear at Brekana's side, his hands holding hers, keeping her veiled and her vault open.

She flailed, kicking, working to scratch or bite him, but he dodged, keeping her at bay. "Hurry, Toria Deel," he said.

She ran, her hands extended as Brekana threw her head back and forth, working to shed the strips of cloth that bound her eyes. Toria reached out, her hand covering Brekana's as Fess held it still. The world disappeared as she fell into the open vault that defined Brekana's personality.

Memories of nights filled with darkness and blood flooded through her. She hunted by the dimmest light of the moon, killing the unsuspecting from the forest, reveling in their surprise and death as they died, pierced by arrows they never saw.

Light flared in Toria's vision, and the sun canted wildly until she hit the ground, retching.

A few feet away from her, Lelwin sobbed softly, her brown hair once more unbound. Fess stood, holding the ruins of the veil he'd used to open her vault.

"My apologies, Toria Deel," he said. "Her kicks had been aimed at me, and I failed to prevent her from striking at you."

Toria clutched at her stomach, fighting the urge to vomit. Gingerly, she waved his concerns away with one hand. "It's alright."

She replayed Brekana's most recent hunt in her mind, counting, and found herself echoing Timbriend's disbelief. She worked to sit up, then fumbled through her cloak for a shard of diamond wrapped in cloth. "I have to contact Rymark." She looked at Fess. "The inner cordon has been wiped out, and the timing is beyond coincidence."

CHAPTER 44

We traveled to the farm where Gehata had hidden the witnesses. It was four days away—far enough to keep them secluded, but close enough for him to visit if he needed additional information. Mirren filled the journey's silences with questions about the Vigil. Custos would answer first, drawing on the information he'd gleaned from the Vigil library. Mirren would pause, her gaze fixed on a spot somewhere just over the top of her horse's head, before asking me the same question.

After two days of travel, during which she endured my confessions of ignorance more than half the time, she turned to me wearing an expression of disbelief. "You don't really know much."

I glanced at Gael, but she showed no inclination to come to my defense. "I've been a little busy for the traditional apprenticeship."

"That's one possibility," Bolt muttered.

My answer didn't seem to satisfy her. "The implications of domere are beyond imagining. How did you survive?"

I winced, certain there was no way Bolt would let a question like that pass without comment. I wasn't disappointed.

"Luck," he said. "Lots of it."

Rory gaped at him. "Luck is a roll of fives a few times in a row. This is divine intervention, yah?"

"You and your companions are strange to me, Lord Dura," Mirren said. "Do they jest?"

I shrugged. "They think so."

On the fourth day, we rode through fields filled with orchards and well-tended vegetable gardens, where we saw men and women of the church watching over those whose penance mandated labor and seclusion.

"I need to delve the witnesses to the attack on Chora," I said, "but I think I'm starting to understand what's happening."

Bolt shook his head in disgust. "But you're not going to tell us just yet, of course."

From Gehata's mind I knew what the witnesses looked like, but dozens, even hundreds of people worked the fields. "I hadn't counted on so many," I said as our horses plodded through an orchard of orange trees heavy with fruit.

We came to the top of a gentle rise, the walled quarters of the farm still five hundred paces distant. Rory turned his horse, searching, his gaze clear and intent. "There," he said, pointing to four people near the southern wall.

"Your eyes must be better than mine," Bolt said. "What makes you think that's them?"

"They're the only ones out here who have a guard for each," Rory said. "They're being kept close to the keep so that they can't escape, and the guards watching over them are probably cosp. They move like gifted."

Bolt sighed. "I'm really not in the mood to kill anybody today. I hope they have sense enough to surrender." He shot a look of disgust at me. "You didn't think to mention that Gehata had put cosp here?"

I held up my hands. "I assumed you knew. He's not exactly the sort of man to trust anyone he doesn't have under his thumb."

"Do they have bows with them?" Bolt asked Rory.

Our apprentice shook his head.

We let our horses approach at a walk. Rory's hands looked as if they were simply resting on his saddle as he held the reins, but there was a dagger in each. If the guards attacked, they would be dead before they realized it. When we were twenty paces away, they snapped some order to the two girls they were guarding, and one of them came out to warn us off.

I told Mirren to fall in behind me. Bolt, Rory, and Gael fanned out, making no effort to conceal just how gifted they were. "Gehata is dead," I said, "and cosp loyal to him are in prison. You can walk away, die, or join them. Don't take too much time deciding."

The guard who had approached us wore a scar that ran the length

306

of his face, which I took to mean either he was experienced enough to see how high the stakes were or he was too stupid to appreciate them. At his signal, the guard behind him stepped behind the girls and pulled his dagger "What proof do you have to offer?" he asked.

I pointed at the two girls. Both dark, with light-colored eyes showing hints of blue and green, they stood frozen by the threat of violence. "They saw something that has to do with Queen Chora's death. I need to talk to them about it." I dipped my head. "That's going to happen whether you allow it or not. So the only question is, will you still be breathing a few moments from now when I do?"

"Willet," Bolt hissed, "I'm not quick enough to get to them."

"There you see?" The man in front said with a smile. "I think you're going to let us pass. Otherwise, the girls will die."

A thought occurred to me, and I pointed to Rory. "If either of these men turn away from us without dropping their weapon, I want you to put your knives to use."

"You think I'm afraid to die?" the man in front asked.

"Probably a little," I said, "but maybe not enough to serve me." I smiled. "That's why I'm telling Rory to put those toys of his in your hamstrings." I dismounted and took a step forward. "I'm not going to let you leave with them, and if you harm them in any way, I'm not going to let you die. I'm going to hurt you in ways you've barely glimpsed in your nightmares. Rory?"

For effect, Rory lifted his left hand and rolled a dagger back and forth across it fast enough to make the edge buzz in the air. "And I'm right-handed," he said.

The guard in back straightened out of his stance and sheathed his sword, stepping to his right, away from the girls. A moment later the guard in front copied him. Bolt and Rory dismounted.

"If you really want to help Aille, go north," Bolt said. "They need men at the forest. If I see you back in Cynestol, I'll kill you."

I took a step toward the girls, my heart pounding with relief and exultation. They backed up against the wall, their eyes wide with expectations of violence. Mirren tugged at my sleeve. "They might prefer a woman," she said, but when she stepped forward they cringed.

"I think they're afraid of everyone, and it's hard to blame them."

Gael dismounted and stepped in front of me. "Go easy, Willet," she murmured. "They're scared. You may be able to see into their minds,

307

but you have no idea what they've been through yet." She turned to the girls. "Let me introduce you to my friend." She pointed to me. "His name is Willet. He's not going to hurt you."

I took a step forward and then another, but at the third they flinched and tried to press themselves into the stones of the wall, their faces turned away. I unbuckled my sword and sat on the ground. "What are your names?"

"Arriella," said the shorter of the two. Her voice was reedy with fear, and the way she flinched when her back touched the stone explained some of it. "This is Oronelle." She touched the other girl on the arm.

"I'd like to talk to you, if I may," I said. "For just a little while, and then, if you like, we can take you back to Cynestol and your family."

Oronelle dropped her head, and a tear caught the light as it fell to the ground. "We didn't protect the queen," she said. "They don't want us anymore."

"Who told you that?" I asked quietly.

Oronelle didn't raise her head, but I heard her sniff. "The bishop."

"Well, Oronelle, the bishop lied," I said. "Your family loves you, and what happened to the queen wasn't your fault."

"How could you know that?" Arriella asked.

I nodded and patted the ground to either side of me. Hesitantly, like skittish colts, they came and sat. "I know what came after the queen," I said. "Your job was to see them, yes?"

They nodded.

I reached out to Arriella, not taking her hand, simply offering mine. She'd taken the lead, speaking for them both, but her fingers trembled even so. "Why don't you tell me what happened?"

"They told us to point at everyone. Everyone," she said. She put her hand in mine.

I plunged through the blue-green of her eyes and into memories that rushed and ran, cascading with all the force of fear and youth. Becoming Arriella, I stood close to the queen along with Oronelle and Bonicia, my sisters. Stern men of the cosp stood around us, tall and unspeaking.

The duty of watching for everyone who approached the queen had seemed exciting and a little scary at first, but the routine of pointing at everyone who approached Chora had grown old. We walked toward the only respite from that duty, the queen's private quarters, where she would sleep for the night. Two of us preceded Queen Chora into her bedchamber, searching out every crack and crevice that might conceal an assassin. Only after we'd satisfied the cosp of the security of the queen's quarters was the queen allowed to seek her bed with us on cots to each side and at the foot. The lieutenant, flanked by the youngest of the cosp, almost boys, nodded to the queen and locked us in for the night.

The first thump against the door woke Oronelle, though she hardly slept anyway. It was her cry that woke me. A second thump, the sound of a body hitting the floor brought Chora to wakefulness. "Guards?"

No answer to her call came from outside the door, but a moment later a key turned in the lock. Relief flooded through me at the sight of the uniformed cosp guards that stepped through, a man and a woman. The woman must have been inordinately skilled with the sword to offset her slight stature, but there was no mistaking the power that resided in the man. His shoulders bulked like hams, and he stood a hand taller than most of the other guards.

Bonicia ran to them as Oronelle and I turned to the queen.

Chora sat up in her bed, openmouthed and watching, her gaze alternating between a wide-eyed stare and a squint, and her head moved back and forth as if she were scanning the room.

A sharp retort of sound by the door shot through me and I turned to see Bonicia on the floor, her head at an awkward angle. The man and the woman darted to us, not slow by any means, but not so gifted as the cosp. Beside me Oronelle whimpered, but I drew breath and screamed.

"Guards! To the queen! Guards!"

Then the man was upon us. I saw the fist coming toward my head, tried to duck, but I was too slow. Pain flared like the sun and everything went black.

I woke to sobbing and light. I recognized that voice. Even as a young child Oronelle had cried in rhythm in her distress, exhaling three sobs before pulling a protracted breath.

I sat up, and the room spun with the effort. I probed twin egg-sized lumps by my temples that felt as if they would split and bleed any moment. The queen stood talking to her advisor, Bishop Gehata.

"He came for me," Chora said, her eyes cold and calculating, "but I couldn't see him. Only providence and the girls kept him from killing me."

"Praise Aer," the bishop said.

But Queen Chora shook her head. "I'd be more inclined to praise Him if Bonicia hadn't been killed." She pointed to a body riddled with arrows that everyone in the room now saw without effort. "I want the other," Chora said, "the woman."

The bishop nodded, his unblinking gaze on me and my sister, his expression sorrowful, but his eyes glittered like splinters of agate. "I think it would be best if we brought fresh guards, Your Majesty. And fresh watchers as well. Oronelle and Ariella are probably too grief-stricken to exercise the diligence needed to watch over you."

The queen nodded. "Go with the bishop, girls."

We stepped over and he took us, one under each arm, and escorted us out of her chambers. At the top of the stairs, the bishop stopped to signal the lieutenant. "Have one of your men go with them. The girls want to go home."

I descended the stairs with my arm locked in Oronelle's, her sobs echoing from the polished stone.

I came out of the delve to see Ariella talking with me, her narrative racing to keep pace with her thoughts. "The next day when we got to the palace we were told to return home." Fresh tears welled in her eyes. "Every day we came back, but it was always the same. The bishop told us the palace had no place for those who were so lax in their task." She swallowed, her throat working against her shame. "Then the queen was killed," she said. "We were outside the hall. The bishop was furious when he found out we were there, screaming at how we'd deserted her." She shook her head. "But it didn't make any sense. He was the one who sent us away."

I nodded without speaking. It made all too much sense. With none but the cosp loyal to him to witness it, he'd had the queen murdered, but I didn't have time to explain, and it would have done nothing to succor the wounds the girls carried. I'd seen something else in Ariella's mind, a room within the protected walls of the farm that no one approached, a room always guarded. "They kept you in the largest building?"

The gesture they both made might have been a nod. Gael herded them toward the nearest entrance, a straight-lined rectangular door in the heavy stone wall surrounding the keep. There was no guard, and the door stood open. We walked through into a community of the Merum church. Penitents and postulates worked at stalls and sheds at whatever tasks the church or Aer devised for them, and across the yard the pinging sound of a hammer came from a smithy.

I paused when my gaze fell across Mirren. The idea of having an apprentice was going to take some getting used to. "Give me your hand," I said.

When I let go, I watched Mirren sort through the memories. "Why are you giving them to me now?"

"I'm safeguarding them," I said. "You said so yourself. I'm lucky to be alive. If anything happens to me, find Pellin or Toria Deel and show them my memories. They'll know what to do." At least I hoped they would know what to do.

"Who's in charge here?" Gael asked a pair of postulants.

"The deaconess," they said in unison as they dropped their eyes to the ground. From their reaction I had an idea of the type of person this deaconess might be. Gael must have had the same notion. Her stare went flat. "Where is she?"

One of the girls pointed to a large squat building opposite the church. Set amid a meticulously groomed flower garden tended by a trio of white-robed postulants, its solidity refuted the adornment. It looked like what it was—a prison. A bell stand stood in the middle of an arc of intertwined rose vines.

"She has a talent for nature," Custos said, "if not nurture."

We tied our horses to the most convenient rail and escorted the girls inside. The postulates tending the garden looked at us with wide-eyed stares, as if we were willingly marching to our deaths.

I blinked twice to let my eyes adjust to the dimmer light and saw a woman of middle years behind a desk, her dark hair shot with streaks of silver. The lines on her face testified to the years she wore, but there remained enough traces of her youth to testify to a luminous beauty. She rose, the motion gracefully imperious, and nodded greeting without smiling.

"Deaconess." I bowed. "The customs of the church here in Aille are unfamiliar to me. How should I address you?"

Her eyes flashed her irritation. "Given that I dislike being interrupted—especially by those wearing steel—as seldom as possible."

"I'm guessing hospitality is not your talent," I said.

Her lips curled. "There is no talent for hospitality in the Exordium," she said.

I smiled. "And you are living proof." I pointed at the two girls. "We're taking at least two of your postulants with us." I moved toward the corridor behind her desk, and thankfully the rest of our company did the same.

The deaconess moved to block me. "What makes you think you can walk in here and give orders to me in my own demesne?"

I tapped the sword strapped to my waist. "That steel you spoke of, Deaconess." She darted a look over my shoulder. "If you're looking for the men Bishop Gehata put here to guard them, you're wasting your time. If they're sensible, they're on their way north. If they're stupid enough to disobey a direct order from the last Errant"—I nodded to Bolt—"they're headed to their own funeral."

Her eyes widened, and she searched Bolt's face. "Errant Consto?" she breathed.

Bolt's expression soured. "I hate it when people look at me that way."

Her steel-shod resolve quickly deserted her, and she nodded to the hallway behind her. "There are four more guards at the end of the hall, but two of them are hardly more than boys."

I looked at Bolt. "I wish that worked everywhere. Who are they guarding, Deaconess?"

"A girl, but Bishop Gehata never said who." She licked her lips. "I don't know. I swear it."

"But you suspect, don't you?"

"Is there another door out the back?" Bolt pointed down the hallway.

When the deaconess shook her head, he nodded to Rory. "Ready your knives, lad. I doubt they'll be willing to walk away." He faced Gael. "If any of them get past us, don't bother with mercy. It's a waste of time."

He and Rory disappeared down the corridor. I pulled my sword and tried to adopt the inherent grace that came with a physical gift. If I was lucky, I'd be able to distract any cosp long enough for Gael to put them down.

"What do I do?" Mirren asked.

I pointed to the far side of the room. "Stand over there with Custos, and don't get killed."

Her eyes widened, and she looked to Gael. "Is he jesting?"

Gael looked like a cat, crouched and ready to pounce. "Not this time, no."

A challenge came from the mouths of one of the guards, and then a scream of pain and the ringing sound of steel on steel. A moment later Bolt beckoned to us.

Gael led the deaconess at sword-point down the hallway. Leaving the girls with Custos, Mirren and I followed. Two men were down and two more—boys, really—were standing to one side, disarmed. I avoided the stares of the dead men, unwilling to deal with whatever horror or recrimination the deaconess might offer.

"Give me the key," I told her.

She stared at the dead men on the floor. "They kept it."

"That might have been a clue," I said in disgust.

Gael bent to search the dead guards. A moment later she straightened to place a key in the lock. She opened the door to the windowless room, but Mirren stepped in front of her. "She might prefer someone who looks like her," she said. "Come here," she called. "You're safe now."

An Aillean girl of thirteen or fourteen, with the features typical of her country came into Mirren's arms. Curious to see if her small cell offered any proof of her destiny, I entered. The Merum order had never believed in coddling their postulants and the interior bore testimony to that philosophy. A raised platform of planks covered with a sheet and blanket served as her bed, and a single ladder-back chair with a miniscule writing desk constituted the furniture. To one side an hour candle had been burned in precise increments.

It was the desk that drew me. Threads had been picked from the sheet and blanket to form a likeness of the deaconess that any artist would have envied. Next to them were portraits of the guards, done in painstaking detail. I stepped back into the hallway.

"Her name is Herregina," Mirren said.

I knelt and watched the new queen of Aille blink against the light in the hallway. "I saw the pictures you made. How long have you been able to do that?"

She blinked, dropping her gaze to the floor. "I did one before," she whispered, "for the bishop." Her voice faded as her chin started to quiver.

I sighed. *Later*, I told myself. I would have time to delve her later, but my imagination conjured images of Chora's death and the desperate passing of her gift.

The deaconess elbowed past me to go into the tiny room. When she came out, she was pale and sweating. "I didn't know," she panted. "I swear it. I had no idea that—"

"I think we should step outside," I said over the woman's fearful babbling. She darted looks at Bolt, as if she suspected he would take her head at any moment. "Gael, would you, Custos, and Rory take Mirren and the girls out to the yard? Bolt and I need to have a word with the deaconess."

We retraced our steps to her office, and as the rest of our company departed, I pointed at the chair. "Sit."

"Are you going to kill me?" she asked.

"That depends," I said. Out of the corner of my eye, I could see Bolt staring in my direction. "I have something that needs doing, Deaconess, and it requires discretion—something you're obviously acquainted with. I watched you go into Herregina's room. You weren't surprised by what you found there, were you?" I moved toward her, and she started to rise. I put a hand on her shoulder and pushed her back into her seat. "No, don't stand up."

I reached for her neck, the skin smooth and unwrinkled despite the streaks of silver in her hair. A moment later, it was done and I knelt by her side. "Are you alright, Deaconess?"

"What happened?"

I looked at her. "You don't remember?" When she shook her head, I went to the door and called to the pair of acolytes working by the roses. "The deaconess has had a spell that seems to have affected her memory. Please see to her." I looked around the yard at everyone sweating in the sun. "I think it would be best if everyone took a respite from their labor for the rest of the day."

I went back in. "We'll be taking our leave, Deaconess. After a few days you should start to feel better."

Outside, Bolt cut his gaze to me for a moment. "What did you do?"

"I reset her memories to just before the girls' arrival." I shrugged.

"Some of them may come back, but even so, she won't be sure of them."

"Good," he said. "I think a little doubt and humility will be good for the deaconess. Let's gather the girls and get back to Cynestol. I want to get this over with. I didn't really care for being the hero of the kingdom when I saved Chora, and I'm pretty sure I won't enjoy having all the nobles fawn over us for finding her heir."

I looked at the sky. Days were longer here in the south, and we probably had enough daylight to make a good start back to the city before sunset, but I shook my head. "Let's find a comfortable inn, preferably one that has some decent ale. We need to talk."

He grabbed my arm. "Willet, we have to deliver the heir—the queen—to Cynestol."

I sighed. "Yes, and I'm sorry that we're not going to be able to do that just yet."

CHAPTER 45

The town of Locallia, two miles from the farm, boasted only one inn, but it had a porch that wrapped around three sides and an affable keeper who might have been Braben's brother if he'd possessed light hair and skin to go with his blue eyes. He escorted us to a private dining room with laughter and jests, bobbing his head and smiling as though our presence honored him.

Bolt waited for me to take a pull from my tankard before he started speaking. I think he wanted to keep me from interrupting him. "We have to get her back to Cynestol."

I nodded. Pieces of a puzzle had started to come together in my head, but I was still too close to it, and I needed to talk my way through my thoughts without being interrupted. I pointed to the room above us. "For now she and the servant girls are safe with Rory," I said. "No one knows where they are, and anyone who tries to force their way in will regret it."

He sighed. "What are you planning?"

"I need to talk to Pellin and the rest of the Vigil, but short of that, I need to know if my intuition is leading me in the right direction." I clapped Custos on the shoulder. "I'm hoping you can help, my friend."

"What did you see, Willet?" Gael asked.

"Something that doesn't make sense," I said. "We knew Bishop Gehata used the attack by the dwimor as a cover to kill the queen, but when I delved his memories the description of the assassin seemed wrong. He was big. Why, when smaller dwimor are much more effective?"

"We knew he was big," Bolt said.

"Yes. What we didn't know was that there were two of them. The woman slipped away when the guards came." I looked at my companions. "She left."

"Two of them," Bolt said.

"Two assassins seems an unnecessary risk," Mirren said.

Gael's eyes widened. "They weren't trying to kill her. They were trying to take her."

"I came to the same conclusion," I said.

"Maybe," Bolt said. "Why would Cesla try to take the queen instead of killing her?"

I took a deep breath. "I need your help again, old friend," I said to Custos. "There's too much to unravel here. Can you tell me what happened when men first came north from the southern continent?"

He nodded, and the light within our room played off the dome of his head. "That's a short question with a long answer, Willet."

I smiled, sharing in the joy that danced in his eyes at the prospect of answering it, and pointed to a bowl of almond-crusted figs perched on the table in front of him. "If you run out, I will pay the keeper whatever it takes to get more."

He took one and savored it, working it from side to side before he answered. "Where do you want me to begin?" His eyes flicked back and forth in that way that told me he searched the library he kept in his mind.

There was no way of knowing what was important without hearing it all, or as much as he could tell me, and I said so.

"Very well," he breathed. "When men from the southern continent took to ships over two thousand years ago, they found the north lush and wild and devoid of men. The first men to settle did little more than build villages on the coast and from there . . ."

Three hours later what remained of the food had gone cold, and the ale had warmed to room temperature. I nodded. Most of what Custos had told me, I'd already known, and though there were interesting details he'd recently gleaned from the Vigil library, there was nothing that truly surprised me.

Worse, nothing he'd told me explained the central question. "Tell me about the gift of kings," I said. "I don't understand how it appeared here in the north."

Custos nodded. "Ah, it's more a question of the south's history than ours. From the beginning, the gift of kings was a part of man's heritage. When the north was discovered, six with the gift of kings left and divided the north between them. The only change in that history came after a particularly divisive political struggle in Caisel. The country decided to split. The kingdoms of the northern continent agreed that the new country, Elania, would have all the rights and privileges of the other kingdoms, except that its monarch would never hold the gift of kings. It's been that way ever since."

"How many still hold the gift of kings on the southern continent?" Gael asked.

"Twelve," Custos said. "But the southern continent is quite monolithic. The twelve choose one of their nobles to act as emperor of the continent. They've escaped the king wars and the order wars, but their internal struggles have been no less violent."

"I think the Fayit created a prison," I said. "Suppose you're one of the last of a dying race of almost incalculable wisdom and knowledge and your job is to guard a prison. Knowing that events often transpire in unexpected ways, you give the civilization that comes after you the means to summon you, despite the oaths you swore to stay hidden."

Custos nodded, his eyes bright. "Yes. They could require the assembly of a circle of four pure temperaments, nine pure talents, or six pure gifts." He shook his head. "But the Fayit must not have counted on the dilution of our race, Willet. The ability to summon them is gone." He pointed to Bolt. "His physical gift is as pure as we know, but in the dim reaches of time, we still have no idea how often it's been split and shared. And we have even less knowledge of what a pure talent or temperament would look like."

I rubbed the top of his head and smiled. "I think your ability, old friend, gives us a clue in that regard." I shook my head. My heart pounded against my chest, constrained by the confines of my ribs. "I don't think the circle is lost to us. I think Ealdor's visits to me—to us—indicates there is still a means of summoning them, regardless of our decline."

"What happened just before the start of the Gift of Kings War?" I asked. I didn't say anything about my guess as to why there were eighteen who held the gift of kings. I might have been wrong. For now, and hopefully forever, it was beside the point.

Gael was the first to answer. She knew my mind better than any other and was the first to see where my intuition and logic had taken me. "They tried to split the gift," she breathed.

Bolt nodded. "It wouldn't split. When they tried to force it, it went free." A moment later he shook himself. "No. It's interesting, but there's not enough steel there to make a dagger much less a blade. Herregina has to go back to Cynestol."

Custos added his objection to Bolt's. "The kings' gifts aren't pure, Willet. Even with the dilution over time the gifts the kings and queens hold don't match those of their strongest subjects in power."

Mirren leaned forward. "Not alone, no, but every king or queen carries a portion of all six gifts. Yes?"

I nodded. "Every new king or queen is tested for the six gifts. It's axiomatic that a king or queen carries a portion of all six. No exceptions. Now work it backward. The gift of kings has been with us since our earliest history. If they can't be split, then it is almost a certainty they've never been split. Don't you see? Every king or queen of the original kingdoms of the northern continent has a fraction of each of the six perfect gifts. If you bring them all together, you have a perfect circle."

"You'll never get the queen of Frayel and the king of Owmead to commit on that basis," Bolt said. "Ulrezia's temper runs as cold as Rymark's does hot, but they share a deep skepticism of any idea that's not their own. They won't come, I'm sorry."

I held up a hand. "Don't be. You want to believe I'm right. If I can't convince you, how can I convince anyone else?" I knew what I had to do, and I hated myself for it. I looked at Gael. "I am so tired of killing people."

Her eyes widened. "Willet . . ."

I reached across the table to where she sat on my right and squeezed her arm, careful to avoid her bare skin. Work with the sword had strengthened her, bringing additional harmony to her willowy frame that I thought beautiful. I sighed, knowing I could put this off, but there was no point. There amidst the mutton and wine and figs, I closed my eyes and shifted in my seat until I faced northwest, aligning myself with the Everwood.

Toward Ealdor's home.

"I'm sorry, Ealdor," I said to the air. "Too much has been lost. We don't know enough to summon you according to your rules."

Though I suspected my friend had a flair for the dramatic, this time he didn't make me wait, and he didn't step from the shadows. He simply appeared.

I pointed to the stole around his neck, the tattered purple one he wore whenever we celebrated haeling together. "I've been meaning to ask you about that," I said. "Why does it look like that? Even the poorest priest keeps his stole in pristine condition."

He gave me a smile, his blue eyes twinkling with mirth and more emotions than I could put a name to. "Do you really want me to expend myself on that question, Willet?"

Surprised laughter came from me almost before I realized it. "Even that?"

He sobered, as though his usual levity had become a burden. "I could tell you what you need to know, but you need to see what happened. The rest of the Vigil can delve any of you for the story."

I delayed. "This is it, isn't it. You won't be able to come back anymore."

A rueful smile played at the corners of his mouth. "Any question I answer will detract from what I'm about to show you, Willet." He sighed. "It will be brief, too brief, but I'll show you all as much as I can."

My eyes stung. "I'm sorry, Ealdor."

The inside of my head exploded into a chiaroscuro of light and sound, but first I heard Ealdor's voice.

CHAPTER 46

"Among the Fayit there were those of us who could sense ripples in time, echoes of the future reaching into the past," Ealdor whispered into my mind. "That inexplicable gift from Aer made me a general when the war broke out. When you came into the forest and when Cailin came after, I felt something in you, a pull from times yet to come that said you would be needed. Perhaps I was just lonely. Millennia ago I stood on the edge of eternity and swore I could bear my solitude, believing my desire for retribution would be enough to sustain me. I was wrong. Time is an implacable torturer."

Tremors still rolled through the deep places of the earth like waves upon the ocean, reminders of cataclysm and war that had fractured the continent. Ealdor strode from the ruined halls with his lieutenants at his side—brothers in spirit, if not by blood—only two at the last.

"Is everything ready?" His voice came harsher than he intended, but grief and ruinous victory clogged his soul as the dust of annihilation filled his lungs. Across the far reaches of their world, nothing remained but ruins.

The fellow priest on his left, who owned the title of the Dara, second priest of Aer, dipped his head and reached out with his bare hand, tempting Ealdor to laughter. Dark in the way of the south, the Dara's height lent elegance even to ordinary gestures. Ealdor sighed. What mattered their manners and deference now, when all was unmade? He thought of the centuries ahead and the long, long grieving yet to come and hungered for speech, as if he could somehow keep sorrow at bay for a moment longer.

"In words, please," Ealdor said as the Dara's thoughts began to convey themselves into his mind.

"As you wish, Altera." Even to the end they used their titles of the priesthood rather than names. The Dara's voice, oddly melodious in the midst of gray choking dust, almost had the power to banish visions of countless dead and destruction. How did one mourn the death of an entire world?

"The last prison is ready." His fellow priest paused. "Your brother and his wife are waiting there for you."

"Why?" Ealdor asked.

The Fayit on his right, similarly titled the Trian, the third priest of Aer, answered in a voice deep and resonant enough to match his bulk. "He's your brother, Altera. He wanted to see you once more." And as he always did, the Trian went on, striving for a deeper meaning that lay beyond the mundane. "Cuman knows that your positions could easily have been reversed, had Gretan survived the last attack."

Ealdor stopped, his feet slipping a bit in the dust and ruins, to bow his respects to the name of his dead wife. Would she have desired Cuman's choice? For a moment grief and doubt overwhelmed him, and he stumbled to find solid footing in the debris around his feet.

"Where have you placed the prison?" he asked. Thinking about his dead wife or the long duty that lay before him served no purpose. He and his lieutenants, bereaved priests like himself, would undertake the peace as they had the long, long war, by shouldering the burden one day at a time until all had been accomplished.

"Two hundred leagues northwest," the Trian said. "As far away from the quakes as we could manage. There's a slip in the earth where the soil runs nearly half a league deep."

"I pray that it holds forever," the Dara said.

Ealdor nodded, but until recently, distinctions of time had held no meaning. For the barest fraction of an instant he sensed the infinite branchings of possibility that overwhelmed him with countless outcomes of a distant future. One stood out from the rest, but it failed to resolve. He shivered. Aer had spoken to him.

"I pray that it does as well," he said, but out loud his voice carried the hollow timbre of doubt.

The Dara and the Trian, ever perceptive, bowed to him as they sketched the profession of belief on their forehead—a single vertical line intersected by a horizontal. "What did you see, Altera?"

Ealdor, weary, waved at the air with one hand. The smell of dust and debris filled his nose. "I sensed a possibility, an impression only, too distant to resolve."

"Good," the Trian said.

"How so?" the Dara asked. "Aer has hinted at a future purpose that we cannot see."

In a time removed from ruin the Trian might have smiled. "But we have a purpose. Still, it would have been a kindness to kill them, and more sure."

"Yes, but not just," Ealdor breathed, hot with anger that still surprised him.

They strode from the empty wreckage of the city of Tolamec, a beacon even during the war, and boarded the fyrlen platform that would take them to the last prison. Ealdor stopped to run the tips of his fingers along the smooth surface, a combination of steel and fiber as light as air and stronger than diamonds. So much had been lost. Soon he and his fellow priests would enter the long dark to ensure the rest of it would be lost as well.

The trip northwest to the prison took less time than he expected, the resonance engine of the platform humming with power. The Dara piloted, skimming the land as if fixing the images in his mind. Outside the burning ruin of the city, the signs of war and destruction lessened, but deep canyons gouged the earth, and sharp rock signaled where new mountain ranges would rise, testimony to the resonance they'd harnessed, power they'd turned on each other.

The fyrlen platform touched the earth, the landing gear flexing on the uneven ground to keep the seating level, and the hum of the engine died away as the rotors slowed. The platforms would have to be destroyed, of course, just as everything else.

They disembarked and walked the short distance to the massive cube where the last enemy awaited. The amount of pure resonant metal they'd committed to the prison still made his mind reel, the wealth of an entire world fashioned into three perfect cubes. The resonance field kept Atol Bealu imprisoned behind shimmering waves of power that diminished sound, but some instinct or premonition must have pulled his head up from unknown contemplations, and their eyes latched on to each other, victor and defeated.

Ealdor resisted the temptation to commence Bealu's imprisonment. Even in this, he would not give Atol the pleasure of believing himself to be the first priority. Though it made his skin crawl to turn his back on the horror Bealu had become, Ealdor willed himself forward to pull his brother and his wife into a clutching embrace.

As if their touch would always hold the power to know him, he voiced his doubt and fear at last. "Are you sure you must do this?"

Soft laughter, amused and rueful at the same time, came from Cuman and Endela. Cuman pulled back from the embrace and swept his arm in a wide arc that somehow encompassed the earth in all its wasted destruction. "Aer gave you and your fellow priests the command that we must surrender our immortality—and now you doubt?

"Look at us, Ealdor." He pointed at Bealu. "Look at *him*. We became too much. Aer placed the earth in our charge, and we failed to stem the ambition of Atol and his like. The choice between departing or living mortal lives is Aer's last, best mercy."

"It seems a hard choice to me now," Ealdor said. "Everyone else has departed. I don't understand why you decided to stay. Your lives will be nothing but a breath, a wisp of morning mist to be burned away by the sun."

Endela, Aer bless her, put a hand to his face, her eyes carrying nothing of grief, her gaze holding only compassion. That incomprehensible strength was exactly why Ealdor wanted her to live on.

"Ealdor, our children will have the chance to be both less and more than us. In their weakness they will come to depend on Aer as we were intended to and didn't," she said. "Their shortened lives will draw them close."

Because he would never see them again after this day, he asked the question closest to his heart. "Does it hurt to know you will be less than you were?"

Cuman nodded. "Yes, but our children will have no reference for it."

Endela added her assurance to his. "With each birth, I will grieve what had to be lost, but I'm hopeful that our sons and daughters will be free from the pride that destroyed our world." Then she shrugged. "But even if they are not, the necessity remains."

"Our strengths will be parceled among our children and theirs and theirs until evil such as Atol's becomes impossible," Cuman said. "The glory of Aer, Iosa, and Gaoithe will fill this world in a new way."

The Trian spoke from behind him. "Imprisoned is not the same as dead."

They all knew the Trian well enough to understand his unspoken question, his accusation.

Endela nodded. "Should the need arise, our descendants will have a way to call you for help. I will craft words to accompany the liturgy Aer has given Cuman. We will teach them to our children, and they will teach them to their children after us, time without end."

"And we will be standing guard," Ealdor said, "should your descendants need us."

The Trian nodded, but whether in approval or acknowledgment, he couldn't tell.

Cuman pointed over Ealdor's shoulder to the prisoner. "Come. Endings and beginnings await us. Our decisions have been made, and the rest of those who have chosen to diminish await us on the southern continent. It is past time we put this abomination away."

Ealdor turned to speak to the Dara and the Trian. "Close the prison." He took a deep breath that felt oddly cleansing, as if his brother's certitude had somehow made a home within him. Odd that Cuman should be able to influence him in such a way after choosing to surrender everything that defined him. "The three of us have countless turnings of work ahead of us, and now I find myself impatient to begin it."

The Dara's brows lifted. "Will you deny Atol his last speech?"

Behind the shimmering wall of force that kept the last of the three imprisoned, Atol glared at him. Perhaps he had been able to discern what they spoke of without sound, but it hardly mattered.

"Yes," Ealdor said, nodding. "I will. I have no desire to hear all the voices he has taken unto himself. Let us see if they are enough to keep him company until Aer makes an end of all things."

Bealu must have caught some hint of Ealdor's decision. Despite the impossibility of breaking the resonance field he thrashed and strained, his face purpling until the pure metal walls of the prison closed around him. At the last, he locked gazes with Ealdor and screamed, his throat cording with the effort as blood vessels burst beneath his skin. Though muted, his words were clear. "Behold! I have a new name!"

Ealdor rebuked the premonition that arose in him. "Then let it keep you company, however you're named, through the endless night."

They stood then, watching as the machines joined the halves of Atol's eternal prison together into a seamless whole and lowered it into the pit.

After the cube had been buried, the canyon filled, and Cuman and Endela had departed to the southern continent, the three of them—priests who'd become beings of war—stood together.

"What are your orders?" the Dara asked.

Ealdor pursed his lips and shook his head. "I have none. From this moment, we are no longer priests or soldiers, but wardens. You know this and the tasks that await us." He straightened, shouldering the burden that would belong to him. "We are the last of our kind. Our memory must pass from the earth."

The Dara and the Trian nodded, and to their credit they paused for only a moment's reflection before they appropriated Cuman's admonition against long farewells, each moving to take fyrlen platforms to the duty that awaited, the Dara leaving first for the south, and then the Trian departing to the western continent, his platform shrinking in the distance.

Despite himself, Ealdor watched them recede into the sky until they were lost in the distant blue. With a sigh he turned to the first task. Though he had countless turnings to complete it, he found himself oddly eager to begin, as if the destruction of the evidence of their race was part of the price Aer had commanded.

He strode over to the machinery that had been used to lower Atol's prison into the depths of the earth. Methodically, he began the penance for his race and commenced the process of taking it apart, reducing it to pieces that would disintegrate to nothingness before Cuman's descendants found their way back.

The vision stopped, and I was Willet Dura once more. My companions wore the same expressions of shock as I. Tears coursed down Custos's cheeks and Mirren wept softly. The remnant of Ealdor stood among us, his stole still draped over his shoulders, but his appearance had changed, the last impression of solidity dropping from him as though he'd become a dying memory. And it continued. My friend became more insubstantial with each passing moment. "Aer forgive me," I choked.

He looked down through his body with no more concern than if I had told him he had a spot on his stole. "I chose to break the binding, Willet. I chose, not you. Aer told us to cleanse the earth, but we—I—wanted vengeance. We buried Atol and those he'd taken unto himself, binding ourselves with our power, constraining our actions with vows that couldn't be revoked."

I shook my head. "I don't understand."

"We held eternity and power that would have made us gods among men." Ealdor nodded to himself. "We had seen what Atol and the rest had become, and more, we knew the long dark of loneliness that awaited us. We had no intention of wasting our victory by becoming god-kings in his place."

"The children's rhymes," Gael said. "You couldn't appear unless you were called."

Ealdor nodded. "We wanted to give you the chance we squandered." He smiled at me. "Your intuition reminds me so much of . . ." he stopped, choking over a name that wracked him with pain. "My friend," he said instead and continued. "We created the gift of kings for many purposes, but the summoning was one of them. You will need all six."

I didn't want to lose my friend. Not again. "Is there any way to restore you?"

He gave me a sad smile. "You didn't meet the requirements of summoning. I came to you because I'm your friend and the thing we imprisoned must not be set free."

Ealdor's face twisted in pain again. His wraith-like hands clenched against his dissolution, struggling to keep it at bay for as long as he could. "When Cesla entered the forest, I had enough strength to stop him or save you, but not both. When he delved the prison, he left himself open to Atol's control, but Cesla's mind still lives beneath the weight of the Fayit who control him."

"You should have let me be taken," I said. But even as the words left my mouth, I shuddered in revulsion and horror.

Ealdor mustered the strength to smile. "I sensed something about you, a suggestion of my old gift. This time I chose mercy instead." Ealdor vanished completely below the waist. "Should Atol gain his freedom, you will find yourself fighting one of the Fayit in truth. I have to return to Aer."

The last impression of him thinned, like a puff of smoke on the air. Panic burst through me. The names! "Wait! I don't know their names. You never used them!" I lurched toward him, reaching, but my arms passed through the mist he'd become.

"Atol's attack on you allowed me to trick the binding," he whispered. "Look inside your mind." He dissipated until nothing remained. Ealdor was gone.

I sat at the table in the village of Localita north of Cynestol and looked around. Nothing had changed. The shadows cast by the southern sun were neither longer nor shorter than they'd been before Ealdor's appearance. My friend's last visitation had taken only an instant.

Yet my surroundings, the buildings, the jaccara trees, even the table where I sat in dumbfounded silence appeared strange to me, their easy familiarity and accustomed solidity riven by memories ancient beyond reckoning.

And my friend was gone.

Panic and grief wracked me, refusing to let me go and I panted for breath until spots gathered in my vision. Gael folded me in her arms, giving me a measure of calm. I gathered Ealdor's memories and placed them behind a door that I marked with his name. Before all else, the history of his race, our ancestors, needed to be safeguarded. I looked at Custos. "You have to go back to Cynestol. Safeguard Ealdor's history. Write it down," I said, "as many times as it takes for you to guarantee its safety."

His eyes were wide with wonder. "I'll write it, Willet, but no one will believe."

My shoulders curled as I tried to protect myself from grief. "It doesn't matter. It shouldn't be lost. If you can't write it as history, then write it as a tale." I had nothing else to say, I was too busy trying to put meaning to what I'd seen.

"We'll have to make arrangements for Ariella and Oronelle to be returned to their family," Bolt said. A moment later, he raised one hand to pinch the bridge of his nose. When he lifted his head, he looked angry, which meant he looked the same as always. "You're a lodestone for trouble, Dura. You know that, don't you?"

"I know," I said. Under the circumstances it was impossible to argue with him. I glanced at Custos. "Can you see the girls safely back to Cynestol?"

After he nodded, I caught Gael peering at me, the perfect arch of her brows phrasing the question despite her silence.

"We have to get the six together," Bolt said.

"North," I said, "at the forest." My insides hollowed out at the thought of coming within sight of the Darkwater. "Most of the kings and queens are there already."

"I'll tell Herregina she's not going back to Cynestol," Mirren said. "The news will be less of a shock coming from one of her subjects."

"What will you do if she objects?" Bolt asked.

Mirren shook her head. "I don't think she will. I'm going to show her Ealdor's memories first. The people of Aille, even the nobility, have a keen sense of duty. It's what allows us to work small jobs in pointless ministries year after year. She'll come."

CHAPTER 47

"We don't have to go to the forest, Willet," Gael said. "Send messengers. Bring the kings and queens here."

"We may not have that much time," I said. "Rymark and Ellias are fighting a battle they can't win. They've set up a cordon around the forest. They'll kill any trying to go in, and they'll kill anyone coming out. Atol's goal isn't to defeat Rymark—he wants to escape."

Bolt's squint turned ugly. "Most of those who get through won't even be trying to come out. They'll be trying to break the prison."

"Do we have time to stop this?" Mirren asked.

"There's no way to know," Bolt said. "We have to hope Rymark and Ellias have realized what's happening. I'll send word by carrier bird."

"It won't help," I said. "They can't go into the forest."

He shook his head in disgust. "I hate it whenever I have to admit you're right. It makes my skin crawl."

"If we can summon the Fayit, we won't have to fight Cesla or the Darkwater. They'll fight for us," I said.

"You don't know that they will," Gael said. "Or if they even can."

"We can't count on having enough time to meet anywhere else," Bolt said. "We're going to the forest, but not directly."

"Why not?"

"King Boclar isn't at the Darkwater."

A flush of anger narrowed my vision for a moment. No one had bothered to tell me. "Pellin's doing it again," I said. "He and Toria Deel. They're keeping me ignorant. Is that ever going to stop?"

Bolt shrugged as if my anger and objections were unimportant.

"Probably after they're dead, assuming you outlive them. Since we can't return to Cynestol, our best chance of contacting the kings and queens will be at Vadras. We can use Boclar's scrying stone rather than sending birds. Rymark's encampment is a long way from Frayel and Collum. We'll need to give Cailin and Queen Ulrezia as much of a head start as we can."

"That's assuming you can convince them of your plan, Willet," Gael said.

"Let's start with Boclar," I said. "If we can convince him, he can help us with the rest. How long to Vadras?" I asked Bolt.

"Four days if we change horses often and ride straight through. But I'm not familiar with this region—we'll need a map."

"My family is from this part of Aille," Mirren said. "I can guide you."

I stood. "In the morning, then." Bolt preceded Gael and me out the door and up the stairs to our rooms. On the third step, Gael's hand found mine and we tarried, waiting for Bolt and the rest to draw ahead.

"You're hiding something from me," she said.

I didn't bother to deny it. Gael knew me too well. We came to the landing, and she took the opportunity to let her lips brush mine. I pulled her close for a kiss that lingered and held her until she pulled away. "While I appreciate and commend your efforts to distract me, Lord Dura, I think you should tell me, one of your guards, what you intend."

The heat faded, sluiced away by fear, and I pulled a deep breath. "I don't intend anything," I said, my voice soft because I didn't want to hear out loud what I'd hidden in my heart. "Have you ever been in a situation and your options keep narrowing down toward a single terrible outcome?" I waited for her to nod, before I went on. "And all along you say to yourself 'everything will be okay as long as *this* doesn't happen.' And then slowly, inexorably, every other possibility and hope is taken from you until the worst outcome happens." I pulled a breath against a weight in my chest. "Then you find in the midst of your despair that you've underestimated your greatest fear."

She kissed me again, her gaze finding mine. "You know that happened to me, Willet, but you changed the game. You saved me." Her fists knotted in my tunic. "What is it? Let me save *you* this time."

I pulled her close and held her. "For ten years I've managed to stay out of sight of the Darkwater," I said. "I haven't even seen it in the distance except in my worst nightmares, but all the other options are fading away, and the forest is pulling me back."

She took my hand and led me upstairs to the oversized room we shared with the rest of our company. Bolt nodded to us as we came in the door and took his position by it in case murder woke me in the middle of the night.

Later, in the dark, I didn't hear Gael come and lie beside me, but I could smell her scent, soft and floral, as she put one arm protectively around me. I cast back for the memories of the last war and lived them again—the desperate run into the forest, the decision to enter the Darkwater, the dying light of sunset. But the memories stopped, and my mind skipped forward to the morning I walked out of the forest alone. I knew the men who ran into the forest had survived, but my mind refused to remember anything at all about my time there.

The next morning we purchased the best mounts we could buy and set a pace toward Vadras that would spend the horses within hours. "Tell me," I called to Bolt, "why we didn't bother to bring supplies with us."

"Because we won't need them," my guard said. "The southern end of the continent is far more heavily populated than Collum or even Owmead. There will always be a village or town within reach, and worrying over supplies will just slow us down."

Behind me, the newest member of Aille's nobility rode sandwiched between Gael and Mirren, her gaze serious but unafraid.

"Does she understand what we're riding into?" I asked.

Bolt snorted. "Do you?"

I nodded. "I've spent ten years dreading the Darkwater Forest, and my time with the Vigil and Ealdor has served to put that decade of fear into a context I'd rather not have."

"True enough, but we have a saying."

I sighed. "Of course you do."

Ignoring me, he continued. "'If you think you've reached the point where you can't learn anymore . . .'"

"'Then you won't,'" I finished for him, shaking my head. "I know how it goes."

"That's not all of it. The rest goes 'because you'll be dead.' Most people conveniently forget that last part."

"You're always so cheerful in the morning. What kind of man is the king of Caisel?" I asked.

"He's old, Willet. Even before the death of Laidir, he was the oldest of the monarchs in the north. The rest are at least twenty years younger." He stilled. "I'm not sure he's in good health."

I swore inside. With Bolt's gift for understatement, that probably meant Boclar was at death's door. "Alright," I said, "he's old, but what is he like?"

"Secretive . . . reclusive," Bolt said. "I'm not sure which. I've only met him once in all the years I've been with the Vigil. Of all the kings and queens of the north, his talent lies most heavily with all."

Surprised, I pondered how to make use of this information. In my studies with the Merum I'd learned that the talent of all, the ability to see connections between seemingly unrelated facts or events and create understanding, was the rarest of the nine and perhaps the most subtle. "Is he a philosopher, then?"

"Not in the usual sense," Bolt said. "I think the gift of kings forces him to be a bit more practical than that."

"Will we be able to convince him to come with us?"

One corner of Bolt's mouth drew to the side. "I'm still not sure how you convinced me."

CHAPTER 48

Pellin had studied Elieve as they made the ride across the outer border of the Maveth and then recuperated at Dukasti's brother's inn. With her vault gone, her maturation had accelerated. In most moments the girl—he would have put her age somewhere between fifteen and twenty—was hardly distinguishable from any other her age. Quieter, perhaps, and more given to observation or thought, but an ordinary girl nonetheless.

Grief and joy mingled within Pellin's heart as he considered their journey and all it had brought. "But that is the way of things," he whispered. "Every joyful circumstance carries a shadow of mourning, however distant it may be, while our griefs hold the hope of something more joyful in the future."

Mark set his glass of date wine back on the table. Since Elieve's healing, the boy had taken a liking to the thick drink. "What did you say, Eldest?"

He gave himself a small shake. "Just the musings of a very tired old man." That last part was an understatement of colossal proportions. The fight within Elieve's mind had taken everything from Igesia and almost all of it from him. His bones and mind ached with a weariness that he doubted rest could cure, a wound that would scar and ache for the rest of his life. "You have a choice before you, Mark, if Aer will allow you to make it."

"The Vigil or Elieve?"

"Yes."

"Are you offering me the right to choose, Eldest?"

Pellin nodded. "Insofar as I can, Mark, but remember, Bronwyn offered Fess the same choice before she died."

"And the gift came to him anyway." Mark took a deep breath of the smoky air inside the inn. "He scares me, Eldest."

Pellin's brows rose at this. "Fess? He is much changed, I'll warrant, but—"

"Not Fess," Mark said. "Aer."

His first impulse was to brush away Mark's statement with some wry observation, an almost-jest to lighten the mood, but his apprentice's objection ran too deep. Regardless of Mark's decision, he should receive the most honest, most truthful answer Pellin could offer. "He scares me as well, Mark. Perhaps for different reasons, but He does."

"You, Eldest?"

Pellin put his hands on the table, accepting the invitation. "I have served the Vigil for centuries, yet in many ways I'm still the stuttering, stammering boy who encountered Aer in his youth. I learned something that day that frightened me and often still does."

Mark leaned forward. "What, Eldest?"

"That something perfectly good can be just as frightening as something perfectly evil. That day, as a boy, I learned how far I was from Aer. And the difference terrified me. I've never recovered, Mark. I don't think I'm supposed to." He lifted a hand to point at Mark's chest. "What is it about Him that frightens you?"

"He's like a thief, Eldest," Mark said. "He doesn't ask. He just takes what He wants."

Instead of arguing, Pellin nodded. His apprentice grew up in the urchins. Naturally, he would see and describe the world from that experience. Who was he to deny Mark his fear, his intuition? Yet, he felt compelled to help his apprentice frame it. "I can see that," he said, "with Lord Dura and even more with Fess. Yet, there is a difference between Aer and any other thief."

"What's that, Eldest?"

"Aer already owns it all."

Mark nodded. "That's cold comfort."

"Agreed," Pellin said. "When I decided to take you as my apprentice, I used it as a temporary solution only. I wanted someone more like me, someone raised to be a priest, to receive my gift. Now I see I was wrong, but if you do not wish the gift, I will not try to force it on you. If you take it, Elieve will age and die while you remain young. Her life will pass you by with a speed you cannot imagine."

Mark looked at him, the clear blue of his eyes earnest in his young face. "You would let me choose?"

He nodded. Inside, he had no idea which choice he hoped Mark would make. "I would, but in the end it isn't really up to me."

"How much time do I have to decide what I want?"

Now, Pellin laughed. "I'm not planning to die anytime soon, but 'Death comes for us all . . .'" he began.

"'And some sooner than others,'" Mark finished.

Seven days later, Pellin fell into a bunk on Captain Onen's ship, spent from the ride. His old man's heart fluttered in his chest like a bird desperate to escape the hand, but more than exhaustion assailed him. No amount of coaxing or volume had been sufficient to make contact through his scrying stone. Yet he could hear a slight buzzing from it at odd moments, a sign, he hoped, that he might eventually reach the others.

The pop and boom of sails filling as Onen brought about his ship gave him some measure of comfort. Favored with a southerly wind, the ship leapt from port. Dukasti had been as good as his word, paying the price for Onen's ship to make the return trip empty. The journey across the sea would be quick, but even afterward, they would have to ride for days more to reach the forest.

CHAPTER 49

We made the trip from Localita to Vadras in three days instead of four, thanks to Mirren's knowledge of the roads that covered Aille and Caisel like a spider's web. On the final day, we hit the coast road, a broad affair built to handle the heaviest merchant traffic on the continent, and came upon the city from the south. Riding through a wall of air that shimmered with heat and humidity we got our first glimpse of Vadras sitting at the mouth of the Mournwater, ascending from the delta like a mountain that had risen from the deeps—and stopped. Soldiers blocked the gates. We queued up with the rest of the travelers and waited.

"Any idea what this is about?" I asked Bolt.

He shook his head. "I could spend days speculating about what Boclar is thinking and never come near the mark. His mind was a labyrinth when I met him twenty years ago. It's doubtful he's gotten easier to understand since then."

"There's your answer." Rory pointed.

At first I didn't understand. Our thief pointed at the soldiers, but nothing seemed out of place until I looked closer. Though the practice had pretty much died out on our continent, it wasn't unheard of for some officers to have pages accompany them to help take care of their mount and equipment. But the young men and women—hardly more than children, really—weren't attending their superiors. They were scanning the crowd, and every one of them kept up a running commentary to the soldier beside them.

"They're looking for dwimor."

Bolt nodded. "Good. That means someone has alerted the kings and queens to be on their guard."

"And bad," I added. "It's going to take us forever to get through."

My guard shook his head. "Perhaps not." He pushed his horse through the press of the crowd—unmindful or uncaring of the comments aimed his way—and dismounted in front of one of the soldiers, a man with a bit more decoration on his uniform than the rest.

After a brief exchange, the man signaled the rest of us forward. "I am Lieutenant Astyrian." He bowed. "You will accompany me to the palace."

Perhaps my experiences in Cynestol had made me overly wary, but I stepped back to give myself room enough to draw steel and nodded to Rory and Gael. Daggers appeared in Rory's hands as if by magic, but Gael didn't move.

Nearby soldiers, seeing Rory's ostentatious display with his daggers, closed in around us, wary.

"Not here," Bolt hissed. "Didn't you see him bow?"

I blinked. "I don't understand."

The lieutenant waved the other soldiers away and bowed again. "King Boclar has been expecting you. I've been ordered to conduct you to him with all speed."

"Expecting us?" I asked.

The lieutenant nodded. "His exact orders were to conduct any to him who were aware of the purpose behind the roadblock."

As we approached the gates, I looked up to view the massive wall and the city beyond. Though not quite as intimidating as Cynestol, its walls were thicker, and it definitely dwarfed Bunard.

"Agin's legacy," Bolt said. "He regarded everyone with suspicion, even his family." He shrugged. "Especially his family."

"How do you know that?" I asked. To me, the Wars for the Gift of Kings were ancient history, buried over five hundred years in the past.

"Pellin knew him, remember?" Bolt's expression might have shifted from stoic to wry, or maybe the light had changed. It was hard to tell. "Whenever Pellin grew tired of his books and wanted to talk, he would tell me about the war and speculate on the reason behind Agin's insanity."

I'd heard discussions of it in my time as a novice in the Merum order. "Did he attribute it to alchemy or inbreeding?"

Bolt cocked his head to one side. "Pellin's theories ran in other directions."

Maybe I saw him glance north, toward the forest. Perhaps I caught the hitch in his speech. For whatever reason, I pulled in closer to my guard, driven by an irrational fear that filled me. "He thinks Agin went to the forest?"

Bolt didn't nod, but for a few seconds he looked at me without blinking.

"Does he *know* he went there?"

"There are few secrets that can be hidden from the gift of domere."

I had to remind myself to breathe. "That casts a different shadow. What did Agin hope to gain?"

"No one knows," Bolt said, "and thanks to the men and women who killed him and his family, no one got a chance to find out."

I couldn't tell if my guard was being sarcastic or not, but in the end I decided it didn't matter. Agin had been defeated, and we were left with the dwimor as the price of our victory.

Lieutenant Astyrian set a pace through the crowded streets that had those on foot jumping out of the way. The city walls straddled the river on both the west and east side. Massive ironwork sealed access to the city from the river, preventing traffic.

Bolt pointed at the gates, black and pitted with age but still staggering in size. "Boclar's serious about the threat of assassination. The river is the lifeblood of merchants in Vadras. Blocking water traffic through the middle of the city and diverting them around is costly business."

If possible, the heat and humidity within Vadras were even worse than Cynestol, but after weeks acclimating to the southern sun, I ignored the weather as best I could. I needed to convince King Boclar to accompany me to the Darkwater and his reputation for seeing through people's motives worried me. Would my flaws cost us his favor?

After thirty minutes, we rounded a corner and came in sight of the citadel, a squat building surrounded on all sides by water.

"It's always reminded me a bit of Bunard," Bolt said. "Not nearly as effective—the land in this region is too flat to make the moat more than a last desperate gesture of defiance—but it also means that Boclar could close off the citadel and the city at a moment's notice to keep anyone from getting out."

"Not exactly a cheerful thought," I said.

Rory laughed. "And you still swim like a rock."

At the far end of the bridge we dismounted. A dozen soldiers, with pages again, waited in the heat. Their blue linen shirts and trousers looked as light as craft and gift could make them but every man kept a waterskin as well as a weapon.

Instead of allowing us to pass through, the soldiers at the gate relieved us of our weapons, and we waited until another twelve men and women with pikes came to take charge before we were herded into the citadel.

The artwork decorating the walls consisted of complex designs and intricate patterns instead of scenes depicting battles or history that I had seen in other courts. Even the sculptures strove for geometric complexity rather than depiction, but it was the music that truly caught my attention. We passed through a hall where a group of merchants or lesser nobles attended a quartet of musicians practicing their art. Instead of the lilting strains that accompanied the formal dances of the north, I heard complex rhythms and dissonance that resolved in unexpected ways.

"Intriguing," I said out loud.

"A different music for a different people," Bolt said.

The music faded, but even after the echoes of the last notes vanished, I kept listening, as if they would somehow continue into the expected finish if I just waited long enough. We kept walking, and in the end, we never turned. The hallway we'd entered from the south gate led us as unerringly as the flight of an arrow to the center of the citadel, the massive domed hall of the King of Caisel. When I remarked on it, Bolt nodded.

"I've always preferred the tor in Bunard. That craggy flat-topped peak forced the builders to use their imagination."

Boclar's court was nearly empty. A few functionaries passed through with the floor-focused gaze of those who have no time or inclination to engage in idle conversation, and no music, juggling, or entertainment of any kind filled the domed space. The lieutenant exchanged a few words with a man in dark blue with a yellow sash on his right shoulder. Together, all of us stepped toward the center of the hall and the round dais that filled it.

"It's empty," Rory said.

Mirren nodded. "It's customary to acknowledge the seat of power in Caisel, even if it's unoccupied." At a look from Rory, she shook her head. "When we get to the dais, just bow toward the throne as though King Boclar were sitting on it."

"Strange custom," he said.

"Most of them are until you learn the history behind them," she answered. "Then many of them just seem outdated."

As soon as we made our bow, the functionary, the lieutenant, and all the soldiers guided us toward the east exit of the hall.

"Our crowd is growing, yah?" Rory said. "If we keep this up, we can just bring the whole kingdom to see him."

A few of the guards eyed Rory with a narrowed gaze, and Bolt reached out to pull him closer. "You might not want to use your fake accent here. It's from Caisel, in case you didn't know, and it's usually a bad idea to offend someone with a pike."

East of the throne room we entered a smaller audience chamber filled with enough people to create the sensation of crowding. Bolt nodded toward the north end, toward a gray-haired man who appeared to be slowly collapsing in on himself. "That's him. This should be interesting."

That last comment caught my attention. I would have asked for clarification, but by that time our escort had formed up in front of the king. Boclar had the same coloring I'd noticed on his countrymen, a swarthy shade between those of Elania and Aille. When he lifted his head, his gaze had difficulty finding purchase. One eye regarded me, while the other roved over my companions. Disquiet threaded its way through my chest as my heartbeat copied the staggered rhythm of Caisel's musicians. Boclar reminded me too much of Myle and Aellyn.

A woman of some forty years stood to his side. Her hair held hints of auburn in the light, but her eyes were a dark, almost violet, shade of blue that fit her expression. She eyed us with the air of someone prepared in advance to be offended.

I hadn't known what to expect, and in the absence of experience I'd assumed some commonality with the only king I'd met. But the only thing Boclar had in common with Laidir was the royal guard. Eight men with drawn swords ringed the king in four groups of two, and four pages filled the gaps at the points of the compass, pointing and speaking to the guards on either side.

Herregina took a step forward, but Gael pulled her back with some whispered advice that brought the girl up short.

The king's gaze refused to focus, and he stared around the hall in wandering patterns. "Light, Erendella," he whispered to the woman at his side.

"Father"—she shook her head—"it's too soon."

For a moment his head dipped, the weight too heavy for him to sustain. Then, trembling with effort, he raised it and managed to force his gaze to serve him. "Now," he said.

With a nod and a glare for our company, the king's daughter snapped orders, and we were herded from the audience hall into a smaller chamber, where we waited until the king, assisted by servants, took a seat at the far end. Instead of being called forward, we were made to wait, the minutes creeping by while King Boclar struggled to make his body obey him and his daughter eyed us with unspoken imprecations.

I stepped forward to speak, but Bolt caught me by the arm. "Wait," he whispered. "It appears Boclar's daughter runs the citadel. If you push too hard, she'll have us thrown out and even the king's personal guards won't gainsay her."

As he finished speaking, a man and woman, each with the narrowed gaze of those who rarely looked beyond the work of their hands, entered the room. They carried a large polished metal bowl and an iron stand. "My apologies, Your Majesty," the woman said to the king, bobbing her embarrassment. She turned to the king's daughter. "Your Highness, I didn't expect your summons for another three hours."

Erendella glared at us, her eyes as hard and brittle as slate. "I didn't expect to send it, Helioma."

The king's hands trembled in a way that Helioma interpreted as a command. "This will take but a moment, Your Majesty."

After the bowl had been set on its low stand, pointing toward the king, Helioma brought forth a bag and measured a quantity of powder into it with enough care to make it seem priceless. I grabbed Bolt's arm. "That's—"

"I know."

With a quick word, Helioma ordered her assistant to retrieve one of the candles that lit the room and with deft movements she touched the flame to the powder in the bowl. I turned away as light like the sun flared in the king's audience hall, throwing the people and objects within it into painful contrast.

Limned in radiance, the king straightened in his chair, his eyes narrowed to slits against the brilliance of the alchemist's art. But his gaze was clear. Clear. "How long?" he asked Helioma.

The alchemist looked from the king to his heir before her gaze settled on Boclar's feet. "About fifteen minutes," she said. "Any more than that and we're cutting the margin too close tonight."

"Excuse me, Your Majesty." I stepped forward and Erendella's gaze latched on to me. "My name is—"

"Willet Dura," the king finished for me. I must have looked startled. "Your likeness has been given to every king and church head on the northern continent." He smiled. "I see this is news to you."

I took another step toward the king, trying to be subtle, but the king's gaze, clear under the burning light shifted to my hands. With a shrug, I surrendered my pretense. "You'll forgive me, Your Majesty, if I seem cautious at your sudden revival. I know of no disease that solas powder can cure."

"Guards," he ordered. "Leave us. Return in a quarter of an hour."

After the door was barred, Boclar spared just enough time to nod. "What is it you wish, Lord Dura? Time is short, as I'm sure you heard."

I struggled to understand what I'd seen, and a seed of fear took root in my mind. I bit my tongue and put away my suspicion. I knelt, going to one knee according to the custom in Collum. Gael, Rory, Mirren, and Bolt copied me, but Herregina remained standing. She might have nodded in Boclar's direction.

"Rise," Boclar instructed.

But when I stood, his gaze was still fixed upon Herregina.

"I hadn't counted on that," I said to Bolt.

"You have to stop saying that," he muttered. "It makes my stomach hurt."

"Lord Dura." Boclar rose from his chair without difficulty, buoyed on a tide of light. "I bid you welcome to Caisel." Without warning a smile wreathed his face. "Bolt, I see you've finally managed to escape Pellin's company. How did you do it?"

My guard shrugged. "I retired. Evidently that's one of those decisions that the Eldest can unmake, if he wishes. He placed me with

Lord Dura. I'm sure it must be penance for something, I just can't remember anything I did that would warrant it."

"Nice," I muttered.

Boclar stared at me. If Laidir had the ability to measure a man with a glance, I could only say that Boclar did that and more, but at last he turned from me with a smile for Gael. "Lady, you grace us with your presence."

"Your Majesty." Gael curtsied.

"You are unknown to me," the king said to Mirren. "Time is in short supply, else I would attempt to interpret your identity by your actions. Who are you?"

Mirren glanced at me and I nodded. "I am Lord Dura's apprentice."

I cleared my throat. "The most recent addition to the Vigil, actually."

The king looked at me. "Truly? You found one of them."

"We did."

"I'm sure there's a tale there, but it too will have to wait." He turned to Rory. "I'd heard you'd taken an apprentice, Bolt."

"Yes, Your Majesty," he said. "This is Rory. He's still new to our company, but he's already one of the deadliest men I've ever met."

Herregina gave Rory another of those appraising glances that he went to some length to ignore. Then the king of Caisel turned his attention to her. "Your presence in this company is a surprise. Do I have the honor of addressing the rightful queen of Aille?"

She bowed from the neck. "Your Majesty. I am Herregina Gestaella, daughter of the second minister of internal protocol in the court of Cynestol."

Boclar smiled. "The traditions of your kingdom are known to me, though I confess that I'm unfamiliar with the exact duties of the ministry of protocol."

Herregina made a discarding motion with one hand. "It's of no import, Your Majesty. Few outside the court of Cynestol would have any reason to know it. We spend an inordinate amount of time on matters of little consequence to keep ourselves out of trouble."

The king laughed. "Well spoken, sister." He turned to the rest of us. "You all look road weary, which I can only attribute to haste and, in these times, fear. Tell me, Lord Dura, what makes a man with your unique talents and gifts fearful enough to come to me in such haste?"

I swallowed the lump in my throat. Any hope of summoning the Fayit hinged on convincing Boclar of our need, and my ability to dissemble with him was probably about as close to zero as it could be. "We need to gather the kings and queens of the north, Your Majesty," I said. "The defeat of the Darkwater depends on it."

He glanced at Herregina. "That you would risk bringing the new queen of Aille here attests to the fact that you believe what you say, but that doesn't make it true. How will having us all in one place accomplish our enemy's defeat?"

At my side, Bolt leaned in to whisper to me. "I hope you've found a way to say this that doesn't sound completely insane."

CHAPTER 50

I hadn't, but I decided it might be a good idea to offer a bit of expla-nation first. "As you know, Your Majesty, the gift of kings can't be split, even though it's been tried any number of times."

Boclar nodded. "I've often wondered why that might be. In my experience, Lord Dura, there's a reason for everything and I consider it the greatest frustration of my life that there are mysteries left un-explained. Are you telling me you've discovered the 'why' behind this particular one?"

"It's still not going to sound good," Bolt mumbled.

"Suppose you found yourself in circumstances you'd never encoun-tered before, Your Majesty."

He shrugged. "By strictest definition, that's a daily occurrence."

I smiled, but inside I was scrambling to find a way to lead Boclar to the same conclusion I'd come to without sounding insane. "Suppose, Your Majesty, you prepared for a distant future as best as possible, but at the last, you were uncertain of your descendants ability to survive. What would you do?"

To his credit, and my relief, Boclar entertained my question instead of laughing. "I would do all I could to ensure that my posterity might live." He leaned forward to rest an elbow on one knee, a gesture that reminded me of Laidir. "Are you telling me, Lord Dura, that you believe the gift of kings is nothing more than a means of ensuring our survival?"

I nodded.

He gave me a thin smile, his eyes bright with the reflected light of the powder. "You've spent a lot of words trying not to say something that you're going to have to say eventually." He leaned back and waved a hand at me to continue. "Let's suppose for the moment that the gift of kings is unique for the reasons you postulate—though you've yet to tell me exactly what those are. Exactly what is it you want us to do?"

I took a deep breath. This wasn't going to work. I didn't know the king of Caisel well enough to interpret his lack of expression, but it was impossible to miss the signs of impatience. "Suppose, Your Majesty—"

"Lord Dura, I find your repeated use of that phrase tiresome. Answer my question. Now."

"Here it comes," Bolt muttered.

I met the king's gaze as best I could. "I want you and the rest of the rulers of the north to help me summon the Fayit."

To Boclar's right, Erendella gasped as if she'd been about to laugh and then thought better of it. Boclar held my gaze for the space of a dozen heartbeats while I tried not to look away. Then he did the same with Bolt, Gael, Mirren, and Rory.

"Lord Dura," Boclar said, "your companions obviously believe you, but that is less convincing than you might think. The power of domere is difficult to overestimate. You hold in your hands the ability to destroy or change the memories of any man or woman you touch. What proof can you offer that does not involve the use of your gift?" He smiled. "Have you spoken with Fayit already?"

I nodded. "I have, and did for years without knowing it. The Fayit are the wardens of the Darkwater Forest, and they always have been. Cesla broke the first commandment, not to delve the deep places of the earth. He used his gift in the forest and by so doing he left himself open to evil. There is a prison beneath the forest, Your Majesty."

"What evil is in this prison?"

"The losing side of a Fayit war that destroyed their world."

Boclar made a show of looking around his audience chamber. "And where are the victors, Lord Dura?"

I lifted one arm. "We're right here, Your Majesty. Most of the Fayit who survived the war surrendered their immortality, willingly becoming less than what they were. Aer told them to split their gifts, talents, and temperaments with each succeeding generation. Their diminishment forged a closer dependence on Him, and we became incapable of the evils they'd perpetrated." Ealdor hadn't shown us the sort of evils that had plagued his world. I didn't really want to know.

The king drew a deep breath and released it slowly. The light in the room dimmed slightly and Boclar glanced at the bowl before he brought his gaze back to mine, squinting. "Lord Dura, you come to me with myths and fables and claim to be the sole person on the face of the earth who comprehends the nature of the forest." He leaned forward. "How would you regard such a man in my place?"

"I'd think he was insane," I said, "but the fact that you haven't rejected my story out of hand says much."

Boclar's thoughts might have been running in the same direction. "Just how is it that these captives are able to reach beyond their prison to infect those who go to the Darkwater, Lord Dura?"

Everything in Boclar's demeanor told me I'd failed to persuade him. "I don't really know, Your Majesty. When Ealdor, one of the last Fayit, gave me his memories, I saw wonders and terrors, but I didn't see everything the Fayit were capable of. Their prison is made of pure aurium. Months ago, I saw an alchemist test a sliver from the forest with the strings of a harp."

The king jerked. I'd finally said something that surprised him. "Can you verify this?" he asked Bolt. "Is there aurium in the forest?"

My guard nodded. "Years ago, before Lord Dura came into his gift, Elwin recovered a sliver of the metal from a dead blacksmith who had entered the Darkwater."

He pointed at me. "Is there any possibility that this is a false memory implanted by Lord Dura to convince you?"

Bolt shrugged. "Anything is possible, Your Majesty, but he would have had to implant it in all the rest of the Vigil. He's never delved Pellin or Toria Deel, and they've both referenced the metal. I don't have the gift, but I've heard those I've guarded speak to this. Implanting memories is far harder than destroying them. Unless the new memory fits seamlessly with all the rest, the mind rejects it."

Boclar's expression settled somewhere between a smile and a grimace. "There is a universal law the liturgy never mentions. 'Destruction is but a moment while creation takes a lifetime.'" Then he settled back into his chair, gazing through us as though we'd become nothing more than mist. Rory fidgeted. The rest of us waited, but time had stopped for the king of Caisel.

"Father," Erendella said, "you're considering this?"

He nodded. "I am. When you become queen, my daughter, you will find two tests of your ability to rule. The first is being able to withstand the tedium of your responsibilities day after day and still give your duties the best of your talent and attention. The second is harder. You must decide how to administer extreme circumstances with wisdom. Lord Dura's tale is fantastic in the most literal sense of the word, but can I afford to ignore it?" He glanced at the polished brazier that lit the room. "How much time is left?"

"Possibly five minutes," Helioma said. "No more."

Boclar, his gaze still sharp and focused, settled himself and waved us to silence, during which he stared off into the space above our heads. Four minutes later, he spoke, his voice breaking the silence like stone hitting glass. "I'm sure you're fatigued from your journey. I will have you conducted to quarters where you can refresh yourselves. I'll have clothing brought to you while yours is cleaned. Now, I would have you depart. I have no wish for you to see my peculiar malady reassert itself."

Erendella guided us firmly toward the door as the light in Boclar's room faded. I didn't look back.

"Is he sick?" Rory asked once we were behind closed doors.

I nodded. "There's nothing about royalty that makes you immune to the human condition, but I don't think he's sick in the normal way." I didn't voice my suspicion. I needed Boclar, but now it appeared I needed Erendella as well.

Three hours later a dozen soldiers came with orders to conduct us to the king. The sunlight had faded, and we walked through the palace to the brilliance of lamps and candles. We bypassed court and continued east through the citadel. The guards had left us our weapons but provided no hint as to why. We were escorted down a slightly smaller hallway that ended in a pair of heavy doors. Men tall and broad enough to have stepped from legend stood watch. The soldiers escorting us stopped, and we were motioned forward into the king's presence.

We entered into a circular room dominated by a huge round table in the center. Bookcases lined the walls, but they held fewer books than I would have suspected for any noble, much less a king. Other than a few other items, the room was surprisingly bare. Erendella waved us to seats around the table.

"I used to meet Laidir in his study," I said to break the silence. "It was filled with books and contraptions so that there was hardly any room."

Erendella must have caught something in my expression. "Of late, clutter distracts my father, Lord Dura."

The doors to the side opened and the king shuffled in with the aid of two of his guards. The alchemist and her assistant came behind him, bearing the polished brazier, but once the king was seated they made no move to light it.

I looked to Erendella. "Why are we here, Your Highness?"

Her eyes flared, and a heartbeat later I realized my affront. I bowed to the king. "Your pardon, Your Majesty. As I'm sure you're aware, the ways of the nobility are unfamiliar to me."

Somehow, whether by palsied wave or glance, Boclar communicated his assent to Erendella to answer on his behalf. Her gaze was still hostile when she faced me. "You are here to place your petition before the rest of the kings and queens, Lord Dura," she said, gesturing to seats around the table. "Please sit. It's almost time to begin." She reached into the folds of her dress and pulled out a pink-tinged scrying stone that she placed on a base in the middle of the table. "If all goes well, all seven of the monarchs will be in attendance."

I bowed without saying the presence of Queen Phidias of Elania was unnecessary. Of the seven rulers, she governed the only country that didn't border the Darkwater, and while she held a gift and numerous talents, she was also the only monarch who didn't hold the gift of kings.

We waited, and the time dragged by until I became uncomfortable. "Your Majesty?"

Boclar tried to smile, and a gesture that might have been meant to be placating sent tremors along his arm. Erendella spoke in his stead. "Rymark and Ellias begin the meetings since they hold command of our forces along the Darkwater."

A hum came from the scrying stone, a vibration that prefaced a voice. "Are we all here?" Rymark's voice came from the center of the table, diminished by distance.

At a nod from Erendella, the king's alchemist stepped forward to summon light that filled the room with the sun's radiance. Once again, I watched the king transform from a man trapped within the eroding confines of his own body to a confident, assured monarch. The fact that all of this seemed to be solely due to the burning of solas powder—the same concoction Myle had given me to fight Cesla's soldiers—sent my stomach into contortions. I could only come up with one explanation. Sweat beaded and trickled down my back, and I prayed that I was wrong.

One by one, beginning with Ulrezia of Frayel, the kings and queens of the north offered perfunctory greetings. Herregina, on Gael's left, leaned forward but demurred at the last moment, her gaze calculating. Clever girl. She would wait and take the measure of her fellows before she revealed herself.

Cailin of Collum spoke last. "I am here as regent for my son and rightful heir, Brod."

"I'll skip the usual pleasantries and obfuscations," Rymark said. "We've been out maneuvered, Your Majesties. We've lost the inner cordon." Gasps came from the facets of the stone.

Boclar nodded to Erendella, and she came to stand close to me and explained. "King Rymark split his forces to create an inner and outer cordon to shut off the flow of people attempting to gain access to the forest."

"The forest erupted," Rymark said. "In a single night, the entire inner ring surrounding it was wiped out almost to a man."

"The battle is lost, then?" Ulrezia asked.

"Not yet," King Ellias said, "but anyone who makes it past the outer cordon will have unfettered access to the forest. Cesla will have his reinforcements and he had more under his command than we expected."

"Why did this attack happen now?" Boclar asked.

"We don't know," Rymark said, "but we noticed a change a few days ago in the tenor of our fight, when our main camp was attacked."

Boclar nodded to his daughter who leaned in to speak to me. "Those who had been turned by the forest concentrated their attack on Kings Rymark and Ellias," she said, "ignoring Toria Deel and Fess of the Vigil, even though they stood close by."

Now I understood why Boclar had entertained my story. He already knew Cesla was concentrating his attack on the monarchs. He just hadn't known why.

"For weeks, Cesla has been practicing a deception, gathering his forces in the forest until he could strike," Rymark said. "The question becomes what has he been doing all this time? And why has he chosen this time to attack?"

CHAPTER 51

King Boclar leaned forward. "Perhaps Lord Dura will be able to shed some light on this."

Rymark's voice crackled from the stone. "Dura! What is he doing there?"

Boclar smiled. "He was kind enough to accompany Queen Herregina of Aille here to make my acquaintance."

Voices erupted, each trying to shout over the other, and Boclar gave Herregina a wink. "You'll discover being queen of Aille entails many duties and few pleasures. On rare occasions, I've been able to surprise my brother and sister rulers. I have to admit, I'm probably enjoying this more than I should."

"What proof do you have that this is the true queen?" Rymark said.

"Lord Dura told me."

"He told you?" Rymark asked. "That's it?"

"I have no reason to doubt him, Your Majesty," Boclar said. "I can guarantee that the unique requirements of his petition preclude deception in this regard."

"Petition?" Suspicion filled Rymark's voice.

Before Boclar could speak again, I leaned toward the stone. If the king of Caisel took offense, I would have to offer my humble apologies and hope for the best. "I believe I know why the enemy focused on you and Ellias during the attacks."

"Of course you do," Rymark said. "I can hardly wait."

"Peace, brother," Ellias said. "Let me tell you sometime of Master Gerimian. Before the gift came to him he was a beggar in the streets of Loklallin. Can you imagine it? A beggar giving instruction to the greatest minds in the kingdom?"

"You're unfamiliar with Lord Dura, Ellias," Rymark said. "The man is a walking curse. You know, Lord Dura, that you're something of a legend in Vaerwold. It's going to take a long time to erase the memories of what happened there. Didn't your masters tell you to be circumspect?"

Cailin's voice came from the stone. "Let him speak."

"Is that an order, *regent*?" Rymark asked.

"Enough, Rymark," Ulrezia said. "We already know of Lord Dura's proclivities. We're at war. Any weapon that comes to hand is a good one."

On my right, Bolt nodded. "Wise woman."

"Oh, by all means, speak, Lord Dura," Rymark snarled.

I took a deep breath. It didn't help. "Cesla is working to disguise his deeper purpose. He's not interested in fighting a war." Perhaps something of my words or tone struck a chord with Rymark. He managed to remain quiet. "At the moment, victory or defeat in battle is immaterial to him. He has a more immediate goal."

"And what would that be?" Boclar asked.

"He wants to open the prison in the Darkwater," I said.

"Who told you there was a prison within the Darkwater?" Rymark asked.

I ignored the question. "The prison is made of aurium. If Cesla manages to free those trapped inside, we cannot win."

"What is the source of your information, Lord Dura?" Rymark's voice scaled upward.

I continued to try and bluff my way through, hoping that something I said would be alarming enough to shut King Rymark's mouth. "Cesla is leading you by your expectations," I said. "His goal isn't to fight you—it's to get enough skilled people into the forest to break the prison."

"How do you know this?" Rymark must have been screaming. Even coming from the stone, his voice echoed in the confines of Boclar's study.

"Ealdor told me," I said.

"Who is he?" Ellias asked.

There was no help for it. "One of the last of the Fayit," I said. "If

354

you don't believe me, inquire of Pellin, Fess, or Toria Deel. They've seen him as well, though not so extensively as I."

"How convenient," Rymark said, "that we are unable to speak with them to verify Lord Dura's story. My fellow rulers, you know his circumstances. Personally, I think it's possible that the forest has already taken him."

"If he had, I wouldn't be here talking to Boclar. I'd have killed him by now," I shot back.

Bolt shook his head. "Someday we have to talk about how you choose your words."

"Fayit and fairy tales," Rymark dismissed. "Just what are we supposed to do?"

I couldn't make myself say it. If the existence of the Fayit had garnered this reaction, what would they say when they heard my plan? Boclar, seeing me flounder, leaned forward. "Lord Dura has shared his counsel with me, at least in broad terms." He paused long enough to give Herregina another wink and smile that made him seem years younger. "Lord Dura requests that all the kings and queens of the north meet so that we can summon the Fayit to aid us."

I gaped at the king, who smiled at me.

"Your Majesty," Rymark's voice cut through the din. "I urge you to take Lord Dura prisoner, now, so that Pellin can arrange for the transfer of his gift. There can be little doubt that the vault in his mind is the source of this insanity."

Boclar shrugged as though Rymark hadn't just tried to put a death sentence on me. "He doesn't *look* crazy. Perhaps we should hear him."

"Has he touched you?" the king of Moorclaire asked.

"No, Ellias. My mind and my memories are still my own."

"Toria Deel and Fess said nothing of this when they were here," Rymark said.

"They've seen Ealdor"—I was desperate to earn their trust and cooperation—"but we have only recently uncovered evidence of Cesla's intetions, of his efforts to prevent a gathering of those with the gift of kings. Since I was given no stone, I have had no means of informing them of this new information."

"The Vigil has always kept its secrets," Ulrezia interjected. "That's hardly proof of Dura's insanity."

"Proof?" Rymark practically screamed. "You require proof?"

The light from the brazier dimmed, and I saw a spasm of pain wash across Boclar's expression before he could quench it. "Perhaps we should adjourn," he said quickly. His words tumbled over each other. "We will take up the matter of Dura's request and its implications again tomorrow. Kings Rymark and Ellias, I thank you for your service. Queen Ulrezia and Regent Cailin, I will speak with you again at the appointed time." Boclar jerked a nod to Erendella and she darted forward to take the stone from its stand and wrap it in thick folds of velvet.

Boclar's gaze latched onto his alchemist. "What's wrong with the fire, Helioma?"

She shook her head, panicked, before donning heavy leather gloves and grasping the polished bowl to shake it. The light steadied for a moment, then flickered again. "I don't know. The powder should have lasted for another hour yet."

Erendella snapped her fingers at the rest of us and pointed. "Leave, now!" The light dimmed further, and Boclar edged toward it until the heat from the brazier reddened his skin.

I stood rooted to my spot. Waiting.

"If you wish my help, or that of my heir," Boclar snapped, "you will leave." A spasm wrenched his expression into something I recognized.

"Guards!" Erendella screamed. "Guards!"

The doors flew open, and Boclar's men poured into the room. "Get them out of here," Erendella said. "Keep them in the north wing."

Half the guards, each of them a head taller than me, ringed us with steel and ran us toward the door. At the exit, I looked back to see the rest of the guards huddled over the supine form of the king as Helioma tried to wrest the last bit of light from her dying powder.

One of the guards paused just long enough to close the doors behind us, but not before cries shattered in the air with glass-sharp edges of sound, an endless series of screams that scaled upward. Through the open crack of the door I saw men twice my size working to bind the king.

Guards ringed us with drawn weapons and kept us at a walk fast enough to force Rory and Herregina to a slow jog. More than once Rory's hands dipped into the folds of his cloak, but each time Bolt or I waved him off. Pride and fear fought to gain ascendancy on Herregina's expression. In the end, the size and gift of the guards cowed her and she kept pace.

Gael shifted closer to my side. "Are they going to imprison us?"

Mercifully, the guards slowed as we put enough distance between us and the king's audience room to muffle the sounds of Boclar's screaming. "I don't think so, at least not in the usual sense." I needed to plant a seed with the guards. Gifted, they would surely be able to hear me, even at a whisper. "I know what afflicts the king, but I don't know if he'll let me free him of it." I turned from Gael and kept my gaze forward.

We came to the north section of the citadel and passed through a room that might have been used for entertaining. Currently, only a few menials were present, working by the light of lamps to prepare it for the next day. The guards led us to an exit, a pair of double doors that met at the top in a point. Despite the scrollwork that gave the wood a delicate look, they were thick enough to comprise an effective prison.

One of the guards waved us through. "We'll let the chamberlain know of your presence," he said. "Food and drink will be sent along with anything else you require."

The door locked behind us.

We stood in a vaulted sitting room with doors to private chambers around the perimeter. I looked at the walls and ceiling. They were of finer, more delicate construction than those in Bunard, but just as capable of concealing any who might wish to spy on us. What I had to do next had to be accomplished with care.

I took Gael's hand in mine, stifling the twinge of regret that came with doing so while I wore my gloves. I nodded toward the girls. "I'm sure Mirren and Her Majesty are unused to such exertions," I said carefully. "Why don't the three of you retire? I'll bring the food and drink to you when it gets here."

Her voice dropped to a murmur that barely reached my ears. "In other words, you're planning something and either you need me out of the way or it's so outrageous you know I'd try to stop you."

I kissed her quickly and without warning. Her eyes widened with pleasure and turned a shade lighter before she could prevent it. "I thought I was supposed to be the one with the gift of domere," I whispered.

"You're not fighting fair."

I laughed and kissed her again. Gael could have stopped me if she'd wanted. "Herregina's going to have questions, a lot of them.

357

Aer willing, we're headed north to the forest, but if she doesn't go voluntarily, this is going to go from difficult to ridiculous."

"What are you going to do?" she asked.

I donned an expression of innocence that probably didn't fit. "I'm going to have a talk with Bolt and Rory."

"Nothing more?" she whispered. She used our proximity to trace one finger along my jawline in a slow caress. And she lectured me about fighting fair?

"Not as far as you know," I smiled.

She nodded and leaned in for a quick kiss. "Be as safe as you can." She turned. "Mirren. Your Majesty." She curtsied. "If you wish it, we can retire to our rooms and Lord Dura will bring us refreshment when it arrives. I'm sure you have many questions."

Herregina's brows lowered, and she opened her mouth as if about to issue some royal objection, but at the last she nodded. The three of them left, taking the first door on the right.

Bolt nodded to Rory, and they meandered around the room, looking both bored and impatient as they surveyed the furnishings. After ten minutes they made their way to me where I stood in the center. "I can't see any spy holes," Bolt said. "Rory?"

His apprentice shook his head. "But they're a lot harder to find on this side," he said. "That's the whole point."

I kept my voice low. "Can you pick the lock?"

Rory shot me a withering glance that said I'd just insulted him. "I was the best thief in Bunard, yah?"

I looked to Bolt. "How well do you know this place?"

A knock at the door interrupted him, and a moment later, a handful of servants entered under the direction of a lean-faced man who wore his reserve like a garment. "His Majesty sends his apologies, but his illness prevents him from entertaining you in the manner you deserve."

I nodded. "No apologies are necessary. The journey here was arduous." I nodded my gratitude at the trays of food and drink. "You've provided everything we require. We will take our rest and meet with King Boclar tomorrow." I stepped toward the door. "The ladies have already retired for the evening. My guards and I will serve them in your stead."

I stopped midstep, pretending an idea had just occurred to me. "A moment," I said. I went through the rooms until I found a writing desk with ink and parchment. After jotting a quick note and blotting it, I folded it and took it to the head servant. "Please deliver this to Her Highness, Erendella."

The servants left, and I waited for the click of the lock. Then I took one of the trays to Gael's door and knocked. When it opened, I gaped. Gael had changed from her traveling clothes into sleeping attire. While it satisfied the dictates of modesty for Aille or Caisel, it would never be fashionable in the cooler climate in Bunard.

"Thank you, my betrothed," Gael said. Her voice dipped into that register that made it hard to think.

She took the tray and closed the door without giving me a chance to reply. I raised my hand to knock again . . . but thought better of it. She probably wouldn't answer anyway.

When I turned, I saw Rory eating like only adolescents could, but Bolt eyed me with an understated smirk. "Never pick a fight you know you're going to lose."

I shook my head, trying to clear the image of the way the silk had clung to Gael's form. "How am I supposed to know when I'm picking a fight?"

"Ha," Rory said. "With you it's not hard. You open your mouth and say something."

I sat and poured myself a glass of wine to go with the meal. "We're going to wait for a few hours," I said. "If nothing happens by then, we're going hunting."

Rory and Bolt donned opposing expressions, one gleeful, the other resigned.

CHAPTER 52

"It might help if you shared exactly what you intend to do," Bolt said.

"I need to see the king."

It was pitch black. I heard a whisper of sound as Rory dropped to his belly next to the door. "There's no light on the far side," he said. "But I can't tell if there are guards or not, and I don't have any oil to keep the lock quiet."

"I'll take care of any guards," Bolt said.

I heard the soft clink of Rory's picks, and Bolt drew a deep breath and let it out in a long sigh. "That you want to do this in the middle of the night says you suspect something important enough to merit imprisonment. Pellin's not here to bargain for your release, and even if he was, he might choose not to."

"The king's illness comes under my authority," I said.

Bolt whispered a curse. "Why do you think that?"

"The solas powder. The light isn't strange or exotic the way I'd expect it to be for court. It gives off the same color as the powder Myle gave us in Bunard. It's artificial sunlight. Boclar is using it to keep his vault from opening."

Bolt sighed. "That would explain why he's here and not with his army."

"Why would he go into the forest?" Rory asked.

"That's pretty high on the list of questions I intend to ask him," I said.

"Fair enough," Bolt said. "But why now? You could just wait until he sends for us."

I didn't answer, choosing instead to let Bolt come to his own conclusion.

His hand found my upper arm without any fumbling, and I envied him his gift. Tomorrow, I'd have bruises there. "What are you planning, Willet?"

"Right now, I want to speak with the king. I might need the use of both arms tomorrow," I added.

He let go at the same time a soft click came from Rory's direction. He opened the door to empty darkness beyond. "They didn't guard the door," Rory said. "That's bad."

Bolt grunted his agreement. "They're probably giving us the opportunity to hang ourselves."

"Can you get us to the king?" I asked Bolt.

"Maybe. I know where the royal quarters used to be, but if they've been moved or if the king has elected not to use them for some reason, we're going to be reduced to wandering around Boclar's citadel. I'll let you imagine what will happen to us when we're caught."

"Let's focus on the next step," I said.

"We'll need to retrace our way back to the audience chamber," Bolt said. "Boclar's apartments are east of it."

Rory stirred beside me. "I'd like to know why they're keeping this wing of the citadel so dark."

Before I could answer, the metallic ping of flint striking steel prefaced a flare of light bursting in front of me.

Pain lanced through my eyes and I screamed. Bolt crashed into my shoulder, sending me sprawling, and I heard the whine of steel as he drew.

"I can't see!" Rory screamed.

"Put down your weapons," a voice commanded, "or Lord Dura dies. I have half a dozen men with crossbows trained on his heart. You can't take them all before one of them fires. At this range they can't miss."

Bolt's shove had put me thirty feet away and left me in a heap. I blinked, trying to see, but my eyes were filled with the green afterimage of solas fire. I stood and bowed toward the voice. "Good evening, Your Highness," I said lightly. "I assumed my message had been misplaced, so I elected to come see you.

"If I wished to see you, Lord Dura, I would have told you."

"You did tell me," I said. "You locked our door but left it unguarded."

She laughed, but there was no sound of humor in it. "You misinterpreted my father's trust for license. You may see him in the morning."

I lifted my hands. "Forgive me. Customs are a bit different up
north." I blinked a few times in quick succession and thought I could
make out dark blobs that might have been people. "You and your
father need me tonight, Your Highness. What happens if the powder
runs out?"

To her credit, she played her hand until the end. "I don't think
the apothecaries are in any danger of running short of anguicaine
powder, Lord Dura."

I didn't answer her in kind. Erendella might use any excuse to
deny me. "That's not the powder I'm referring to, Your Highness."

"I could have you shot and tell my father you were mistaken for
thieves," she said after a moment.

Silence fell in the room, and I felt rather than heard Bolt and Rory
tense. Smudges of light intruded on my vision. How well could Bolt
and Rory see?

"Is the solas powder burning for him now?" I asked.

"No," she said softly. "We have to husband what we have. There's
not enough to last each night."

"There's nothing I can do while he raves," I said. "But if you have
even a few minutes' worth, I can help you."

Silence stretched while I tried not to think about a half-dozen
crossbow bolts punching through me as if I were wet parchment.

"Your guards will be returned to their quarters," Erendella said.

"Where he goes, I go," Bolt said.

"Not this time," I told him. "I'll come back to you."

"No," he said, his voice flat.

"Dura alone, or no one," Erendella said.

"Why?" Bolt asked.

The princess, tall as most men, might have shrugged. The haze
from the solas powder had yet to clear. "You're gifted." She pointed
to me. "He's not. My father's life is in my care."

Bolt looked as if he might object again, but in the end he relented.
"Understand that I am making you personally responsible for Lord
Dura's safety, Your Highness."

362

"Is that a threat?" Erendella's voice sharpened to an edge.

"Interpret it however you wish," Bolt said. "Just don't forget it."

"Beorgan." She pointed to one of the guards. "Take these two back to their quarters and rejoin us. If I do not see him within the minute," she said to Bolt, "Lord Dura will bear the consequences."

The remaining guards formed up around me, but they didn't draw their weapons. Evidently, I was so obviously ungifted that I didn't constitute a threat.

Unlike the court in Cynestol, which ran until nearly dawn, the citadel was quiet, devoid of courtiers or courtesans making the rounds. I remarked on the difference.

"Court life in Vadras is a more serious affair," Erendella said. "The citadel is the residence of the king, and the audience chamber for those whose petitions cannot be resolved by anyone with less authority. Ceremonial occasions are no longer held in the citadel but in the grand hall across the moat."

Some inflection within her voice, a hitch in her speech, gave me the impression this was a recent development. "How long has that been the case?" I asked.

Her reserve receded just enough for her to glance my way. "Since father returned from the war."

We came to the chamber where we'd held conference with the rest of the monarchs earlier, but instead of departing through the east entrance, Erendella and the guards led me north to an inconspicuous door that opened to reveal a stairway heading down. "The king's illness requires a measure of solitude," she said. "I hope you're not uncomfortable with enclosed spaces, Lord Dura."

"No, it's forests I've learned to fear."

Her eyes widened at that, but she led the way down into the rock foundation of the citadel without speaking. We came into a room composed of a single arch running its length, and we gathered in the middle so that we could stand upright. At the far end of the room, four guards held vigil by a door. No light showed beneath it.

Closer, I noticed that the door and frame had been padded with heavy felt. Erendella nodded to the guards, and they parted as she pulled a heavy key from within her dress. "You said you could cure my father of his sickness."

I nodded.

Her mouth tightened as a prelude to anger. "And what is the price of your aid, Lord Dura?"

I needed Boclar's gift to help me call the Fayit. If I answered Erendella with the plain truth of my intention, she wouldn't let me within arm's reach of the king. She'd likely imprison me instead. I took refuge in the fact that I didn't *know* what was wrong with Boclar, telling myself I only suspected. "The price depends on who pays it," I said.

"You sound like a priest."

I nodded. "There's probably a good reason for that."

Erendella opened the door and we stepped into madness.

A small room, hardly more than a niche within the rock, had been equipped to host the king of Caisel. Boclar stood on a thick pile of blankets in the middle of the room, bound by heavy chains anchored to the four walls that offered him just enough slack to sit, but no more. At the sight of his daughter, he threw himself toward her but moved no more than a few inches before the heavily padded manacles drew him up short. The whites of his eyes showed all around, and he strained, working to get his hands around his daughter's throat. Rents showed in his clothes, and bruises discolored his flesh, testimony to the extremity that had burst the blood vessels beneath his skin.

Just inside the door the king's alchemist waited with fire, but her mirrored bowl was empty. "Please, Your Highness, let me light the powder," she begged. "He's killing himself."

Erendella watched her father, her expression cold and still like snow piled on a mountain before an avalanche. "How much do you have?"

The alchemist dropped her gaze to stare at her hands as if they accused her. "An hour's worth. No more. The shipment of phosine from Owmead has been delayed. It will be another week in coming."

Erendella was wavering.

"Your Highness," I said, "if you have any hope of defeating this illness, light the powder and let me work." Inside, I retched at the deception I'd just perpetrated.

She pointed to Helioma, who placed a measure of powder into the bowl and lit it with a taper from one of the lamps. Shadows fled. "My compliments," I said to her. "The best alchemist in Bunard sought in vain to find a way to make the powder burn more slowly."

Erendella paused just long enough to turn to me. "Helioma is the foremost alchemist on the continent."

The king's struggles ceased, and he looked around at us, his eyes clear. "Aer have mercy," he cried. "I hurt all over." Erendella ran to him, holding a cup. "Not too much?" he asked. "I have to be able to function come dawn."

She swallowed. "Not too much, Father. Drink."

I steeled myself for what I had to do and tried to ignore the fact that my justifications sounded too much like Pellin's or Toria's. "You spent a night in the forest," I said. If Boclar or his daughter noticed the absence of his title, they gave no sign. "Why?"

Boclar looked like a patchwork of a human, used up. "I doubted," he said. Screaming had reduced his voice to a croak.

I waited, but he seemed to think his explanation sufficient. "What doubt led you into the forest?"

"I've been to Bunard," he said, scraping the words across his throat. "Years ago I visited Laidir. Bunard was smaller than I expected, but I thought the way the engineers had diverted the river to divide the city and defend it ingenious."

He paused, and I wondered if Boclar's mind had broken under the unique strain he bore. I looked to Erendella, who signaled me to be patient.

"I remember thinking the tor was magnificent, the way the tower of rock soared toward the heavens. I had a carriage, of course, but I wanted to *feel* the height, so I ordered my captain and his men accompanying me to dismount. We ascended the road." His laughter came out as a soft bark. "When we finally got to the top, the view took my breath away and refused for the longest time to give it back. The men and women of Caisel live their entire lives on the plain, Lord Dura. We are unaccustomed to the extremity of height."

"Your Majesty," I interrupted, the weight of time pressing on me. "The forest?"

But he went on as if I hadn't spoken. "Most of my guard recoiled from the sight our lofty vantage point offered, but it drew me onward to the edge of the parapet, Lord Dura. I stood there with my head as close to the clouds as it had ever been and wanted nothing more in the moment but to jump and fly." His eyes lost their abstracted look and focused on mine. "That's what happened in the forest, Lord Dura."

I shook my head. "You knew what would happen."

"The threat of the forest is less real to us in the far south than to those in Collum," Boclar said. "The reality you experience daily is an abstraction to us. I didn't view the forest as evil but as a sickness."

"What did you do?"

Boclar nodded toward Helioma. "I surmised that if darkness was the means by which the forest infected its victims, then light would be the means by which the disease could be prevented. I went into the forest equipped with enough solas powder to last the duration of my stay."

Boclar's gaze bored into mine, and the tenor of his voice carried accusation. "If a soldier of Collum could survive the forest, then surely a man with phos-fire and the gift of kings could. I expected to learn the means by which to conquer its disease."

I gaped. "You dared the forest because of me?" I put my hands on my head, but I couldn't think, couldn't order my thoughts. "You . . . Your Majesty . . . how could you do anything so stupid?" Rage I couldn't contain worked its way up my chest and into my throat. "You didn't think to ask? I would have told you how I survived the forest!"

The king stiffened at my tone, but he managed to smile. "Foolish, yes. Perhaps even as foolish as Cesla, but I believe in the mercy of Aer, Lord Dura. It may surprise you, but I have faith that He offers second chances to everyone." His nod was deep enough to be considered a bow. "Hasn't He brought you to me? You've been to the forest. Pellin and the Chief of Servants have testified to it, and though I have no means to test them in this, I believe them."

"My daughter brought you out of darkness and walked you through lightless halls." He smiled, his teeth wet and shining by the light of the solas powder. "Yet no hint of madness came upon you." He nodded to the guards, and they drew weapons. "You are Aer's second chance for me," he said. "I am king of Caisel. I cannot continue to rule in this manner, Lord Dura. You will tell me the secret to your survival."

CHAPTER 53

I gaped at the king. Under different circumstances I would have accused him of jesting in poor taste and at my expense. "What have you done?" I asked. My voice rebounded from the rock of the citadel and came back to me, hollow and desperate. "You dared the forest because I survived?"

Any trace of humor disappeared from Boclar's face, and his expression grew stiff and haughty. "I hold the gift of kings, Lord Dura. When you survived the forest, you were just a man. Now, release me from this disease."

"That's just it," I said. "I was and still am just a man. It wasn't me at all. He must have seen you, but he was too weak to prevent it."

"Who?"

"Oh, Aer," I wanted to weep. "Ealdor. You've destroyed yourself for nothing."

The king pointed, and one of the guards closed with me, the point of his dagger working through the cloth of my tunic. "If this Ealdor saved you, Lord Dura, he will save me. Bring him."

"Don't you understand?" But of course, Boclar couldn't possibly understand. "Ealdor's gone, dead, *because* he broke his vow in order to save me."

My arguments had no effect on the king or his daughter. They looked at me, implacable and merciless as iron. "Then bring another like this Ealdor."

A desperate laugh escaped before I could stop it. "Ealdor was one of the Fayit."

"The Fayit?" The king gaped at me, his expression caught between mocking and incredulous. He nodded to the brazier. Half the solas powder had burned away, leaving streaks of soot to mark its passing. "Lord Dura, my patience and time are limited. If you wish to be believed, then summon the proof of the Fayit and have them release me."

"I can't. Not without a perfect circle," I said.

Boclar pointed to the brazier. "Lord Dura, there was a flaw in the last shipment of solas powder. The brazier holds the last of our supply. My body is bruised and spent, and I'm at the last of my strength. Without healing or more powder, I won't live beyond another week. Have I not said the gift of domere is powerful beyond measure? Either heal me yourself or summon one who can."

My hands were bare, and I held them up for the king's inspection. "I'll have to touch you."

At the king's nod the guards stepped back, and I took a moment to speak to Erendella. "I'll need your help as well, Your Highness." I had no hope of healing the king. Ealdor's knowledge of the Darkwater so far surpassed mine it precluded hope, but I needed all six monarchs with the gift of kings in one place.

I approached Boclar and his daughter, who stood to his immediate right, the two of them basking in the light of a false sun. "Hold hands."

"Why?" Boclar asked, suspicious.

"Do you love your father?" I asked Erendella.

She nodded once, solemn. "I would die for him. He's already proved he would do the same for me."

"There are mysteries I can't explain, Your Majesty," I said, "because I don't fully understand them. But Pellin and Bronwyn and Toria Deel went to lengths to tell me the importance of love. It undergirds our gift. I bear you no great love, so it's imperative that your daughter be close. Hold hands." I waited until they'd done so and stepped forward.

I reached out to Erendella, and she mirrored the gesture, but instead of taking her hand in mine, I grasped her sleeve, protecting myself from her memories. Some lasting suspicion must have remained with Boclar. When my hand was close enough to feel the warmth of his skin, he turned to his daughter. "You remind me so much of your mother, full of fire and strength."

I reached out and gripped his hand, roughly, desperately. The phosfire of the king's powder receded as my consciousness hurtled through his dark, dark eyes, and I stood before a wide stream of memory. What I meant to do would take little time as those with Boclar reckoned it. Before I destroyed the king's vault, I wanted to see what circumstances had driven him to the forest.

Our talk of the Darkwater had brought those memories to the surface of his mind—they flowed close by me. I dipped my hand into the stream and let myself become the king.

The trees rose all around me in the fading light of day, a mass of twisted trunks so large around it would take half a dozen men to encircle one of them. Leaves the color of midnight blocked all but the barest hint of the dying sun. Erendella, my heir and heart, waited.

"She'll never forgive me for this, Woruld."

"As long as she's safe, Your Majesty," he said. His voice carried strains of effort from hauling the polished brazier and the heavy sack of solas powder. "Your Majesty, if this doesn't work . . ."

He didn't bother or need to finish. "We have enough," I said. The light dimmed further, and we were far enough into the forest that the darkness had become almost complete. "We should light the brazier now."

Quickly, with the economy of motion that came from practice, Woruld threaded two rods through the holes on either side that would allow us to carry it while the fire burned. Then he poured a quantity of powder that would last for the duration of the night into the bowl and struck his steel with a glancing blow that sent a handful of sparks dancing through the air.

The darkness leapt away from us, held at bay by a circle of light, a sun in miniature that rested on the forest floor. Together we picked up our burden and threaded our way through the undergrowth.

"Which way do we go, Your Majesty? Woruld asked.

We'd entered from the south. Our exit and safety still lay just a few hundred yards, no more than half a mile, behind us. It would be simple to walk away—but for the fact that any reason I had for living was ahead of me. "In," I said, "to the center."

Twisted trunks, blackened with age and malice surrounded us, their roots overlapping each other, struggling for preeminence. "Careful of the bowl," I said, but my warning was more for my own ears. I was a child of the delta, and the forest was as strange to me as Vadras would

369

be to any from Collum or Frayel. Nothing stirred. The malevolence of the forest had extinguished every creature. Only trees possessed the requisite fortitude to grow here. I glanced up by the light of the phos-fire to the hatred-blackened leaves above me. Yes, the trees grew, but even the durability of wood was insufficient to keep the evil at bay. The trees' strength had done nothing more than allow them a life of corruption.

We worked our way toward the center of the forest for hours. I nibbled on chiccor root, wary of the danger it presented. After a night comprised of putting one foot in front of the other, Woruld stopped to snuff the fire in our brazier.

"We can rest, Your Majesty." He pointed overhead to the merest hint of sunlight could be seen through the canopy.

I stopped, my legs shaking from unfamiliar use. "Have we come far enough? Is there still enough powder to get us there and back?"

Woruld nodded. "Yes, Your Majesty." He looked around. "We should have brought more men."

I swallowed my indignation. "I was ordered not to."

"Sleep, Your Majesty," Woruld said. "I will wake you when it's time."

I dozed for a few hours and rose before Woruld summoned me. Fatigue flowed through my veins with every beat of my heart, but every step we could take in the daylight was a bit of powder we could husband at need. We spent the second day as we had the first. And most of the next.

As the third day died, Woruld lit the brazier again, and we marched toward the smell of water. The ground grew marshy under our feet, though no frogs or turtles disturbed the black-leaved plants. After a mile or so, we stepped through the stench of moss that hung from trees like a curtain and onto the muddy shore of a lake.

"And so the name of the forest is the name of the lake," Woruld said. "Darkwater."

"Come," a voice called from outside the glow of our brazier. "The water is shallow."

"Father!" Erendella's voice cried. "Run! It's a trap."

Laughter rebounded from the surface of the lake. "Of course it is," Cesla said, "but he knew that when he entered the forest."

"We have light," I called, but my intended defiance met only more laughter.

"Yes, my servants told me." Scorn, a trace only, filled Cesla's voice—as though my defiance didn't merit anything greater. "Bring your light, if you wish."

We stepped into the cold of the water, our boots splashing before sinking into the mud. After a few paces, the footing became firm, unyielding, as though I walked on stone.

"Sire," Woruld said.

I nodded. "I feel it."

After a hundred yards, I saw figures arrayed in an arc around Cesla, the man who had been Eldest for centuries. They were men and women of no particular note or gift, but they held themselves ready, their hands on knives or swords. All of them wore layers of gauzy cloth over their eyes.

I pulled the stench of death and decay into my lungs and lifted my voice. "Release my daughter."

Cesla threw back his head and laughed his scorn until the canopy of leaves above him fluttered. "But of course, Boclar. Here." He flourished a bow and motioned Erendella forward.

She took a few tottering steps, unsure, suspecting treachery, but Cesla made no move to interfere, and his men raised no weapons against her.

"That's it?" I asked. "You've taken her simply to release her to me?"

He lifted one hand, tapping his chin with his forefinger. "What would you have me do, old friend?"

A hint of sound came from behind us. Woruld turned and I heard him sigh. "Your Majesty."

I nodded. "We're surrounded." And we were. Cesla's men were arrayed in a broad arc that I and Woruld with all his gifts could never hope to defeat. "What do you want?"

Cesla cocked his head, a smile playing around the corners of his mouth. "Erendella's mind is her own, though she has spent a week here in the forest. Am I not merciful?" He paused to give a theatric shrug. "Even the liturgy says that Aer's mercy has its price. Mine is no different. Your daughter and your man may go with my blessing." His face contorted into a parody as he made the sign of the intersecting arcs in the air in front of him. He stopped just short of completing the gesture. "But I think I would enjoy the pleasure of your company for a time."

"Sire," Woruld said, "you cannot stay here."

I turned to my faithful guard, my friend. "Take her."

"Yes," Cesla said, "by all means. I assure you, your sovereign will be only a day behind you, though it's a pity you only brought the one fire."

Woruld shifted. If need be, the brazier holding the fire could float for a time. I heard movement behind us.

"If you make any move to threaten the king or his daughter," Cesla said. "I will kill you where you stand."

My last hope died. "Take her Woruld. Protect her as you have me."

"Father." Erendella threw her arms around me to whisper in my ear. "Kill me, then yourself. We must not leave here."

"What has he done to you?" I asked.

"Please, Father," she begged. "I cannot."

Her hands fumbled in the inside of my cloak, but when she touched the hilt of my dagger she jerked as if burned.

"Please," she sobbed.

I pulled my head up from the wealth of my child's hair. "Woruld, take her and the light and go."

My friend and my heart, both of them, walked away, heading south until the light of solas powder vanished and I was left in darkness. "Ah, Boclar," Cesla crooned my name. "Do you know what you have done?"

I tried to laugh my defiance at him, but it died in my throat. "My soldiers will not surrender the field because you hold me, Cesla. You and yours will die here in the forest, cut off from light and love."

Cesla's laughter succeeded where mine failed, held genuine mirth. "I have lived uncounted centuries, Boclar."

The canopy of leaves overhead blotted out the light from the moon and stars, but splashing sounds came to me, near and far across the lake. The sound of shovels hitting earth and water accompanied grunts of effort, and I strained to see.

"My purposes are myriad, Boclar, and I give you the honor of being a part of them. Centuries from now your descendants—if I allow you any—will mark this as hallowed ground, and I will have them worship me here."

"Worship? You're insane."

"Do you know the problem with your world, Boclar? It's not a lack of faith—it's the lack of will to create the singularity of it. Even before the Merum split from the southern church, your leaders allowed people their doubt, their moments of disbelief. There is a new faith coming, Boclar, one that will unify the world, because I will place it in every mind."

I knew the reference from the liturgy. "And every heart?" I asked. The nearest of Cesla's men were at least three paces from me. Escape from the Darkwater was impossible, but I clutched my dagger and contemplated freedom of a different sort.

"No, I will allow them to keep their hearts, just as I will allow you to keep yours. Why kill a man when you can torture him? Behold!" From the throat of every man and woman around me, there arose a low moan of infinite despair that grew in intensity until the forest shook with the wail of countless damned souls. Cesla laughed his counterpoint.

I turned to run, but his hand caught my bare arm with the strength of a vise. Frantic, I reached for my dagger, desperate to open the arteries in my wrist or throat.

"Try," Cesla said, releasing me.

My hand stopped as it touched the hilt, powerless.

"What have you done to me?"

"Night has fallen on you in the Darkwater, Boclar," he said. "And you are here at the center of my power. Now I have a disciple and more. You will be the instrument of my release." He put his hands on my head in a parody of blessing. "Sleep now, my blessed one."

CHAPTER 54

The stream of Boclar's memories skipped to a vision of leaving the forest at dawn, the thread changing color from the black of despair to a bright green of hope without transition. Beneath the stream lay a vault, a scroll of deepest night. I drew closer to examine it, searching for some clue of what the writing meant.

A thread of black, thick and sluggish, snaked away from the scroll, suspended in the depths of Boclar's mind—then it came for me.

I jerked, breaking contact, and my eyes found the king's as I struggled to breathe. Shaking, I put my hand on the sleeve of his arm, my skin no longer touching his, but ready. It would take me no more than an instant, the barest touch, to break Boclar's vault and destroy his mind, but my training as a priest had given me the conviction that a man should be allowed to confess before he died.

"You brought Cesla's plague back with you from the forest, Your Majesty." I waited for him to speak. Even kings were granted the rite of confession.

He nodded. "The morning I came out of the forest I dared to hope that I might have escaped its evil. I was alive and by the grace of Aer so was Erendella. I regained the safety of our lines and men. Even after night fell, nothing untoward happened. I didn't rave. No madness descended upon me. I slept like any other man, exhausted from my ordeal."

"But the second evening, as the sun dipped below the horizon, I gathered my captains, declared that my journey into the forest and my escape had revealed the enemy's weakness." Boclar looked at me and shouldered the burden of his guilt. "I told them I'd seen a talisman in the forest, large beyond comprehension, that must be destroyed at all costs."

My heart stopped, and I gaped. "Aer in heaven," I whispered. "What have you done?"

"You don't know?" Boclar demanded. "Is your gift nothing more than pretense?"

"I saw you in the forest with Cesla. I released the gift because there's a vault in your mind," I rasped. "My last memory is you leaving the forest at dawn because the evil in your mind sensed my presence and came for me, Your Majesty!"

He flinched and his guards advanced.

"Stop," I said. Of a wonder they obeyed me. "Tell me what you've done," I repeated. "I will make no attempt to cure you until you do."

His eyes held threats, but with a sigh he relented. "Seemingly in my own mind I ordered my men to return to the forest with me. We stopped at the nearest village, and they equipped themselves with the ironmongers art to return and destroy Cesla's talisman."

"It's no talisman, King—it's a prison."

Boclar shot me a withering glance. "I surmised as much." He turned to his daughter. "Something in my manner must have alerted Erendella. When night fell at the next city on our journey south, I began to repeat those same orders, only this time I commanded the aid of every alchemist in Vadras. Erendella, suspicious, lit a brazier of solas powder." He licked his lips. "I felt it, Lord Dura, the evil you saw. I felt it withdraw, sensed its frustration."

"You've kept your vault from opening ever since by lighting your nights with solas powder," I said. "What of the men you sent to the forest?"

Boclar shook his head. "By the time I realized what I had done, they'd passed through our lines."

"If they open the prison, Your Majesty, the world is theirs."

Boclar nodded. "We have time yet. The prison is vast and the tools from the village were crude." He pushed himself back in his chair. "Now, Lord Dura, you know everything. You will cure me of this vault. I am out of solas powder."

Powder or not, I had no wish to have the king's death on my hands. "Your Majesty, I—"

"Now, Lord Dura."

The guards closed in. "Very well, Your Majesty. Take your daughter's hand. I will perform the same healing on you as I did on Regent Cailin."

Boclar gave a satisfied nod. "Proceed, Lord Dura."

I took Boclar's hand in mine.

The river of memories lay before me once more, comprising all the loves and losses of the king, but the threads were no more brightly colored than they would be for a common laborer. I dove beneath the flowing stream to the vault beneath them. Wary. The evil had become aware of me.

The lure of the king's memories dropped away. I turned, warned by some instinct. A thread came out of the dark for me, but it oozed, sluggish. I retreated to the far side of the black scroll that had birthed it and watched as it tried to reverse direction. Another thread lifted from the scroll like a worm freeing itself from the soil and came toward me, writhing as it followed my scent. I swallowed my revulsion and tried to think.

I moved through Boclar's mind, edging toward the vault. I caught sight of the myriad threads that sprung from it, linking the vault to every part of his mind. Experimentally, I slashed at one with my gift, hoping.

But the memory attached to it flared and died, taking a small portion of the king's mind with it. I wanted to rage at Boclar, but he wasn't there. In his ignorance he'd asked for something beyond my ability. Only the Fayit, through the grace of Aer's power, had kept my vault from destroying me. Only his intervention had kept Cailin's mind intact when I destroyed her vault.

And Ealdor was dead. If Boclar was to live, it would only be through the will of Aer.

Pressure. I felt pressure on my leg.

In horror, I looked down to see a thick tentacle of black wrapped around my thigh. Gagging in panic and revulsion, I reached out with my mind to throw it from me, slashing with my thoughts. More of them came for me, but under the influence of phos-fire they were too slow.

I paused, standing there in the dark of the king's mind to say the antidon for Boclar. His vault was nothing more than parchment. My merest thoughts tore it, destroying the withering snakes that tried to reach out. With every stroke of domere, more of Boclar died. I slashed over and again with my gift until nothing remained, not even dust.

It was finished.

I stood in the empty ruin of his mind, the vault gone, the river gone. With a last act of will, I envisioned myself letting go of Boclar's hand in the real world.

Light from torches surrounded me as the last of the solas powder flared and winked out. Boclar stared, his mouth gaping. Next to him, Erendella stood, her gaze trying to find purchase, now looking at me, now at her father, now at her hands. Before she could refuse or react, I brushed my fingers along the back of her hand, just long enough to confirm her mind was her own. No sign of a vault existed beneath her memories.

Then I stepped back, knowing my danger. I'd reduced Boclar to idiocy, his mind ruined by the vault he'd kept at bay, but ruined nonetheless. Erendella—queen now—would be grief-stricken beyond reckoning and angry enough to kill the man responsible.

But the rage I expected never came. Instead, she ordered the guards to escort me back. Bolt, Gael and the rest were waiting for me, but the king's death had used me up. Explanations could wait. I groped my way to bed.

Sunlight, warm and yellow, came through the nearest window to show luxurious furnishings that still managed functionality. Figures stirred, but the first person I noted in my vision wasn't Gael—it was Mirren. Only then did I look down and notice she held my arm.

"Boclar is dead," I said. My voice cracked with disuse.

"We managed to figure that out," Bolt said from somewhere behind me. "Pellin's going to want to have a long conversation with you about the way you use your gift. You're picking up some bad habits."

"He had a vault. Doesn't that fall under our authority?"

I still couldn't see him, but I heard him snort. "You understand people, Dura, but you have no idea how to deal with them. How is that possible?"

My body felt fine, but my mind still screamed with fatigue. Even this limited conversation tired me. "How long have I been asleep?"

"A day and a half," Mirren said.

"We have to leave for the forest."

"We're leaving this morning," Bolt said. "Mirren arranged it."

He came into view and gave my apprentice—the thought struck me oddly—an inscrutable look.

She nodded. "The rest of the monarchs are on their way as well."

I managed enough strength to look around the room. "Where are Gael and Rory?"

"Rory's guarding the door," Bolt said. "Gael is probably with Erendella."

"Why?"

"Because the guards were ordered to alert her the moment you woke."

"That doesn't sound good," I said.

"That's because it's not."

The door opened before I could think of anything clever to say. Outside, Erendella stood, flanked by Gael and six guards who carried enough meat on their frames to pass for livestock. Nobody looked happy to see me.

"Willet Dura," Queen Erendella said. "Time, as your apprentice keeps telling me, weighs heavily upon us. You will ride with me today and offer such defense as you may for the death of my father. We will leave within the hour."

Relief flooded through me, but I'd learned to be distrustful of good news in any guise. "Why the change of mind, Your Majesty?"

Erendella gave me a look accompanied by a slow blink of annoyance. She'd been queen for all of a day and a half, but that was enough for her to don her royal demeanor. She wasn't happy to have her orders questioned. "Your apprentice showed me the memories you were given from Ealdor."

"I don't understand."

Erendella sighed. "Obviously not. Suffice it to say, Lord Dura, that you could not have contrived those memories. They were filled with wonders for which you have no reference or imagination."

It took me a moment to figure out that the queen had just called me stupid. She gave me a thin smile. "I mean no offense." She shrugged. "Or very little of it. My point is that no one could have created those memories. They are too far removed from our existence."

CHAPTER 55

Well after the sun had burned off the morning mist, Toria felt as much as heard Pellin calling her through the scrying stone she carried. With a nod to Fess, they made for a nearby copse of trees that would shield them from observation. Lelwin remained silent on her horse, her eyes uncovered, her head bowed. Fess positioned her in a pool of light, despite the fact that the shade of the trees was weak. Then they held their stones before them.

"Hear me, Toria Deel," Pellin called from the stone, but his voice wavered, becoming louder and then indistinct through the call.

"I hear you, Eldest, but your voice is—"

"There was an accident," he said. "My stone was damaged. Praise Aer I can reach you at all."

"I am here as well," Brid Teorian's voice announced. "Where have you been, Eldest? I have half the Servants on the continent searching for you."

"Then it should come as no surprise that I've been on the southern continent," Pellin said. "We're about to land in Cynestol."

A stream of invectives poured from the stone, and Fess's brows rose in appreciation. "I haven't heard some of those insults since I left the urchins. The Chief has a very ecumenical vocabulary."

"Are you finished?" Pellin asked when the Chief paused to take a breath.

"Temporarily, Eldest," she snapped, "but this isn't over. You have a responsibility to safeguard the forest, and I fail to see how that duty entails going to the southern continent."

"You will." Pellin's voice held notes of confidence Toria had seldom heard before. "With the help of the Honored One, we've learned how to cure Lord Dura of his vault."

Toria's heart leapt at the announcement as she caught his phrasing. "Cure, Eldest? Not break?"

"That's impossible," the Chief said.

"I'm surprised to hear you say that," Pellin said. "Don't we say that with Aer all things are possible?"

Toria's heart struggled to find its rhythm. "But that means that it was always possible. Oh, Aer, what have we done? How many thousands have we broken and thrown away? We could have saved them."

Either Pellin had already worked through his grief and culpability, or he'd shouldered enough guilt in his long life that more hardly mattered. Regardless, his voice came through the stone, weak with damage and distance, but commanding.

"Grieve later, Toria Deel," he said. "Ealdor told me to find what was inside Lord Dura's vault. We now have the means to do so. I need you to get word to him in Cynestol."

The Chief of Servants muttered imprecations but managed to curtail herself a moment later. "That's just the point, Eldest. Lord Dura is no longer in Cynestol. He's on his way to meet Rymark and the rest of the monarchs. He claims he's found the means to summon the Fayits' help in fighting Cesla. He's managed to convince them that the gift of kings creates a perfect circle. Desperate people will believe anything, it seems."

"Where are Cailin and Brod?" Toria asked. "Surely, the regent of Collum has more sense than to take the heir anywhere near the forest."

"Have you *met* Cailin?" the Chief's voice grew brittle. "She is as reckless in her own way as Dura. We're five leagues from the edge of the forest and withdrawing south and west as fast as men and horses can move."

Toria leaned toward the stone as realization flooded through her. "Wait. If he has plans to create a perfect circle, that would mean he found Chora's heir."

"Yes," the Chief said. "I received word from Bishop Serius. It seems Bolt has managed to add another historical footnote to the Book of Errants."

Toria's mind reeled, but before she could speak, Pellin's disjointed voice came from the stone. "Where's Ry . . . mark?"

"Treflow," Brid Teorian said.

"Why is he so far from the forest?" Pellin asked.

"The Darkwater erupted," the Chief said. "Every outpost on the inner ring was wiped out. Here in Collum they came within a hairsbreadth of breaching Cailin's camp."

Pellin's voice came through the stone, shrill with the effort of making himself heard. "Cesla knows we have gathered the means to defeat him."

"Doubtless," the Chief said.

"Eldest," Toria asked, "what happened to make him so desperate?"

Toria's stone grew still, and she could sense the Eldest gathering his thoughts. "When we broke Elieve's vault, we broke it from inside."

"Whose vault?" Toria asked.

"A dwimor we discovered outside of Cynestol," Pellin said. "Mark persuaded me not to kill her."

"You left one of those things alive?" the Chief asked. "Have you been taking lessons from the reeve, Eldest?"

"You forget yourself, Chief," Pellin snapped. "The defense of the forest is in my hands."

Toria didn't speak. She had never heard Pellin assert his authority that way before, not with any of the rulers or heads of the church.

"Your pardon, Eldest," the Chief said. "Can you turn Dura aside from his plan? If we bring all the rulers together, the risk is unacceptable. If Cesla should manage to take or kill them, the north will fall into anarchy overnight."

"No," Pellin said. "The risk must be taken. Ealdor told me the secret to defeating Cesla was hidden inside Dura's mind. If he can call the rest of the Fayit, the knowledge Ealdor placed within his vault will defeat Cesla. The evil in the Darkwater knows this, Brid. The Honored One and I, along with another member of the southern Vigil, fought the evil in the Maveth for the duration of an entire night within Elieve's mind. And we won."

"I have to tell Cailin to get in contact with the other rulers immediately," Brid Teorian said.

"Before nightfall," Pellin admonished. "Cesla won't wait before he strikes again. If Dura is correct, then Cesla only needs to capture one of the monarchs to prevent the call."

"Speed, Eldest," the Chief said. "Rymark cannot hold. Without the inner cordon the foolish and the greedy are flooding into the forest. Cesla will have all the reinforcements he needs."

A moment later Toria caught the barest sound of sighing through the stone. "My heart tells me we are in midst of Cesla's last desperate gamble," Pellin said. "Secrecy avails us little at this point. What did Ealdor tell you to do, Toria Deel?"

"To keep the forest defended for as long as possible," Toria said. "We have a weapon, Eldest, but we need more men. I don't know how long we can hold at Treflow. Cesla has been teaching blacksmiths how to make tools stronger than aurium."

"Do whatever you must," Pellin said. "So long as the six are safe and Dura lives, we have the means to fight. I will come to you as quickly as I can."

The stone went silent. Toria turned to see Fess looking at her, his expression inscrutable. "Lelwin is the weapon you spoke of," he said.

His tone had been neutral, but she couldn't help but read condemnations into it. She pushed it aside. Grieving and guilt would have to wait. If she lived, she would make time for both. "Come, we must gather what forces we can and make for Treflow."

CHAPTER 56

Hours later Toria Deel held a leaf in her hand, working to think against the panic that made her heart race. Black spots disfigured the oak leaf—and every one of its kin still attached to the sapling. She knew the boundaries of the forest better than any save Pellin. She tore her gaze away from the diseased leaf to stare north, to where blue skies met the black canopy that defined the Darkwater Forest.

"How far away are we?" she asked Fess.

"Five miles," he said. "Perhaps a bit more."

His estimate confirmed hers. "It's growing." She turned a slow circle, taking in the destruction of yet another outpost. In truth, there hadn't been much to destroy. Everything that could have been removed prior to the attack had been and there were no bodies. None.

"Where did they go, Lady Deel?" Fess asked.

She dropped the leaf and crushed it beneath her boot, obeying some obscure impulse. "South. The commander either received word to withdraw or was wise enough to notice the encroachment of the forest, probably the latter." She pointed to the sapling. "The dirt around the trunk is freshly dug. Clever man."

She glanced at the sun, noted they still had two hours until dusk, and considered their course of action, weighing Ealdor's command against the desire to find the men who'd fled their outpost. For the moment, those two objectives aligned. She paused. Perhaps there was a way to ensure that continued. Mounting her horse, she lifted her voice and called. "Wag."

"I don't see him," Fess said. "Can he hear you?"

Toria nodded. "The sentinels are physically gifted, just as you are. Imagine adding a pure gift to an animal whose senses of smell and hearing are already far greater than your own." She pointed east, to where a blur moved across the ground at frightening speed. "You see?"

A moment later, the sentinel stood before her, his tongue waving in time to his panting. "Wag, track the men who fled from here, not the attackers."

With a yip that should have come from a smaller dog, he entered the compound, pausing to smell the ground where the grass had been disturbed and flattened by the presence of tents. Then he returned and started south, setting a pace that forced the horses to a quick trot. Toria breathed a sigh of relief. The possibility that the evil from the forest had caught the men unaware, corrupting them, had lain on her heart, nagging at her and refusing dismissal.

A half hour before sunset, Wag went on point facing a thick copse of trees. Fess dismounted. "They don't know us, Lady Deel. Wag and I will go first." He approached, stepping slowly with his hands in sight and Wag on his right. "We're seeking the men from the outpost north of here," he called.

A woman wearing the blue and black of Caisel stepped out from behind the nearest tree, an arrow nocked and trained on Fess's heart. "Move along, stranger, and we won't have any trouble."

Fess halted his advance. Toria dismounted and edged closer, keeping him between her and the woman. "We've been looking for you."

"Why?"

"Because you won't survive the night without us," Toria said.

A man stepped out from behind a tree to her left. "I'm Commander Oriano. You tracked us here so you could help us?" He darted a glanced at the woman on his left. "You hear that, Serana? They want to help us." He barked a laugh. "I have two score men in these woods. We can care for ourselves. Tomorrow we'll make the outer cordon."

"No, Commander," Toria said. "You have fifteen, and when the sun goes down the fields north of here are going to be filled with the enemy." She took a step forward, away from Fess's protection and made a point of gazing at the copse of trees. "At the approach of dawn, your hiding place will draw them like a flame draws moths. They'll need shelter from tomorrow's sun, and when they find you here, Commander, you will die."

Doubt filled Oriano's gaze as Toria waited.

Serana's arrow dipped toward the ground. "And what can you do to help us?" the woman said. She pointed at Wag and then Fess. "The dog is big enough and he moves well, but your sword won't be much help in the dark. And as for her . . ." She nodded to where Lelwin sat her horse. "The snap of a twig would have her screaming."

On Toria's left the sun touched the horizon. "Commander, if you want to live, you need to let me help you. I can show you how to fight those from the forest, but you have to do exactly as I say, and you have to do it now."

His eyes narrowed to slits. "And if I refuse?"

Toria turned her back on him and returned to her horse, ready to mount. "Then we will leave you to your own protection and circle around." She nodded to Wag. "He sees well enough in the dark to get us to the outer ring of Rymark's defense. We'll send someone back for your bodies."

She gave him all of two heartbeats to decide, then put her foot in the stirrup.

"Alright." He stepped forward. "What do you want us to do?"

"Take us to your camp," she ordered. "Then, gather or make long strips of heavy cloth, about a hand wide." His expression clouded, betraying his confusion, but he turned and waved Toria and Fess into the copse.

Ahead of Toria, Fess turned, his expression dark. "What do you intend?" he said. "They do not have the knowledge to fight like Lelwin. You'll be sending them out to be killed."

"No," Toria said. "They will fight nearly as well as she does."

He stopped, as if entering the trees might signal surrender. "What do you intend, Toria Deel?" he repeated.

Conscious of the soldiers waiting for them, she edged closer. "At sunset Lelwin's vault will open and she will become Brekana once more. With your help, we will delve her and place her knowledge and experience into Oriano and all his soldiers."

He shook his head. "If you mean to do this without their permission, Toria Deel, I will not help you."

She nodded. "That is your choice, Fess, but men and women will die who would otherwise live. What I am proposing to do is taxing. I can only transfer Brekana's experience to half of Oriano's men, perhaps a bit more."

Without waiting for an answer, she turned to follow Oriano and Serana deeper into the woods. Fifty paces in, she came to a small clearing where the commander waited for her with Serana and thirteen more, strips of cloth clutched in their hands. A small fire burned in the center of the clearing. "That's a good idea, Commander, but the wrong time," she said. "Cover your eyes, you and all your men. For the next few hours, light is as much your enemy as those from the forest. Fess, kill the fire."

Oriano stood before her. "Without the fire to keep them at bay, we cannot hope to fight."

Instead of answering her question, she turned to Fess. "Bring her," she said. Then, taking three of the strips from Oriano, she moved to Lelwin's side and began wrapping her eyes in the heavy cloth. Without the fire and with the setting of the sun, it only took one. She stiffened, straightening from her curled posture, her mouth twisted with contempt.

"Do you think I will consent to help you, Toria Deel?" Lelwin rasped, her voice dropping into the deeper register that defined Brekana. "Am I your hound that you may send hunting whenever you desire?"

"Yes," Toria answered. "However much you may hate me, Brekana, I know you hate the forest and those who fight for it even more." Toria stretched forth her bare hand, then stopped. Brekana hated her, but it would be a mistake to justify that hatred by taking what might be freely given. "We're caught between the ruins of Rymark's inner cordon and the outer defenses. The sun has set, and it's likely that Cesla's men will find us before dawn. There are fifteen men and women, soldiers of Caisel, who are hale and whole, around you. Will you tell them how to fight?"

Lelwin's head moved from side to side. "Tell them, Toria Deel? It took weeks of experience and heavy losses to teach those who fought with me how to stay hidden until the right moment, how to position themselves in the moonlight to see the enemy."

Toria stepped closer so that none but Lelwin might hear her. "While you teach them, Fess and I will give them your memories. They will have your teaching and experience to draw upon."

"Ah, yes. Your mind tricks. For all your skill, you couldn't take the memories that broke me."

"I could have," Toria said. "But our pain defines us, for good or ill.

If I had taken those memories from you, it would have broken you in the end. Taken from your mind, but present in your spirit, you would have been unable to understand the terrors that came upon you at random times, unaware that some chance sound or smell triggered a memory you no longer had, but still held in your spirit."

"Yes," Lelwin mocked. "I'm sure you have an excellent reason for your failure." She pointed at Toria's hands. "And if I refuse, will you take what I haven't offered?"

"Yes," Toria said, but she made no move.

Lelwin held out her arm. "You fool yourself if you believe that you've offered me a choice."

Her fingers hovered above Lelwin's arms. "I'm sorry."

"Yes," Lelwin said. "Of course you are. Take them, Toria Deel."

Just before contact, Toria spoke once more. "I need you to think about how you fight those from the Darkwater."

A predatory smile split Lelwin's face. "I think about little else."

Toria dropped into the delve to see the memories that comprised Brekana's personality. Sparkling recollections flowed past, savored memories streaked with black, testimonies of their dual nature. "Someday," Toria promised, "I will see you healed of this." She paused to amend her vow. "If Aer wills."

Sighing, she dipped her hands into the memories that defined Brekana's personality, sifting for those she would use to teach Oriano and the rest how to fight. After she had placed them behind a door within her mind, she willed herself to release Lelwin's arm and blinked to find herself in the darkened clearing.

Oriano, possibly sensing her movement, spoke, turning to face her despite the veil he wore. "How are we to fight?"

"A moment, Commander," she said. "You and your soldiers must acclimate to the dark, and the embers of the fire are still too bright."

She moved to Fess's side. "Will you consent to help me?"

When he didn't speak she held out her arm. "You will have to touch me." When he came into her mind, she was waiting for him in the midst of her sanctuary.

"You left me no choice but to help you," he said. "You knew I would never consign those men and women to death." Strangely, his tone was gentler than she expected.

"You don't condemn me?" she asked.

"No," he said. "I realize you had no choice either. Without Lelwin's knowledge, Oriano and the rest will die. My apologies, Lady Deel. I spoke without thinking."

She'd been prepared for judgment, not understanding, and tears gathered at the corners of her eyes. Ignoring them, she stepped forward. "Make a door within your mind, a place for the memories I'm about to give you." When he nodded, she released them.

Finding herself in the clearing once more, she spoke to Lelwin. "Speak to them, Brekana. Tell them how you fight those from the Darkwater. Tell them everything you've learned, however long it takes."

Lelwin stepped forward, her voice strong, assured. "First you must understand the enemy you face. The moonlight that is hardly more than a phantom of barest argent to us is as bright as day to our enemies. That is why you must wear the veil until you're ready to fight. You must guard your eyes from light, any light, if you want to live."

As she spoke, Toria and Fess moved to each member of Oriano's command, touching man or woman, releasing Brekana's memories into their stream. Over and again, they touched them, reinforcing the instruction they heard with her memories.

Hours later, after the embers of the fire had gone completely out, Lelwin stopped. "That's all," she said.

Toria touched the soldier nearest her, a tall, lanky woman with sinewy arms. Brekana's memories had merged with the memories of her instruction within the woman's mind, but the threads held an ephemeral quality, as if they might be forgotten at any moment. "That's enough," she said, speaking with false confidence.

"Is the fire out?" Lelwin asked. "Is the moon up?"

"Yes," Toria said, "on both counts."

Removing her veil, Lelwin retrieved her bow and quiver. "Come, all of you. It's time you began your apprenticeship in truth. Once we have departed, Toria Deel, relight your fire. It will draw them to you. Outlined against its light, they will make easier targets."

CHAPTER 57

Lelwin and the rest melted into the night, each armed with a short bow and as many arrows as they could carry. Toria stood in the dark, squinting to see, straining to hear, but any noise that might have come to her from outside the copse of trees was swallowed by the wind coming out of the north. "Wag, come here."

Because he was hidden by darkness, she didn't know he'd responded until she felt him press against her, his bulk of muscle hard beneath the fur. A thousand different smells came to her as she dropped into his awareness. *Wag, I want you to guard Oriano and Serana and all the rest, but don't kill.*

Within the delve her impression of the woods around them pitched as the sentinel tilted his head. *Mistress, I don't understand.*

They need to hunt, Wag, and if you kill those from the forest, they won't learn how. Keep them safe, but don't kill any from the forest except to save our soldiers.

She could see herself from his perception, hints of yellow and blue in the moonlight. His tongue came out and found her cheek, leaving a trail of wet a hand wide on her face. *As you say, Mistress. Knowing how to hunt is important. I will guard your pups.*

Moments after he ghosted from her side, she heard the repeated clack of flint against steel. A tiny flare of light bloomed in the woods as Fess relit the fire.

When the flames had strengthened to the point she could see again, Fess stood facing her. "Bronwyn never mentioned such a use of the gift, Lady Deel. She maintained that any attempt to give one person's memories to another would fail."

"There are too many unspoken questions there for me to know which one you intend to ask," she said.

When he dipped his head in acknowledgement it cast his eyes in shadow, making him appear older. "If we are found, it will be some hours from now," he said. "We have time, I think, for you to answer all of them."

The scent of cedar, fresh and burning, filled the air. He stared at her, waiting for his answers, but she found it easier to speak if she watched the fire. "Our gift allows us to enter another's mind and live their memories and emotions as though they were our own. In the annals of the Vigil it is recorded that the early holders of the gift believed it could be used as an instrument of instruction. They thought to use the gift to bring peace to the world."

A frown passed over his expression. "Peace?"

She nodded. "The men and women of the Vigil have never been accused of lacking ambition, Fess. The early fathers and mothers in the gift surmised that if the knowledge of the devout, those men and women who were strongest in their faith, could be given to kings and nobles, the world would see an end to war."

"Ah," he said. "Perhaps if you had gathered the memories of soldiers who'd experienced it and discovered only grief at its end, it might have worked."

She gave a rueful laugh. "Oh, that was tried as well, along with the memories of healers wielding their saws on the battlefield, and wives and mothers grieving endlessly over loved ones lost. Then the Vigil tried combining them until the load of implanted memories was nearly as great as those the kings and nobles already carried. The early Vigil spent over a hundred years working to eradicate war from the world."

"It's just as well you failed," he said.

She searched his tone for irony or sarcasm but found none. "How so?"

"Centuries of peace would have created a world the Darkwater and Cesla could have destroyed in a fortnight," he said. "The evil would have emerged from the forest to find a warren of rabbits." He paused briefly. "If our instruction was doomed to fail, Lady Deel, why did we attempt it?"

She turned to regard the fire. "Failure and success are connected by any number of possibilities between them. Over the years we found that we could gain some measure of success if the implanted memories were strengthened with instruction."

"The power of story," he said. "That's why you had Lelwin tell them everything she knew."

"And why we continued to give her memories to Oriano's men throughout," she added. "The memories are transitory, but her stories conjured images within their minds. By giving them Lelwin's memories as they created their own, we can give them some measure of permanence."

"Some measure?" he asked. "How long?"

The temptation to shade the truth kept her silent until he stirred, probably to ask the same question again. "If those under Cesla's control attack tonight, the combination of real experience with Lelwin's instruction may be enough to cement Lelwin's memories as their own."

"May?"

"We are at war, Fess," she said. "As Bolt would say, we must use any weapon that comes to hand."

"They could all die out there tonight, Toria Deel."

She summoned the courage to face him at last. "And doubtless some of them will, Fess, even under the best circumstances." She would have added some qualification, but anything else she might have said would sound dishonest. She waited in the silence for some response, but none came.

"Brekana hates you," he said later. "Have you considered she might allow some from the Darkwater to slip past their defense and attack?"

"More than once," Toria said. "I thought the possibility likely enough that I wanted to—"

His hand closed on the upper part of her arm, dragging her so that they stood against a tree on the far side of the fire. "They're coming."

Suggestions of movement flitted among the shadows cast by the fire. They broke from the darkness into its dim light, two men racing toward them across the clearing. Fess broke from her side as they leapt, springing into the air, but Fess kept his feet on the ground, changing direction so swiftly it made Toria's head hurt to follow him. The two attackers flew toward her, daggers out and screaming.

But one would land first. Earth flew from beneath Fess's boots as he came behind him, his sword moving faster than Toria could follow and the first man was down, taken by a stroke that cut him almost in two. With the first man's blood still in the air, Fess intercepted the second, lunging as his feet touched the ground.

Toria pulled a ragged breath. "Th—"

"Quiet," he said.

She held her breath, stifling any sound as Fess stood with his head cocked to one side, listening. He straightened from his fighter's crouch a moment later to sheathe his sword, and her breath gusted from her. "Is it done?"

"At least for now, Toria Deel. If there are any more out there, they are too far away for me to hear."

She looked up through the thin canopy of leaves overhead, hungering for daylight. "How long until sunrise?" she asked.

"Three hours."

Her eyes burned with a desperate need for sleep. "And therein lies the flaw," she said.

"Lady Deel?"

A memory of war decades old slipped from behind one of her mind's doors, a door whose memories belonged to a long dead captain of Owmead. "'Fatigue can defeat an army as easily as superior force,'" she quoted.

Fess assented after a moment's thought. "Oriano's men will have to march all day after fighting all night. How long can a man last on chiccor root and fear?"

She searched through memories—her own and those she'd collected over the last century—before she answered. "It depends on the man. Three days, perhaps four. After that, the ability to discern friend from foe disappears. Often men and women will see visions conjured by the mind, images born of fatigue that don't exist." She searched his face across the fire. "Without horses for Oriano's men it's four days hard marching to Treflow, and men without sleep can't do it."

"We need a wagon," Fess said. "With our horses, it would allow Lelwin and Oriano's men to rest while we traveled during the day."

"We're half a day away from the outer cordon if we head straight south," she said. "They'll have wagons for their supplies."

Lelwin led Oriano and his soldiers back to the copse of trees as the sky lightened to charcoal. Of the thirteen, eleven came back, all of them stumbling with fatigue. Wag trailed them to the edge of the trees before breaking into a lope that brought him to Toria's side. She slipped a hand from her glove to scratch him behind the ears. *How many did you have to kill?*

Four, Mistress.

Two of the pack have died.

Yes, Mistress. A pair of scents, both belonging to men, came through the link. *The man-things panicked, making sounds of a frightened pup, and were killed before I could safeguard them.*

She pulled her hand from his head to greet Lelwin, who stood next to Oriano, wrapping the cloth around her eyes. "How many did you kill?" she asked.

But it was Oriano who answered. "Ten." He shook his head. "I wouldn't have thought it was possible, Toria Deel." His mouth pinched. "It's not war the way I've read of it. In the tales, you don't put an arrow in a man's back."

Lelwin, still under the influence of Brekana's personality, laughed a harsh sound just short of a bark. "You left the tales behind when you left your home, Oriano. In the tales, you're fighting men with a sense of honor and everyone has the decency to die quick and clean."

Oriano, visibly shaken, turned to Toria. "Cold, that one is, but this is the first I've heard of any outpost getting the better of the Darkwater. I'll stay with you."

"Thank you, Commander," she said. "You and your men need rest. We're half a day from the outer cordon. Sleep now. Fess and I will wake you in four hours."

After they woke, Oriano guided them south toward the nearest camp on the outer cordon. As they crested each hill, Toria found herself clenching her knees to her horse while she searched the sky for telltale signs of fire, but there were none. When they cut through a stand of hardwoods, they found the camp in a broad clearing, the stumps of trees and saplings stripped from the palisade that defined its walls. Beyond a few scorch marks on the green wood, there were no signs of fighting. Guards stood at the gates, and in the distance she could make out the mounted men patrolling the countryside for those attempting to sneak into the forest to search for gold.

Fess stared in disbelief. "They weren't attacked. Does the Darkwater boast so few men?"

"No," she said. "There is something deeper at work here. Oriano, stay here with your men. Fess and I will see if we can search out the meaning of this."

A few minutes and two escorts later, she and Fess stood in the tent of the commanding officer, Warena, a lieutenant of middle years with a heavy bandage around one leg and a pronounced limp. If her current wounds concerned Toria, the faded scars that crisscrossed her forearms provided some measure of comfort. The commander was a veteran.

"What news do you have from King Rymark?" Toria asked.

Warena bent to retrieve a small sheet of parchment with Rymark's signature at the bottom. Her close-cropped gray hair hardly shifted with the effort. "This came three days ago." She licked her lips. "I don't usually question orders, Toria Deel, but this one came with less explanation than most."

"'Hold your position at all costs until you receive orders to withdraw,'" Toria read out loud. "'Keep the enemy within the cordon and await orders.'" She turned the parchment over, but there was nothing written on the other side.

"There's no explanation for the change," Warena said. "Without the inner cordon, we can do little more than defend against attacks."

Toria kept her expression neutral, unwilling to divulge Rymark's purpose. Instead, she turned her attention to her purpose. "Lieutenant, we'll require horses and a cart."

Warena signaled her consent. "You'll have them."

"One thing more," Toria added. "How many men can you spare?"

The lieutenant lifted her hands. "That's impossible to know, Lady Deel. I have a hundred under arms here, but only half are veterans. We've seen little fighting to this point, but King Rymark's orders are worrisome."

"They're necessary," Toria said.

"If we extend the time on patrol, I can spare ten percent of our force without compromising the king's orders," Warena said. "But if it comes to fighting, I'm going to need every veteran with even the slightest physical gift."

"Then we won't take any veterans."

"Begging your pardon, Lady Deel, but I don't see how you can get much use out of conscripts who haven't been tested yet."

"I appreciate your concern, Lieutenant, but our requirements are different. How well do you know your soldiers?" Toria asked.

"Any commander spends as much time learning about their men as we can. Our lives depend on each other."

"Set aside your veterans," Toria said. "Of those remaining, I want those most comfortable in the darkness and who have a talent for space and temperaments for observation or impulse—preferably both."

CHAPTER 58

The fact that Erendella contrived to have me ride next to her without Bolt or Gael nearby wasn't lost on me. Even Mirren had been systematically shunted outside the ring of guards that enclosed us. Only Herregina rode in our company, a circumstance that I attributed to her royalty. Despite Erendella's earlier admonition, we rode in silence, and I locked whatever questions I had behind my teeth. I had no desire to give the queen further cause to despise me.

An hour later she spoke without turning her head, her voice directed between the twin peaks of her horse's ears. "You might wonder at my affection for my father," she said. "His nobles noticed his weakness. Many regarded him with disdain."

I caught the carefully worded indignation that included me and chose my words as carefully as I could. "Your father did something no one has ever been able to do, Your Majesty."

In silence, I waited, hoping that Erendella's curiosity would compel her to ask the obvious question. I had learned over time that the etiquette of inquiry often served as a balm to the emotional wounds people carried. If Erendella trusted me enough to ask me a question, she might forgive me for failing to save her father.

"What?" she asked finally, but without breaking away from the contemplation of the landscape before us.

"He found a way to keep the evil of the Darkwater at bay for weeks on end," I said. "No one's done that before."

She shook her head. "If the tales are true, Lord Dura, you've done it."

"No, Your Majesty," I said. "My survival has nothing to do with me. I owe my life to chance or providence or both."

Now she looked at me, her gaze searching me for motives. "Your manner is strange. Given an opportunity to claim some skill or favor and elevate yourself in the eyes of one of the seven monarchs of the north, you opt instead for humility."

"It's safer," I said. "If I pretended to some virtue I didn't have, it wouldn't take long for you to find me out."

"There it is again," she said. "You hold the most powerful gift in the world, and yet you continually offer me deference."

I took a moment to gaze at the ring of guards that rode around me. "I have reason."

She might have laughed or sighed or sobbed. It was difficult to match her expression to the sound she made. "Lord Dura, my father threatened you because he had nothing to lose. I do." Her expression turned curious. "Are you that ignorant of the authority the Vigil holds?" She didn't wait for an answer. "If I harmed you, the church and the rest of the Vigil would break my mind like a twig and my rule would pass to another."

"They might thank you," I said. "My guard tells me with every other breath that I'm a nuisance."

"A nuisance who saved my life," Herregina said.

I'd forgotten that the young queen-apparent rode with us. She'd adopted a similar posture of speaking over the head of her horse. Perhaps the affectation came with the gift of kings. Regardless, the comment carried an edge to it, like a dagger still in its sheath, but present, and Erendella took note. I wondered what conversations I might have missed.

"To be fair, Your Majesties, I'm leading you both into danger," I said. "Whatever gratitude or regard you feel you owe me should wait until you're safe in your palaces again."

Erendella shook her head at me. "You're either the worst negotiator I've ever met or the most skilled."

"Perhaps I'm just honest," I said.

"Regardless, Lord Dura, you're in no danger from me."

Herregina added a nod that might have been due to nothing more than the gait of her horse. A bit of Erendella's reserve slipped, and instead of a middle-aged queen I saw a girl who missed her father.

"I would have saved him if I could have, Your Majesty."

She blinked several times, quickly, and returned her attention to the road ahead. "Thank you, Lord Dura. I believe you."

We rode until an hour before sunset, stopping at a small town along the Mournwater River and set out at dawn the next day. We followed that routine each day after, pushing the horses as hard as we dared and buying or commandeering new ones when we had to replace them.

A week after leaving Vadras, we saw the first soldiers retreating from the forest. Two men, each with an arm that would need the healer's saw, led a horse-pulled cart filled with soldiers on the edge of death. The horse, ridden and worked to exhaustion, clopped past us, its head barely off the ground. The smell of blood filled the air, and it was difficult to tell who would die first, the horse or the men.

Our company, nearly twenty strong, stepped off the road to let them pass. From my spot next to the queen, I caught Bolt's attention and gestured toward Mirren. With a nod, the pair of them peeled away and left to speak to the men leading the cart.

They caught up to us about a mile later, Erendella's men parting to let them through. "Bad?" I asked Bolt.

"Not good," he said. "It's not the type of war we want to fight." The planes of his face hardened.

"You mean it's not the kind of war we can win."

He scowled at me. "I think I just said that."

"Errant Consto," Herregina cut in, "please explain."

He dipped his head toward Mirren. "I think I'd better let her tell you what she saw. You'll need the context. There's not much I'll need to add."

Mirren wet lips that had gone bloodless, and I knew something in those memories had done more than just scare her. "Ten nights ago their outpost came under attack. Men and women bearing the look of ordinary craftsmen and laborers broke through their palisade. Before they could organize resistance, the enemy was in their midst, moving like gifted. The entire post was wiped out except for the men we saw in the cart."

"How did they survive?" I asked. Bolt nodded his approval at the question.

"They huddled by the watch fire," Mirren said. "The attackers avoided the light, but that ploy only worked to a point. They came under arrow fire that poured into them until an hour before dawn. Then the attackers left."

"Which way did they go?" I asked, hoping that Mirren would tell me they'd gone back to the forest. I hoped that the attack was nothing more than Cesla's desire for blood and vengeance.

"Southwest," Mirren said, "toward the nearest town." She started to say something more, but her voice broke.

"They stripped the dead," Bolt said, "swapping clothes."

"This is what you meant," I said. "This is the kind of war we can't fight."

He nodded. "Not unless we're willing to kill our own," he said. "Not unless we're willing to become the thing we're fighting."

I turned to Erendella and Herregina. They looked at Mirren and me as if we had the right to command their obedience and expect it, but I had no desire to shoulder that responsibility. "Your Majesties, I would *suggest* that we expend whatever effort required to conceal our passage. It would be wiser if we supplied ourselves at each town we passed through, but made our camps in hiding."

"Is the forest after us, Lord Dura?" Herregina asked.

"I think so," I said. "At least in part." I started thinking through all the different ways my plan could fail. Two leapt out at me.

"If Cesla can kill me, he's won. The knowledge of how to call the Fayit would die with me. But that knowledge is useless without the six kings and queens who hold the gift of kings. I can't call them without all of you. Cesla wants us badly, and the best way to keep us all safe is to hide our journey."

They didn't speak. "It's just a suggestion," I added.

"But if you're smart, you'll listen to it," Bolt said. "Eight men and women from the forest made tatters of an entire outpost of a hundred soldiers. And that was in an enclosed space where they didn't have room to move. Out in the open and in the dark, they'd go through us like a sword falling through water."

Herregina and Erendella regarded each other in silence for a moment. "Your advice is sound, Lord Dura," Erendella said. "Since it is a mere hour until sunset, I suggest we make for the nearest concealment and endeavor to contact the other monarchs."

Hiding proved the least of our worries. Thick stands of trees covered much of the northern half of Caisel. We sent scouts before and behind to ensure we were unobserved and then left the road, riding for a large copse of cedars to the east that offered cover. Erendella's men made what defenses they could in the fading light, but we didn't light a fire and we hadn't brought tents.

We huddled in our cloaks as Erendella pulled the scrying stone from her pack. I tried not to think about sleeping under the trees. My experiences in the Darkwater and the Everwood had taught me to be wary. The two forests couldn't be more different, but the trees attracted power.

"King Rymark," Erendella called into the stone. "Hear me."

We waited. Gael edged closer, her hand worming its way into mine. My gloves kept me from dropping into her thoughts, but I could feel the warmth of her skin through the thin leather and it comforted me.

"King Ellias," Erendella called. "Regent Cailin. Queen Ulrezia, hear me."

We waited. After a few moments, the queen of Caisel repeated her call.

"I hear you," Rymark said. "King Ellias is with me. Where's Boclar?"

"King Boclar has died," Erendella said.

"Who rules in Vadras?"

"I do," Erendella said. Rymark couldn't see her, but she stiffened, her shoulders moving back.

"I mean no disrespect, Your Majesty," Rymark said. "It's imperative to know if you hold the gift of kings."

Erendella looked at me in the fading light, and I leaned toward the stone. "This is Willet Dura," I said. "I was present at Boclar's death. He passed the gift to his daughter."

"Dura." Even through the stone, Rymark's voice held a growl of disapproval. "You seem to be cutting a wider swath than usual. Tell me, Lord Dura, just how many bodies have you left in your wake?"

Erendella's eyes flashed, but she held up a hand to Herregina who appeared on the verge of yelling at Rymark through the stone. "Lord Dura's presence during the king's passing was my father's doing." She glanced at me. "My father hoped Lord Dura could heal him of his affliction."

The scrying stone didn't do much to lessen Rymark's derision. "Dura is hardly a healer."

Erendella nodded. "As it turns out, King Rymark, you are correct,

400

but that fact didn't prevent him from trying to cure my father of the Darkwater's evil."

"Boclar went to the forest?" Rymark and Ellias said together.

"I was taken," Erendella said. "Father thought to outwit Cesla by bringing solas powder to keep the effects of the Darkwater at bay. It almost worked."

"Foolish," Rymark said. "He should never have risked the forest."

Erendella's mouth tightened. "You'll excuse me if I don't agree. I didn't contact you to offer justifications, Your Majesty. We encountered soldiers today, returning from the cordon you placed around the forest. They were the sole survivors of an attack on their outpost by men and women who then took clothing off the dead. Lord Dura thinks they're coming for the Vigil and the monarchs."

Intermittent sounds of Rymark's swearing came through the scrying stone. In between we could hear orders being given in staccato bursts. "My compliments to Lord Dura's insight," Rymark said. "He's a fount of welcome news. If they're stealing uniforms from the dead, we have to suspect our own. Where are you now?"

"A few miles north of the city of Leogan," Erendella said.

"Queen Erendella, Lord Dura, meet us in Treflow as soon as you can," Rymark said.

The scrying stone went silent. "It's difficult to decide what troubles me most," I said to Gael. "I've got a long list to choose from."

Bolt spoke into the pause. "If Cesla has enough men and women to put this plan into place all along the border of the forest, it's going to be impossible to tell friend from enemy. There's no way for you and the rest of the Vigil to delve every threat."

I sighed. "That's one."

"Cailin and Queen Ulrezia didn't answer the call," Gael said. "Where are they?"

I nodded. In the silence my fear had conjured the worst. If Cesla had taken even one of the rulers captive, we were beaten. "That's two," I said. "There's one more."

"Where are Fess, Toria, and Pellin?" Mirren asked.

"And that's the list," I said. "I thought Fess and Toria would be back with Rymark and Ellias by now."

Rory cleared his throat. "Whoever heard Rymark knows where we are."

Everyone turned to look at our thief in the last charcoal light of dusk. "If I were Cesla," Rory said, "the easiest way to find you would be to place a spy in Rymark's camp."

I didn't want to admit that our situation could be so precarious. "There's no way for them to know exactly where we are," I said. "And our camp is dark."

Rory shrugged as if my argument didn't really matter. "If he's got enough people, he'll find us. They can see in the dark."

I looked around, the stand of cedars no longer comforting me. Cesla's soldiers would slip in and out of the woods like ghosts. Most of us would be dead before we knew we were being attacked. "Get everybody down," I said. "No sentries. A man patrolling the perimeter might as well be waving a torch." I turned to Rory. "If there is a spy, and they're coming after us, they'll expect us to be near the road. Can you hide close enough to spot them?"

He grinned as he nodded at me. "There are trees near the road. People never think to look up."

His words put a sudden itch between my shoulder blades, the expectation of a stroke I wouldn't see coming. I checked the branches of the cedars above us, sighing with relief when I found them empty.

"You see," Rory laughed. He took just long enough to check his knives and sprinted away.

Bolt grimaced. "We'll have to put the horses on the far side of the trees. That should keep them hidden from the road." He shook his head. "'Never ask how things could get any worse . . .'" he quoted.

I didn't bother to finish it for him. I didn't want to hear it out loud.

CHAPTER 59

We spent the night huddled on the ground, hoping the trunks were thick enough to hide us. Gael lay beside me. If we were found, my safety would depend on my betrothed, a thief, and a Vigil guard who'd been put out to pasture nearly six years ago. The soldiers Erendella had brought with her, gifted and semi-gifted guards, were tasked with keeping the two queens and Mirren safe.

I'd given Mirren all the memories she needed to call the Fayit. Deep in my chest, I hid the certainty that I wouldn't survive the attempt to destroy Cesla's power. He knew I was a threat. The best use I could make of myself was as a decoy, allowing Cesla to expend his energy against me while the rest of the Vigil brought about his downfall.

My throat tightened. I'd really wanted to marry Gael. Months earlier, she'd offered me herself in marriage. I'd refused, citing my need to focus on my fight with the Darkwater. That decision seemed foolish now.

Sometime in the deep of night I started awake, unsure of where I was, but knowing darkness had drawn near.

"What is it?" Gael whispered. The crisp words communicated that she hadn't slept.

I resisted the urge to stand and point. "They're here." I couldn't hear anything, and the sliver of moon in the sky couldn't alleviate the night for a *gnath*, a physically ungifted person like me.

Slowly, I watched Gael shift, sliding away from me until she could peek from behind the tree. Then she became so still she might have been part of the forest.

"I don't see anyone. It's too dark," she said, her mouth next to my ear once more. "Are you sure?"

I nodded. I didn't want to tell her what was inside my head had opened up to tell me. "I can feel them. How long is it until dawn?"

"Three hours."

We huddled in the darkness as I willed time to go faster, praying snatches of the liturgy and the soldier's prayer for fools.

In the midst of my prayers, Gael's mouth rested against my ear. She spoke so softly I felt as much as heard it. "I hear footsteps in the grass."

She tensed beside me, a coiling of muscle that presaged violence. Bolt, hiding behind the next tree a couple of paces away, would be watching. Now I heard the steps as well, a shuffling gate through the grass to brush aside any twigs that might give them away.

A distant snap, a cascading crash of something falling through a tree, broke the heavy silence, and I heard the muffled sound of footsteps, a lot of them, pounding away. I let a trembling breath loose and pulled its twin into my lungs.

"Don't move," Gael whispered in my ear. "They're not all gone."

Footsteps, a solitary pair, continued toward us from the other side of the tree. The moment he stepped around the trunk, he would see us. Gael curled into a crouch without making a sound, her legs coiled beneath her.

I groped for a dagger, though how I would be able to use it in the darkness, I had no idea. The footsteps stopped. The air filled with restrained violence. One sound from our attacker would bring the rest. Gael gathered herself, waiting.

The footsteps moved away, slowly at first but gathering speed.

After a few moments, Gael resumed her place at my side. "Don't move," she whispered. "I don't know how good their hearing is."

About an hour later, my heart resumed its normal rhythm and I dozed until someone nudged me awake.

"Let him sleep for a few more minutes," I heard Gael say.

"He's going to want to see this, yah?" Rory's voice came from right beside me. "I'll get Mirren."

I stood up, my hands shaking from too little sleep and the rush of fear, but I didn't see any immediate threats. "What's he talking about?" I looked around. "Where's Bolt?"

Gael shook her head.

Rory came back with Mirren in tow. Erendella and Herregina followed, each with a pair of hulking guards looming protectively over them. "Hurry, before they move," Rory said.

We ran toward the road half a mile away. Well before we got there, I saw Bolt standing near a figure in a soldier's uniform. He had his sword in hand, his posture threatening. The soldier shifted his feet as if he wanted to run away.

Rory pointed to a solitary tree by the road that stood a bit taller than the rest. "It's easier to see from up there, but you'll understand in a moment."

I stepped up onto the fitted stones of the road. Checking south, I saw a solitary figure, moving away from us, with backward glances, the universal language of flight. A moment later, he left the road to disappear into the trees. To the north, the road ascended a slight rise that went on for over a mile. Along that stretch, I saw two soldiers, moving as if their lives depended on evading capture.

"Were those the men hunting us?" I asked Rory.

He nodded. "Came within a hairsbreadth of spotting you, I think." He pointed to a stretch of woods on the far side of the road. "I threw a stick to draw them off of you. At first light, they split up and fanned out, running away along the road."

I still had enough fear coursing through me that my hands trembled. I checked to make sure the sun was visible over the horizon before I walked over to Bolt and the soldier he guarded. I stripped off my glove.

"Every minute you take is one we lose," Bolt said.

When I reached out, the soldier's eyes went wide and he gathered his legs and jumped, his arms straining for my throat. Bolt's stroke took him through the heart, and he fell at my feet, the life draining from him. His gaze, already beginning to empty, locked with mine, and one hand reached for me, curling into a claw. With a sigh, his arm fell to the ground and he lay still.

That's when I noticed his eyes were a light brown, like tea with cream. "What's your eternity like?" I asked him. His gaze went through me, just like all the others. "What's out there?"

"Willet," Bolt's voice broke the spell the dead man had cast over me. "It's time to go."

"Yes," I said looking up the road. "I want every man or woman in a soldier's uniform brought to me."

Bolt shook his head. "That's going to take time we may not have."

"There's a way a man looks at another he knows or has been taught to recognize," I said. "This one knew who I was, but there's more to it than that." I pointed ahead and behind. "Why did they split up?"

His mouth opened to reply then closed. "Why wouldn't they?"

"Because it's not what people do in war—especially injured ones," I said. "They stay together."

"But they're not in enemy territory anymore, yah?" Rory said.

"It doesn't matter," I said. "By the time I got done with the war ten years ago, you couldn't pry me away from my squad. In battle, stragglers die. So why is this man alone?" I wedged my knife beneath the thick, bloody bandage around the dead man's leg and cut it away, making sure I kept the knife edge away from his skin. Then I ripped his breeches up to the groin. The flesh was already pale with death but unmarked.

"Should have expected that, I guess," Bolt muttered.

"I don't understand," Rory said. "Why would they pretend to be injured, yah?"

"The only reason I can come up with is that they're casting a net and they don't want people to know it," I said. "If you give someone a wound to look at, they won't notice much else—they let down their guard." I looked at Bolt. "Can you think of any other reason healthy men and women with vaults would separate and line the road?"

He shook his head.

"But that means they knew exactly where to look," Rory said. He didn't bother with the fake accent this time.

"Not exactly, thank Aer," I said. "We didn't tell Rymark that much."

"It still means someone within earshot of the king is a spy," Bolt said. "Rory was right."

I nodded. I had no way of warning Rymark short of getting to him. "I don't understand how Cesla is doing this."

"Doing what?" Rory asked. "Aren't these people acting the same as the ones at Bas-solas?"

"That's his point," Bolt said. "Laewan was able to control the people with vaults because he was in Bunard—near them. If Cesla were anywhere near here, he could have killed us himself."

Rory nodded, but Bolt had missed an important detail. "There's more," I said.

Bolt snorted. "There usually is. What?"

"A man with a vault acts normal during the daytime," I said. "Something about their behavior is off." I looked down at the dead soldier near my feet. "I wish I'd had the chance to delve him."

"Let's go, Rory," Bolt said. "We'll have to hunt down the rest on foot. They've scattered into the forest by now."

I backtracked to our camp. Everyone was ready to travel, but the mood had turned sour, and Queen Erendella's men wore the grim expressions of soldiers who didn't hold much confidence in returning home alive.

Gael came toward me. "How bad is it?"

"I don't know yet, but we saw the men and women who were searching for us last night. They separated and lined the road—waiting for us to show ourselves, I think. I'll know more as soon as Bolt and Rory catch another one."

The morning sun caught the wealth of her hair and skin, and I smiled. Few men could boast that their betrothed looked as beautiful outdoors as well as in. Then, because we had a few moments, and because I wanted Gael to know how I felt, I peeled the gloves off my hands. "I'm going to show you something," I said.

I took her hands in mine and escaped into her thoughts. She appeared in front of me, younger, as everyone did, but in the full flower of womanhood. "I can see you," she said.

I nodded, keeping myself from the river of her memories. "That's because you knew I was coming. This gives us a measure of privacy."

She laughed, a seductive, deep-throated sound that set fire to my skin. "You know I've never been shy about my affections for you, Willet."

That much was certainly true. "But time flows differently here. An extended conversation in the delve takes but a heartbeat or two in the real world."

She tucked her chin to her chest and looked at me through her dark lashes. "And what would you say here that cannot be said there?"

I kissed her.

"I've always enjoyed the fact that you're a man of few words." She laughed. "But you could have kissed me there as well."

I smiled and swam in the glorious blue of her eyes. "I wanted to tell you that I regret not taking you as my wife when you suggested it.

I thought I needed to concentrate on this task, but that was my pride speaking, thinking that I had to be the one to defeat Cesla and the Darkwater. The truth is it's not up to me. It's up to Aer—however, and if, He intends to do it."

She sighed. "Think of all the opportunities we missed. The beds in Cynestol were very comfortable."

I kissed her again. "I can't rewrite the past," I said, "but I'm yours whenever you wish."

She shook her head. "I don't know what you mean."

"This," I said. Like any man, I'd imagined what union with my betrothed would be like. There, in the privacy of the delve, I let those imaginings flow through the bond, images of sight and touch and all the senses, the future hope that had given me strength.

I blinked and found myself in the midst of our camp. Gael had broken the delve and stepped away, staring at me with her eyes wide and a flush on her cheeks. She exhaled quickly, almost a pant. I couldn't tell whether she was angry or pleased, but I knew I'd crossed a line that couldn't be uncrossed. My betrothed knew exactly what, and how, I thought of her.

"Lord Dura," Gael said, "you are the biggest fraud on earth."

"I . . . um . . . how so?"

Her brows lowered and a dangerous tint came into her eyes. "For months you've bantered with me, pretending embarrassment at my flirtations." Her hands balled into fists, and she shot a pointed glance at my head. "Is this how you've pictured me in your thoughts?"

I'd never been able to lie to Gael, but I was tempted to try anyway. "Yes," I said, "many times."

She closed the distance between us so quickly that I didn't have time to defend myself, her fists coming for my head. I tried to brace for the blow, but at the last second, her hands opened and she cupped the sides of my face and kissed me, laughing. "Oh, Willet, do you think to shock me?" She shook her head at me. "We're betrothed. If you've never seen how I've imagined you, it's because you never looked deeply enough."

She stepped back and looked around the camp. "It's time to go." Looking at me, she laughed. "It's customary during wedding vows for the bride and groom to hold hands during haeling. That should prove interesting. I do hope you'll be able to make it through the ceremony without spilling anything."

I didn't respond. I was too busy wondering what imaginings lay in Gael's thoughts that I hadn't seen. Then a different thought occurred to me. For months I'd cudgeled my brain, trying to figure out a way for Gael and me to enjoy centuries of life together such as Toria Deel had desired with Volsk. The prospect of outliving her by centuries had daunted me. I didn't wish to face the reality that she would grow old while I remained young. Now, I realized there might be another way. Of course, while it solved our problem from Gael's point of view, it did nothing to solve it from mine.

CHAPTER 60

A mile down the road, Bolt and Rory were waiting for us. I made to dismount, but Bolt waved at me, telling me not to bother. He and Rory grabbed a couple of spare horses and swung up to join us. With a word to Queen Erendella, we were thundering north at a canter, working to put distance behind us.

"Nothing?" I asked.

He looked more than a little annoyed, the planes of his face harder than usual. "No. Rory and I aren't gifted trackers, but with no more of a head start than they had, we should have been able to run a couple of them down. It's like they disappeared."

"What are the chances that every one of the people who came looking for us last night had been trained in woodcraft?" I asked.

Bolt snorted. "Most of those in Cesla's army are common men and women who wandered into the forest looking for treasure. I'm guessing few were trained in anything."

That description might have been apt enough to describe me ten years earlier. "That means someone taught them."

"Cesla?" Rory asked. "Do they teach you how to track in the Vigil?"

"If they do, nobody's mentioned it to me," I said. "But we're not really fighting Cesla. The fool did the one thing he wasn't supposed to do. He delved the Darkwater and opened himself to the Fayit imprisoned there."

"How strong are they?" Gael asked.

"There's no way to know," I said. "My conversations with Ealdor never touched on them, except to say that if the prison is breached,

410

the war's over." I pulled a breath heavy with mist and the scent of cedar. "I think the Exordium of the liturgy gives us the best clue. After their war, the Fayit divided their gifts, talents, and temperaments among their offspring until they felt they were weak enough. Imagine someone possessing all of them," I said. "They would be so much more than human."

"That's what Laewan meant," Rory said. "Just before we killed him he said he would show us the depth of our diminishment."

I tried to imagine fighting someone equipped with every gift, talent, and temperament that Aer had created—and got just far enough in the process to feel sick. "I think I'd rather not find out." I looked at Bolt. "Can we push the horses hard enough to escape their net?"

He shrugged. "That depends on whether or not the people coming after us can find mounts. If I were them, that's what I would do."

"They're probably still trying to hide," Rory said. "How can they possibly catch up to us?"

I looked at Bolt. "You tell him."

"Training a replacement didn't used to be like this," he grumbled. "All I had to do before Cesla's sin was beat my apprentices black and blue until they learned to keep me from doing it." He turned to Rory. "If they find horses and track us, they'll run us down long before dawn tomorrow. We'll have to stop at nightfall. They won't. So, tell me, apprentice, what should we do?"

Rory's eyes narrowed in thought. "I've never had to deceive someone smarter than me before."

I laughed. "Modest."

But Rory didn't laugh. He just looked at me with that brown-eyed stare that saw everything. "Pretending to be less than I am isn't modesty. It's a lie." He looked at the earth on either of the road. "How well can a gifted tracker follow a trail?"

Bolt's expression grew sour. "Well enough to make it look like magic, even without the Fayits' help. I've seen men who could look at hoofprints and tell you how heavy the rider was."

"So you're saying there's no way to lose them?" Rory asked.

"Not if they're that good."

He sighed. "And since we've seen them, they've seen us."

As I watched Rory think through the problem, I willed our mounts to go faster, but a horse can hold a canter for only so long and a full gallop for even less. At a signal from Erendella's captain, we dropped into a trot.

"We need a village, a river, and supplies," Rory said.

Bolt caught my eye. "What do you have in mind?"

Rory waved a hand at our company, some twenty strong. "There are too many of us. We can't help but leave a trail a blind man could follow. If we leave the road, there's no way they'll miss it," he said. "The earth is soft enough to betray us. We need to buy enough horses at the next village to split up without making it look like we have. We can load the horses so that the weight is the same and then divide. We can send the queen's guards one way while the rest of us head the other. A stream or a river would help cover the deception."

Bolt nodded in approval. "It's not perfect, but it's probably the best we're going to be able to do."

Rory looked offended. "It's a pretty good plan, yah?"

"As far as throwing the trackers off the scent, it's fine," Bolt said. "But how are we going to disguise the fact that we bought up most of the village's horses? That's pretty hard to miss."

"Mirren and I can take care of that," I said, "but it's still going to be obvious something happened. We're going to leave a lot of muddled villagers behind us."

"And we're leaving the bulk of our protection behind," Bolt added. "I'm not a big fan of voluntarily putting myself in a weaker position."

It took me the better part of two hours to convince Erendella of the necessity of the plan. She kept echoing my own concerns, and try as I might, I couldn't shake my fear of fighting a being vastly more gifted than anyone in history, but on the outskirts of Cleofan, we split our forces.

"Was that really the best we could do?" Gael asked as she watched Erendella's men leave by the north road. "Most of those mounts are ready for pasture."

"Or the tanner," Erendella said.

I couldn't help but agree. "They can buy more at the next village. They'll get a few leagues out of them."

"We hope," Bolt said.

I nodded. "If we didn't, we would have given up a long time ago."

Rory knelt, looking at hoof impressions in the earth, comparing the village mounts to ours. "I can't tell the difference," he said. "Will they be able to?"

"I don't know."

We mounted and put the nose of each horse east. Gael rode next to me with Mirren on the other side. Rory took point, despite the low likelihood of meeting a dwimor here in the pastures and fields of northern Caisel. Erendella and Herregina rode behind me with Bolt guarding our rear.

The fact that I rode with the most concentrated collection of gifts in the north failed to cheer me. Mirren and I were spent. The presence of so many armed men and women passing through the village had aroused the curiosity of most of the populace. We'd had to muddle the memories of nearly every resident, at least those we could get to. The children who'd seen us had sensed something amiss and had run away before we could touch them.

We crested a hill a few hours after noon, and I heard Rory's shout of satisfaction. Below us lay a small branch of the Dirgewater. "Thank Aer," I said.

Bolt rode up beside us to take a look. "It's about time something went right, but there's bound to be farms along the banks. We won't be able to completely disguise our passing."

"At least it will buy us some time."

He nodded. "Let's get the horses into the water and ride north until dusk. When we leave the river, do it separately, and look for rocks so you can hide the tracks." He sighed. "We'll still have to find a place to hide our camp."

The rolling farmland of this part of Caisel didn't offer much in the way of forests, but we managed to find a hollow between two hills that offered concealment. The fold of land had caught the windblown seeds of a few trees and brush so we were able to hide the horses.

"Will they find us?" Gael asked.

I pretended confidence I didn't have. "No, I don't think so." If they found our tracks coming out of the river, they'd be on us before daybreak.

She tapped me on the head. "Whatever Ealdor put in here is the key to defeating Cesla and the Darkwater. You have to live."

I hoped she would stop there, but she didn't, of course. When Gael wanted to make a point, she didn't do it by half measures.

"My life isn't as crucial," she continued. "I'm not going to ask you to be less than you are, but don't die for me."

The argument wasn't one either of us could win, so I let it go. If Cesla's men found our tracks, they'd be coming from the west, so we put the horses to the eastern side of the little stand of trees, and the six of us bedded down for another dark camp.

Two hours into the night, I woke and stumbled my way to Erendella.

"Your Majesty," I called softly.

"Yes?" Erendella answered, but so did Herregina on her far side.

"Have you contacted Rymark recently?" I asked.

She might have shifted in the darkness. "There's trouble in Treflow."

"What is it?"

"Treflow is the closest major city to the forest," she said. "Gold fever hit there pretty hard, and Toria Deel and Fess haven't returned yet."

"So he has no way of knowing who's been to the forest," I said. "The tidings keep getting worse."

"Not all of them," Erendella said. "Queen Ulrezia is only two days away, and Pellin has returned from the southern continent."

"Is there any word about Regent Cailin and Brod?"

"No, I'm sorry, Lord Dura."

I gnawed the inside of my cheek. "We need all six."

I heard what might have been a soft chuckle from Erendella. "It's amusing to think that we and all the kings and queens before us have been so wrong about our place in history."

"How so?" I asked.

"Lord Dura," she said, "you're being polite. I'm sure you've noticed a certain arrogance in the kings and queens of the north."

"I've seen it in nearly everyone who holds power," I said. "But King Laidir was a man of uncommon humility for all the power he held."

"I wish I had known him better," she said. "Still, it's humbling to realize that my position as queen is hardly the gift of divine right that our history claims. Instead, it's a creation of the Fayit, an artifice against the evil of the Darkwater."

I shook my head. "A construct, perhaps, but the gift does more than just provide a last hope. It provides the people of this continent with wise rulers."

"Wise?" she asked. I couldn't see her, but I could hear the smile in her voice.

"Well, I hope so—most of the time, anyway."

"I would like to be worthy of that hope, Lord Dura. Thank you. I will keep the scrying stone at hand. If I hear anything, I will let you know."

Hearing the note of dismissal, I went back to my blanket. Gael put a hand protectively over me but didn't offer any conversation to go with the gesture, and I fell asleep.

I couldn't breathe.

Frantic, I reached for the hand covering my mouth. Warm breath covered my ear. "Don't move," Gael said. "They've found us."

Bolt crouched a couple of paces away. The sky lightened from a sea of black to charcoal. Dawn would be coming soon, but not soon enough.

A figure materialized. Rory.

"There's only the one," he whispered. "He passed by our hiding spot and then doubled back. I don't know if he heard us or smelled the horses."

"Where there's one, there's more," Bolt said.

But Rory shook his head. "Not anywhere close. I would have seen them from the top of the hill." He paused. "It's not one of the men we saw before."

"Willet Dura!"

I flinched. "That's probably not a lucky guess."

"Willet Dura," the man's voice called again. "I know you're there and your scout has already confirmed I'm alone. Will you parley? You may bring your guards."

"If you move," Bolt said. "I'll knock you unconscious."

I looked at Rory. "Is it Cesla?"

"No," he said. "This fellow is short and probably in his thirties. If he wasn't wearing a uniform, I'd spot him for a tanner or some such."

"Willet Dura," the voice called again. "Dawn approaches and our opportunity for conversation is short. Will you waste it?"

I looked at Bolt.

"You know this has to be a trap," he said.

I nodded. Already the sky showed hints of blue and all but the brightest stars had winked out. "Yes, but what kind?" I looked at Rory. "You're sure he's alone."

He nodded. "And unarmed as far as I can tell."

Bolt let loose with an impressive string of curses.

"You never told me you had a talent for language," I said.

"I should have stayed in Arinwold," he said. "I liked it there. Quiet. Mostly sheep. No fool-headed reeves to watch over." He looked at Rory. "You're coming. If this fellow even blinks wrong, kill him."

"Not you," I said to Gael. "If anything goes wrong, you have to get Mirren and the queens to Treflow."

She nodded, but her eyes were slits. "We're going to talk later, and I can guarantee you're not going to enjoy it."

I walked out of the thicket with Bolt and Rory. In the predawn morning, I saw a solitary figure in Owmead's colors, standing where the hills flattened out to level ground. A bird cried once, a questioning call that went unanswered.

"How close do we have to be for you to guarantee a kill?" Bolt asked Rory.

"From ten paces in, I won't miss."

We stopped at eight.

"Greetings, Lord Dura," the voice said. "I've come to offer you terms of surrender."

"Why should I accept anything but unconditional surrender from you?" I asked.

The man smirked. It might have been a trick of the light or its absence, but it seemed an intelligence old beyond imagining glittered in his eyes. "Glib to the last," he said. "Gabbanal Ador, Ealdor's brother, thought to show me the back of his hand when I surrounded his forces and called for his surrender. Time has no meaning for us, but I took enough of it to teach him all the variations of pain before I let him die."

Cold spread through my middle, as if I'd swallowed a lump of ice. "But you were defeated yourself, Atol. Were you not?"

The man laughed. "Do you think to cow me with Ealdor's knowledge? I have given myself a name that no one knows." He cocked his head. "You really don't understand. Allow me to enlighten you. Your battle against me is hopeless, Lord Dura. In fact, each day—"

"How so, infinite one?" I mocked. I didn't feel overly inclined to hear about the hopelessness of my situation.

A spasm of irritation twisted the man's expression. "My power grows with each passing day, Lord Dura. You will not reach Treflow alive. The greatest human to live was still far less than the least of the Fayit, and I am far more than Ealdor and his kind ever thought of being. The stroke of their vengeance has twisted in—"

"It usually does," I broke in. "You really do go on, don't you." I drawled. "Oh well, there is no gift of conversation."

"You worm!" the man said. "You think to bandy words with me? I will teach you—"

"Yes, yes, yes," I waved my hand as if his anger was nothing more than smoke on the wind. "You were going to tell me the terms of my surrender before you got distracted with your own magnificence."

"Interrupt me again at your peril, Lord Dura," he said. "I can use you, but I don't need you."

I smiled. "The terms, exalted one."

"You will deliver the kings and queens of the north into my hands at Treflow."

I stared at him, working to understand his request. "Your solitude has driven you mad, Atol. Instead of asking you why I would do such a thing, I think I'd rather know why you want them."

The man Atol inhabited shrugged, glancing at the sky. "This time grows short, but as a token of my goodwill, I will tell you. There is, after all, nothing you can do with the knowledge. The kings and queens are the last holders of pure gifts. Upon my freedom, I will use them to re-create the race of the Fayit."

"What about the talents and temperaments?" I asked. "Were you not endowed with all?"

He smiled. "The gifts, Lord Dura, are what I require, and though you did not ask why you would do such a thing, I will tell you. It is within my power to ensure Lady Gael's life is as long as yours."

I let my face go slack and filled my eyes with hunger, waiting until the smallest glimmer of hope showed in his eyes. Then I laughed. "So wise and such a fool," I said, "to tempt me with a gift that would kill her love for me."

The sky on the eastern horizon showed a hint of orange. Despite our relative safety, I hungered for dawn.

The soldier coiled and launched himself, coming for me with his arms outstretched, his hands curled into claws that strained for my throat.

Beside me, Rory blurred into motion as Bolt jumped to meet the attack in midair. Spinning and twisting, he hit the soldier with his feet, knocking him to the side, but the man was already dead. One of Rory's daggers had found his eye, the other his heart.

I had no inclination to fall under the spell of the dead man's stare. Turning to Rory, I bowed. "Nice throws."

"That depends," Bolt said, walking up to us from where he'd landed. "How close did you come to your target?"

Instead of being insulted, Rory went to the body and retrieved his weapons. "I might be a quarter of an inch off on the strike to the heart."

Bolt nodded. "As soon as I can get you up to speed with the sword, I'll be ready to retire." He sighed. "Again."

Chapter 61

"Move!" Rory blurred into motion a split-second before I heard the sound of air whistling through fletching. Bolt crashed into me, knocking me aside just before he hissed in pain. Arrows whistled through the air and hit the ground near us, too many to dodge.

"Run, you fools!" Gael's scream came from the distance.

A score or more archers lined the hills on both sides of us. Gael fired arrows from the right, drawing and releasing so quickly her hands blurred. But there were too many targets.

"Into the woods!" Bolt yelled. With a snarl he broke the arrow sticking through his thigh and ripped it free. Rory grabbed my arm and pulled me toward the protection of the trees as he pulled his sword. He and Bolt swatted arrows from the air as they ran.

The soldiers charged, firing in volleys as they came. I stumbled, felt a door open in my mind. I tried to close it, but the memories came for me. In the space of time between heartbeats, I realized it was my own door that was opening.

"No," I begged. "Not now."

An arrow from their volley flew by me close enough to hear the air whistling through the fletching. I lifted my shield out of reflex and took the impact of a second arrow on it a moment later, like the blow of a fist. Twelve men copied me, mercenaries from the southern continent whose commander lay facedown in the mud. . . .

I blinked. A shaft of sunlight had cleared the hills to land on my face.

"*Kreppa*," Rory snarled as he dragged me along by my arm. "Have you forgotten how to run?"

Arrows hit the dirt around us. Twenty paces away from the meager protection of the trees, Bolt fell behind, favoring his leg. The rain of shafts had thinned but hadn't stopped. Broadheads tore chunks of bark from the trees.

"Stay here and hold them off as long as you can," Bolt told Rory. Pain put a crease across his brow and his voice rasped with each step. "Then fall back to camp. I'll be waiting."

"No—" But I never got any further. A blow I never saw coming took me across the chin and the world spun.

"I don't have time for arguments, Dura," Bolt said. Despite the limp and the blood running down his leg, he hauled me along like an undersized sack of turnips. When we got to camp, he shoved me toward the largest tree. "Get behind it and stay there until they're all dead."

He hobbled to his belongings and gathered the short bow and quiver. Marking his path with curses and blood, he hid behind the tree next to me.

Moments later Rory came crashing through the brush, pursued by a flight of arrows. Twice, I saw him turn and twist in midair, dodging shafts I could barely see, swatting at them with the flat of his hand to send them falling to the ground. A moment later, a dozen soldiers broke into the small clearing. Bolt moved out from behind the trunk of his tree and loosed six arrows within the space of a heartbeat. Six soldiers fell.

He nocked again, holding three more between the fingers of his draw hand, but he never fired. The rest of the soldiers toppled forward, shot from behind. Gael came charging into the clearing with her sword drawn. Her eyes blazed darker than I'd ever seen them, searching.

"Are you insane?" she screamed. Her gaze swept across the three of us. "You didn't think to put someone on the heights to watch for a trap?"

"Rory checked," Bolt said. "There weren't any."

"And how long does it take to move men into position?" she snarled. "The three of you would be dead if I hadn't climbed the hillside."

"The sun was coming up," I said. "Their vaults should have been closed."

She lifted her hands as if she wanted to throttle me. "Of course," she snapped. "They were counting on you to think that. Every one of those men kept shooting at you after the sun rose. Don't you think an ordinary man can kill you? Idiot. A man doesn't have to have a vault to be evil."

The world tilted under my feet. "We're not safe anywhere."

Gael drew breath, but I waved her off. "Yell at me later," I said. "We have to tend to Bolt and get out of here. They saw us before the sun rose. If we're not a long way away by the time the sun sets, they'll track us down again."

"How?" Rory asked.

"It's what Laewan did at Bas-solas, except stronger. Cesla sees through the eyes of his servants when their vaults are open. He's throwing a net around the entire area. We have to move."

Bolt limped over, a thick stream of blood covering the bottom half of his left leg. "I'm going to need help with this." His eyes took on an unfocused look.

"Oh, Aer," Gael breathed. "You're bleeding to death."

"I sure hope not," Bolt said, his face white. Then his eyes rolled up and he fell forward.

Rory darted over to catch him and lay him gently on the ground. "He's heavy."

I'd watched men bleed out before, but I'd also seen battlefield surgeons save those they got to quickly enough. I pulled my dagger and slit his breeches, exposing the wound. Already the flow pulsed more weakly. Turning him, I pointed to the inside of his thigh. "Press here," I told Gael. Then I remembered she was gifted. "Don't press so hard that you crush the artery or we'll lose him anyway." I turned to Rory. "Build a fire and heat the end of your sword until it glows."

"It'll ruin the temper," he said.

"A dagger won't work," I said. "It will just make the wound bigger. The arrow hit an artery. We have to cauterize his leg."

Rory nodded. "I don't really like swords anyway." He darted away, gathering tinder and branches. Blood leaked out of the wound, but Gael had applied enough pressure to stop most of the bleeding. Either that, or Bolt was already close to dying. Mirren, Erendella, and Herregina came through the brush from wherever they'd been hiding.

"We saw the attack," Erendella said. "They came after you, Lord Dura."

I nodded without looking up. I was busy cutting strips from my cloak to make a bandage. "Yes. Cesla had a message he wanted to deliver."

My answer didn't seem to calm her much. Considering that we had left a member of the Vigil and two queens unprotected in the midst of a battle, I wasn't feeling too calm myself. But they'd stayed hidden and were unharmed—thank Aer.

Erendella continued, clearly none too happy. "Those weren't the men we saw before."

"That's right," I agreed. "This was a whole new batch."

She darted glances at the hills, the woods, the horizon. "We can't stay here," she said. Panic threaded its way through her voice. She spoke as if she couldn't get enough air.

"No one's arguing with that," I said. "But I have a situation with my guard here that you may have noticed requires my attention."

"They could come for us any moment," Erendella said. "We have to leave now."

Gael turned from her contemplation of Bolt's bleeding to give Erendella a cold stare. "Save your breath, Your Majesty. He won't leave anyone behind. You can take comfort from the fact that this particular philosophy includes you."

"I'm a queen, and he needs me," Erendella said. "The guard has fulfilled his duty nobly. Would you dishonor his sacrifice by having us all die?"

"Stop," Herregina said. "This is unbecoming of you, sister. The guard is our companion and responsibility, not a resource or commodity to be used up and cast aside."

I nodded my thanks to Cynestol's new ruler. "If you want to leave here, Your Majesty, help Rory with the fire. The arrow went all the way through Bolt's leg, and I'm going to have to cauterize both sides of the wound. We'll have to heat it twice." I looked at Mirren. "Have you ever delved a healer?" When she shook her head, I tried a different tack. "Do you know what bation trees look like?"

Her brow furrowed and her eyes darted from side to side without seeing. "Is that a small tree with light bark and teardrop-shaped leaves?"

I exhaled. "That's the one. If you can find any, bring the leaves."

Herregina came and knelt by my side. "What can I do?"

"Do you have any training as a healer?"

She shook her head. "No more than any other noble of Aille."

I sighed as I tore another strip from my cloak. "I was hoping you could tell me how to do this. I've seen it done any number of times, but a little instruction would be helpful."

Bolt stirred. "Robin?" A string of nonsense syllables followed that I couldn't make out.

"That's probably not good," I said.

"Who's Robin?" Herregina asked.

"His dead son."

Herregina's face paled. "Is he talking to him?"

"Probably," I said. "Let me know if Robin answers. It would settle a question I've had for some time now." I saw Rory and Erendella coming back from the fire. Herregina was all of thirteen and probably wouldn't care for what was about to happen. "Check Bolt's saddlebags and pack. He might have healing supplies in them."

I held out my hand, and Rory handed me the sword. Even through the hilt I could feel the heat that had blackened the last third of the blade. "Hold him." Rory pushed down on Bolt's hips, and to her credit, Erendella sat on his uninjured leg to keep him from thrashing.

I didn't know if Bolt could hear me, but I leaned forward to speak to him anyway. "Hold still. I've got to cauterize your leg."

Blood boiled and steamed around the wound and the smell of roasting meat filled the air. At the first touch, Bolt screamed, pounding his arms against the ground, but nothing below his chest moved. I pressed the flat of the blade against the side of the wound toward his heart and held it there until the sound of quenching metal faded.

Then I handed it back to Rory. "Again."

Bolt groaned and beat the ground with his fists. "Aer have mercy," Rory said. "Isn't that enough?"

"I don't know," I growled back. "I'm not a healer. Now go heat the sword!"

Gael never flinched. She kept the pressure on the upper part of Bolt's leg, doing her best to keep him still.

"After I finish I want you to ease off the pressure," I said. "Do it as slowly as you can—I don't care how long it takes. I'll check for bleeding."

"Erendella's right," Gael said. "We can't stay here. How is he going to be able to ride?"

"You're going to have to hold him in front of you," I told her. Besides Rory, Gael was the only one of us strong enough to keep Bolt mounted and still enough to keep his wound from opening.

She nodded. "I understand. You know what this attack means?"

I nodded, irritation making it more of a jerk. I'd been trying very hard not to think about that very thing. "It means we can't afford to let anyone see us," I said. "And it still might not be enough to get us to Treflow."

Erendella's head came up at my bleak assessment. "What do you mean?"

"Those men kept attacking us even after sunrise," I said. "That means that even in their right minds, they've given their allegiance to Cesla." I pulled a deep breath and tried to focus on the task at hand. "This is why I never ask how things can get worse."

Rory returned carrying the heated sword with Herregina in tow. She cradled a few potions in her arms. "I recognize paverin sap, but I don't know what any of the rest of these are," she said. "I brought them all, just in case."

I took the sword from Rory. "Brace yourself, Bolt, I'm going to cauterize the other half of the wound." He didn't respond. I stepped over his leg and knelt by the outside of his thigh, worried about going too deep with the sword. What if I disturbed what I'd already done? I shook my head and focused on the memory of the battlefield surgeon and how he'd done it.

The hissing sound of hot metal against flesh filled the air again. Bolt dug at the ground with his hands as his uninjured leg convulsed. I pulled the sword slowly out of the wound, and he relaxed, unconscious but gasping. I looked at Gael and nodded, but inside my guts twisted into knots. If that hadn't sealed the artery, I didn't know what else to try.

So slowly that I could hardly see her moving, Gael eased the pressure on the inside of his leg, allowing blood to flow back in. I checked both sides of the wound. Aside from a bit of seepage, it stayed clear.

I loosed a breath I didn't know I'd been holding, but fear still took most of the air from my voice.

I smiled weakly at Gael. "Herregina has medicine from Bolt's pack. See if there's anything in there that stops bleeding."

She went through the bottles and vials, not nearly as many as Bronwyn or Toria had carried. "No, just paverin sap and chiccor extract."

"No surprise there," I said. "Alright, let's get the paverin into him. Hopefully, his gift will keep him from dying on us."

Mirren returned, carrying a double handful of bation leaves. "Thank Aer," I said. "If these work as well on people as they do on dogs, it'll keep the wound from fouling." I pointed. "Pack the leaves on both sides of his leg while I wrap it."

Thirty minutes later we were mounted. Gael rode with Bolt cradled in her arms like an oversized child.

CHAPTER 62

Toria glanced back at the wagons following her. In another day, they would make Treflow with the men and weapons she'd managed to beg or borrow from each outpost they'd encountered along the outer cordon. Fifty men and women slept in the wagons, their eyes shielded against the light of day.

"If Rymark has withdrawn to Treflow, why did he order the outer cordon to remain?" Fess asked.

"Cesla has his forces pinned," she said. It had taken her two days of musing on the orders Warena had received to come to a firm conclusion. "The kings and queens of the north are coming as quickly as they can along the outer cordon," she said. "In order to buy the monarchs safe passage south, he has to keep the cordon in place. If he doesn't, he puts them at risk."

"But why keep them there?" Fess asked. "Once Regent Cailin and Prince Brod have passed south of each outpost, those soldiers could withdraw and accompany them to Treflow."

"Such a move would pinpoint their location," Toria said. "Cesla would be able to concentrate an attack and kill or capture them. The kings and queens must move quickly, but quietly."

Her apprentice fell silent, musing. When he spoke again, his voice held concern that mirrored hers. "If Cesla knows Rymark has fallen back to Treflow, he can concentrate his entire force on an attack there before Rymark can pull reinforcements from the perimeter. What are the odds the king will win, Lady Deel?"

"The specifics of the mathematicum are beyond me, Fess," she said, hoping he would be satisfied.

"I don't really understand the mathematicum myself," he said. "Can Rymark win?"

"Yes."

"If you were a betting man, Toria Deel, where would you place your wager?"

When she didn't answer, Fess sighed and resumed his inspection of the landscape. "I thought so."

Pellin stepped from the quay in Cynestol's port, stumbling as his legs worked to find their land rhythm again. For as far as he could see, people pushed and fought to board any ship that could make the trip south. Desperate passengers argued and sometimes fought, bidding up the price of passage. Ahead of him, Mark walked with Elieve, Allta a pace behind.

"Rumors are flying as thick as gulls over garbage," Captain Onen said as he walked beside him. "I don't know what business you're on, Master Pellin, and I don't wish to, but your coin is appreciated and you're better company than most of those who live on the land. Are you sure you don't want to go back to the south?"

He'd turned to respond when Mark's cry cut through the air. "Get down!"

Pellin heard the whistle of displaced air just as Allta crashed into him and Onen, sending them sprawling across the stone pier. His guard stood above them, swatting at arrows that came from different directions.

"Dwimor!"

Screams echoed in the streets. Mark's yell of rage threaded through them. Onen rolled, drawing his hooked knife and searching. An arrow appeared out of thin air a dozen paces away to come streaking for the captain's heart. Allta's sword whined as he lunged to knock it aside. It deflected from his blade to take the captain through the arm, and his knife clattered to the ground.

Reaching up, Pellin pulled at Onen's clothes. "Get down! You can't see them."

A gurgle prefaced the sound of a body hitting the quay, and a man appeared, a knife lodged in his throat.

"Allta," Pellin yelled. "Help Mark with the others."

"I can't," he answered. "If I move, the archers will have you."

Mark's screams of rage filled the air as people fled. Pellin looked to see his apprentice charging empty air, his knives flashing. An arrow appeared in midflight, but Mark threw himself to the side at the last moment and the shot went wide.

Allta parried another arrow, then grabbed at his belt and threw in a motion too quick to follow. Pellin watched the knife spin end over end. The hilt struck with a muted thump and the knife dropped harmlessly to the stone.

But the throw had given Mark enough time to close the distance and an instant later another body came into view, a woman. Even at this distance, Pellin could see her colorless eyes.

Arrows came from a single direction now. Between parries, Allta threw whatever he could at the attacker. Mark had disappeared behind a row of crates. Elieve lay still on the pier, an arrow jutting from her side.

Moments later the last dwimor was down, cut from behind.

Pellin made to rise, but Allta prevented him. "There may be more."

Mark huddled over the form of Elieve. "Get a healer. Somebody get a healer!" But the pier continued to empty as people ran from the blood and bodies.

Pellin rolled out from beneath Allta's presence and stood. Onen joined him a moment later, pressing against his arm where the arrow jutted out. "Captain," Pellin said, "we need your youngest sailors with us."

Onen bawled a pair of names in a voice that made Pellin wince, and a moment later two men, both under a score, stood beside them. As he ran toward Mark and Elieve, with Allta hovering over him, Pellin explained what he needed.

The two men surveyed the area, searching as Pellin knelt. Mark looked at him, his gaze demanding and frantic. "She's so pale."

The arrow had not gone through, and blood pulsed weakly from the wound. Elieve's eyes fluttered. "Give me a moment," Pellin said. He retreated into his sanctuary, searching for every set of memories that belonged to a healer, especially those who'd served in war.

"Allta, pick her up."

"Eldest, I can't protect you with my arms full."

"I'll protect him," Mark said. "Please. She jumped in front of me."

Pellin turned. "Captain Onen, do you have medical supplies on board?"

"Aye," he said, "but no healer."

"That's alright, Captain," Pellin said. "Let's get her back on board the ship. Have your men keep watch. No one boards but us. No one. She's going to be fine, Mark. I promise."

An hour later, Pellin exited the cabin to find Allta standing guard just outside. "The girl?" he asked.

"The arrow took her in the side, but missed anything vital. Come, we need to see the captain. I'm a fool."

"How so, Eldest?"

"When Igesia and I freed Elieve of her vault, we put the evil of the Darkwater on guard. It knew where we were, but more importantly, where we would be."

"Cynestol," Allta said.

"Cesla had all the time he needed to get his dwimor into place." He stopped at the captain's quarters and knocked.

"Come."

Pellin followed Allta into the room to find Onen at his desk, his left arm in a sling. "How are you set for provisions, Captain?" he asked.

"We're running lean, Master Pellin." Suspicion laced his voice. "We have less than a week of food and water remaining. The crossing was quick or we'd be even lower. As soon as we victual the ship, I'll be putting as many passengers aboard as I can hold. Have you heard what the other captains are charging for passage? It's insane."

"I have. Do you have enough food and water to get us to Haefan?"

The captain nodded. "Moorclaire? That's hardly more than a fishing village. As much as I'll hate having a bunch of passengers, Master Pellin, the profit on this could—"

Pellin reached into his purse and pulled two gold pieces. The captain's response, though silent, spoke volumes. "We're your cargo, Captain, your only cargo."

Onen stood. "I've only seen gold twice in my life. May I hold them?"

Pellin placed the coins in his palm. "They're yours if we leave now."

"I'm no stranger to trouble," Onen said, "but it usually does me the favor of showing itself. Who were they?"

"Enemies who know how to stay hidden," Pellin said. "I should have known they would be here. If I'd ordered you to continue northeast to Haefan to begin with, they wouldn't have found us."

Onen nodded, staring at the gold in his palm in disbelief. "And who are you?"

"A passenger. I'd like to leave, Captain," Pellin said. "Now."

Onen pocketed the gold and moved past them, bellowing orders to his crew.

"This may serve us, Eldest," Allta said. "It's a shorter ride to Treflow from Haefan than Cynestol."

He nodded. "Tell the captain we need all the speed he can wrest from his ship and pray Rymark can hold Treflow until we arrive."

Chapter 63

The sun might have been a few degrees past noon when I saw Bolt stir, jerking to wakefulness.

"I've got you," Gael said.

Pain put years on his face, but his gaze seemed lucid enough. "Water."

Rory lifted a skin to him, and he drank, emptying it before he handed it back. "More." He skewered Rory and Gael with a look that promised retribution. "I fully expected him"—he pointed at me—"to spout some piffle about not leaving anyone behind, but it's your job to stand against that kind of fool-headed mush."

"Save the speech," I told him. "We had to cauterize the wound."

He scowled at me. I couldn't tell whether the sour expression came from his pain or because he was irritated with me for saving him, but I would have put money on the latter. "Really?" he asked with his eyes wide. "I think I might have picked up on that from the smell of burnt meat coming from the vicinity of my leg."

"Is the pain bad?" Gael asked.

Bolt rolled his shoulders, twisting in Gael's hold. "It's not the kind of thing I'd volunteer for, but it's swimming upstream against whatever you gave me."

"Paverin sap," she said.

"Is there any left?" he asked. When she nodded, he held out a hand. "Let's have it."

We stopped the horses, and Bolt hopped down and landed on his good leg without letting the other touch the ground. While Gael retrieved the medicine, he probed the bandages around his wound. "Not bad for battlefield surgery," he said to Gael. "What did you use?"

"Not me," she said. "Willet."

Genuine surprise lifted his brows. "Where did you learn to do that?"

"I watched a healer do it after my first battle with Owmead," I said.

"You watched it and you thought you could try it out on me without being trained?" he said. "You could have killed me."

"You were dying anyway." I shrugged as if the decision had been of minor importance. "It wasn't like we had much to lose."

"Humph. What did you use to cauterize the wound?"

"My sword," Rory said.

"You've ruined the temper," Bolt said to him, his face stoic. "What have I told you about taking care of your weapons?"

Rory lifted his hands. "I tried to tell him."

Bolt almost smiled. On anyone else it would have been a grin that split his face from ear to ear. "That's alright. We'll get you a proper sword as soon as we can. The balance on that one is atrocious."

"What?" Rory said "You've had me train with that sword for months."

Bolt nodded. "I wanted to make sure that I could beat you without trying too hard. Your gift runs at least as pure as mine, and your talents are better."

I couldn't help but laugh at the look on Rory's face as he realized he'd been conned for the last six months into working far harder to master the sword than he had to.

"You would have made a good urchin," he said finally.

Bolt nodded as though Rory had paid him one of the greatest compliments of his life. "That particular set of skills is another reason why I chose you," he said.

Gael handed him the vial of paverin sap, and he held it up to the light for an instant before pulling the stopper and downing the contents. "Where are we?"

"About forty leagues southwest of Treflow," Erendella said.

"Two days hard riding if we change horses often," Bolt mused.

"Can you ride that hard?" Gael asked.

He shrugged. "Do I need to?" He looked at me. "Will you have all six of the rulers in place when we get there?"

I shook my head. "I don't know."

432

"That's probably the kind of question you'll have to ask. The net's closing in, and they know we're headed for Treflow. We'll have to ride at night as well." He turned to Rory. "You should probably go ahead and cover an eye. I don't know how much light you'll have."

Erendella pulled the scrying stone from the folds of her cloak. "King Rymark, hear me."

We waited there in the middle of the rolling hills of northern Caisel without a farm or village in sight. The wind whispered out of the west. "King Rymark," Erendella called, her voice rising. "Hear me."

"I'm here," his voice answered from the facets of the stone. "Who calls?"

"Erendella. Are you still in Treflow?"

"Yes," he said. "We're holding."

"Are the rest of the rulers with you?" Erendella asked.

I held my breath, waiting for his answer.

"Ulrezia not here yet, but she's close. The problem is Pellin. The Eldest was attacked by dwimor in Cynestol. He says he's on his way north now."

I leaned forward to ask a question, but Bolt's look of warning stopped me.

"Make haste," Rymark said. "Our losses are mounting."

Bolt moved to Erendella's side to whisper into her ear. When she hesitated, he donned a look that said plainly he meant to be obeyed.

"Can you hold for five days?" she asked into the stone.

"Aer willing. I've sent messenger birds for reinforcements," Rymark said. "But if I try to hold the city for that long, I won't have enough men to buy us our retreat."

Bolt held up four fingers and nodded toward the stone.

"We'll be there in four," Erendella said, "even if we have to ride the horses to death."

"Better," Rymark said. "I hope I'll be here to greet you when you arrive."

None of us said anything until after Erendella had wrapped the scrying stone in cloth and tucked it away again.

"He has a traitor in his camp," I said. "That's why you told him four days instead of two."

Bolt took a step on his injured leg and winced. "That and something might go wrong. It usually does."

I shook my head. "True, but it's a lot easier for men to hold out for two days instead of three or four."

Bolt nodded. "Since there's a spy in Rymark's camp, getting into the city is going to be a challenge. If they're looking for us I want to make sure they're doing it at the wrong time." He hobbled over to his horse and mounted. "Let's go. Our only hope is to ride fast enough to leave Cesla's net behind."

I locked gazes with Gael and gestured. She understood. When we set out, she made a point to ride at Bolt's side.

We began our dash to Treflow.

Ten miles from Treflow, Toria signaled Fess and Oriano to bring the wagon train to a halt. Wag sat on his haunches, his tongue lolling in the morning sun. She dismounted then stripped her gloves. "How many people do you smell in the direction of the sunrise?" she asked.

Many packs, Mistress, but they are still some distance away. His thought came with an image of a field covered with hundreds upon hundreds of men.

"And how many of those have the smell of the forest on them?"

Also, many packs. But the field contained less than half as many now.

"Can you guide us into the city and keep us away from those with the scent of the forest on them?"

Yes, Mistress.

With the sentinel in the lead, his nose into the air and twitching, they circled around to the south. Soon after the city came into view, they spied their first patrol, a group of seven soldiers with their heads bared. A weight lifted from her shoulders as the men in Caisel's colors caught sight of them and headed their way.

Fess pulled his horse in front, his hand raised in greeting, when Wag burst into motion. The men tried to draw weapons as their horses reared.

"Stop," Toria ordered Fess as he pulled his sword. "You'll only get in his way."

"Toria Deel, there are seven of them."

"Not anymore." She pointed. "Look."

Three of the soldiers were already down, and the other four were galloping away, toward Treflow. With grim efficiency, Wag ran them down from behind, leaping to take each rider from the back of his horse, his jaws crushing their throats.

She nudged her mount forward and stopped next to Fess where he stared as Wag loped back toward them. "This is why they're the guardians of the forest," she said, "and why Cesla's first stroke was to kill them."

He nodded. "Why not let him cleanse the area around the city, Lady Deel?"

"Because he's the last of his kind," Toria said. "And even a sentinel can be killed. We have to get Wag into Treflow. Cleansing the city is more important."

Fess nodded. "Whoever betrayed us will have the smell of the forest on them."

Onen's ship slipped into the dock at Haefan's small harbor. Because it was more of a fishing village than a trading port, their approach had been hampered by the deeper draft of their ship. The lights on the pier had barely been sufficient for them to find their way. Except for the harbormaster, the town slept, dawn still two hours distant.

"Will it work, Eldest?" Allta asked him.

It had taken them a day and a half, even with the favorable wind and an empty ship, to make the dash up the coast to Haefan. The time had given him and Elieve the opportunity to heal and gather strength. "Cesla and the Fayit intelligence within him will have no choice but to hunt for us along the routes from Cynestol. Even if he suspects we've taken ship to another port, he's more likely to search for us in Loklallin or Vadras."

Onen, lighting his way with a lantern, found them where they waited for the gangplank to be made fast. "That's the fastest trip I'll ever make, Master Pellin, and sure enough."

"I hope so, Captain," Pellin said. "There's usually not much money to be made sailing empty."

"True enough, that," Onen said, "but it's a thrill I wouldn't have missed, racing across the sea that way." He stuck out his hand. "Fair winds to you."

"And you, Captain," Pellin said. "Find whatever cargo you can and make for the southern continent."

The light of Onen's lantern cast the planes of his face in stark relief. "For how long?"

Pellin smiled. "You'll know when it's safe."

Allta left to fetch Elieve and Mark, and they spent the time until dawn combing the town of Haefan for horses and supplies. By the time the sun crested the horizon, they were riding across the moors of southern Moorclaire.

CHAPTER 64

Two days after our conversation with Rymark, we came in sight of columns of thick black smoke that marked Treflow like a pyre. We crawled up the backside of a low hill and looked down on a city under siege. Treflow sat at the junction where the Darkwater River split into branches that flowed south, southwest, and southeast. The wall of the city encompassed the junction. Around the perimeter, a thick cordon of men and women in both soldiers garb and civilian clothes guarded every bit of land. Even more were concentrated on the roads going in and out.

"How come they're not attacking?" Rory asked.

I knew and felt my stomach drop toward my legs. "Why attack during the day when you have the advantage in the dark? They can see better and fight almost as well as the gifted."

"If Rymark has the advantage during the day, why doesn't he come out and attack?"

"I can think of a couple of reasons," I said.

"And neither of them good," Bolt added.

"Rymark's forces are so depleted he should have retreated," I said. "He's waited for us."

"Oh," Rory said in a small voice.

"How are we going to get into the city?" Erendella asked.

Bolt sighed and then turned to look at me. "You're really not going to like this."

I swallowed against a knot of panic in my throat. "I bet it has something to do with swimming."

"Why is that a problem?" Mirren asked.

"He doesn't swim so well," Rory said.

She frowned. "Doesn't Bunard straddle the banks of a big river?"

Rory nodded. "Oh yes. There's water everywhere."

She shook her head. "How can someone—"

"Stop," I said. "Just stop. We can't swim into the city anyway. They'll spot us from the banks and fill us with arrows." I looked at Bolt, expecting agreement. He disappointed me.

"I said you weren't going to like it," he said. "They're not going to see us."

I pointed to everyone in our group and then myself. Holding up seven fingers, I said, "They can't *help* but see us."

"Not if we go in at night."

We traveled north until we were miles from the main siege and the heavy patrols of those who belonged to Cesla in both daylight and darkness. A few hours before sunset we found a burned-out farmstead and set our horses loose in the pasture. The ruins of the house and the barn we avoided entirely. I tried to keep from imagining unseen eyes watching us from their shadows as we made our way to an isolated copse of trees by the river.

Bolt nodded in satisfaction. "We'll wait here until dark."

Gael's hand clamped on my arm, and I followed her point to the leafy canopy. The trees and river spun as I tried to draw breath. "Aer help us," I breathed, searching for some prayer in the liturgy for the hopeless. "Bolt."

Everyone turned to look first at me, then at the black-spotted leaves overhead. "It's here," I said. "The Darkwater is here."

"Stop staring and move," Bolt ordered.

"What do we do?" Erendella asked.

My guard looked at her, his face devoid of expression. "The basics," Bolt said. "We don't let the sun set on us while we're in the Darkwater." He turned and led us south along the bank of the river, but I could feel the evil of the forest creeping up on us from behind every time we stopped.

After a few hundred yards we came to another stand of trees whose leaves were whole. The rest of us hid on the banks of the river while Rory and Gael went hunting, leaving Bolt to defend the four of us—still badly injured, but his gifted body was performing a miraculous recovery.

I watched the leaves, each shift in the breeze conjuring images of black, but they were still green when Rory and Gael returned a couple of hours later wearing the uniforms of Caisel soldiers. They carried five more sets, along with several lengths of river reed.

We marched along the river, pretending to be one of the patrols until the sun touched the horizon to the west.

Bolt brought us to a stop. "We have to get into the water. In less than half an hour these fields are going to be crawling with Cesla's troops." He handed me a length of hollowed reed. "Gael will stay with you. Rory and I will safeguard the queens and Mirren."

"We're too far away," I said. "I'm going to drown."

Gael put her arm around my waist. "I will make sure you don't. Just remember to stay below the water and breathe normally. You don't have to swim. You just have to float."

There was no point in arguing. No one there understood that slipping beneath the dark surface of the water was too much like stepping into the darkness of the forest. I took my first step into the river, surprised at its warmth. I put the reed to my mouth and the water, murky with rain, slipped over me, blotting out the light. We stayed there for an hour until the sky turned black. Then Gael's hand grabbed my belt and we drifted with the current, my feet slipping from the bottom, taking any sensation of motion away. I tried to focus on keeping everything still, as if I were a living piece of driftwood. Time stopped.

Questions came at me in the dark, accusing. Would I be able to call the Fayit? I shoved the thought away.

But even if I was able, would they consent to help? I didn't know. Did they have to answer the summoning and give aid or did the calling only give them the opportunity? If the Fayit were anything like their human descendants, they might very well refuse. Worse, I might find myself summoning beings who'd long ago gone insane from their self-enforced isolation.

I pushed that doubt away, but others took its place. Drifting like a piece of human detritus in the river, I had no distractions I could use to hide from them. Lulled by the water, random memories passed through my mind.

Even in the depths, I could tell when the current took us beneath the city wall. The water chilled, lacking the memory of the sun that would have warmed it. Then I struck iron. Gael lifted me above the surface, and I found myself in a shallow air space created by the arc of the stone wall over the water. Black iron pitted by age and elements blocked our way into the city. A moment later the rest of our party surfaced, gasping and shaking the water from their eyes.

"We've hit the water gate," Gael said.

Bolt's eyes narrowed. "I was hoping they wouldn't have one, but it's probably just as well. The city would be impossible to defend without it. I'm going to see if there's a way through." He took a few deep breaths and dove.

Bereft of light, I shivered. Time passed while my doubts returned to assail me. "It's taking him too long," I said. "How long can you hold your breath?"

She shrugged. "I've never tried it, but I've seen even ungifted swimmers stay under for three minutes or more."

I looked at the water. Despite my enforced familiarity, I still couldn't see it as anything other than an enemy.

Bolt surfaced, cutting my reflection short. "There's no way through. We're going to have to make a gap."

I looked at iron bars as thick as my wrist. "Even you can't bend that."

Bolt nodded. "Not alone, but there are three gifted here and two more with partials. We just have to bend it enough to wiggle through."

Mirren and I moved to one side while Bolt gave instructions, positioning each person and telling them where to brace their hands and feet. By the time he was done, Erendella and Herregina faced each other like human spiders suspended sideways, clinging to the bars. Bolt, Rory, and Gael each took three deep breaths and dove to grab the bars beneath the queens.

I didn't see or hear any signal, but I saw Erendella and Herregina strain until veins corded in their necks. Still they pulled, working against the iron until their skin turned red. Then Bolt, Gael, and Rory surfaced, gulping air with shaky breaths.

"It moved," Bolt said, "but not enough." He looked at me and Mirren. "We're going to need your help. Can you take the surface positions?"

I nodded, feeling like a boy lending his strength to the blacksmith, but I grasped the bar, determined to pull until my heart burst if I had to. Erendella and Herregina submerged beneath us. Bolt, Gael, and Rory went even deeper. One of them must have hit the bar of iron I held with their dagger. I felt it vibrate. I threw my weight against the pitiless metal, pushing with my feet against one bar while I pulled with my hands against the other until I thought my back would break.

I didn't stop until Bolt broke the surface, gasping for air on the far side of the gate. Hands gripped the bars as Gael and the rest broke free of the water, sucking air and trembling. One by one we slipped through, floating just beneath the surface with our reeds once more. It was only a moment before Gael's hand tightened on my belt and I lurched, dragged toward the surface. Cool air kissed my face. I blinked away the water of the river and looked around. We were inside the city. A few paces away, five more figures emerged from the water by torchlight, dirty, wet versions of some mythical sea creature rising from the deep.

Sounds of fighting came from all around us, smoke heavy in the air from fires burning wherever the defenders could keep them lit. Cries went up and soldiers scrambled toward us from the street, their swords drawn.

"Down!" Bolt ordered. The whine of arrows screamed past me as I dove for the mud.

"Halt! Halt!" an unfamiliar voice screamed. Slowly, we rose, surrounded by bedraggled and bloody soldiers with arrows trained on our hearts.

Erendella stepped forward, her hands above her head. "I am Erendella, queen of Caisel. King Rymark is expecting me."

No one moved. Treflow's defenders were too scared and we were too tired.

"They're not putting their weapons down," Rory said.

Bolt sat on the bank of the river, favoring his injured leg. "They can hold them on us every step of the way to Rymark, for all I care—just so long as we get there."

CHAPTER 65

They kept us on the bank of the river for an hour, until Rymark came to us, barking orders as runners brought reports from each section of the city. Memories of the last war threatened to break loose from the room in my mind where I'd locked them away. The screams of death and dying were too close, too loud. More than anything, I wanted to close my eyes and put my hands over my ears.

"You're early," he said to Erendella.

She nodded. "Errant Consto thought it best to sneak into the city before resistance could be organized against us."

Rymark nodded. "You're referring to the traitor in our midst. He's been dealt with." He nodded toward the river. "That was quite a risk."

Erendella didn't bother with accusations or criticism. "Under the circumstances, it was the best we could do."

The ride to Treflow and our entrance to the city had left me weak. I could have used the riverbank for a bed, but I pushed myself up to stand before half the kings and queens of the north. "We have to call the Fayit."

Rymark nodded, but doubt clouded his expression. A runner, his right arm hanging useless, ran up, not stopping until he came within reach of the king's circle of guards. "We're losing the west wall," he said.

Rymark barked an order that sent four dozen soldiers running into the night before turning back to us. "Whatever you wish to do, Lord Dura, will have to wait until morning. We're holding for now."

"But we can call them now," I said.

The king's face clouded. "Lord Dura, when dawn comes, I will be more than happy to entertain your fancy, but if I leave, more of my men will die, and I don't like it when my men die. We'll hold through the night." Without waiting for a reply he barked an order and another injured soldier, this one on makeshift crutches, came forward to lead us away.

The slow pace through the city afforded me the opportunity to see the extremity of Rymark's defense. Rings of palisades and barriers had been set every hundred paces, lines of retreat made with whatever materials could be scavenged. More than one building had been razed to build barricades and clear lines of fire for archers.

"I hope you know what you're doing, Willet," Bolt said. "Rymark's gambling everything on buying you enough time to call Ealdor's friends."

On our way to the center of the city, we passed a watchfire that threw the lines of his face into stark relief. "How do you know that?"

He pointed south, but I couldn't match his vision. "He's left no avenue of escape, which means either he thinks *he* can win, or that *you* can."

"Where are we going?" Gael asked our escort.

"The counting house," he said. "It's the closest thing this city has to a citadel."

"Any tunnels?" Bolt asked.

He kicked a piece of rubble out of the way as he placed his crutches for another step. "No, and there's only one entrance."

Bolt shook his head. "That's not a defense—it's a death trap."

Everything about the counting house fit our escort's description, but he'd neglected to mention that Prince Maenelic's head would be on a post out front. The prince somehow looked surprised, but his eyes were closed and I had no desire to speak with him.

I caught Bolt's attention. "That's another sin we can place at Gehata's feet."

"Perhaps," he said.

"A little compassion might have kept Maenelic from this," I said. "For that matter, trusting me with one of the scrying stones might have as well."

"Water through the gate, Willet," Bolt said.

The doors to the moneylenders' guild were high, but they lacked the arch at the top favored in the keeps and holds of the nobility. Heavy bands of iron gave their rectangular shape the look and feel of forbidding solidity. Rymark's escort crutched his way past a heavy contingent of guards and rapped three times on the door, paused and struck twice more.

"The code changes every day, in case the defenses fail," he said. "But I wouldn't want to fight my way free even in the daytime."

We entered into a grand hall, and the doors boomed shut behind us. Barrels of food and water lined the walls, and medical supplies filled the tables. "They'll be near the holding room," our guide said.

We turned a corner, and I saw Toria and Fess standing near Cailin, queen regent of Collum. At her side the prince chewed on a chubby fist, his eyes wide, taking everything in. Brid Teorian stood on her other side. A tall woman I didn't recognize—with dark eyebrows and hair so blond it was almost white—observed us from a few paces away.

There was no sign of Pellin.

"Welcome to Treflow, Lord Dura," Toria Deel said.

The blond woman turned to regard me with a lift of her dark brows. "That's him? That's the man who's upended the Vigil and trapped us in this killing field?" She pursed her lips as her gaze took the leisurely route to my feet and back. "I expected someone more imposing."

"I think that's his secret, Your Majesty," Bolt said. "He looks so ordinary it never occurs to you that he could cause so much trouble."

The woman I assumed to be Queen Ulrezia nodded, her expression serious, as though my guard hadn't been jesting. I looked around. Nobody smiled except Gael. I listened for the clamor of fighting, but the walls of the counting house, built to confound thieves and burglars, blocked all sound.

I took the opportunity to introduce the newest member of the Vigil to Toria Deel and Fess. "This is Mirren, my apprentice." Toria Deel jerked and I nodded. "One of the bishops in Cynestol had certain ambitions we needed to curtail. You can get the memories from her." Toria Deel and Fess were removing their gloves as I turned away.

Silence fell again, grating on me. I saw Herregina and Erendella making the acquaintance of their fellow rulers and decided to make my way to the street in front of the counting house. The sounds of battle set my nerves on edge, but the fear I might be taken unaware lessened. I stood behind the last barricade and waited for dawn with a desperation that surpassed any hunger. Bolt, Gael, and Rory flanked me.

I stared east, willing the sun to rise. When the sky lightened from black to charcoal, the sounds of fighting stopped. "Thank Aer," I breathed. I don't know if I'd ever meant it more. Another hour passed before Rymark and Ellias approached the counting house, leaning toward each other with their heads bowed, the way men do when they're in conference.

Both kings were free of injury, but they wore the look of men who might drop at any moment. "Well, Lord Dura," Rymark said, "you've got your gathering." Without saying anything more, they walked into the counting house, and the rest of us followed.

"Is there some sort of ceremony that comes with this calling, Lord Dura?" Ulrezia asked when we rejoined the rest of the monarchs.

Maybe it was because she ruled a kingdom even farther north than Collum, but Ulrezia was as cold as her castle. "No," I said. "All that's required is the presence of six perfect gifts and the name of the one being called." I didn't tell them that the only Fayit whose name I had was dead. I prayed Toria Deel could help me.

"And it's your belief the gift of kings satisfies that requirement?" Ulrezia asked. I doubted whether snow would melt in her mouth.

"Give over, Ulrezia," Rymark said. "Of course he believes it, or we wouldn't be here."

"I do," I said. "The Fayit are our ancestors. They parceled out their gifts, talents, and temperaments among their descendants, among us."

"That's probably as close to blasphemy as anyone has dared to come in my presence," Brid Teorian said.

I bowed in her direction. "It's only blasphemy if it's not true. Against the day we might need to call them, the Fayit created the gift of kings, a perfect alloy of all six gifts that couldn't be divided."

Ulrezia had a way of raising one eyebrow without speaking that called my sanity into question. "And do you want us to hold hands and chant the children's song?"

"Maybe," I shot back. "The fact that you're here means you've given at least some credence to the idea."

Her expression turned colder, if that was possible. "Let's try it without the singsong," she said. "If that doesn't work, you can strip us of the rest of our dignity."

"If you don't mind," Rymark said, "I'd like to get on with this. Lord Dura. We won't last another night. I've sent messages to every commander along the outer cordon telling them to get here with all haste. None of them have replied."

Queen Ulrezia noticed my hesitation. "You can do what you've claimed, can't you, Lord Dura?"

I nodded, but inside I felt sick. "Toria Deel, I need the names of the other Fayit."

Her eyes widened. "I don't have them, Lord Dura. That is not the task I was given."

I tried to smile but I couldn't get my face to cooperate. I tapped my head. "They're in here. Inside my vault. Ealdor told me."

She backed away from me. "I don't know how to free you from your vault. We have to wait for Pellin. He's still a day away."

"Didn't you hear me?" Rymark's face flushed with anger. "I said we can't hold. For the love of Aer, I've ordered the dead to be propped up on the wall to make it look as if we have more men than we do."

Toria Deel spun to face him. "If I try to pull the information from his vault, I'll destroy his mind in the process. He'll die."

"We cannot hold for another night," Rymark said. "The attempt must be made or you doom us all to die here."

Toria Deel thrust out her hand to point at me. "Hear *me*, King Rymark. Only Pellin knows how to cure a vault. The knowledge we require is inside it. If I break Dura's vault we *will* die."

"Fool man, you've brought us to our doom." Ulrezia turned to her guards. "We're leaving now, while it's light. King Rymark, if we combine our forces we stand a better chance of fighting our way clear of the siege."

"No!" I pleaded, reaching toward the queen. "If you leave we can't call them."

"A token," Ulrezia demanded. "Show me some measure of proof that what you say is true."

The kings and queens of the north—all six that held the gift of kings—looked at me, all of them wearing expressions of expectation, even Herregina and Erendella. Ulrezia's demand had taken hold. "Form a circle," I said. "Hold hands."

CHAPTER 66

They joined together. Of all those assembled, only Cailin—standing behind Brod, where he held hands with Ellias and Herregina—gave me a nod of confidence. I searched my mind for some hint of the names Ealdor had buried there, but nothing came to me. Desperate, I retreated into the gift and entered my sanctuary. I needed time to think.

I replayed the memories of my life from almost eleven years ago, sifting through my memories as though I was delving another, but every time I saw myself going into the forest, they stopped at sunset, only to skip forward to the morning I walked out of the Darkwater.

I opened my eyes.

"Well, Lord Dura?" Ulrezia asked.

Please, Aer, I pleaded in the depths of my mind. *Please let Ealdor come to me one more time. Give the kings and queens, your appointed rulers, something to believe in.* I turned to face the Everwood and called. "Ealdor, please. Come to me one more time. Whatever is left of you, show it to us. Please."

I waited, my imagination conjuring hope from each hint of movement at the edge of my vision, but each time I turned to it, it resolved into the shift of a guard or a queen or a king. I called again, but within seconds Ulrezia dropped her hands. "Well, King Rymark?" she asked.

Rymark turned to me, his expression unexpectedly beseeching. "Unless you can conjure some men or stratagem, Lord Dura, we must abandon Treflow."

I shook my head. "You can't win if you quit the field now, Your Majesty," I said. "You know this."

447

"I do." He nodded. "When's the best time to die, Lord Dura?"

"Later," I sighed.

Toria Deel stepped through the remnant of the circle. "Give me every man or woman you can spare."

Fess shouldered his way through the press to stand next to her. "There are too many, Toria Deel," he said. "They'll all die."

She turned to him. "Then you decide, Fess. I will support whatever decision you make."

I didn't know what they were talking about, but it didn't take a gift to see a long-running contest of wills in its final battle.

"And if I elect to fight alongside Lelwin and the rest?" he said.

Toria nodded, but I could see grief in her expression, even if I couldn't understand it. "Then you must, but for selfish reasons I hope you will try to live."

"With Wag then," he said.

She stiffened, and I saw refusal in her expression before she conquered it. "Very well." She turned to speak to Rymark and Ulrezia. "With the help of Lord Dura and Mirren, Fess and I can equip your men to fight in the dark nearly as well as those from the forest."

Rymark's face filled with doubt and fear. "What sorcery is this?"

An hour later I stood in the ruins of a cavernous building near the city wall with a thousand men and women wearing blindfolds against dim candlelight. Time after time, I released the memories of Lelwin's alternate personality and tried not to be horrified at the change in the urchin I'd known.

"Clever," I murmured to Bolt as I stepped outside of the building and flopped against the wall, grateful for the break. At Mirren's suggestion, we worked in shifts with three of us moving among the soldiers while the fourth rested. It wasn't as taxing as a full delve, but I was still sweating from the exertion.

"How so?" he asked.

I pointed. "Rymark knows what he's about. There are dozens of men and women there on crutches who can't fight, but with Lelwin's memories and a bow on top of a building . . ."

"They can shoot in the dark and make the enemy pay."

Time dragged by in a procession of delves interrupted at intervals by breaks where I talked with Bolt or Gael and worked at not saying what every man and woman inside the city knew. A half hour before sunset, Rymark approached, his steps quick.

"We have to go," he said.

I pointed at the setting sun. "It's still too bright."

"It's going to take time to get everyone into position. Cesla has scouts out there that have given him their unconditional allegiance."

Bolt nodded. "You'll have to take out as many of them as you can so they can't see where your men are hiding."

"That's it," Rymark said. "This sortie is going to be expensive, Dura. I hope this idea of yours works."

I gestured my agreement, even though it hadn't been my idea and he knew that. "Any word from Pellin?"

"No." Rymark's expression soured.

"What?" I asked.

"Cesla's shifting men to the south of the city." He disappeared into the building, and moments later, ranks of men and women exited wearing the heavy veils I'd come to associate with those who'd been poisoned by the forest. I suppressed a chill and waited. Lelwin came out followed by Fess, whose eyes were covered. Wag trotted by his side.

I called to him and he came to my side. *Master!* He thought in welcoming. *We hunt.*

Yes, but I have a special job for you.

Mistress has already given me one, Master. I picked up an image of Toria Deel, accompanied by her scent. *I'm supposed to keep Fess and Lelwin alive. Should I not?*

You should, I thought back. *But do you remember the way Pellin smells?*

Old master.

His scent came to me in more nuanced detail than I could have imagined. *That's him. If you smell him out there, I want you to bring him into the city.*

Wag sat on his haunches with his head tilted to one side and I had to reach to maintain contact. *Which is more important, Master—keeping Mistress's pups safe or bringing old master to you?*

Bringing old master to me, I thought. I couldn't ignore the fact that I might have just condemned Fess and Lelwin to die. I wanted to be angry at myself or the Vigil. Anger felt powerful, but as often as I'd slipped into that defense, it wouldn't come. I felt only the grim necessity of keeping the evil of the forest in check. If we failed, saving Fess or Lelwin or anyone else would be pointless.

I lifted my hand from Wag's head and pulled him close for a hug that I couldn't give to anyone else. *Keep yourself safe, if you can.*

He barked once, his tongue lolling out to one side, and turned to follow our last hope to the gates of the city. "I've become one of you at last," I said softly.

I hadn't counted on Bolt's sense of hearing. "How so, Dura?"

He stood in the dying rays of the sun like a living statue, as absolute and unyielding in his sense of purpose as granite. "The lives of my friends are nothing more than ficheall pieces on the board," I said.

"If you enjoyed it, you'd be the wrong man for the job," Bolt said. "We should get back to the counting house."

"No. I need to see what's happening."

"Why?" Bolt asked. "You can't do anything about it until Pellin gets here."

When I didn't answer, Bolt let out his breath in a long sigh. "Very well, but we're going to do this on my terms."

I blinked. "What would those be?"

"We're going to stay as close to Rymark as his shadow," he said. "If you want to know what's happening, that's the place to be, and if the king of Owmead falls, we've lost anyway."

We found him talking with Toria Deel near the north wall of the city. Rymark held a pink scrying stone he used to communicate last details to Ellias. Toria held her own scrying stone, this one with a green cast. I could hear a voice coming from the stone, but I was too far away to make out the words.

Rymark nodded to me. "Lady Deel's idea," he said. "Her apprentice is far more useful to us as a scout. If he can stay hidden and tell us where Cesla's men will be, we can shift men to the point of attack."

The sun sank below the horizon, an inexorable death that cooled the air with its dying. I tried to ignore the symbolism. From the north and the south I heard a moan that built into a wail as thousands of voices cried in their damnation. We followed Rymark as he ascended ladders to the tallest roof on the northern wall. I looked out over the low parapet to darkness. No one had lit the watchfires.

I waited for my eyes to adjust, and after a moment I could see smudges of color shifting on the outer wall.

"Any injured soldier who can still draw a bow has been placed there," Rymark said. "We'll see how well Toria Deel's hunters do."

A door in my mind from the last war tried to open, and I forced it shut, strained with the effort to keep it closed. One of the memories escaped, and I relived the terror of being hopelessly outnumbered. Like Fess, Lelwin, and the rest. "Can they last until dawn?"

Rymark turned from his inspection of the wall to face me. "I don't know if *we* can." Something in my expression, some fear or resignation must have spurred him to continue. "The practice of war will always be an exercise in managed chaos, Lord Dura. I've seen great warriors die in their first battle, undone by circumstances they could never have anticipated, and I've seen fools live to old age after surviving countless battles and their own idiocy."

The king's diplomatic answer only served to confirm my fears. "How outnumbered are they?"

He shook his head. "At least ten to one."

"They're all going to die," I whispered.

Rymark looked at me, a reminder one of his gifts was physical. "I heard you were a priest," he said.

"Almost."

"Then say a prayer or light a candle, Lord Dura. We're not dead yet. Neither are they."

Moments later Cesla's men came pouring out of the fields in a wave, howling for blood, and there was no time for talking. Still favoring one leg, Bolt left to help man the wall. I moved to follow, but Gael and Rory closed ranks.

The hours passed in a series of attacks, each defended with the aid of Fess's scouting and those who fought in the fields outside of Treflow. Untutored though I was, I understood the flow of battle. "It comes down to this," I said.

Rory shook his head. "How can Rymark make sense of this?" he said, peering into the dark. "It's just people running in to attack and retreating."

"Cesla's probing," I said. "Rymark doesn't have enough men to man the entire city. He's counting on Fess to tell him where the next attack will be."

Gael's face blanched. "How long will it be before Cesla attacks from two directions at once?"

I'd been trying not to ask that question or even think it. "If he suspects Rymark is short on men, not long," I said.

CHAPTER 67

On the streets below us, men with torches came running from the west to climb ladders and man the wall. I edged closer to the king. "We're halfway to dawn, Lord Dura," he said. "Most of Lelwin's men we put on the walls are down. We're going to have to light the fires."

He spoke into Toria Deel's scrying stone, a warning for Fess and those beyond the wall. Then, at his signal, men on the parapet dropped torches. They spun and fluttered to land on piles of broken furniture and wood scavenged from the buildings in Treflow. Bluish flames licked at the naptha and oil and leapt across the dried wood. The area beyond the walls emerged from darkness accompanied by screams of frustration.

Hundreds of the cries changed into roars of pain, and grim satisfaction wreathed Rymark's expression. He turned to me. "We may yet make it through the night."

"What did you do?" I asked.

"I had Lelwin hide her men behind them, keeping them in reserve. When we lit the fires, his men were temporarily blinded."

I looked east and west, hopeful. "Will it work again?"

"No," Rymark said. "Not against any commander with sense, and if I was foolish enough to try I'd lose Lelwin and all the rest. We've put a dent in his forces on the north wall, and if Lelwin and her men are still alive, they're going to be more than just a distraction for Cesla."

Fess's voice came from the stone, piercing the air. "We've lost Wag."

The blood drained from Toria Deel's face, and she wavered on her feet. "How?"

Fess's voice reverberated through the crystal. "He ran off to the east side of the city."

Unexpected hope took my breath, and I reached out to grab Rymark's arm. "It's Pellin. Wag's found him. You have to get everyone you can to the east gate."

He shook his head. "That's exactly what we have to avoid. Cesla thinks he's coming up from the south. We need to make sure he continues to think that." Rymark spun away, snapping orders that sent men. "Have Fess get as many of Lelwin's men around to the east as he can," he told Toria Deel. "Have them stay hidden."

"For how long?" she asked.

Rymark's head jerked in a single nod. "He'll know."

I watched as the king pulled his scrying stone free and hailed Ellias. "Pull together any men you can spare by the south gate," he said. "Have them mounted for a sortie."

"How many?" Ellias asked.

Rymark paused to look at me. "You know Cesla's mind as well as any here, Dura. Too few men and he'll know it's a feint. Too many and we're throwing away lives we'll need later."

"Your Majesty," I said. "I'm not a man of war. I don't know."

"Ellias," Rymark called into the stone. "Use volunteers unless you're short of two thousand. If needed, draw the rest by lot. Give them the best horses and have them ride in wedge formation as deep into the enemy as they can."

"When do you want me to send them out?" Ellias asked.

"On my order," Rymark said. He turned to Toria Deel. "The second Wag finds the Eldest, I want to know how far away they are."

Silence descended on the rooftop, and I could hear the rush of my heartbeat in my ears. Bolt rejoined us, sweating and smelling of smoke. Rory handed him a waterskin, his words rushing over each other. "Is war always like this?" he asked.

Bolt gestured toward me. "Ask him. My fights have always been a bit more private."

I checked the door in my mind that led to my memories of the last battle I'd been in. "Every man interprets the fighting and bloodshed in his own way, but if you're referring to bursts of action followed by tense waiting, then the answer is yes. War is quiet dread followed by moments of abject terror. Even the winners are marked by it."

Gael shook her head. "What's taking them so long?"

Foolishly, I looked east, searching from some sign of Pellin in the darkness. "Wag can pick up a scent from miles away, but he's trying to protect Fess and Lelwin as well. They can only travel as fast as she can."

I waited there on the rooftop while my heartbeat rocked me, looking east where the sun refused to rise. Bolt's hands flexed over and over again, his right drifting across his body every few seconds to touch the hilt of his sword. Rory spun daggers through his fingers as he gazed into the darkness. Gael reached out and took my hand in hers.

"We have him." Fess's voice, quiet, broke the silence, and we exhaled in unison. "We're about four miles out." Tears coursed down Toria's face as she held her stone aloft.

"Bring the Eldest to the east gate," Rymark ordered. "We're going to lure Cesla's men to the south." He pulled his scrying stone free. "Ellias, can you hear me?"

The king of Moorclaire's voice answered in return. "I can."

"Send them now," Rymark said. "Have them push south until you signal them to retreat."

We descended from the rooftop and moved to the east wall, where Rymark took command of the watch. Half an hour later, Fess's voice came through Toria's stone. "We're within bowshot," he said. "Open the gates."

By the time I climbed down from the wall, Pellin and the rest were streaming inside. Wag came in last, a gash in his left shoulder. Blood spatters covered Lelwin, but oddly, she hadn't redonned her veil against the dim light near the gate and I wondered which personality held ascendancy.

A dozen paces away, I saw Rymark speaking into his crystal.

"Ellias's volunteers?" I asked.

The king shook his head, once. "Gone."

I bowed my head to say the antidon, but Rymark's voice cut across my prayer. "If you want to honor their memory, Dura, make sure we don't join them."

Pellin approached and took me by the arm. If a man could look more used up than the Eldest, I didn't know how. "It's time for us to take care of your vault," he said.

I looked at Toria Deel and attempted a smile that probably didn't take. "Congratulations, my lady," I said. "I'm about to grant you your fondest wish."

I'd hoped she would smile or respond in kind, but banter didn't seem to be part of Elanian culture. "Not my fondest," she said.

In the square outside the counting house, Pellin stopped us. "It has to be done here, where we can see the light of the sun and we have to hurry. Dawn is coming."

The rest of the Vigil gathered around me with our guards and the rulers standing watch over us. "How is this done?" I asked Pellin.

He looked to each member of the Vigil. "The fight to free Elieve's mind took everything from Igesia, and he was stronger in the gift than I." He took a deep breath. "We must fight our way inside the vault in your mind and use the power of our gift to hold it open until dawn. The threads that came for you before, Lord Dura, are as nothing. Now, they will be as thick as vipers."

Pellin turned to Rymark. "We must expose Lord Dura to the light of day, while his vault is still open."

The king of Owmead issued orders to his guards. "Create a defensible perimeter around the square," he said, "and put every archer we can on the buildings." He turned to address the Eldest. "If Cesla's men don't withdraw at dawn, that's going to make for an interesting confrontation. They'll be ordinary, but we'll be outnumbered. We can't defend the square for more than a few moments."

Pellin nodded. "Consider the worst possibilities and plan for those," he said.

"That's the soldier's maxim," Rymark replied.

Gael shouldered her way between Ellias and Rymark to stand by me. "I'll stay by your side as long as I can," she said. Then she leaned in close so that only I could hear her. "You must live."

For once I had no desire to dispense with the polite pretensions others used to hide from their grief. I didn't say anything about being dispensable or how the need for Cesla's defeat outweighed my need to live. She knew. "Your eyes are like slate," I said. "They only look that way when you're angry."

One of her hands found the back of my neck and pulled me close. Our foreheads touched. "Or scared."

"When you're bantering with me, they're a deep rich blue, like the sky at sunset," I said.

Her mouth quivered as she tried to offer some lighthearted jest, but after a moment she shook her head. "Then come back and see them that color, Willet." She pulled away, making room.

Pellin and the rest of the Vigil closed in around me, and I prayed in desperation. Mirren and Fess had less experience in the gift than I, and the only time I'd fought within another's mind, I'd been trapped there.

Pellin paused, looking at me. "Your vault has to be open."

I knew what he needed. "My memories from the war are the key."

Bolt came forward to wrap his arms around me. "It seems to me I've done this before."

As one, Pellin, Toria, Mirren, and Fess put their hands on my head. Within the confines of my mind, I welcomed them to my construct and showed them where I kept my memories of war. I'd modeled it after Custos's sanctuary in Bunard. Pellin opened a door into my past and lifted a stack of parchment sheets. Oddly, I wondered what had happened to Custos—and if he had anyone to bring him figs.

Then the past came for me.

I stood rooted to the spot, my feet refusing the command to run. The forest, the arrow, or the mercy stroke? "No one survives the Darkwater."

The sergeant smiled, the long puckered scar across his forehead dimpling with the expression. "We have a saying south of the strait, Norlander. 'If there is no second, it's because the first hasn't been tried.'"

The hiss of an arrow broke the spell binding my feet. "I hope you have a saying for surviving the forest." I ducked behind a bole two paces across. The mercenaries followed and we headed deeper into the gloom.

The men gathered into a tight mass as the light faded from the thick canopy and the dying sun. "Ben, split the men into two squads of six, four to watch each point, one to watch the floor, and the last to watch overhead." Strange smells, sweet and acrid, filled my nose, and I turned westward in an attempt to make our stay in the forest as brief as possible. "I'll take the point on the lead group."

Just before night fell, we improvised torches. Darkness closed in. A hundred paces in, some instinct warned me. I turned searching for the men behind me. Ben's squad had vanished, no longer trailing behind us. "Curse it," I said. "Where are they?"

"We have to return for them," one of the men said. "We do not leave our countrymen behind."

"We can't stay here," I said. "If we can get out of the forest quickly enough, we might escape its poison."

The southerners around me nodded. "Then let us find our brothers quickly."

We backtracked to the last spot I'd seen Ben's squad, but there was no one there, and when I bent to examine the ground by torchlight, the forest floor was undisturbed. Panic made the air thick. When I stood, only three men stood with me. My torch made enough light to see perhaps twenty feet in any direction. Nothing moved.

"This place is cursed," I said. "Stay if you want, but I will not." I ran, trying to retrace our steps, but the forest betrayed me. Everywhere I went, the floor appeared undisturbed. Alone, I turned, trying to find west, but in searching for Ben and his squad, I'd gotten turned around. I peered harder, searching the darkness for any hint of light that might indicate the setting sun.

There! A glow in the darkness like the faintest witch light appeared, but it eluded me. For hours I ran until my soul became parched for light, but the black canopy of the forest never receded, and I imagined that I had died on the battlefield and some lightless hell had taken me as punishment for forsaking my vow to be a priest.

I slowed to a walk as my feet hit mud. Then they splashed water. How many days had I been in the forest?

I came to the shore of a lake bordered by massive cypress and sycamore trees, their trunks and leaves twisted and blackened. Dim moonlight glinted on the surface, but the glow I had chased was gone. A man knelt in the distance, his arms thrust to the elbows in the water. The cords of his neck strained as though he worked to lift a ponderous weight, and his eyes stared through me, unseeing, witnessing horrors.

I left the footing of tree roots to approach him, flinging my arms for balance as my feet sank through a depth of mud to find purchase on something smooth and hard. I reached down through centuries of detritus and decay, curious.

"No!" the man kneeling in front of me cried. "I cannot hold!"

But I was dead already. Too much time had passed since I'd entered the forest. I pushed through the mud until my hand touched the foundation I stood upon, metal smooth beyond the ironsmith's art.

My head filled with the presence of another.

"You are mine, little one," a voice said. Pain erupted in my thoughts as strand upon strand of black evil spun a web through my mind, attaching itself to every memory I owned. Not one remained free. "I have claimed you and sealed you to me with the power of my name." Fire flared in my mind as though I'd been branded, marked to the depth of my soul. "Sealed with my name," the voice said, "you are ever and always mine."

"No," a second voice whispered, for my ears only. "You are not, though your redemption will be incomplete and its cost beyond calculation." A song ghosted through my mind as black strands snapped, freeing most of my memories, but not all. "We will meet again, Willet. I am Ealdor."

"Return to your people," the first voice said.

I rose from the water, relinquishing my touch. The man before me still strained, caught in his motionless struggle. I could do nothing for him or for the figures passing me, as I stumbled from the waters, on their way to damnation.

Light tore through the forest.

CHAPTER 68

Pellin slipped behind Dura's eyes to be joined an instant later by Toria Deel, Fess, and Mirren. The river of memories and emotions that defined Dura flowed by—broad, swift, with the multicolored strands that indicated the strength and tenor of his past. A strand so dark that it ate the surrounding light floated near the surface. "That's it," Pellin said, reaching for it. "Be ready. The evil of the Darkwater will try to consume you when his vault opens. It will know we're here. Focus your thoughts like a blade and slash any of the attacks that come for you. They may appear as thin as strands or as thick as vipers, and they're quick."

He grabbed the memory and entered Dura's descent into the Dark-water, holding it so that Dura would experience the memory over and over.

Violence exploded with a soundless concussion. Threads darker than pitch came from everywhere, but the Vigil were ready. Slashing with their gift, they cut through the threads in midflight.

"We have to go to his vault," Pellin said. Entering the stream that defined Dura, he sank below the river of recollection until he saw the black scroll. Sensing their presence, the vault no longer sent threads against them, but ropes as thick as Pellin's arm. Fess and Mirren slashed with their gift, but they lacked the strength and focus that came with years of practice. Their strikes landed but failed to cut all the way through. Each rope that came for them required two or three cuts to sever.

And the ropes were coming faster.

Two attacked Fess simultaneously, one taking a high line as the other wrapped around his leg, pulling him from his feet. Toria and Mirren cut them away and Fess stood, but his strikes were weaker.

"We have to get inside," Pellin said. He broke into a run, his gift slashing before him with Toria, Mirren, and Fess following, cutting their way through a hedge of evil. The sounds of whiplike strikes and snapping threads filled the cavern of Dura's mind.

Dura's vault loomed above them, larger, far larger than Elieve's had been. Pellin searched for some snatch of prayer from the liturgy, but panic filled him. "Aer, help me," he gasped. Thrusting forward with his gift, he tore a hole in its surface and stepped through.

And found the image of Willet Dura standing inside. Toria, Fess, and Mirren slipped in beside him and the tear closed behind them, trapping them. There would be no retreat—victory was their only hope.

Dura shook his head. "I was in the forest."

Pellin gathered his strength and slashed, using his gift as a broadsword that cut through a swath of waving tentacles, but the effort left him gasping. "We're inside your vault. Somehow, you're here as well." A rope shot out of the darkness, coming for Dura's back like the bolt of a crossbow. Toria cut it from the air. "Help us," Pellin said. "We have to read the writing on the inside of your vault and keep it open until dawn."

Dura turned as a tentacle as thick as his leg came for him, and he slashed at it, severing it with one strike, but as the end fell, writhing, to disappear in a puff of oily smoke, he doubled in pain, clutching his belly. Agony twisted his face and put him on his hands and knees. A moment later, he pushed himself to his feet, his face deathly calm.

"I understand," he said to no one.

A sinewy rope of purest black came out of the darkness, wrapped around Toria's middle and lifted her from her feet. She screamed as it coiled, tightening. Fess leapt, catching her and hacking at it with his gift, but while his strokes injured it and thick smoke poured from it like ichor, it remained intact.

Dura stepped forward, his hands raised, and spun, cutting the air with his arms as his gift lashed out. The tentacle holding Toria parted like silk beneath a sword, and she fell. Dura curled in agony, screaming as though he'd been gutted. Mirren crouched by him, searching as he thrashed in pain.

461

She looked at Pellin. "There's no wound."

"Guard us," Pellin said to the others and knelt by Dura's side. "What, Dura? What do you understand?"

Tears streamed from him as he spoke through clenched teeth. "It's not just the forest," he said. "It's me." He clutched his midsection. "Oh, Aer, have mercy."

Strands came at them for what felt like hours, numerous as threads in a spider's web. Toria panted with each strike of her gift and Mirren tottered on her feet. Fess wore the look of a man who knew he would be used up long before the battle ended.

"Help me lift him," Pellin cried. Ropes curled around his arms, pinning him.

Fess slashed at them, hacking desperately, but it was as though he wielded a dull cleaver now. They pulled Dura to his feet. Agony stretched his face as he saw the multitude of strands. "Oh, Aer, again? Do I have to do it again?"

He raised his hands, his fingers curled like claws, and brought them raking down toward his side. Dozens upon dozens of ropes fell severed to the ground and the air filled with oily black smoke. Dura threw back his head and screamed. On it went, his cry scaling upward until Pellin covered his ears.

"We have to help him, Eldest," Toria said. "He can't do this on his own."

He slashed at a group of threads that came for him. Were they weaker now? For a moment, there was a lull in the attack and he gestured at the walls. "Memorize the writing." Glyphs and runes filled the inside of Dura's vault just as they had Elieve's, but Pellin couldn't tell if they were the same and tentacles of black obscured the writing, a writhing nest of snakes that blocked his vision. "Move. We have to see the rest."

At his feet, Dura whimpered, huddling over hurts they could neither see nor heal. Weeping, he struggled to his feet, half bent to protect his middle. "Read it," he said, his face consumed by pain Pellin couldn't understand. "I'll help clear the threads." Screaming as though he eviscerated himself, he wielded his gift, recoiling in agony with the death of each strand.

"This is killing him, Eldest," Toria cried. "What's happening?"

Pellin shook his head. "I don't know. Elieve was absent in the battle for her mind. Some aspect of the gift enables Dura to be present and aid us, but each thread he cuts wounds him in some way."

Threads shot out of the darkness toward them, pulling Pellin's attention away and the four of them worked to keep themselves free while Dura aimed strokes of excruciation at the walls of his vault. Pellin turned, taking just enough time to memorize the writing. For a moment almost too brief to be real, he thought he spotted writing that differed from the stylized glyphs and looping whorls of the Darkwater. "There." He pointed. "Willet, aim there."

Dura's mouth stretched in agony as he slashed at the black vines that pulsed where Pellin indicated. The threads receded, recoiling in pain beneath the strikes of Dura's gift. Then they returned in a boiling mass. "Again!" Pellin extended his hand, aiming the focus of his thoughts.

"There!" he shouted. Dura's gift opened a section of the wall and Pellin stared. Names. Words he recognized as names stood outlined against the unrelieved black of the wall.

"Eldest!" Toria screamed. "Help us!"

Pellin took just long enough to commit the names to memory before turning. Threads encompassed Fess, working to crawl into his mouth and nose. Already he was choking and though he worked to free himself from the strands, the blows of his gift no longer cut the tentacles that came for him. He coughed, struggling to breathe.

Anger fiercer than any Pellin had experienced in the long expanse of his life flooded through him. Always the innocent died to save the guilty. How many had died for Cesla's pride already? How many more would perish for the Fayits' arrogance? No, he would not bear it any longer! He slashed with the fire of his gift, his anger giving him strength that burned through tentacles of evil and left them smoking, writhing to escape.

Given respite from the attack that had choked him, Fess tried to renew his assault. Lines of fatigue etched his face. He had used too much of himself. Beside him, Toria and Mirren stood back to back. The newest member of the Vigil defended against the threads that came leaping at them from the dark, while Toria strove to clear the walls.

Each time the battle stalled or threatened to go against them, Dura would fight, screaming in agony.

"Stop this," Toria yelled as he fell again. "You're killing yourself."

Dura shook his head, scattering tears as he squeezed his eyes shut and pulled a shuddering breath. "You don't understand. It's my fault there are so many."

Sensing their momentary weakness, a cascade of black came for them out of the dark. Pellin's anger, so fierce a moment ago, guttered, waning, and his heart shuddered, laboring to find its rhythm.

He turned to the prostate figure at his feet. "Willet, I don't have the strength of Igesia. I'm sorry. We must have your help."

He didn't answer.

"He can't help you. He's mine, and I'm coming to collect what belongs to me." The voice emanated from all around them as threads and ropes of black stopped just short of them. Pellin stilled and the rest of the Vigil mirrored him, searching the walls for the speaker.

"He belongs to Aer," Fess yelled his defiance.

"If he is Aer's," the voice mocked, "then let Aer show himself and aid him."

The threads surrounding them coalesced into a trunk of glossiest black, shimmering in the air, a colossus of evil that threatened to sweep them away. As Pellin watched, the threads unwound to stand suspended in the air once more. Cesla stood among them, his eyes purest black. "If Aer will not deign to show himself, I will." He smiled. "Greetings, brother."

"I know you, Atol Bealu," Pellin spat. "You may wear Cesla's likeness, but it is no more than a mask."

"How little you know," Cesla crooned. "Are you surprised that I claim your kinship even now?" He laughed. "Your brother hasn't died. He lives still within this shell, horrified at the cost of his pride." His black eyes glittered. "Like him you will all live and be mine. You cannot win. With every entrance into the forest, my power grows. Even if your defenses hold, you will all belong to me when the Darkwater engulfs your city. Do you think your kings and queens, huddling around you in fear, will save you?"

A realization came to Pellin, and he pulled Fess close and whispered into his mind. "Cesla must be somewhere close. Find him."

CHAPTER 69

Fess blinked, surrounded by the monarchs of the north. Runners flooded into and out of the square. In the eastern sky the first hint of the coming dawn marked the horizon. "Cesla is close," he yelled at Rymark. "We need to attack."

The king of Owmead shook his head. "The best we can do is hold until sunrise. I don't have the men for a counterattack."

Fess grabbed the king's arm, desperate to make him understand. "He's too strong. If we can't get to Cesla and distract him, it won't matter."

Rymark spun, knocking his hand away. "The walls are falling! I don't have the men!"

Fess searched the square. Willet stood, surrounded by Pellin and the rest of the Vigil, their hands still on his head. Ringed around them were the monarchs, waiting for their opportunity to call the Fayit, an opportunity growing less likely by the second. Outside the ring stood their guards, the most physically gifted of each kingdom, waiting, the last line of defense. Standing to one side in the shadows, Lelwin waited with the remnants of the force she'd taken outside the walls.

"I don't need your men," Fess said to Rymark. "Wag!"

The sentinel came running out of the shadows covering Lelwin. Fess put his hand on his head. *The man who stole your litter mate is here in the city,* Fess said. *Can you find him?*

His smell is everywhere, Master. The scents of him and the forest are all over the city.

Is there a direction where it's stronger than any other?

The sentinel broke contact to trot around the boundaries of the

465

square, stopping at each alley or street that led away to raise his muzzle and test the air. He came back and put his head beneath Fess's hand, staring. *The wind is swirling, but it's strongest from there, Master.*

Guide us as quickly as you can, Wag. We must find Cesla before sunrise. He raised his hand, pointing at Lelwin. "If you want vengeance that matters, then you and your men will come with me."

They ran through the darkened streets toward the west wall. As they turned the last corner, the sounds of battle swept over them. Soldiers screamed in pain and fury, fighting to contain men from the Darkwater who moved among them, darting shadows who left death in their wake. Light blazed and died in pockets as the defenders fought for advantage.

"Where is he, Wag?" Fess yelled above the clamor of steel and butchery.

Wag scented the air for a moment before going on point toward a shadow of a building where the torchlight failed to penetrate. Fess grabbed Lelwin's arm and pointed. "There!"

She barked an order and a hundred of her veiled soldiers nocked and fired into the shadows.

Screams of pain and rage shattered the air.

Threads erupted from darkness, coming from the walls, coming from everywhere. Pellin slashed, but already the black snakes had wrapped around Mirren and more were coming. Dura pulled himself to his feet like a man being forced to his own execution, but the edge of his gift cut through the threads and tentacles that threatened them. The severed ends dispersed into greasy smoke that thickened around them until they were lost to sight.

When the smoke cleared, Dura lay on his face like a dead man, but the rest of them stood. A solitary thread, no bigger around then his wrist, came for Pellin out of the darkness, but he destroyed it with a thought. Stillness settled on Dura's vault.

"Is it over, Eldest?" Mirren asked.

Pellin shook his head. "No. We must clear the walls."

"Why?" Toria asked. "The writing is beyond us."

He held his answer, fearing the evil that lurked in the darkness of Dura's vault would hear. Instead he turned from the center to face the nearest wall. "Guard me. If you need help, summon Lord Dura."

"If he can be summoned," Mirren said.

466

"He's alive," Pellin said. "Everything here ends if he dies." Raising hands that trembled with exhaustion, he cut at the mass of black that covered the wall. Perhaps it was because Dura's vault was older than Elieve's. Possibly, the disease in Dura's mind ran far deeper than any of them could guess, but the vines shrugged off his attacks, and he feared exhaustion would take him before he was halfway done. One by one the other members of the Vigil turned to help him, but the threads refused to give ground.

"If we cannot uncover the walls before dawn," Pellin said, "the light will destroy his vault and the information within it. We must not fail in this."

But their progress was too slow. Even as their gift reckoned time, they would never clear the walls of Atol Bealu's malice before sunrise. "Willet," Pellin cried. "Stand and fight!"

Dura groaned, gasping in pain as he struggled to rise. "Cesla," he panted. "The key."

"What do you mean?" Pellin asked. "How is Cesla the key?"

Dura doubled over in pain as he reduced another attack to wisps of smoke. "He didn't want us to know who he was." He ducked his head. "Why? Why would it matter?"

Pellin's mind raced. "Atol is torturing him."

Dura, curled almost in two, shook his head as he gasped in pain. "They wouldn't care."

A memory of Elieve came to Pellin, on the ground and shaking as she tried to reconcile memories that didn't match her body or spirit. Intuition burst in his mind like a flash of phos-fire. "They needed his mind to make his body work."

Dura nodded. "He's still there, trapped."

Pellin whirled, but there was no sign of Cesla now, only the attacks that came from Dura's vault. "Cesla!" he screamed. "Fight with us. We need you." He turned, searching. "I always loved you. I know you're tired. Help us!"

Toria stumbled, falling to one knee. "Was it so difficult with Elieve?" she gasped.

Pellin shook his head. "No, but Igesia was powerful beyond reckoning. He used himself without regard." He thought about that for a moment. "No," he amended. "Even before his final apotheosis, Igesia's attacks were far stronger than mine."

"Why?" Toria pressed.

Pellin would have demurred, feigning ignorance, but his instinct told him differently. He knew. "Igesia had a capacity for love that surpassed me. In the few hours he knew Elieve, he loved her like a favored daughter."

Already, Pellin's mind accused him, throwing comparisons to Igesia at him, and he desired nothing more than to return to his fight rather than admit he was so much less than the Honored One who died for a girl he hardly knew. "His love gave him strength in the gift that astonished me."

Toria lifted her head, calling with the longing of a child. "Cesla, I loved you. You never wanted this. Please!"

Turning to the wall, she raised her hands and attacked. Wherever her gaze landed, threads and tentacles withered and fell away. Writing appeared, strange glyphs comprising a language of vast complexity. Instinctively, Pellin realized the authors of the language would have to be immortal. The writing made his language appear crude and rushed by comparison.

Tears streamed down Toria's face. He added his strength to hers. With slashes of their gift the vines parted from the walls, and each time they were slower to return. The attacks ceased and Mirren added her strength to theirs. Together they wielded domere with the grim efficiency of executioners.

Then it ended.

Dura lay on the floor of his vault, unmoving. Pellin turned to the others. Each of them would bear scars within their souls of the battle, and it would be turnings of the moon before any were strong again. Toria and Mirren sat, watchful of the darkness, untrusting of their victory. He couldn't blame them. He turned a slow circle, his gaze taking in the glyphs of the Fayit language, memorizing it.

"Go," Pellin said to Mirren. "See how the kings and queens fare. Time passes strangely in the delve and even more so in battle. Determine the hour and return."

Pellin settled himself to wait. Even a few moments might feel like hours within Dura's mind, but Mirren returned almost immediately. "Dawn is here. The sun is about to clear the horizon."

He had only to wait for a second. Light flared in Dura's mind.

CHAPTER 70

I opened my eyes to wan sunlight outside the counting house in Tre-flow. While Gael and the rest of the Vigil stared at me, I searched my mind. "It's gone," I held out my hands. They touched me, briefly, and I couldn't help but notice the pain of fatigue that pinched their expressions. Even so little effort was beyond us. The thought of ever using my gift again made me want to weep.

The sun continued its rise off the horizon, its light strengthening as it changed from red to orange to yellow. I heard the sound of footsteps just before I saw Fess and Lelwin come into view from the west quarter of the city. The bodies of men and women were strewn everywhere.

Fess bowed to Pellin and the assembled kings and queens.

"Genuflections can wait for another time," Rymark said. "What happened?"

Wonder lit Fess's eyes, and he wore a smile. If it was less carefree than he would have worn months ago, I was still gratified to see it. "We were beat, Your Majesty," he said. "They came pouring over the west wall, spending men and women until they took control. We fell back and fought house to house, slowing them with bow fire." He looked at Lelwin. "Several times Cesla sought to withdraw and we pursued."

"Just before dawn the enemy went crazy. They started attacking each other." He gestured west at the bodies strewn everywhere. "I thought it was a trick at first, but they kept on. We put down as many as we could."

"Is Cesla dead?"

Fess shook his head. "Just before dawn, he took the last of his men and fled back over the wall of the city."

I turned to the rulers. "We have to hurry before he gets too far away."

"You all need rest, Dura," Rymark said. "And there are men and women who need whatever healing we can give them. This can wait."

"No," I said. "It can't. They're still trying to open the prison."

"It's daylight," the king of Owmead said.

"Not in the Darkwater," I said, looking at Pellin. "I remember."

The sunlight did little to relieve his pallor, and tremors worked their way up and down his arms. Only Allta's support kept the Eldest upright, but when he spoke his voice was clear. "Lord Dura is correct. We cannot wait."

They formed the circle there in the light of the morning with Pellin and me inside. "I remember the names," I said.

He nodded. "I have them as well, along with the writing on the wall."

"The name of the Darkwater."

"Aer willing." His expression turned grave. "I can't read it, Willet."

Something too desperate to be called hope ran through me. "I think they can teach us." I turned to face the Everwood, missing my friend, but unexpected lightness filled my heart as I lifted my voice. "*Daelean Eriescu Allorianae Rihtmunuc*, answer the call. According to the binding you placed upon Fayit, you are summoned." I didn't wait for him to cross whatever distance separated us before I continued. "*Storan Midriashech Zelwaunil Rihtmunuc*, come! As you have sworn and bound yourself, aid us."

Within the circle they appeared, larger than men, overshadowing us all, but with their heads bowed in submission. "What is your command?" they intoned.

I pointed to myself, Pellin, and the rest of the Vigil as I replied. "Teach those of us in the Vigil the language of the Fayit," I said. "Then abide until you are released."

When they lifted their heads, the light in each gaze was fierce, jubilant. They passed among and through us, imparting the knowledge of their language, much as Custos had shown me how to read the ancient language of my own race.

When they finished, they returned to the circle where Pellin and I waited. Equipped with the knowledge of their language, I bowed

my apologies. "Your pardon for pronouncing your names so poorly,"
I said.

They smiled in return. "The binding Aer had us weave on the
Fayit is incomprehensibly powerful, but also elegant. It recognized
your intent," Daelan said. "Yet I thank you for your graciousness. It
has been a long time since I heard my name in full. I'm surprised by
how much I've missed it."

I nodded. "That brings me to my first question. The binding you
created—is it designed to be used only by the descendants of Cuman,
the first man?"

Daelan and Storan nodded as one, but I saw the ghost of a smile
begin to play over their expressions. They may have suspected my
intention. "And does the binding apply to any and all Fayit, no matter
who or how changed they are?"

Now their smiles shone like the sun. "Eldest," I said. "Before you
make the calling, might I suggest that you share the knowledge you
hold with the rest of the Vigil."

Pellin nodded, but grief clouded his eyes. "Toria, come," he called.
"Fess and Mirren, I need the two of you to delve me as well." He
pointed south. "But I command that you, Fess and Mirren, withdraw
immediately afterward. We will contact you if we are successful. If we
fail, get to the southern continent as quickly as you can." He turned,
searching until his gaze landed on his apprentice, and he pointed.
"Take Mark's memories with you as well. Seek out Dukasti. Tell him
the north has fallen."

Without ceremony we touched him, receiving his memories of the
writing within my vault. Impatience thundered with each beat of my
heart. I had no idea how far Cesla might have gotten or how close
those in his power were to breaking the prison.

But now that we came to the moment, Pellin turned to face me.
"This is your victory more than any other, Willet. Why do you defer
to me?"

"Because he's your brother," I said. "His pride destroyed him, but
Atol trapped him within his own mind, taking pleasure at his pain,
denying him the release of death. I thought it would comfort you to
know that he received his final mercy at your hand."

"Thank you." Pellin raised his hands and began the call. As long
as Daelan and Storan's names were, Atol Bealu's far exceeded them.

It took me a moment before I realized his new name was a twisted compilation of every Fayit whose spirit he'd taken unto himself, but Pellin never flinched or faltered.

Later, much later, the cadence of syllables cascaded upward, signaling he'd come to the end of Atol's name. "You are summoned," Pellin commanded. "By the binding placed on the Fayit and by the grace of Aer, you are bound. You are commanded to come to me with all haste. You must answer the call."

Pellin lowered his arms, and we waited. Toria and the rulers cast about, searching. "It will take some time," I said. "They are bound to Cesla's body. He will have to travel here physically." I looked up at the morning sun. "I pray the binding forces him here before dark."

An hour passed before Daelan and Storan jerked and turned to face north. Within minutes we heard a keening wail, and from the northern part of the city we witnessed a figure racing toward us, his legs churning faster than the purest gifted among humans could run. But his hands covered his eyes.

As he grew closer, it was clear rage and fury comprised his scream, not grief. He emerged from the rubble and ruin of Treflow to stand before us, wet from crossing the river and panting with fury.

"Greetings, Atol," Pellin said. "I would offer you the chance of repentance and the rite of haeling, if you wish it."

Daelan and Storan shook their heads. "It is not possible."

Cesla jerked and writhed, straining against invisible bonds. "You and your kind are motes of dust. Nothing more."

"You are defeated, Atol," Storan said. "Again."

"Defeated?" Cesla said. "Do you think our war is over? Do you presume to believe you've won?" Scorn twisted his features until I thought the bones in his face might break. "Look at you. Deprived of corporeal presence, you've reduced yourselves to shadows." He flung out his arm, using the other to keep his eyes covered against the light. "True—you've won a great battle." He laughed. "But how will you ever erase its memory from those who fought it? They will come to me seeking gold or aurium or knowledge. At the last, you will not be able to stand against me."

"He has spoken his coda," Storan said to Pellin. "According to the binding set on the Fayit, he is yours to command."

"For how long?" Pellin asked.

472

"A day."

I watched him shake his head. "I have no wish to be in your company for so long," he said to Atol. "But I do wish to speak with my brother. Step aside and make room for him to talk to me. Now."

I watched as the malevolence faded from Cesla's expression, and the man who had been the greatest holder of domere in the history of the Vigil emerged.

"Greetings, brother," Pellin said. "Well met this fine morning."

Cesla lowered the arm covering his eyes like a man expecting pain and turned his face toward the sun. "It is." He smiled past rue and pain. "It is a very fine morning."

I hoped I didn't imagine the joy and relief that abided in his features as well.

"Why did you delve the forest?" Pellin asked him.

Cesla dropped his head until he gazed at his brother once more. "For every reason you might suppose, and more, but mostly because I wanted to know the truth of the forest. That was my fatal mistake. I equated knowledge with truth." He looked around. "So much blood on my hands."

"Was it?" Pellin asked. "A fatal mistake, I mean."

"Thank Aer, yes," he said. "As soon as you banish Atol and his kindred spirits back to their prison, I will die. Only their life force has sustained me this far. I should have perished at the first touch of their prison." He glanced toward me. "I heard you in his mind. And Toria. I helped as much as I could."

"I've missed you, Cesla," Pellin said. "I'm sorry I let my jealousy and self-doubt keep me from telling you how much I loved and admired you."

"Your admiration is misplaced," he said. "You have acquired knowledge and achieved a victory that was beyond me." He sighed. "I'd like to go now, brother. You'll have quite a mess to clean up, but it's better than the alternative."

"Farewell, Cesla," Pellin said. "May Aer grant you mercy."

He blinked. "I hope so." When he lifted his arm to cover his eyes, his face twisted with contempt once again. "Banish me then, before your cloying sentiment makes me retch."

"As you wish," Pellin said. No gestures were required, but he raised his hands. "Atol, you—"

"Stop!" I yelled. Panic brought my heartbeat to a standstill.

Pellin lowered his hands as he turned to face me. I struggled to find breath. "Oh, clever, clever snake," I said. "Almost you succeeded." I turned to Pellin. "There are still people in the forest."

The Eldest's eyes went wide as the blood drained from his face. "Dear Aer in heaven." He turned back to the prisoner, his expression grim as iron. "You are commanded to restore all who are enslaved to you, Atol. Remove their vaults and erase their memories of gold and aurium in the Darkwater. Further, I command you to drive everyone from the forest before sunset and immediately kill any who remain when night falls."

Atol threw back his head and howled with rage, screaming his defeat and frustration at the heavens until his breath ran out. "Eternity is on my side," he said. "After you have returned to dust, I will be free, and I will make a mockery of Aer's intent."

"You are banished," Pellin said. "Return to your prison."

Cesla collapsed, falling to the ground, a marionette whose strings had been severed at last, but as he hit the earth his arms fell away from his eyes. His head rocked with the impact, but when he stilled, sunlight illumined him and he stared at the sun. I turned away before his gaze could capture me.

Pellin spoke to Daelan and Storan. "Is it done?"

Their gazes grew distant and they disappeared briefly before they returned. "It is. Those who sought to free Atol are leaving the forest."

"What about the prison?" I asked. "Is it intact?"

I had no experience by which to judge their expressions, but I sensed they were troubled. "It is," Daelan said. "Though it is damaged somewhat. Common iron is too brittle for aurium. The forest is littered with broken tools."

"Beware of his knowledge," Storan said. "The lure of the Darkwater will remain. The rumors of wealth within its boundaries will be hard to erase."

Pellin nodded. "Centuries of work lie ahead," he said, but joy blazed in his eyes that couldn't be denied.

"What about this pleases you, Eldest?" Toria asked.

"Something new comes," he said. "Lord Dura is cleansed of his vault. We don't have to kill those who stumble into the forest. Like Elieve, they can be healed."

474

I drew closer to the Fayit so no one else could hear me beg. "Daelan, Storan, is there any way I can talk to Ealdor again?"

"This day you will be with him where he has passed beyond the sphere of our world," Daelan said. "Have you forgotten the price that must be paid?"

I heard Gael gasp and sensed movement, but when I turned toward her she stood frozen, her face clenched and sweating with effort. The Fayit shook their heads, their hands raised in forbidding. "The price must be paid. This too is part of the binding."

Gael's cry of loss shattered the morning, a needle of sound that pierced my heart. Daelan and Storan reached for me.

CHAPTER 71

In a futile gesture, Pellin stepped between us as though he had some power or lore that could prevent Daelan and Storan from extracting the cost of their aid. "A question, if you please," he said.

For some reason they forbore, waiting. "You cannot use the binding to prevent us from collecting the price."

I pulled Pellin around to face me. "Eldest, even with you the Vigil is pitifully young, and the peace will be very nearly as difficult as the war."

He smiled. "Therefore you and Toria Deel and the rest of the Vigil will adapt to it." He turned to the Fayit. "I will pay the price."

Gael's sob of relief tore at me. She didn't see the Fayit's expression, their refusal.

"You were not part of the circle," they said. "Nor did you make the call."

Pellin's smile dropped from him. "It was I who used the knowledge of the circle to bind Atol back to his prison."

"Indeed," Daelan said.

Pellin nodded. "Will Aer allow me to pay for Lord Dura?"

Daelan and Storan withdrew from speech, but from the way they looked at each other, I suspected they were having an extended conversation. I tried to resign myself to their decision. In my heart I knew that Gael had always been too high and lofty a prize for me. I wondered if they would let me say good-bye.

"We consent," the Fayit said together.

I drew a shuddering breath that provided counterpoint to Gael's, but Pellin drew back. "A moment more, if you please."

Storan's expression showed almost human exasperation. "We will not tarry at your convenience, Eldest."

"A moment," Pellin said, "no more." Without waiting for their permission he scanned the crowd of people outside the counting house, then pointed. "Come."

Mark disentangled himself from Elieve's arms and came forward until no more than a pace separated him from the Eldest.

Pellin smiled through the tears coursing down his cheeks. "The choice is upon us, it would seem."

Mark nodded. "Too soon."

"That is the way with change, my apprentice," he said. "It is always too soon and often takes us unaware."

"What should I do, Eldest?" Mark asked.

Pellin smiled. "Trust Aer, Mark, and trust your heart." Laughter worked its way through Pellin's grief. "It is a very good heart, indeed."

Mark faced the Fayit. "Is there any way to know where Aer will send the gift once it goes free?"

Daelan and Storan grew quiet before answering. "No."

Mark glanced back at Elieve, his face rent by love and doubt. "I don't know what to do, Eldest."

Pellin nodded. "Then simply trust that Aer does. If the gift does not come to you, then know that it has gone by Aer's will to another."

"And what should I do then?"

Joy filled Pellin's expression. "Marry Elieve when the time is right and fill your house with love and children."

Pellin placed his hand on Mark's head, not in the rite of passage, but in simple blessing ancient beyond reckoning. "May Aer bless you and keep you, always."

He stepped toward the Fayit. "It's in your tradition to allow the condemned a last coda, yes?"

At their nod, Pellin turned to give us a wink and extended his arm to Daelan and Storan. "Here is mine. Will you honor it?"

They touched him and nodded to each other, sharing in his smile.

Pellin nodded. "I'm ready now, I think."

Together the Fayit extended their hands over him. At the moment they touched each other, they disappeared. Pellin collapsed, but his body fell more slowly than it should have, some grace or waning strength working to lay him gently on the ground.

I would have married Gael that very day, fearful as I was that some other calamity would prevent me, but the rulers of the north took it into their heads that a traditional wedding in Bunard would give them the opportunity to plan for an uncertain future. We dispersed the soldiers back to their kingdoms under the command of their captains—with the exception of Rymark, who insisted on gathering those few men of Owmead still able to wield a sword and march to the forest.

"Trust, but verify," he said. I couldn't fault his soldier's wisdom.

Regent Cailin and Toria Deel prevailed upon Gael to allow them to plan our wedding ceremony in Bunard. I tried to make myself scarce as we journeyed north and west through signs of war. There, I took the only stand concerning the wedding that I refused to negotiate. Custos, a priest of the Merum order, would perform the ceremony. We resigned to wait until he could be brought from Cynestol with all speed.

In the interim, Bas-solas came and went. Bunard no longer celebrated the festival, but the eclipse of the sun passed without incident. No one went mad, and most of the citizens made their way to one of the four cathedrals below the tor to pray. I think they might have actually listened to the criers this time. The Clast was nowhere to be found.

Fall had begun to give way to winter, and Custos was still a week from Bunard, when a pounding at my door startled me. Bolt and Rory seldom knocked so loud, and they rarely let others approach me. Despite our victory over Atol, they continued their vigilance, concerned that some dwimor still lived to hunt the Vigil.

I opened the door to see Jeb filling the frame, a blond-haired girl clutching his oversized hand with one of hers. The other held a charcoal pencil and a dirty piece of parchment.

I heard the pop of knuckles and checked the distance between Jeb and my guards. "Cailin refused to let me go fight at the Darkwater," he growled. "She said she'd have Aellyn taken from me even if I survived." He shifted, and I took a step back. "You did that." It wasn't a question.

I shrugged. "I did. I wanted to make sure we won the peace if we won the war."

Gael came up to put her arm around me.

"Ha! I heard you were getting married, Dura," Jeb said. He gave Gael a leering glance. "I'm surprised to find you unoccupied."

Gael smiled, and her eyes lightened to a startling blue. "What a charming suggestion. Thank you, chief reeve."

Jeb grinned. "Not anymore. The title and the headaches that go with it belong to Gareth now. I'm just a shopkeeper." He looked down at Aellyn. "I like not having to use my fists for a living."

I followed his gaze, preparing myself for sorrow, when Aellyn lifted her head to peer at me. "Who's this, Poppa?"

Jeb laughed at my expression. "An old friend, little one, and a better one than he knows."

I knelt, amazed at her focused gaze. I had no wish to intrude on the mystery of her healing, so I didn't touch her with my bare hands. "My name is Willet."

She smiled as she turned to bury her face into Jeb's leg. "She's still a little shy, especially in crowds," Jeb said. His gaze grew intense enough that I had to look away. "But I wanted her to know you, Dura." He shifted on his feet as though he were about to leave when his arms shot out to catch me in a hug that threatened a few of my ribs. "Thank you . . . for both of us."

Before I could say anything, he turned to Rory. "Watch after him. He's worth it." Then he left.

Rory laughed. "Now there's a miracle right enough, yah?"

The door closed behind Jeb and Aellyn. "And more than one, I think."

Toria Deel came to see me a few days later. By happenstance or design she found me alone in my rooms. Well, not precisely alone. Bolt and Rory still kept themselves close, playing ficheall while I read *The History of Errants*. Gael had absented herself with the excuse that she needed time away from me to put some of the finishing touches on our wedding plans.

"It's just as well she's not here," Toria Deel said.

My hackles went up, and I braced myself for a familiar argument.

"Rest easy, Lord Dura. I have no intention of talking you out of your decision, but there are matters that need to be discussed, and the fewer people involved the better."

"Such as?"

She sighed, still showing signs of a deep fatigue that all of us would carry for months. "Where to begin? Our crisis has passed, but the Vigil's purpose remains."

"To guard the forest," I said. "We know more of its nature now, but what did we accomplish?"

She cocked her head at me. "Our world was a hairsbreadth from being destroyed, Lord Dura. Atol's prison is intact, the forest has receded to its original boundaries, and for the first time in over a year we can say that no one in the north has a vault."

"But all we've done is hold," I said. "Is there no way to achieve victory?"

"You might as well ask if you can eradicate evil from the world," she said. "Be careful, Lord Dura. Cesla's thoughts ran in such directions as he grew older, and you have much in common with him already."

She turned away before I could object to the comparison. "However, I must admit," she continued, "that there are more problems coming out of our victory than I'd hoped. There is still the matter of the missing gift we've yet to find, and then there's our larger concern."

"The Fayit," I said.

Toria nodded. "Our newfound ability to call them will certainly awaken ambitions among the kings and queens, if not with those we have now, then certainly with their descendents. On top of that, we still have the problem of the forest itself. The rumors of gold Cesla planted made deep roots, and we have exactly one sentinel." Where Pellin would have paced the room, Toria simply stood and faced me. "The world is changing faster than we can manage it, Lord Dura." Her gaze became painfully direct. "How do you wish to proceed?"

My unease grew until realization hit, then it changed to horror. "You want me to be Eldest?" I couldn't seem to stop shaking my head. "Have you lost your mind?"

She tossed her wealth of dark hair and regarded me, her stare inscrutable. "That's an interesting question, considering the source, but no, I don't think I have. By tradition the most experienced member of the Vigil takes the title of Eldest, but there have been exceptions. I won't elaborate on the reasons for my decision to refuse leadership. If you accept the title, you will, of course, have the right to know them, but not change them."

"Let someone else do it," I said.

She laughed at me. "You would place this burden on one of the others? They're far too young."

I gaped. "I'm thirty."

"You have acquired centuries of experience," Toria said.

I shook my head. "Well, aren't I a lucky guy?" I ignored the barks of laughter that came from the ficheall board. "I don't want it."

Toria Deel blinked. "That is beside the point. You never wanted any of this."

"There's another reason," I said.

Her expression said plainly that she thought I was stalling.

"I went for a walk last night."

Her eyebrows communicated the depth of her unconcern. "What of it?"

I waited until she made the connection.

"Is this true?" she asked Bolt.

My guard nodded. "I followed him. We ended up near Braben's. A merchant had a pointed disagreement with a footpad. The point found its way into his chest. By the time we got there, the city watch was already on the way."

Toria Deel shrugged away my objection. "Then it's part of who you are and has nothing to do with your vault."

"I refuse."

Rory laughed. "Ha! Refusing won't do you much good if people bow and scrape while they call you Eldest and stand around waiting for you to tell them what to do."

Toria Deel allowed herself to join Rory's amusement. "He's right, you know."

In the end, I was beaten, though I did manage to wring a few concessions from her—the most important of which was to order Bolt to remain in my service until he'd trained guards for each of us. He tried to refuse, but I got the impression he objected more out of form than conviction.

When Toria turned to leave, I pulled a deep breath and called her name. "Before you go, there's something I need to show you. A promise I made to . . . a friend." The title didn't quite fit, but I didn't know what else to say. I held out my arm.

Toria looked at my bare skin, suspicious. "Is this a command, Eldest?"

I nodded, but just before she touched me I spoke again. "I'm sorry."

Her gaze narrowed, but she reached out and rested her fingers on the back of my hand. I opened the door where I'd stored Volsk's last memories and let them flow through the delve, watching as her eyes welled with the knowledge of what he'd done. She pulled her hand away, blinking tears.

"You called him friend," she accused.

"He saved Custos's life," I said. "That's good enough for me."

She nodded. "Perhaps I was hasty, comparing you to Cesla. It was more in Pellin's nature to grant mercy and forgiveness to his enemies." She curtsied, lingering before she rose and left.

A knot of distrust I'd been carrying for months loosened and disappeared. I turned from the door and made preparations for my wedding.

Toria Deel stood next to Fess, wishing she were someplace else. According to custom, the reception would be held before the ceremony. The throne room in Bunard was filled with too many people for her taste—and too many of the insincere—but the heads of the church had accompanied the kings to Bunard. Too many of the Vigil had fallen too quickly for the rulers of the clergy to feel comfortable. They needed a familiar face in which to find comfort, and Lord Dura, while familiar, rarely made those around him comfortable. Knots of red, brown, blue, and white marked the different orders of the church where they stood in the throne room, each leader with their personal attendants.

Even the new head of the Merum had come, leaving the basilica in Cynestol in a rare gesture of humility. Archbishop Serius stood in rich red robes next to Brid Teorian of the Servants, who wore her customary brown, and Hyldu, her Grace of the Absold, resplendent in blue. Collen, the head of the Vanguard, had died during the fighting in Frayel. Per his request, his body had been buried in sight of the forest. His successor, Gaberend, broad and a head taller than anyone present, save Cailin's guards, managed to convey even more discomfort than Toria.

Fess stood at her side as the crowd milled about, waiting for the signal to take their places. He would never again be the carefree boy Bronwyn had apprenticed. His experiences precluded it, but his eyes were less guarded and he laughed easily now. As usual, he saw too much. Toria attributed this to a temperament of observation, which she found interesting, given that his talent lay so obviously with others.

"You're not happy," he said.

She pulled a deep breath of the cool northern air into her lungs and opted for honesty. "I'm conflicted. Lord Dura has obtained something I've desired for a hundred years," she said. "I'm finding it hard not to be jealous."

He nodded, but in a way that gave her the impression her gambit had failed. His next words confirmed it. "You surprised Pellin with your show of strength."

"When was that?" she asked and immediately regretted it.

"When you fought for Dura's mind," Fess said.

"Pellin should have expected it," she said. "He's the one who told me love was the key to Elieve's deliverance. I delved Lady Gael when we found Lord Dura in the caves beneath Bunard. I had access to her memories and her love, and my own, and that of all those I'd delved."

Fess's eyebrows, so blond they were almost invisible, narrowed for a fraction. "Couldn't Pellin have accomplished as much?"

She groped for words to explain a facet of their gift that she understood only through intuition. "There are mysteries within us, diminished as we are, I think the Fayit for all their power cannot comprehend. We know much about gifts, and nearly as much about talents. Libraries are filled with the ruminations of scholars and theologians about their properties and combinations."

"But not temperaments?" he asked, noting her omission.

"No, not so much," she said. "Pellin believed his strongest temperament to be thought, and I think he was correct. He prized learning above all else."

"But not you."

A small laugh escaped her as she searched for words to describe the obvious. "No. Anyone who has known me at all would say my strongest temperament is passion."

"Was it passion that allowed you to free Willet's mind?"

She took a slow, deep breath. "I've wanted love of my own for a long time, Fess. In its absence I've collected the memories of love from those I've delved and made a habit of visiting them, reliving them as though they were mine." The confession forced her to look away as she finished her explanation. "Inside Dura's mind, I released them, relived them all at once until I thought they might burn me to ash where I stood, but they gave me strength I could never have summoned on my own."

"And this shames you?"

She nodded. "Within the traditions of the Vigil, we regard that practice as a type of theft, a traffic and intrusion on the sanctity of another's memories."

He cocked his head to one side, a slight movement that accompanied the narrowing of his eyes. "Is this why you refused the position of Eldest?"

"Only in part." She nodded and cursed the tears that threatened to betray her. "When I resorted to poisoning the wellsprings of those who took Lelwin against her will, I forfeited any right I might have to lead."

"How is she?" he asked.

"She sleeps with a light and avoids the shadows to keep Brekana at bay, but we talk for hours each day."

"What of her vault?"

Toria pulled a deep breath. "It is diminished somewhat. Lelwin's healing will be long in coming, and I doubt it will ever be complete on this side of eternity, but I made a vow to see her healed, as much as possible. I won't leave her until I have." She lifted her head to see him looking at her. "I used her, Fess, and that's the third reason I deferred the position of Eldest to Lord Dura." She shook her head, forcing herself to make the admission. "He would never have done such a thing. I've used my gift for war and stolen memories. I am unfit to lead."

He stepped closer as he laughed, and she felt his breath fall across her face like a caress as he brought her into his embrace. "Do not expect any condemnation from me, Toria Deel. I have thieved for most of my life."

She stiffened at first so that he must have felt her reticence. She lifted her gaze and found it to be true, and wonder filled her. How could an urchin offer such grace? "Please," she said, stammering and putting her arms around him. "Call me Toria, just Toria."

He nodded, as she'd known he would, but she hadn't expected the comprehension that warmed his gaze. "Yes, sister. I would be honored."

I stood outside the throne room with Gael, waiting for the last of the monarchs before we made our entrance. "Stupid custom," I said. "We should have fled to the southern continent and paid the first village priest we found to cord us."

Queen Ulrezia chose that moment to arrive, resplendent in a deep blue gown with her lustrous snow-white hair piled up to look like a crown. "This attitude is unbecoming of you, Lord Dura. The north has been delivered from a threat greater than any in its history. Your marriage is a welcome occasion that allows us to celebrate it." She looked away as she sighed. "And to plan for the future. I shudder to think of the time it will take to forge a consensus between the nobles, the heads of the church, and the Vigil." She swept past me with a swirl of blue satin.

The throne room door closed behind her, leaving me nominally alone with my betrothed. "This isn't what I envisioned when I asked Laidir for your hand all those months ago."

Gael leaned forward to kiss me, the brush of her lips warm and soft against mine. "If I recall correctly, Lord Dura," she said with an arch of her brows, "I told you not to be boring. You've succeeded admirably." She tapped her lips with a finger. "In fact, I see I'll have to exercise some caution about my instructions in the future. You're such an enthusiast."

Before I could respond, she signaled the guard at the door and we entered the throne room, the brazen-throated call of the chamberlain announcing our presence. The collected monarchs of the continent and the nobles of Collum turned from their private amusements to applaud.

Gael left my side before I could stop her. "Where are you going?"

She looked back at me over her shoulder. "Tradition dictates that we mingle before our vows, ostensibly so that those married women in attendance may give me advice and the men may counsel you."

I nearly asked what type of advice, but the slightest curl of her smile warned me and made my question moot. "I hate this place," I muttered.

Bolt and Rory were at my side, appearing as though they'd been spun out of air. "I can't blame you," Bolt said. He wore his Errant's medallion on his chest, but hadn't bothered to clean the tarnish from it.

I commented on that.

"If I polished it every time it got a little dirty, there wouldn't be anything left."

We progressed through the throne room, and for once I didn't have to suffer the insults or jibes from the nobles of Collum as I made my way without destination. The throne and the regent's seat next to it were empty. Cailin and Brod were somewhere within the throng on the floor.

Yet my fellow nobles managed to disperse as I approached. No one seemed overly anxious to engage me in conversation until I came upon Rymark where he stood with Timbriend. "I don't understand," he said, pointing to me. "You think the mathematicum will someday be advanced enough to predict the behavior of someone like him? The man's a study in chaos."

She nodded. "Perhaps not in our lifetimes or even several after, but the fight at the Darkwater opened new fields of study we never dreamed of before."

I'd begun to stammer my greetings when a voice I'd come to despise intruded.

"Ah, Lord Dura," the Duke of Orlan said as he stepped forward on my right. "I see that you've managed to impress the king of Owmead with your particular brand of charm."

King Rymark turned to the duke, a man two hands taller and more physically imposing than any in attendance except the guards. "Who is this?"

I began to bow to both of them—a habit of survival that had been ruthlessly instilled in me upon my elevation to the nobility—but Rymark's furious glare stopped me. I straightened. "Your Majesty, this is His Grace, Duke Orlan, the most powerful noble in Collum after Prince Brod and the regent."

Duke Orlan managed to bow in acknowledgment rather than obeisance.

King Rymark, despite his stature, conveyed the impression that he had to look down at Orlan in order to see him. "Ah, a duke. I have quite a few of those." He offered nothing more, just continued to stare at Orlan until the duke, his smile turning sickly, stepped away.

Rymark stepped close enough for me to touch my forehead to his. "You are *Eldest*," he hissed. "You will bow and scrape to *no one*." If possible, he managed to inch closer. "Hear me in this, *Eldest*. The balance of power in the north is as precarious as it ever has been. If the heads of the church see that you can be cowed by a puffed-up piece of conceit like Duke Orlan, they will assume they can put you in their cloak pocket and tell you what to do. I didn't sacrifice a quarter of my men just so the church could tell me how to run my kingdom."

His tone could have tanned an ox hide.

"You make peace sound like war, Your Majesty."

He snorted his contempt. "Peace *is* war, Eldest. Every boundary and trade negotiation is an attack and counterattack. I have no intention of having to put men back in the field because you lack the will to use the power in your hands."

I let my surprise show. "You *don't* wish to fight, Your Majesty?"

"I've had my fill of fighting, Eldest." He pointed around the throne room at the other members of the Vigil. "The first rule of war is to know and train your forces."

My forces. Mine. I looked out across the throne room, searching for reassurance. I found it at the back, where Wag and Modrie sat in repose, watching. Modrie's gaze, filled with budding intelligence, swept over the throng, and I thanked Aer for the miracle of the Fayits' unexpected gift. We would have to find trainers for their pups when they had them, but the forest would be guarded once more.

To one side, Toria Deel and Fess stood close in quiet conversation. He still wore his vigilance like a guard, and I made a note to speak with him about surrendering his physical gift and ending the conflict between duties. Across the room Lelwin stood in the light, ill at ease, but unveiled. King Rymark wasn't the only one who'd had his fill of bloodshed, it seemed. Near her, Mirren watched the crowd while appearing to be part of it, her temperament for observation apparent. I would have to resume her training soon, a laughable thought. Perhaps I could delegate that task to Toria Deel and Custos.

Yet the difficulty of those tasks paled in comparison to another. I turned toward the rear of the throne room to a young man and woman, hardly more than children, who stood close enough to touch and spoke in hushed tones, oblivious to all else around them—even Allta, whose bulk and demeanor were enough to discourage others' approach.

"As Aer is my witness," I said. "I can't see the path forward there."

Bolt followed my gaze to where Mark and Elieve stood. "I overheard Ellias considering the probability that the gift would come to each of them by chance. After the first fifteen minutes of his explanation I lost interest."

"He shouldn't have bothered," I said. "There was no chance. None at all, but how are they supposed to be members of the Vigil when they're not even aware of the world around them?"

"You worry too much, Willet," Rory said. "If Aer can arrange for the gift to go to them, He can tell you how to train and use them. You know what we say in the urchins."

I sighed. "No, but I'm sure you're going to tell me."

He laughed. "'Each day has enough trouble of its own,' yah?"

I laughed. "You little thief. That's not yours. You lifted it right out of the liturgy."

He eyes went wide. "That's in the liturgy?"

I nodded, and he grew thoughtful.

"I'll have to make it a point to read it then. Maybe there's something to all this religious stuff after all."

I was sure he was bluffing me. Almost.

Custos performed the wedding, eschewing the tradition in Collum for the priest to charge a silver crown for joining members of the nobility, opting instead for the memories I'd gathered since we were parted.

And a packet of figs, of course.

"We are gathered here in the presence of Aer to cord these two together," he intoned, his voice surprisingly strong. "And tradition dictates that we offer praises and prayers for a long and bountiful union, for in the blessing of children we find that renewal in physical form that Aer promises our spirits if we join in union with Him."

Gael cocked her head at me, her eyes filled with surprise. "He's a poet."

I found his delivery more impressive than his prose. Custos probably had a dozen books of wedding speeches tucked away inside his head. "I bet he's quoting," I whispered. "Where do you want to live?"

"Someplace warm." The smallest catch in her voice told me she thought of Kera. "I will age, Willet. Even with my gift, time will exact its price and at the last, I will grow old and infirm while you remain young." She swallowed, and I saw fear in her eyes. "Will you love me for the rest of my life, Willet?"

We turned to face each other across a narrow bench to partake of haeling, and as Custos recited the liturgy and fed us bread and wine, I couldn't help but search the shadows of the buttresses for my friend Ealdor. He never appeared. I would have asked him what he'd found on the other side of eternity, but that question would have to wait.

Gael looked at me, waiting for an answer, but I couldn't give her what she wanted. Not yet.

While Custos waxed eloquent, I found myself tallying the questions that remained and the tasks to be completed before the world would be normal or safe again, if it could ever be. When the time finally came for Custos to cord our hands, I held out my left and Gael her right and he tied them together with seven loops of purple braid.

At the touch of her skin, I fell through her eyes and found her waiting for me within her mind, tall and lithe and glorious. There, in the time between heartbeats, I took her into my arms. "I will do more than love you for the rest of your life," I said. "I will love you for the rest of mine and past its end as well." I smiled. "And here, you may picture yourself however you wish. You can be forever young. I am, and always will be, yours."

There in the privacy of her thoughts and memories, I taught her how to construct a room within her mind. With a smile that set my blood on fire, she created a wedding bower, complete with a canopy of delicate purple flowers entwined over a broad bed on a raised dais.

If we were lucky, very lucky, we would have decades together, and I intended to make the most of every moment. But outside the delve, in the world of Bunard's throne room, we faced each other, motionless while the crowd of witnesses looked on. "You do know that time is passing, however slowly, in the throne room while we tarry here?" I asked.

Even in her thoughts, her physical gift made her strong, though I wouldn't have tried to resist anyway. Her laughter caressed its way over my ear, my lips, my throat.

"Let them wait."

ACKNOWLEDGMENTS

The Wounded Shadow is complete and THE DARKWATER SAGA has drawn to a close (at least for now). One of the things that may not be apparent (and it shouldn't be since it would defeat the purpose of the story) is the difficulty of creating and maintaining consistent world-building with a series this long. To say it's difficult is a vast understatement at best. Put in another way, the task is so far beyond the capability of one person (as far as I'm concerned anyway) as to be laughable. I had a ton of help along the way.

Steve Laube is my agent. I've lost count of how many times he's calmly listened to me and my complaints and given me the benefit of the experience and peace he carries with him.

Dave Long is my interface at Bethany House and a friend. I'm not sure what he heard in that very first pitch that made him decide to take a look at my work (I was too stressed with nervousness and caffeine to remember the conversation), but I'm so thankful he gave me a shot.

Karen Schurrer is my editor, and her ability to spy inconsistencies in plot and characterization is amazing. I don't know how she does it, but I'm glad she's willing to do it for me.

Mary Carr is my wife, but that is far too short a word to describe everything she is and means to me. For the purposes of *The Wounded Shadow*, Mary brought her incredible attention to detail to bear on the galleys. She managed to find small mistakes I'd missed even after I'd made multiple passes through the manuscript.

Ramona Dabbs is my alpha reader and has been ever since I started writing well over a decade ago. She's read everything, good and bad, polished and raw, and she's never failed in her encouragement. What a gift.

Finally, dear reader, if you've made it this far, I want to thank you. You have no idea how your letters, emails, and kind reviews have encouraged me to strive to improve as a writer. The goal is and always will be to write a story that you come to regard as your best friend. I hope someday to succeed.

ABOUT THE AUTHOR

Patrick W. Carr was born on an Air Force base in West Germany at the height of Cold War tensions. He has been told this was not his fault. As an Air Force brat, he experienced a change in locale every three years until his father retired to Tennessee. Patrick saw more of the world on his own through a varied and somewhat eclectic education and work history. He graduated from Georgia Tech in 1984 and has worked as a draftsman at a nuclear plant, did design work for the Air Force, worked for a printing company, and consulted as an engineer. Patrick's day gig for the last nine years has been teaching high school math in Nashville, TN. He currently makes his home in Nashville with his wonderfully patient wife, Mary, and four sons he thinks are amazing: Patrick, Connor, Daniel, and Ethan. Sometime in the future he would like to be a jazz pianist, and he wrestles with the complexity of improvisation on a daily basis.

Sign Up for Patrick's Newsletter!

Keep up to date with Patrick's news on book releases and events by signing up for his email list at patrickwcarr.com.

More from Patrick W. Carr!

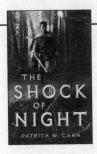

When one man is brutally murdered and the priest he works for mortally wounded, Willet Dura is called to investigate. As he begins to question the priest, the man pulls him close, cries out in a foreign tongue—and dies. This strange encounter draws Willet into an epic conflict that threatens not only his city, but his entire world.

The Shock of Night by Patrick W. Carr, THE DARKWATER SAGA

◊ BETHANYHOUSE

You May Also Like...

As a dynasty nears its end, an unlikely hero embarks upon a perilous quest to save his kingdom. Thrust into a world of dangerous political intrigue and church machinations, Errol Stone must leave behind his idle life, learn to fight, come to know his God—and discover his destiny.

THE STAFF AND THE SWORD: *A Cast of Stones, The Hero's Lot, A Draw of Kings* by Patrick W. Carr
patrickwcarr.com

Prince Wilek's father believes the disasters plaguing their land signal impending doom, but Wilek thinks this is superstitious nonsense—until he is sent to investigate a fresh calamity. What he discovers is more cataclysmic than he could've ever imagined. Wilek sets out on a desperate quest to save his people, but can he succeed before the entire land crumbles?

King's Folly by Jill Williamson
THE KINSMAN CHRONICLES #1
jillwilliamson.com

BETHANYHOUSE